**Also available from Rhenna Morgan
and Carina Press**

Rough & Tumble
Wild & Sweet
Claim & Protect
Tempted & Taken

Coming soon in 2018

Stand & Deliver
Healer's Need

Also available from Rhenna Morgan

Unexpected Eden
Healing Eden
Waking Eden
Eden's Deliverance

For Abegayle and Addison.
There's so much magic to be found in life,
but the two of you are the most powerful
and beautiful demonstrations of it I've ever found.
i love you, forever and always.

GUARDIAN'S BOND

Rhenna Morgan

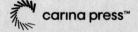 carina press™

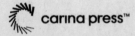 carina press™

Recycling programs
for this product may
not exist in your area.

ISBN-13: 978-1-335-01655-3

Guardian's Bond

Copyright © 2018 by Rhenna Morgan

www.CarinaPress.com

Printed in U.S.A.

GUARDIAN'S BOND

Chapter One

Safe with the Keeper. Guarded from the dark.

Over and over, Priest repeated the protective words in his head, merging his magic with the ancient symbols he inked at the base of Jade's nape and down her spine. Black and red swirling links with shades of gray joined each sacred talisman. No one would hurt her. Not her or Tate so long as he drew breath.

His forearm ached from his constant grip on the tattoo iron, but the steady drone and vibrations from the coils as he worked deepened his trance. Beneath his free hand, Jade's body trembled from the rush of pain-induced endorphins she'd endured for nearly four hours.

Safe with the Keeper. Guarded from the dark.

He swiped the excess ink away from the intricate design. The same intertwining scroll and symbolism that marked his shoulders, back and collarbone—and likely the only thing that had saved his life and sanity in the early days. Had Jade's and Tate's parents not guarded him after his brother's betrayal and marked him with the sacred symbols, the darkness would have consumed him entirely.

"Priest?" Jade pushed to her elbows on the padded table and peered over one shoulder. "Are you done?"

The art was perfect. A sufficient start in hiding her from the threat he sensed closing in. A malevolence he'd first felt with an unexplained summons to the Otherworld. Never since he'd been named high priest had he ever been called there so abruptly. Without warning or purpose.

Priest set his equipment aside and peeled off his latex gloves. As eerie as the memory had been, even if he covered Jade in ink, it wouldn't feel like enough protection. "For now."

Jade grinned, swiveled on the padded table, and snagged her blue tank top off the counter next to them. "How does it look?"

The tiny chimes above the front door jingled before he could answer, and Tate stalked through, his hands laden with yet another haul of the fast-food breakfasts Priest detested. The coffee, though—that he could use in abundance.

Through the open door, morning sunshine glinted off the storefronts on Eureka Springs's Main Street, only a few cars and Harleys motoring down the main drag. Not surprising for a Thursday, but by late tonight or early tomorrow they'd be flooded with tourists and bikers soaking up the spring weather.

Tate kicked the door shut and threw the bolt. The fifties throwback neon clock showed straight up eleven o'clock, only one more hour until the shop opened.

"Tate, check it out." Jade shifted in front of the full length mirror behind her and held the blue hand mirror higher for a better angle on Priest's work. "Mine's as badass as yours and Priest's."

Ignoring Jade, Tate set the orange and white paper bags and cardboard drink holder aside and stalked to the window overlooking the street. "Hey, Priest. Have you got an early gig today?"

A prickling awareness danced across his skin. Not danger or evil. Either of those would have stirred the darkness trapped inside him. Instead, it lay still and dormant like midnight fog. He turned from cleaning up his tools. "First client's at noon. Finishing up that biker from Fayetteville I started last weekend. Why?"

Tate twisted enough to meet his gaze. "'Cause there's a little old lady and two people about my age outside in the parking lot. They keep staring up here."

Jade sidled up beside Priest. "You sure you didn't schedule an early one?"

Hell yes, he was sure. Appointments before or after hours were only for customers needing more than art. Those needing protection, peace or comfort woven into his coveted designs. "Get away from the window."

Tate stayed put and studied the parking lot. "Looks like the old lady's coming in."

"Get away from the window. Now." Two weeks he'd waited, petitioning the Keeper as much as he dared for guidance. For some insight into the danger he sensed or Jade's subsequent terrifying vision. The Keeper's only answer was a promise that messengers would be sent to guide him, but his instincts screamed to brace and prepare. "Stay behind me. Say nothing until I know who they are."

"But I locked the door. We're fine."

The bolt flipped before Tate finished his argument, the remnants of air Priest used to unlock the mechanism fluttering the paper want ads on the corkboard beside the door.

"I want to know who they are, but I want you out of the line of fire," Priest said.

Footsteps sounded on the wooden stairs to the shop's raised patio, a light tread that would have gone unnoticed to someone without the benefit of a predator's keen hearing.

The door latch clicked and the chimes overhead tinkled as an older woman eased through the door. Her attire seemed more on par with something from Jade's closet—comfortable cotton pants the color of a robin's egg and a fitted, white T-shirt. Around her neck hung three charms, each dangling from simple black leather cords.

Charms fashioned in the symbols he'd honored since birth.

His gaze snapped to hers. Deep blue-gray eyes he remembered from his youth stared back at him, the woman's shoulder-length gray hair framing her delicate face. "Naomi."

"Eerikki," she whispered, the emotion behind the sound so deep and fraught with bittersweet memories his knees nearly buckled. Countless nights he'd wondered if she was safe. If she and her children had survived the night his brother murdered so many—Naomi's mate included.

Before he could shake the surprise that held him rooted in place, she closed the distance between them and wrapped her arms around him. "I'd hoped you were alive. I tried to track you through my visions for years, but couldn't find you until a few weeks ago."

The messenger he'd been promised.

Finally.

His arms tightened around her, and the solitary weight

he'd shouldered since Tate's and Jade's parents had died eased a fraction. As if the presence of someone from his own youth altered the gravitational pull around him and soothed his beleaguered soul.

Jade's and Tate's quiet footsteps sounded on the tiles behind him, their curious stares a tangible press against his back.

Begrudgingly, Priest released his old friend and stepped aside, bringing his two companions into view.

Naomi studied them. "These are your children?"

By now, he should be used to it. Everyone asked the same question, and yet it still knifed through him. He loved his wards. Would do anything to protect and guide them and never regretted their place in his life, but he craved his own mate. His own children.

A dangerous proposition with the tainted magic trapped inside him.

"No," he said. "These are Lisana's and Rani's children. Lisana and Rani healed me after my brother's attack."

Naomi blanched, but tried to mask her response with a weak smile. He couldn't blame her for her fear. The mere thought of his brother, Draven, still flayed his insides.

He motioned to his wards. "Naomi Falsen, meet Jade Mitchell and Tate Allen. They've lived with me since their mothers passed."

Hand outstretched, Tate stepped forward first. "Not too many people know Priest's real name."

This time her smile was genuine, and her eyes lit with joy the likes of which Priest had long forgotten. She cupped Tate's hand with both of hers. "I've known Eerikki since before the Keeper named him high priest.

My mate, Farron, mentored him before his soul quest and afterward served him as warrior primo."

Tate released her hand and puffed his chest up a little broader than before. "I'm warrior house."

As soon as the words were out, Tate's excitement deflated, the reality of Naomi's information belatedly connecting with Priest's history lessons. How Priest's failure to ferret out Draven's plans before it was too late had cost every house primo their life and countless clan members as well.

Naomi patted Tate's shoulder, her petite stature compared to Tate's towering height making the gesture almost comical. "It's okay, Tate. Let it go. My mate faced his destiny the same way Eerikki and all the rest of us will."

"You mean Priest," Tate said.

Naomi swiveled toward Priest and frowned.

"The world's different now," Priest said. "Eerikki's not exactly a name that blends in. Rani started calling me Priest in the seventies." He shrugged. "It stuck."

"Ah." She scanned him head to toe, obviously connecting how the name tied with his image. He might have been an innocent when he'd stepped into his position fifty years ago, but now he reflected the hardened years in between. "It stuck because it fits. In more ways than one. Though for your mother's sake, I'll use the name she gave you unless we're outside our clan."

Decision made, she turned her gaze on Jade and studied her aura. "You're a seer. Who's the primo for your house?"

Jade hung her head, and it was all Priest could do to stifle his flinch. "We have no primos," Priest answered for her. "Our numbers are down. Most from the last generation refused their quests."

Naomi frowned and opened her mouth as if to share something, then closed it just as fast and dug in her purse. "Give me a minute. There's someone I want you to meet." She pulled out her phone and typed out a message fast enough to rival Jade and Tate on a texting frenzy.

The same warning buzz he'd wrestled for weeks surged between his shoulders, both beast and man sensing a shift on the horizon. As though the answers he sought crouched nearby in thick shadow, poised to launch into the light. Whether the change he sensed was good or bad remained to be seen, but the sensation was too big to ignore. An emotional stirring that warned whatever lay ahead would pack a serious punch.

My mate faced his destiny the same way Eerikki and all the rest of us will.

If he remembered right, Naomi and Farron's son had been eight or nine at the time of Draven's betrayal. And yet Priest had never been summoned to join his soul quest. "Your family has always led the warrior house. Where's your son?"

She averted her face and dropped her phone back in her purse. Her aura dimmed, the vibrant gold of the seer house paling as though a cloud had moved across it. "My son and his wife couldn't come."

His wife. Not his mate. More evidence her son had shunned his gifts like so many others.

Before he could question her further, the shop door opened and sent the chimes overhead jingling. A tall and oddly familiar looking man with short dirty-blond hair and a beard in the making stepped just inside the entrance, one hand braced on the knob. He scanned the room, his muscled torso locked tight until his gaze snagged on Naomi. "Everything's safe?"

"It will be now." Naomi shot the man a relieved smile and waved him in. "Get your sister and come inside."

Priest tweaked at her choice of words. "Why wouldn't it be safe?"

The man ducked outside, leaving the door open, and soft voices murmured from the raised porch beyond.

Naomi subtly inclined her head toward Jade and Tate. "I'll explain later. After you meet my grandchildren."

Well, that explained the familiarity.

Her grandson strode back through the door and stepped to one side, holding it open for the woman behind him. The second she came into full view, Priest froze.

"Eerikki, this is my grandson, Aleksander, and my beautiful granddaughter, Kateri. Kateri, Alek, this is our clan's high priest, Eerikki Rahandras. Though, now, he just goes by Priest."

Granddaughter.

Beautiful.

Kateri.

Some dim corner of his mind registered Naomi had shared more with her lighthearted words, but those were the only three that mattered. Except the woman in front of him wasn't just beautiful. She was perfect. Dressed in a flowing tan skirt and fine white linen shirt tied at the waist, her willowy body gave the illusion of fragility, but strength beamed from her intelligent blue-gray eyes. Her hair fell well beyond her shoulders, a soft blond the color of endless wheat fields.

But it was her aura that gripped him most. No colors

to represent a house, but powerful nonetheless. Shimmering as though the moon shone directly behind her.

My mate.

His beast stirred and scented the air.

"Eerikki?" Naomi's touch pressed just above his elbow, her fingers light against his skin, but trembling. "Is something wrong?"

Nothing was wrong. Not anymore.

Seventy-seven years he'd been alone, but now she was here. His to win. To protect. To provide for and pleasure.

The darkness rose, and crude, devastatingly vivid images blasted across his mind. Him above her. His cock powering deep and her breasts bouncing with each thrust. Her soft cries filling his ears.

Kateri crept forward and held out her hand. A lifeline and a temptation. "My nanna's told me a lot about you."

He should step away. The evil was too close, waking with a devastating hunger and licking the edges of his control. To hurt this woman would be the end of him. The annihilation of his soul. He clasped her hand in his anyway, the contact zinging through him as profound as his connection with the Otherworld. He needed more. Wanted her hands pressed against his chest. Her nails scoring his back and her palm working his shaft.

Tugging gently, he pulled her to him.

She stumbled slightly, but didn't resist, splaying her free hand above his thrashing heart. She lifted her face to his, her beautiful eyes wide and mouth slightly parted, her soft pink lips ready for his kiss.

His panther chuffed and purred, the uncontainable response rumbling up the back of his throat and filling the room.

Two seconds. No more than that and his mate was

ripped from his arms and thrust behind the unknown male, her startled gasp still lingering in the air around him.

"What the hell?" The stranger's terse voice slashed through the otherwise quiet room.

Priest's cat screamed and clawed for release. The tingle and burn that came scant seconds before each shift raced beneath his skin, and his breath crept up the back of his throat in a hot hiss. He stalked forward, his prey mirroring each advance with a step backward.

Logic tried to surface, a flicker of knowledge as to the man's name and who he was clawing at the back of Priest's mind.

It doesn't matter who he is, the darkness whispered. *He took her from us. Kill him.*

Through his beast's lethal focus a movement registered. A woman blocking him from his target. "Don't move, Alek. Not so much as a step."

Priest stopped. He knew that voice. Trusted it. He fought the thickening black haze around the edges of his vision and focused on the woman in front of him.

Naomi.

An innocent.

An elder and a friend.

Her words pierced through the murderous fog, a pinprick at most, and echoing as though she whispered from the depths of a cave. "He's her sister, Eerikki. Their parents were killed two weeks ago. He wants only to protect her."

Her brother.

One of his clan.

Safe.

He touched her, the darkness countered.

His cat growled in agreement.

Eliminate him. Take what's rightfully ours.

Naomi inched closer. "Alek, take your sister to the car. Wait for me there."

The two shifted for the door, but froze at the warning growl that rumbled up Priest's throat. "No."

"He'll bring her back." Lowering her voice, Naomi crept within killing distance. "Your companion is angry. Insulted and raw. He doesn't care that he's her brother. Only that he's a stranger he doesn't know. But *you* know, Eerikki. Take the time to find your balance. Tate and Jade can go with them. Tate's a warrior. You can trust him to keep her safe."

As though she'd summoned him with her words, Tate stole closer to Priest, the wary nature of his coyote obviously sensing Priest barely held his panther in check. He kept his silence, but his watchful amber eyes burned with curiosity and confusion.

Never in all the years they'd been with them had Priest ever lost control. Hadn't sunk this deep into the darkness in years.

Still braced protectively in front of Kateri, Alek stared Priest down. Such innocent bravery. Clueless of the torture Priest could wield with little more than a thought.

End him. The dark encouragement danced all too enticingly inside his head and sent fire licking down his spine.

Behind Alek, Kateri watched him with wide eyes. Not afraid. Surprised, yes, and curious given the tilt to her head, but not afraid. She swallowed and flexed the hand clutching her brother's shoulder.

His panther bristled at the sight, jaws aching to sink its teeth into the usurper who enjoyed her touch.

"Go," he ordered Tate, not daring to break eye contact with his mate for fear he'd lose what little control he had left. His muscles flexed and strained, blood pulsing with a ferocity that left an aching throb in its wake. Naomi was right. If he didn't find his balance, he'd slaughter Alek where he stood. "Stay close, but don't let her out of your sight. No one touches her." The darkness and his beast coalesced with his own voice and unleashed a feral claim. "She's mine."

Chapter Two

It couldn't be real. None of it. Katy padded down the wooden steps from the tattoo shop, her footsteps nearly silent in comparison to those resonating from the three people behind her. The crisp spring morning temperature kissed her sweat-misted skin and the sun beamed just shy of its zenith. Normal. Safe. The same world she'd grown up in.

Except that the world wasn't what she'd thought it was. For the last two weeks, her scientist's mind had insisted that the things Nanna had told her—even shown her—weren't possible. But that man. Eerikki. Priest. Whatever his name was. Her logic couldn't ignore that. Had heard the animalistic sounds roll past his lips and felt the power emanating off him. Electric like the snap and tingle that came before a lightning storm. That was no trick of the mind. No figment of her imagination or wishful thinking as she'd tried to explain her grandmother's foresight and shifting abilities.

And his body...

She shuddered at the memory of the hard muscles she'd felt all too briefly. The heat of him. Between his edgy biker appearance, loose black hair well past his shoulders and deep olive skin, he was every deep, dark fantasy rolled into one. Had her brother not yanked her behind him, she had no doubt she'd have happily pressed herself flush against him and purred like a desperate cat in heat.

Talk about illogical responses.

She released her shaky grip on the handrail and stepped onto the aged asphalt parking lot, praying her adrenaline-overloaded body could navigate without the extra support.

Behind her, the woman she'd yet to formally meet asked, "Are you guys hungry? We've got some great cafes and coffee shops on Main Street."

Katy paused on the sidewalk that ran along the west side of the street and rubbed her arms to ward off the chill. The traffic had picked up since they'd pulled into the parking lot, but the quaint storefronts nestled along the softly sloping street and massive budding trees that framed it on either side seemed to ground the bustling area in a quiet peace.

And, boy, did she need peace right now. Even with the rumble of motorcycles and chattering tourists milling up and down the street, the fresh air and birds chirping soothed her as nothing else could. Nature was what grounded her when nothing else could. The simpleness of it. The soul-calming beauty. Two weeks ago, she'd been a few formalities away from making it the foundation for her future, her Bachelor of Science in Environmental Science and the coveted environmental protection internship she'd fought for almost guaranteed.

But then her parents had been murdered and her neat, tidy life had been turned on its head. "Is there somewhere we can sit outside?"

Alek's deep, clipped voice sounded a second before

his hand clamped onto her shoulder and redirected her to the parking lot where his red Jeep Wrangler waited. "We're leaving."

Before Katy could even dig in her heels, Tate was between them and the cars lined in orderly rows. When she'd first seen him in the shop, she'd thought him a cross between a male model and a hipster—his long hair pulled back in a low ponytail and a honey-blond color a lot of women paid hundreds to achieve. Now, seeing his slightly darker beard framing bared teeth as he growled at Alek, he was pure predator. Shoulders back, arms tense at his sides and braced on the balls of his feet, he appeared only seconds from taking Alek to the ground.

Jade shoved Alek's hand off Katy's shoulder and positioned herself between Katy and Alek. She was shorter than Katy, five-two at best, but the soft blue tank top and tight-fitting jeans accented firm muscle and curves the likes of which always left Katy envious. "Keep your hands off her." She studied each of the men and shook her head like they'd both lost their minds, the same silver clan charms her grandmother wore woven into small braids in her long dark hair and glinting in the sun. "Jesus, don't you know *anything* about our race?" she said to Alek. "Priest said no one could touch her. Tate's coyote takes that literally."

Maybe Katy *should* have followed her brother. Or at least put a little extra distance between her and Tate. Instead she stepped forward, her indomitable curiosity overpowering the need for caution. "Your animal's a coyote?"

Tate scanned the distance between her and Alek and relaxed enough to jerk a terse nod. Only after he'd drawn a few more breaths and straightened from his fighting stance did he shift his attention to Alek. "Your family has always anchored the warrior house. Why don't you know about us?"

Alek frowned and gritted his teeth so hard the muscles at the back of his jaw looked as if they'd snap. "I don't know. Nanna said our dad made her promise not to tell us. Said he didn't do his soul quest, or whatever you call it. Something about not wanting his gifts. After what I've seen the last few weeks, I'm starting to see why." He glared at Katy. "We should go. Nanna can finish her big reunion with Mr. High-and-Mighty and call us to come get her." He huffed out an ironic chuckle and shook his head. "Oh, wait. She's a hawk, right? She can fly to us when she's done."

No way was she leaving. Not when she had a chance to pry information out of two people who clearly knew what they were talking about. Even if she didn't have a solid motive for wanting to learn more, the scientist in her insisted on digging deeper. On finding some reasonable explanation for the things her nanna had summarized as simply *magic*. "Don't you want answers?"

"What I want is for my sister to not end up like our parents. Have you seen the way these people act?"

Memories of the blood-splattered walls and coppery stench that had filled her parents' living room fired as bold as real-life, pricking her carefully buried rage. To lose control was unacceptable. The worst offense she could show her parents after what they'd suffered. "What I want is justice. The only way we're going to get it is if we talk to the people who can help us find him. I don't care if they have spots or shift into unicorns. I'm staying."

"Justice for what?" Jade shifted her gaze to Alek,

confusion clouding the green depths that matched her namesake. "What happened to your parents?"

Mouth pressed in a hard line, Alek stared at Jade for all of two seconds, then spun to face the street, a muttered curse Katy couldn't quite make out drifting on the wind.

"Our parents were killed two weeks ago." Two weeks that felt a lifetime away and yet her words still shook with barely contained fury. "It was bloody. Gruesome."

Jade glanced at Tate as if to gauge if he was following the topic any better than she was. "What?"

"Murdered," Alek said, shifting enough to scowl at Tate. "By a Volán. You really think I'm inclined to trust anyone from your race after what happened to them? After the whacked-out shit I just saw from Eerikki or whatever his name is?"

Tate smirked and cocked an eyebrow. "He goes by Priest. And I hate to point this out, but if you're Naomi's grandson, you're Volán, too. One from the warrior primo family."

"A warrior what?" Katy said.

Jade's gaze cut behind Katy to a couple meandering down the sidewalk. She cleared her throat and motioned for Katy to step out of the way. Only when the couple was out of earshot did she speak, but her voice was still hushed. "Warrior primo. Every house has a leader that serves the high priest and mentors their people. Your family has led the warrior house for as long as anyone remembers."

Alek scoffed, stuffed his hands in the pocket of his jeans and glared into the distance. "This is bullshit."

Katy understood the sentiment. Had echoed the thought more times than she could count since Naomi first shared her family's mysterious heritage and shifted into a hawk for the first time. But this was the first time she'd seen Alek struggle with the concept of their race. Yes, he'd grieved and wrestled with anger the same as her since they'd found their parents slaughtered in their family home, but he'd seemed more open to the idea of magic. Even eager to learn more about it. Or he had been—until he'd come face-to-face with Priest.

"Call it whatever you want," Tate said. "But it's reality. If you don't accept what's yours, the Keeper will hand the honor to someone else."

"Who's the Keeper?" Katy asked.

"Wow." Jade's eyebrows hopped high, and she scrunched a handful of her soft black hair on top of her head. After considering Katy and Alek for a second, she planted both hands on her hips, scanned Main Street from left to right, then made pointed eye contact with Alek and Tate the same as a scolding mother would her errant sons. "Okay, can you two hold your shit in check long enough for us to find a place to talk?"

"I'm fine," Katy said. "It's the men doing all the flipping out, not the women." Although, if she was honest with herself, Alek's attitude had been getting worse even before their parents were killed. Like the quiet patience he'd always shown growing up had sprung a slow leak that showed no signs of stopping.

Jade crooked a grin that spoke of a saucy attitude Katy could absolutely appreciate under normal circumstances. "Not exactly a trait unique to our clan, but still true." She glanced back at Tate, a genuine concern and question in her soft gaze. "You good?"

Tate paused long enough to scrutinize Alek who still

refused to look at the rest of them. He nodded. "Yeah. Just keep him at arm's length."

That got Alek's attention. He squared his shoulders toward Tate and started forward, but Katy held up her hand before he could get two steps in. "Stop it." She lowered her voice. "Whatever it is that's going on with you, let it go. They're not going to hurt me. No one's going to hurt me. But I want answers and they've got them. If you can't deal with that, go wait in the car, and I'll find you after we're done."

It took a good fifteen seconds and more pride than Alek was likely comfortable swallowing, but he finally dipped his head, the tiny acquiescence leaving his features hard and pinched.

Jade sighed and motioned toward the top of the main strip where a pub sat on the opposite side of the street with motorcycles lining the front of it. "Let's hit the Cat House. Breakfast sounded good thirty minutes ago, but right now a drink sounds better than coffee, and we can sit on the patio."

Less than fifteen minutes later, they were seated at a balcony table overlooking Main Street. There'd been another tense moment when Tate had claimed the seat beside Katy—effectively caging her between the balcony rail and him—but between the give-it-a-rest glower she aimed at her brother and Jade's placating demeanor, Alek took a seat beside Jade on the opposite side of the table. If the waitress found it odd they all ordered hard liquor at straight up noon, she didn't show it.

Eureka Springs truly was a beautiful town. The soft rolling hills, quirky shops and buildings from a more peaceful era was a place she'd enjoy exploring. But while she loved the thick foliage and the winding streets, what she wanted most right now were answers. Checking the proximity to make sure no one could overhear them, Katy started with Jade. "Can you shift, too?"

One blink and the watchful tension that had gripped Jade nearly nonstop since Alek had yanked Katy out of Priest's arms flashed to bright happiness. "I can. My soul quest was just a little over a month ago."

"What's your animal?"

Her smile grew bigger. Prouder. "My companion's a lynx."

Alek snickered. "You mean you're a cat."

Katy shot him a warning glare. "A full-grown Eurasian lynx would come up to your thigh and could spot you coming as much as 250 feet away. They're also superb hunters. I'd hardly call her a cat."

Tate's reply wasn't nearly so subtle, the low growl of his coyote winding around them all.

"Let it go, Tate," Jade said then turned her attention on Katy. "How do you know so much about them anyway?"

"I took an advanced zoology class before I declared my major in Environmental Science." She glared at her brother, still more embarrassed than she cared to admit. "I don't know what's up your ass lately, but I've just about had it with your attitude."

"I don't have an attitude, I'm just tired."

"Trust me. You have an attitude. All the time. And when you're not biting everyone's head off you're passed out in bed."

Jade and Tate shared a look, one borne of many years together and unspoken understanding.

"What?" Katy asked them both. "Does that mean something?"

Ducking her head, Jade tapped her thumb against the scarred wood tabletop.

"How old are you?" Tate asked Alek.

Alek hesitated as if he sensed a trap or a prank coming on. "Twenty-five, why?"

"Bad temper? Sleeping a lot?"

Alek glanced at Katy and shrugged. "I guess. Yeah."

Tate nodded. "Most Voláns are called on their soul quest between twenty-one and twenty-six. Most never make it past twenty-five and men almost always share the warning signs of fatigue and anger. If you're not generally a giant dick, I'd say you're close."

For the first time since he'd gone all protective-big-brother with Priest, a little of Alek's bravado faded. An especially surprising response considering Tate's blatant verbal taunt.

"You really don't know much about our race at all, do you?" Jade asked quietly.

Alek shook his head, barely meeting her eyes. "Nanna told us about the magic and the basic houses. She said she was a seer and showed us she could shift, but other than that... I think she was afraid to share more."

"You said you went on a soul quest," Katy said to Jade. "That's when you learn to shift?"

"Sort of." Jade stared at the table for a second, her eyes distant while she seemed to struggle for the right words. "In the Otherworld, you face the parts of yourself the Keeper feels are necessary for you to navigate this realm with magic. Once you do, you're assigned a house and the magic that goes with it. It's only after your quest that you meet your companion."

Odd. She'd heard that expression several times since her grandmother had divulged their race's shapeshifting gift and it still didn't make sense. "I don't get the companion part."

"If you think it's weird now, wait until you have one." Tate chuckled and crossed his muscled forearms on the table. "Think of it this way. Today there's just you. When you think to yourself, all you hear is your voice. After you're given your companion, you'll hear two. Yours and your animal's. It's the Keeper's way of ensuring our race stays in tune with nature and magic."

Fascinating. Far-fetched and completely insane, but fascinating in theory nonetheless. "And there are four houses, right? Seer, warrior, healer and sorcerer?"

Jade nodded. "The sorcerers are rare, though. Very powerful and highly respected. Or they were. We don't know of any that are still alive."

Alek shifted in his seat, obviously uncomfortable. "The primo thing. You said our family led the warriors. What's that about?"

While he'd directed his question to Jade, it was Tate who answered. "Your grandmother's mate was the last primo for the warriors. Unless the Keeper deems otherwise, each primo stays within a family line. No clue what she'll do since your father refused his gifts."

"And what do primos do, exactly?" Katy asked.

"They're the strongest in their house and serve as mentor for the people they lead. But they also serve as Priest's advisors and share their magic with him at presect."

"At what?"

"Huh?"

Both Tate and Jade smiled at Alek and Katy's dumbfounded responses, but it was Tate who answered. "When the seasons change, our clan comes together for a sacred rite called presect. It's simple really. An exchange designed to honor, balance and keep the Earth's magic thriving. Only, we don't have any primos right now. Without them to help Priest, the rites aren't as effective. We need them. Bad."

"So, what happens without the primos?" Alek asked. "Our race's magic dies out?"

"Not just ours," Jade said. "The Earth's magic."

Katy groaned, planted her elbows on the table and planted her forehead in her palms. "Earth magic. That's insane."

Tate chuckled. "Seriously? You've seen your grandmother shift into a hawk, and been up close and personal to Priest fighting back his panther and you don't believe in magic?"

He was right. She'd seen Nanna shift. Watched her as a trance pulled her under and followed what she'd learned in her visions guiding them right to Priest.

And Priest...no one could ignore the power inside him. She'd felt it the second she'd stepped across the shop's threshold. Had been drawn to him in a way her mind still couldn't find a decent way to categorize.

She rested her forearms on the table and sighed. "I don't know what I believe anymore. Maybe the Volán have magic, but you can't tell me it's out there for everyone. Normal life is just that. Normal."

Cocking her head, Jade studied Katy with a quiet intensity. "Maybe your definition of magic is too limited."

"Too limited how?"

Jade scanned the parking lot below, her gaze lingering on the clusters of patrons milling beside their bikes and laughing like they had all the time in the world to enjoy the day. "The magic is everywhere if you're open to it.

The comfort you feel when you're with your friends. In the quiet of a spring day or the rumbling thunder of a violent storm. That's not just for the Volán but for the singura, too."

"The singura?" Alek asked.

"Companionless humans." Tate grinned. "Basically, what you thought you were."

Warming up to her explanation, Jade motioned to a couple on the lower patio. The woman was perched atop the wide protective rail that separated the patio from the parking lot, and the man stood between her spread knees, his arms possessively coiled around her. It was an intimate moment. Powerful in its simplicity. "Look at them. You can't see something like that and not believe in magic."

Warmth blossomed beneath Katy's skin, the all-too-vivid memory of how Priest's muscles had felt beneath her palms and how his presence had enveloped her in a protective cocoon lifting to the height of her awareness.

And his scent. She pressed her knees together under the table and fought back a groan. She could still smell him on her. A mix of summer storm, leather and the deepest woods. Her voice came out softer, when she answered. Deep and husky. "That's just attraction. A chemical response in the body."

Jade grinned. "Is it?"

She's mine.

The remembered words sluiced through her in the most exotic caress. Possessive at a level she both craved and railed against. She cleared her throat and laced her fingers together on the table, forcing a detached expression. "Priest said I was his before we left. What did he mean by that?"

Jade looked to Tate, a request for guidance without a word spoken.

Tate shook his head. "I can't know for sure."

"But you *think* you know."

He hesitated, glanced at Alek as if gauging how well his temper was holding, then shifted his compassionate amber gaze back to Katy. "It's not up to me to share. Priest will tell you."

"But the way he acted…how he lost control," Katy pressed. "Surely, you can see why I want answers."

For the longest time, Tate merely studied her, consideration and concern marking his handsome features. "I do. It's still something he should talk to you about, but I will tell you this." He paused as though carefully considering his words, not just for her but for her brother who'd drawn scarily motionless beside her. "Of all the people who walk this Earth, there is no one safer than you."

Chapter Three

White walls covered in Priest's favorite artwork. His custom black tattoo bed still configured for the protective symbols he'd inked on Jade's back. Gloves, glass jars filled with ink caps, rubbing alcohol and prep pads lined up with all the other equipment he used in his job along the side shelf.

Bit by bit, the private room where he did all his work came into focus, the depth of the trance he'd escaped into with Naomi's help leaving him numb but blessedly centered. Which meant Kateri's brother was safe—for now.

A soft indrawn breath sounded nearby followed by hushed movement. "You've been gone a long time," Naomi nearly whispered, her voice both gentle and concerned. "How do you feel?"

Like he needed to stretch and let his beast run for a good long while. Though the latter was impossible in town and during daylight, the color and sheer size of his massive panther a beacon guaranteed to send the singura into full-scale panic. "Better," he said instead. He rolled his shoulders and craned his head side to side, loosening the tendons in his neck. "What time is it?"

"One-thirty."

Fuck.

Two hours he'd been out. Far longer than he'd intended or could afford with his mate unattended. Forcing his mind back online faster than was wise given his near-loss of control, Priest rose from the guest couch he'd collapsed on and scanned the empty shop.

"I flipped the sign to closed before noon," Naomi shared from the chair Jade usually manned behind the register. "I found some paper and put a note on the door, too, explaining you'd had an emergency and all appointments were cancelled for today." She paused long enough to shrug one shoulder. "Not as professional as you might have liked, but I didn't want to risk anyone interrupting your meditation."

Wise, considering even the slightest provocation could have set him off in the state he'd been in. "It doesn't matter. They'll come back." They always did. Priest's designs were legendary in this area. Highly coveted. Which was ironic considering the most sacred ones he gave were often executed without the recipient even knowing the gift they'd received. "Where's Kateri?"

Naomi lifted the phone she'd left on top of the display case filled with the charms Jade sold and waggled it. "Safe with Tate and Jade and apparently getting a crash course about our clan."

Priest grunted at her sly omission of Alek's name, yet again proving what a wise woman she was. He prowled to the refrigerator at the back of the shop, his magic homing in on Tate and Jade's location through the marks he'd given them.

Two blocks down the street.

The Cat House.

He snatched a bottled water and downed nearly all of it in one go. Probably a smart place for his wards to take his mate. After the way he'd reacted to her and Alek's subsequent interference, most people would need a fifth of whiskey to steady their nerves. Though the idea of his mate being exposed to unknown males without him there to warn them off made his panther bristle.

But what if she wasn't there? What if she'd left with Alek and they were just feeding Naomi texts to keep her unaware? He tossed the empty bottle to the recycle bin and stalked back to the front of the shop. "You're sure she's there?"

Naomi smirked. "I might be old, but I've stayed up to date with technology the way you wanted us to. Her GPS shows her a few blocks down the street."

"And Alek?"

"He's there, too."

He settled in the rolling chair he used for work, the plastic casters whooshing on the industrial tile floor. His gaze snagged on the custom bed Jade had lain on only hours before and his right hand fisted. He wanted to see Kateri there, stretched out on the supple leather. To watch the ink take shape on her skin and pour his magic into every line. If he marked her, she wouldn't be able to hide from him no matter where she went. Would have his protection even without his presence.

Naomi stood and padded toward him. "Are we going to talk about it? Or just pretend this morning didn't happen?"

"Which part? The fact that I almost lost control, or that you were almost minus a grandson?"

"If Alek had been brought up with knowledge of our clan, he'd know better than to step between a high priest and his mate."

Priest wasn't sure what surprised him more—the reminder that Naomi's grandchildren knew nothing of their race, or that she'd so readily figured out why he'd acted as he did. "You knew?"

"Of course, I knew. You forget I once had a man look at me that way." She grinned. "And given the way Tate put himself between her and Alek on the way out the door, your wards figured it out, too."

Another colossal fuckup to add to his day. He was their high priest. The one who was supposed to keep himself in check no matter the provocation. Not let himself get thrown sideways by a male who'd not yet accepted his gifts.

"As to almost losing control," Naomi continued, "I'd say you're being overly hard on yourself. You're a powerful man who was caught unaware. It's only natural for your beast to be protective when it senses a threat."

"It wasn't just my beast."

The second the words were out, he wanted to snatch them back. Of the few elders still living, Naomi was the last he wanted to know of his situation. Of the ugly taint that moved inside him.

Naomi kicked off her pretty flip-flops and settled on the couch across from him, crossing her legs under her the way many of his younger customers did when they watched him work. "What do you mean it wasn't just your beast?"

She deserved the truth. Deserved to know the risk her granddaughter would face if Priest pursued her the way his instincts demanded. But he sure as shit wasn't looking forward to the fear and disappointment in her eyes once she heard it. "Because Draven's darkness is in me."

No response save two slow blinks. As though she needed to rewind what she'd heard. "How?"

The biting cold that always came with memories of that night rushed him. Smoke from the bonfire had streamed high into the star-filled velvet sky, one primo for each house anchoring north, south, east and west. Clan members sat on the ground behind them, as many as five hundred gathered for presect, only his second as high priest.

And he'd failed them all.

He shook away his memories. "You understand Draven's intent that night?"

"To steal each primo's magic and take it as his own."

Priest nodded. "And to use their combined power to kill me. Without me in the way, he planned to lead our clan and retain our old ways."

"But you stopped him. You took their magic back, which means it lives in you."

He swallowed, hating how the truth tasted on his tongue. "I did and it does, but with it came all the taint from the things he'd done. I can't get rid of it. No matter what I try or how many times I ask the Keeper to free me, it's still there." He paused long enough to let Naomi fully process what he'd shared. When she still looked on him only with slightly raised brows, waiting as if to learn the fatal blow, he added, "Fifty years ago I might have been fit for your granddaughter. Now it's a *very* dangerous proposition. If you knew the way it wanted Kateri—the things it urged me to do when I saw her— you'd put her in your car and drive like hell from here."

She huffed a sharp laugh. "Hardly. More like I'll cart her back here and start over. Only this time I'll make sure Alek keeps his distance." She paused and cocked her head, a sly grin tilting her lips. "You forget, I know how protective a Volán male can be. I don't care how much darkness is trapped inside you, you couldn't hurt her if you tried. She's exactly what you need to find balance. More than that, *you're* exactly what *Kateri* needs."

The response couldn't have shocked him more if she'd stood and slapped him as she said it. "Come again?"

Naomi sighed and reclined against the couch's leather back, her shoulders sagging as her words flowed free. "My son shunned his gifts. Forbade me from sharing about our race or any of our ways. Kateri's grown up too distant from her feelings."

She paused a moment, clasped her hands and studied them. "He never intended to share their heritage with them. Even urged them into mainstream society when they both wanted more free-spirited careers." She looked up and a small smile crept back in. "It never worked with Alek. He flies only on instinct. More so lately than normal. But Kateri always wanted to please her dad and ended up locked in her self-discipline. She's passionate. Almost frighteningly so. But she's too afraid to let it out. She wanted a much different life for herself when she was young, but the way my son drove her to be rational—logical and methodic—he choked the passion right out of her."

The darkness stirred, tightly contained under the barricades he'd refortified, but testing every nook and cranny for an escape hatch.

His panther stretched and purred, more than a little pleased at the challenge presented and eager to take it on.

But it wasn't just Kateri he had to look out for. Whether his beast had wanted to gut Alek a few hours ago or not, he was still a clansman. And an important one at that. "How old is Alek?"

"Twenty-five."

"And no call to his soul quest?"

"No, but he's close. You saw how quick his temper fired, and he sleeps nearly as much as he's awake." Her face brightened. "He's a natural at fighting. Every bit as skilled as Farron was, if not more so. Started martial arts when he was only six, though he had to beg his father for a year before he was allowed to enroll. If the Keeper wills it, he'll make a fine warrior primo."

Outside the shop's wide window overlooking Main Street, the treetops clustered around the old business fronts swayed in a soft afternoon breeze. A perfect early spring day.

Except even the bright sunshine coating the cloudless sky couldn't mask the emptiness encroaching. The lessening of magic that held the beauty of their world together. Without the primos, he'd never be able to restore it to the levels they'd enjoyed fifty years ago. If Alek was the first to bring him closer to a full council, he'd take him no matter what his skill set. But Naomi was probably right. The way he'd braced himself in front of Kateri and prepared to fight spoke volumes about his character. But there had been genuine fear there, too. Fear apparently triggered by their parents' death. "That's why you're here? Your son and his wife are dead so you've brought them here to learn?"

"That's part of it." She studied him a moment, as though gauging if he'd really gained the balance needed to withstand more. Whatever she saw must have been enough, because she nodded, stood and padded to her purse beside the display case. Carefully, she pulled a folded white felt cloth free and faced him. "Mostly I came to keep them safe."

The darkness inside him surged, an alertness on par

with his panther scenting danger. Only the most sacred objects were stored in white.

Or the vilest to protect the bearer.

Moving closer, she unfolded the cloth. "I found this beside my son the day we found him and his wife murdered."

Nestled in the center of the fabric was the symbol he'd found only moments before their last full presect. A dagger with a serpent coiled around it.

His brother's mark.

"You may have thought you killed Draven that night," Naomi said, "but he's alive. If my visions are correct, he's out to find the house primos and finish what he started fifty years ago."

Chapter Four

Draven was alive. Alive and hunting Priest's primos all over again. In the time it had taken Priest to reach Kateri and Alek, usher them from the pub and get them all on the road, the harsh truth had pummeled him unmercifully, every instinct lashing him to move. To hide them both from his brother's reach until he could figure out what to do. But it wasn't until they'd settled into the thirty-minute drive to the home he shared with Tate and Jade near Beaver Lake that reality had thrown its harshest punch.

Kateri was the biggest target.

More so than all the primos rolled into one. Because if Draven ever learned she was his mate, he'd stop at nothing to capture her. To use her to control Priest's every move and the future of their clan.

At the front of their mini-convoy, Tate rounded the last curve on the winding roads that lead to Priest's isolated property, his souped-up, semi-restored '69 Camaro roaring loud enough to match Priest's Harley taking up the rear. Alek navigated between them, the minimalist sunscreen-only top to his Jeep leaving the rest of the occupants in full view—Naomi beside Alek up front, while Jade chatted up Kateri in the backseat.

As she had many times throughout their trip, Kateri twisted in her seat and glanced back at him. Where some people hated the idea of so much wind, Kateri seemed to thrive on it, often canting her face upward as if to honor the air and sun on her skin. Not at all the rigid woman Naomi had painted her to be. She'd pulled her hair back in a haphazard ponytail, but bits and pieces whipped in the wind. Her blue-gray eyes were hidden behind a classic pair of silver-rimmed aviators, a barrier he wished like hell his powers allowed him to see through.

Hell, if he'd had his way, she'd have been behind him on his bike for the ride home, her arms and legs wrapped tight around him and her heartbeat solid against his back. He'd almost insisted as much, but had opted for the expediency of getting her someplace safe over another head-to-head with her brother. Not to mention Kateri had eyed him with a wariness that rubbed both man and beast raw. Considering he'd been in her presence all of five minutes the first go-round, he'd apparently created some sizable relationship obstacles to overcome.

Tate slowed and pulled into the drive, Alek tight behind him. Only then did Priest draw his first decent breath since he'd laid eyes on his brother's talisman. The land Priest had bought after relocating to Eureka Springs was vast—enough to give his panther room to roam at will—but protective wards covered every inch of it.

Priest backed his Harley into the custom shelter he'd built for his Heritage Softail, dismounted and headed straight for Alek's Jeep.

Wise woman that she was, Naomi had already hopped from the front passenger's seat and all but dragged Alek out of Priest's path toward Kateri. "Alek, get my bag for me. Priest will get Kateri's."

Yep. Wise *and* crafty. Although, she couldn't act as the buffer between Priest and Alek forever. Sooner or later, he'd have to set things straight with the male, and as irritated as his cat still was with the challenge Alek had thrown down, sooner was the better bet.

He reached Kateri just as she started to jump out of the raised Jeep. Rather than offer the hand he'd intended to help her down, instinct took over and he gripped her by the hips and lifted her to the ground.

The darkness purred in chorus with his cat, pacified for the moment by the contact, but urging him for more.

Kateri's hands covered his, the tenuous touch as soft as her startled gasp. "I could have managed." A rebuke on the surface, but still breathy enough to give him hope.

Mindful of her brother still in earshot and the obvious need for damage control, he lowered his voice and leaned in close enough her scent surrounded him. Something exotic that reminded him of the jasmine Tate's mother had grown. "You could have, but then I wouldn't have been able to touch you."

A nearly infinitesimal shudder moved through her, and her lips parted. While wariness still weighted her gaze, there was more behind it now. Curiosity and resounding inner strength.

He could work with that. Assuming he could keep the darkness and his beast in check long enough not to kill her brother. He gently squeezed her hips. "I won't hurt you. Despite my cat's way of showing it, he was actually happy to meet you."

Her gaze sharpened to match the snippy drawl of her voice. "He didn't sound happy."

"Oh, he was happy. So was I."

Blanking her expression, she pushed his hands away

and stepped out of his hold. "That doesn't make any sense. And I don't think the way you growled at my brother had anything to do with being happy to see me."

"I doubt much of anything makes sense to you right now, but it will. Soon." He'd see to it in the most personal fashion possible. "And my response to your brother is a different issue, but I won't hurt him either."

At least he'd try not to. For Kateri's sake.

Forcing himself to back away, he plucked the last remaining suitcase from the Jeep and motioned her toward the house. "Come on. Let's get you inside before your brother comes looking to tempt fate again."

Whether she agreed with the wisdom of cutting short another run-in between Priest and her brother, or just wanted neutral ground, he couldn't be sure, but she wasted little time putting her long legs to good use. Like everything else about her, she moved with an understated grace. Smooth and easy as water over a pebble-lined creek. She'd made it all of two steps past the front door when she paused and removed her sandals, her gaze adeptly perusing the open entry and massive living area beyond.

Staring out the windowed wall that lined the back of the house and overlooked the natural terrain beyond were Naomi and Alek. Tate stood rooted next to Naomi and pointed out his favorite details below. Neither Naomi or Alek were barefoot, so either the shoeless indoor routine was a mandate of Kateri's parents that Alek had already brushed off, or she simply preferred to be without them. Given the way she'd seemed to enjoy being outside, he was betting the latter.

As if sensing their arrival, Naomi glanced over her

shoulder and beamed a huge smile at Kateri. "Come look, Kateri. It's beautiful."

Kateri glanced at Priest and hesitated, one of those awkward pauses that spoke of discomfort and uncertainty. Another thing he'd have to work on between them.

"My home is yours." He motioned her ahead with a lift of his chin. "Go. Enjoy whatever suits you. Though, if you explore the property, take me, Jade or Tate until you learn the boundaries. We can talk about everything else after you've had a chance to settle in and look around."

"Thank you." With that, she hurried to take in the view beside her family. His home was really more of a lodge built on piers that butted up to a large bluff, but the landscape was exceptional no matter the time of year. Especially with the thick unspoiled woods that stretched between here and Beaver Lake in the distance. Scoring five square miles had taken a whole lot of negotiating and just shy of a miracle, but every headache it had taken to seal the deal had been worth it.

Jade bounded down the open staircase with an enthusiasm far outside the norm for when she was at home. Likely centered around the fact that she wouldn't be outnumbered by men for once. "Hey, Priest. I put Naomi's bag in my room. I figured I'd sleep on the couch and give her and Kateri my room."

"No." His sharp rebuke came out before he could censor it, the near-growl that came with it so grated, everyone spun to face him at once. He tried to soften his tone, but his words still came out gruff. "Alek and Tate will bunk together. I'll take the couch and Naomi will share your room with you." He locked stares with his mate. "Kateri sleeps in my bed."

Her gaze shuttled from Jade, to Naomi, then Alek before rooting back on Priest. "That's not necessary. I can sleep—"

"In my bed."

Alek spun to Naomi. "I've got a better idea. How about we get a hotel room and keep her the fuck away from this asshole?"

"Kateri goes nowhere without me," Priest said before Naomi could so much as open her mouth. "If my brother's alive, it's not safe."

"No offense, but I think I can keep my sister safe just fine."

The room fell quiet.

Inside him, his panther bristled and flicked its tail. "You think so, do you?"

Naomi started forward. "Eerikki—"

He held up his hand to stop her, but kept his attention zeroed in on Alek. "No. We need to deal with this. Now. He needs the release and the knowledge."

The timing was absolute shit, but nothing was more volatile than a Volán male bordering on coming into his powers. Either Priest handled what needed handling while he was still in control, or he risked breaking his promise to his mate and gutting this generation's most likely warrior primo.

He held Alek's stare a second longer, then shifted his gaze to Jade. "Start dinner for us, *nahina*. Show Naomi and Kateri the house and make sure they have whatever they need." He cut his attention to Tate. "Stay with them. Especially Kateri."

Tate nodded, the knowing behind his amber eyes

making it clear he understood the reason behind Priest's request even if he'd yet to share what Kateri was to him.

Priest eyeballed Alek and jerked his chin toward the raised back porch and the wooded terrain below. "You come with me. We'll see how ready you are to face off with my brother."

Rather than wait for an answer, he stalked out the wide sliding glass door. That Alek would follow was a given. The young man might not have accepted his gifts yet, but he was full of unspent anger. A sure sign his soul quest was imminent. If Priest hadn't been knocked for such a damned loop by Kateri, he'd have noted the chaotic energy pouring off Alek a hell of a lot sooner.

Sure enough, Alek's heavy footsteps descended the wooden steps that lead to the wide gorge. Their weight didn't lessen when he reached solid ground. Even with the thick leaves still damp from rain the night before, his steps crunched unnervingly loud against nature's quiet.

"You walk loud enough a deaf man could hear you coming," Priest said.

"You know damned good and well, I'm right behind you. Why try to mask it?"

Ah, youth. Always so quick with the attitude. Particularly when they didn't have a clue what they were dealing with. But Alek was about to get a good dose of reality. "So you can hear the threat headed your way before it hits."

"What's that supposed to mean?"

"It means this." Priest shoved a sharp gust of wind against Alek's chest, the thrust of it powerful enough it knocked him on his ass. With fifteen feet still between them when it hit and Priest's back to Alek, the man never saw it coming. Or more to the point, never heard it.

Priest turned in time to enjoy the utter shock on Alek's face and the awkward way he pushed himself upright. "What you're feeling right now," Priest said, "the caution and awareness—*that's* what will keep you alive with Draven. That and understanding the depth of his powers. He won't meet you face-to-face. He'll corner you. Slip up behind you. Lure you into a trap and suffer no conscience while he slits your throat and steals whatever magic the Keeper gives you. And you damned sure won't hear him coming tromping around like an elephant."

Pausing only long enough to brace his feet, Priest motioned Alek forward then let his arms hang loose at his sides. "You think you can protect your family, then bring it. Show me what you know."

Alek glanced back at the house.

Priest didn't dare follow his gaze. Just the thought that Kateri might be watching through the picture windows offered too much distraction. Not to mention, if he actually got a visual confirmation she was watching, he'd be too tempted to forgo this task, and Alek needed this confrontation. His skepticism and impending change was too dangerous to leave unattended. For now, he'd have to hope that Naomi was as skilled at running interference with Kateri as she was with her grandson.

"You're fucking kidding me," Alek said, all righteous indignation and bravado. "We're gonna beat our chests and duke it out like knuckle-dragging idiots?"

Priest grinned and his panther practically purred at the challenge. "You can think of it that way if you want. Or you can accept it for what it is."

"Which is?"

"You learning your place."

The taunt worked. Alek's face flamed a violent red and he stomped forward, his fists engaged at his sides and ready for action. "You think I'm some stupid punk you can push around?"

Priest's magic surged. One more little nudge and Alek would lay it on with everything he had. Not that it would be anywhere near enough. "Quite the contrary. You need the release. The confrontation against someone stronger and more capable than you."

Alek lunged, the move generated more from frustration and anger than any decent strategy.

Countering easily, Priest shifted out of Alek's trajectory and added a humbling tap to the back of his head as he passed. "Surely that's not all you've got to show for your training. The way Naomi talked you up, I'd expected more."

Rather than pause and get his bearings, Alek spun and re-engaged, this time leveraging his skills and letting loose with a string of attacks.

Priest blocked them all, never once throwing his own punch or kick. Merely let his opponent take the release he needed.

Naomi hadn't misspoken. Alek did have talent. Even if it was hindered by the unfocused rage that fueled his every move.

It took a solid minute of back-to-back blows before Alek frowned and backed off. His chest heaved from the nonstop advance and his eyes burned with barely leashed fury. "You wanted a fight. Why the fuck won't you engage?"

"Why waste my strength and skills when you're so willing to show me what I want to know without the effort?" Priest circled Alek where he stood, subtly herding his prey deeper into a sizable space along the center of the gorge. "Do you know what your grandfather was for our clan?"

Still braced on the balls of his feet, Alek kept himself squared to Priest as he moved. "Tate said he was the warrior primo."

"Your father would have been as well, had he answered the Keeper."

"My dad didn't want his gifts. Didn't trust it after what he saw your brother do."

"Didn't want them, or was afraid of them?"

"Does it matter?"

Priest sprung forward, a blade-hand strike aimed at Alek's temple but tempered enough he had at least a chance of defending himself.

Alek's block was too slow to completely avoid contact, but lessened some of the impact. To his credit, he shook it off and repositioned, but there was a difference in his gaze. A whole lot of shock and a flicker of respect. Whatever he'd expected of Priest where fighting skills were concerned, moving faster than the human eye could follow apparently hadn't been on the list.

"Everything matters where it affects our clan," Priest said, answering Alek's question as he prowled forward. "Odds are good you or Kateri will be the next warrior primo if you answer the Keeper's call. Though with your interest in fighting, I'm betting on you." He feigned a jab and Alek wisely didn't fall for it. "I need my primos to protect our clan and the Earth's magic. So, I need to know—are you afraid?"

The taunt jarred Alek into motion, his grated words mingled with each strike. "You didn't see my parents.

What your brother did to them. They had everything. Deserved to live their lives left alone."

Priest parried with a twisting move that left Alek scrambling to keep up. "So, you are afraid."

"I'm pissed." More punches and kicks, each one growing in intensity and aimed for maximum damage.

When he aimed for Priest's face, Priest dodged, manacled Alek's wrist and spun him into a choke hold. "Enough to answer your call and help me end my brother?"

Alek's training kicked in and he twisted out of the hold, going for a counter assault to the vulnerable back of Priest's leg.

Before he could connect, Priest was already free and poised behind him.

Alek faced him and all but spat, "Tate said the same darkness is in you. What's to stop you from being any different than Draven?"

Finally, the real issue. The fear that fueled Alek's anger.

Slower this time, to rebuild Alek's confidence, Priest started in with a string of punches and kicks, each one building faster and more powerful.

At first Alek met them easily, but with each point of contact, his strength weakened and his eyes grew wide in concern. Over and over, each strike grew more complex. Faster until Alek slowly began to retreat.

Priest kept pushing. Naomi was right. Alek was no ordinary fighter. He was a warrior through and through. An alpha who'd bow to no one unless they were stronger. Faster. Worthy.

He unleashed his power, hitting Alek on all sides with snaps of fire, electricity and air, while raining physical

punches in rapid succession. Just when Alek was about
to break, Priest rippled the earth beneath Alek's feet.

Alek stumbled backward.

Priest's cat burst free in a brilliant burst of silver and
pinned its prey to the cool, damp leaves. His panther's
massive paws weighted Alek's shoulders and his bared
teeth hovered inches from Alek's face.

The beast wanted to linger. Wanted to toy with the
male who'd dared keep it from its mate.

The darkness urged for something uglier. Tempted
him to cross an unforgivable line.

But Kateri's image as he'd lifted her from the Jeep
flashed to the forefront of his thoughts. Grounded him.

Priest forced his human form back into place, but the
growl from his cat lingered in his voice. "What stops
me from being like Draven is my brother lives only for
himself and power. I live for my mate and my people."

Up and down, Alek's chest heaved, his heart pumping so hard it was visible at his neck. His eyes were wide
with wonderment and shock. A fighter who not only accepted he'd been bested, but was too awed by the strategy and strength that put him on his back to hold any
remorse for his defeat. "Holy shit. How'd you do that?"

Priest shoved back to his knees and stood, towering
over Alek still flat out on his back. He offered his hand.
"It's my heritage. Yours, too, if you accept it."

Alek volleyed his attention between Priest's face and
his outstretched palm.

Priest waited until logic won out and Alek took his
hand, then pulled him to his feet. "Your skills are solid.
Fitting for a warrior primo."

For the first time since they first met, Alek refused
to meet his eyes head-on and a vulnerability laced his

voice. "I don't know anything about us. What it means to be Volán."

"Then I'll teach you."

"Why?"

There he was. The real man underneath the change brewing inside his soul. A teachable youth with the tenacity and courage to face whatever fate threw them. "Because I'm your high priest. It's what I do. What I was born for."

The only *thing I existed for until five hours ago.*

Instincts honed by his beast bristled along his shoulders.

He twisted and scanned the horizon behind him, but froze at the sight of Kateri standing in the breakfast nook's window. Naomi stood beside her, blatantly trying to catch her granddaughter's attention, but Kateri was having none of it. Not if her crossed arms and angry scowl were any indication.

"What is she to you?" Alek asked beside him.

Priest held Kateri's gaze, sorely tempted to skirt the truth a little longer. The newly formed bond between him and Alek was too new. Too fragile to risk too much. But if the Keeper chose Alek to serve alongside him, he also couldn't risk losing the young man's trust. Not with the undoubted battles in their future.

He faced him, trusting Naomi to do what she could to explain what Kateri had witnessed. "Your first lesson—Volán men who've accepted their powers know their mates on sight. Instantly. There is no doubt. No hesitation or misunderstanding."

Alek's head snapped back, the unexpected change in topic visibly throwing him for a loop. "So, what? It's like some cosmic arranged marriage?"

"An arranged marriage implies the woman is aware. In our case, only the male knows. At least to begin with. It's the man's responsibility to win his mate. Her respect. Her trust and her heart. Only when her soul accepts him is the bond formed."

"What happens if she doesn't?"

The thought cut through him with all the kindness of a jagged blade of ice, and the inky ugliness that drifted and swirled inside him went deathly still. As though it, too, waited for the answer. "The same as any other person who denies their destiny. They suffer. Live half a life. Empty."

Still rooted in front of the window, Kateri and Naomi watched them. His mate might not be scowling and seconds from charging out of the house to interfere, but her focus was intent, taking in every little detail. Logically, he knew she couldn't hear him. Not yet anyway. But the part of him that existed only for her didn't care. Relished the chance to say out loud his new truth. "I would put your sister above anyone else. Would give up my life and my clan to keep her safe. It's why she needs to stay protected. Draven can never get his hands on her or he'll use her as leverage."

Alek frowned and shuttled his gaze between Kateri and Priest. "What are you saying?"

Priest met his stare, the beast and darkness merging with him to make his claim. "I'm telling you, she's my mate."

No response. Just stunned silence.

Not exactly a surprising development considering Alek had been raised with zero knowledge of their ways, but it spoke volumes of how far Priest had to go in teaching him. He motioned Alek to follow him and started toward the house. "Come on. Jade will have dinner ready soon. She might not have given me grief for putting her on food detail, but she'll rip us both a new asshole if we're not there when it's ready."

He'd made it all of two steps, when Alek clamped him on the shoulder and tugged. "Hold up. You can't seriously plan to keep Katy in the dark on this."

Priest pointedly dropped his gaze to Alek's hand.

Alek released him and stepped out of slugging distance, but crossed his arms in a show of stubbornness Priest couldn't help but appreciate.

"Your parents died two weeks ago," Priest said. "Likely by my brother's hand. You know almost nothing of our race and Naomi tells me Kateri barely believes even what she sees with her own eyes. When I tell her what she is to me, it will be in my way, when my instincts tell me it won't scare her more than she already is."

His logic must have resonated with Alek because he unwound his protective stance, raked one hand through his hair and shook his head. "Man, this is whacked. Seriously, insane shit. Though, after everything else I've heard and seen, I guess it shouldn't be all that much of a shock." He planted both hands on his hips, checked the window, as if to ensure Kateri couldn't really hear them and lowered his voice. "Any other surprises you need to throw me? 'Cause I'd just as soon field 'em now and only have to unscramble what's left of reality once."

Priest huffed out a chuckle. "Nope. Not today. Though I'll give you some damned good advice." He started for the house.

Alek fell in step beside him. "Yeah? What's that?"

Priest hesitated only a beat. "If you value your life, don't ever step between me and my mate again."

Chapter Five

Normal. For the last thirty minutes the world around Katy settled into a nice normal rhythm. No fantastical conversation about companion animals or shifting. No growling, hissing or flame throwing like she'd watched take place in the giant gorge outside Priest's home. Certainly no mammoth panthers flashing in and out of existence in the space of seconds. Just regular people eating dinner like normal people. Even the simple tacos Jade and Tate had whipped up while she'd stood rooted in terror by the kitchen's wide window were beautifully ordinary. Exactly the balance she'd craved since finding her parents dead.

And here she was eager to push things back off-center again.

Because you want justice.

Katy tightened her grip on her fork and pushed a bite of taco salad around on her plate. Her cheeks heated and the cold fury she'd kept buried deep shoved harder against her control. She couldn't lose sight of her goals. What had been done to her parents was an abomination. Pure evil. She owed it to her parents to find their killer and make sure he paid for what he'd done. Only she'd do it the right way. Not give way to the dark need that pushed her to pay Draven back with the same cruelty he'd dealt the people she loved.

Across the large trestle-style table, Alek handed off the bowl full of seasoned ground beef to Tate beside him. The last streaks of sunshine danced through the softly swaying treetops outside the large window, lending a semblance of peace to her rioting thoughts.

Something had happened outside between Priest and Alek. Something deeper than just two men beating their chests and acting like idiots. For the life of her, she couldn't figure it out. But Alek was different. Calmer than she'd seen him in weeks and deferring to Priest like he'd been his wingman for years.

Very weird.

Not that everything else in her life these days wasn't beyond the realm of belief.

She stole a peek at Priest beside her. As it had when he'd helped her from the Jeep, the slow, pulsing warmth blossomed low in her belly, and her heartbeat fluttered in an unsteady, but eager rhythm. It didn't make sense. She'd known him only hours, but just looking at him stirred her in an inexplicable way. Never mind the breath-stealing response when he actually touched her.

His gaze slid to her plate and her barely touched salad. He'd done that a few times since they'd settled in. Both times he'd followed up the cursory study by frowning and handing her another food option off the table. This time he stood, prowled to the kitchen and yanked open the refrigerator door. He rummaged around inside and pulled out a medium plastic tub. The last thing she expected was for him to jump into the conversational lull he'd created by leaving the table, but he pulled down a clean plate from the cabinets and focused on Naomi.

"You said you had a vision after you found your son. Tell me about it."

Katy straightened in her seat, the impatient part of her eager for any kind of information that might lead to action instead of more waiting.

Priest's gaze cut to her, considering, before he went back to laying out whatever was in the tub on a plate.

"There were two, actually," Naomi said. "One the morning it happened alerting me to trouble, and another when I saw Draven's talisman."

"You saw him?"

Naomi shook her head, eyes aimed to the table but unfocused. "I saw the marks of primos from our past. I felt the chill of Draven's magic, and I saw a jaguar stalking through the dark."

Priest put the lid on the plastic tub and put it back in the fridge. "You're sure it wasn't a memory?"

"No. It was the present. Our old world had a different feel to it. Today's world is more electric and connected. The darkness was thick, but there were newer buildings in the distance. Someone was being chased. And there were screams. A man and a woman."

Priest moved her taco salad out from in front of her and slid a plateful of fresh fruit in its place. For late March, the quality of what he'd selected was impeccable—plump strawberries, blueberries and blackberries mingled with cantaloupe and watermelon.

Such a simple gesture. Uncomplicated and done without any fanfare, but deeply thoughtful.

He eased his big body into his seat with a grace that echoed the panther she'd glimpsed, braced his elbows on the table and shared a tense look with Jade across the table.

Something in the unspoken message that moved between them prodded Katy's instincts. Spurred her to do something. "What's that look mean? What do you know that we don't?"

Priest paused long enough to cast a pointed look at the fruit and cocked an eyebrow. A tit-for-tat nudge if she'd ever seen one.

Barely fighting back one of the scoffs her father had always called uncouth, she snatched a blueberry and popped it in her mouth.

Priest's mouth twitched as though he wanted to smile, but his eyes countered what he'd kept in check, a healthy amount of mirth shining behind the odd gray color. "Jade had a vision around the same time your parents were murdered. It was her first after earning her gifts."

"What'd she see?" Alek said.

Jade ducked her head and focused on what was left of her taco. Considering how outgoing she'd been throughout the day, seeing her so uncertain and vulnerable rubbed Katy all wrong. "Someone hunting. Lots of blood, but no details. It only lasted a minute. Maybe less."

"A new seer's early visions are always brief," Naomi said. "Especially an uncomfortable one. They'll get stronger. Longer. And you'll learn to disconnect from the emotion as you grow." She turned her focus to Priest. "But the feelings she felt confirm my belief. Draven is hunting our primos."

Everyone at the table grew silent.

Elbows still planted on the table, Priest laced his fingers and rested them against his mouth. Thoughtful and distant.

"You don't believe her?" Katy said.

Priest's gaze slid to her and this time his mouth crooked in a semi-wry smile. "Your grandmother is one of the strongest seers I know. I wouldn't question her judgment."

"Then what are you thinking?"

His expression sobered and the gray in his eyes seemed to shift and swirl like an early morning fog. Only that couldn't be right. Eye color might change based on lighting or other environment elements, but to actually move?

Then again, she'd watched her grandmother shift into a hawk and witnessed the biggest panther in history pin her brother on his back—even if it had only been for a handful of seconds. So, what did she know?

"The same day Jade had her vision," he said, "I was pulled into a soul quest. It was fast. No warning. But when I got to the Otherworld there was no one there. At least, not that I could see or feel. I was just about to return when a scream sounded from somewhere out of sight. The next thing I knew I was here."

Jade shifted in her chair, the creak of the wood overloud in the room's otherwise quiet. "My vision happened at the same time."

"Maybe what you heard was my parents," Alek said.

Priest considered the suggestion for a moment then shook his head. "Your mother wasn't Volán and your father refused his quest. There aren't any second chances with the Keeper. Refuse her once and you'll never go back."

Done with the overloaded plate of food he'd taken on, Tate tossed his paper napkin to the table and reclined against his seat back. "I don't understand. If Draven's hunting primos, why wouldn't he go for the sorcerer line first? Outside of Priest, they'd hold the most power."

"A better question is why aren't *you* hunting the primo lines?" Alek said to Priest. "If they're so important, then shouldn't you be doing the same thing?"

Not the least bit ruffled, Priest met her brother's stare head-on. "I had no need. I thought my brother was dead, and I'm called to the Otherworld when anyone answers their soul quest." He shifted his attention to Tate. "As to why he started with the warrior line instead of the sorcerer line, it could simply be the only lead he had."

Sighing, Naomi leaned into the table and cupped the mug of herbal tea she'd made shortly after Priest and Alek had finished their he-man one-on-one. She'd tried to foist the allegedly calming concoction on Katy, but the lavender and chamomile combo was no match for a decent cup of coffee. "I've only kept in touch with a few other families since our clan broke apart, but I've heard many changed their last names to better disappear."

"But yours didn't?" Jade asked.

Naomi shook her head. "We believed Draven was dead. My son just wanted as far from his heritage as he could get. To forget the things he'd seen that night."

Katy couldn't blame her father. She'd only seen glimpses of the power her race was apparently capable of. None of it ugly, but all of it shocking. If that night was on par with the carnage she'd found at her parents' house, she'd have distanced her family from all of it, too. "So, you think Draven tracked us by name?"

"Or through his gifts," Naomi said.

As he had with all his other questions the last half hour, Alek turned to Priest for answers. "What house is he?"

"Sorcerer."

One word, but the ominous undertone behind it stirred more than Katy cared to process. A flight instinct her father had no doubt wrestled his whole life combating with a white-hot need for vengeance. "The most powerful house. And now he's looking for me and Alek, right?"

"He won't touch you." Priest's gaze bore into hers, the strength behind it instantly seizing her chaotic thoughts and anchoring her on solid emotional ground. "My brother is powerful, but there is absolutely no gift I won't use—no advantage I won't leverage—to keep you safe. He will not beat me. Not if you're at stake."

The same electric surge she'd felt the two times he'd touched her reignited. A pull that seemed rooted in the center of her chest and urged her forward, all the while nudging a dormant part of herself to life.

And why such importance on her? Why not Jade or Tate? Or even Alek, for that matter. He was the fighter in her family. If this Keeper person was going to put a primo label on anyone, it sure wouldn't be her.

As soon as the questions surfaced in her head, she tamped them down. Emotions and physical responses weren't important. All that mattered was finding the person who'd wrecked her family and the reality that went with it. "So, outside of records and technology, how would he trace us?"

Priest studied her, the intensity of his scrutiny so deep it felt as if he'd stripped away her flesh and peered straight to her soul. "If he had something of your line—something of significant meaning or filled with emotion—he could use it. But only if the person had accepted their gifts." His gaze dropped to the mostly untouched plate in front of her and he nudged it an inch closer. "Since your father never accepted his, he'd have had to use traditional means."

Katy ignored the fruit, her stomach churning too much to even consider adding food to the mix. "He's your brother. If he has something of yours, what's to stop him from finding you?"

"Priest marked us," Jade said, cutting through the thick connection between her and Priest. Not the least bit concerned with the mixed genders gathered round the table, she twisted in her seat and pulled her tank top up and over her head.

Alek coughed as though he'd nearly swallowed his tongue and all but gaped at Jade's now exposed back across the table.

Tate and Naomi chuckled, but it was Priest who spoke. "Another lesson about our race—modesty doesn't carry the same weight it does with the singura."

Scoffing, Tate stood, plucked his and Naomi's plate off the table, and sauntered to the kitchen. "And if you do have any, you learn quick to get over it the first time you shift back to human form in front of other people and forget your clothes."

"Sorry." Jade peeked over her shoulder, but the mischievous grin on her face said she really wasn't. "You have to admit, the marks are pretty awesome. I just got mine today."

Awesome was an understatement. Done in red, black and every shade of gray imaginable, they exuded power, yet held a feminine grace that matched Jade's personality.

"Tate has them, too?" Katy said.

"Hell, yeah," Tate answered before Jade could so

much as nod. Rounding the kitchen counter that separated the dining nook from the kitchen, Tate peeled his T-shirt off and bared his heavily muscled torso. She'd barely had a chance to appreciate the artwork dipping over his shoulders in a half-arc along his collarbone before he turned and displayed his back.

"Whoa." Gone was Alek's awkward response to Jade's bold behavior, replaced with pure appreciation.

Like Jade's, the design exuded tremendous strength. But where Jade's featured soft feminine lines, Tate's was pure male. A mix of Nordic and tribal influence. The detail was so impressive anyone who saw it would be tempted to touch and trace each bold line. She forced her gaze away from the beautiful work and found Priest's attention rooted on her. "You did that?"

His lips didn't move, but something in his expression shifted. Something important she couldn't quite categorize.

"Everything Priest does is awesome." Tate turned, jabbed his arms back into his shirtsleeves and pulled his T-shirt over his head. "You wouldn't believe how much people pay for his ink. And that's without the extra mojo added to it."

"That's why I couldn't find you before the Keeper gave me direction," Naomi said. "You put protection spells in the marks."

Priest nodded. "And a locator so I can find them if they ever need me."

"Well, your brother can't find us yet outside traditional means," Katy said, "but shouldn't you at least start looking for the others and beat him to the punch? Maybe see if you can find someone still around from Nanna's generation?"

"We'd need a sorcerer to help us," Naomi said. "Do we have any?"

"None," Priest said. "I thought the house was dormant until I learned Draven was alive."

The heaviness in his answer drew Katy on a visceral level, a foreign impulse to soothe and comfort him pushing against her tight control. To wipe away the thick regret in his voice with a soft touch. Which was absolutely insane. She barely knew this man. Had zero obligation to him or his troubles except where it aided in finding her parents' killer.

Undaunted, Naomi crossed her arms on the table and narrowed her gaze. "Jade and I could see if our visions bring us anything. We wouldn't be able to pinpoint as clearly as a sorcerer could, but if there are other seers nearby, we could pool our strength and perhaps narrow the area to search. Surely we have active seers in the clan?"

"Some from the new generation and the old," Priest said. "Tate's and Jade's parents got word out to a handful of families when we settled here. The news hasn't traveled as far as we'd like for it to, but most of those who've heard relocated with us."

Jade grinned and waggled her eyebrows at Katy. "It's a hoot. Lots of the elders have built a reputation with the people in Eureka Springs. They're known as people who've gone off the grid and everyone thinks they live without electricity or running water."

"Do they?" Katy asked, the scientist in her rising up in interest.

Tate scoffed. "They're elders. Not stupid. They like their hot water and internet as much as everyone else, but the rumors help keep people away so they can shift whenever they want. In the time since Jade and I were born, we've taken up Ozark land from the Ouachita Forest to just south of Springfield."

"But none of them are from primo lines?" Alek asked.

Priest shook his head. "We've got twenty families at most and only eight of those in your generation."

"Do you have anything from the primo lines?" Naomi said. "Something Jade and I could use to help narrow our focus on each family?"

"We've got the primo medallions," Jade said. "My mom saved them."

Naomi brightened. "Those are perfect. The more power and history, the better."

Katy straightened in her chair, all the information shared throughout their meal and opportunity clicking together at once. "Wait a minute. If Draven is the problem then why wouldn't we just go straight for him?" She locked gazes with Priest. "If we stop him, then everyone else is safe."

"If my brother gets control of our primos, no one is safe. Not our clan and not the singura."

"But you're high priest and Draven already has his gifts. You can do everything the other houses can do and you don't have to worry about ticking off this Keeper person."

Priest waited, patiently listening.

Seriously? He didn't see it? It was easy. Assuming he could really do all the stuff everyone claimed he could. "So, we've got his charm. You use it, find him, and we bring him to justice."

In the silence that settled around them, Katy wasn't sure if she'd hit the idea lottery, or inadvertently stepped on the mother of all land mines, but the tension and awareness in the room grew supercharged in a second.

When Priest finally answered, his voice seemed not just to register in her ears, but as an echoed thought as well. "What does that justice look like for you, Kateri?"

Brutal.

Bloody.

Painful.

She shoved the raw, uncensored thoughts and the cold fury that went with them into the dark well she'd built to keep her life in check. Balanced and responsible. "We find him and have him arrested. He can stand trial and be judged like everyone else."

"And do you think a singura jail could contain my brother?"

No. Absolutely not. And the fact that her anger had blinded her to such a harsh truth made her cheeks burn with embarrassment.

But it's not what you really wanted anyway. You want him to pay. To experience every pain your mother and father felt.

Not waiting for her to answer, Priest kept going. "This will end with my brother's death and it will come by my hand."

"But she has a point," Alek said. "If you can use the same skill as a sorcerer to track him, then why not use the charm and short-circuit any need to find the primos? You find him and we deal with him ourselves."

Priest shared a look with Naomi, a question unspoken.

"You should tell them," she answered. "They need to know the truth. All of it."

He sighed and clasped his hands in front of him on

the table, his thick biceps clenching as though it took every ounce of control to hold himself in place. His gaze stayed rooted on the table, though his eyes were distant. "I learned of my brother's plans to steal each primo's magic too late. My only recourse the night he acted was to strip from him the magic he'd stolen." He paused and lifted his head, meeting Katy's stare head-on. "With it came his darkness. It's in me. It took nearly twenty years after his attack for me to find balance and keep it contained. I don't dare touch anything of his. Not without risking letting it loose again."

"He could have bespelled it, too," Naomi added. "If Draven is smart enough to find my son, he has to know I'm alive and that the first place I would come would be to Eerikki. It's why I wouldn't let either of you touch it when we found it beside your father's body."

Still watching Katy, Priest lowered his voice, the softness behind it that of a man trying desperately to pull a punch he sensed would hurt. "You want retribution. It moves inside you the same as his darkness does in me, even though you hide it. But finding the primo families first is the wiser course. Draven will come for me eventually and, when he does, I'll deliver your vengeance. Gladly. Both for what he's done to you and your brother, and how our clan has suffered."

Vengeance.

The word resonated through her, carried on the deep rumble of his voice and strangely placating the incessant need that had prodded and driven her for weeks. How he saw what she'd fought so hard to contain, she had no clue. It terrified her. Made her want to put as much distance as possible between them.

But it also comforted. Offered an ally and acceptance free of judgment.

He pushed away from the table and stood, the legs of his chair grating against the stone floors that so perfectly fit his home's wilderness lodge design. "I have a client who'll take most of the day tomorrow, but most of our local families will be here on Saturday for training. I'll reach out to the seers in our clan, make sure they're joining us."

Standing as well, she blocked him from wherever he was headed. He couldn't just up and leave, expecting her to bide her time until he was ready. "Why waste a day? Let's start tomorrow." Well, maybe *she* wouldn't. Without any powers of her own, the best she could do was leverage her technical contacts from college, but she'd be on that first thing for sure.

He scanned her head to toe and his lips curled in the barest grin. "Tomorrow won't be wasted, kitten. You'll need it to rest and get ready for Saturday."

"Why?" A quick check of those still seated around the table showed Alek didn't have a clue what he meant either. Naomi, Jade and Tate, however, either kept carefully blank stares, or outright avoided her gaze. "What's so important I need a day to gear up for it?"

"For starters, you've had a long trip here and need time to unwind. To settle yourself in my home." He cupped her shoulder, the contact so careful and tender it seemed as if he barely trusted himself to allow the connection. "But more than that, on Saturday you start your training."

Training? Like exercise and fighting the way Alek did every day? Or Volán 101 and all the undoubtedly weird stuff that went with it?

Before she could so much as open her mouth and clarify, he turned her and guided her from the kitchen. "Tate, you and Alek handle clean up. Jade, take care of Naomi and make sure she has whatever she needs. I'll take care of Kateri."

A command.

The same authority he'd exerted since he'd prowled into the pub and issued his plans for getting them all safely home. Though, oddly, she didn't bristle at it. Nor did anyone else. The authority simply surrounded him. Created a natural order with those he came into contact with. No different than a predator stalking among less capable beasts.

Well, except for Alek. And Priest had handled that, too. Establishing a hierarchical order in a way that seemed to have helped her brother level out.

Too distracted by her thoughts, she let him guide her from the room, obediently putting one foot in front of the other as if some unknown part of her had already high-fived his plans even while another part insisted she dig in her heels and interrogate him for the rest of the night.

His footsteps were eerily silent beside hers, his power a tangible presence between them as he guided her through his home toward the open staircase at its center. The lodge feel suited him. Contemporary in its lines, but grounded in openness and nature. Exactly the kind of place she'd want for herself someday—isolated from the world's chaotic hubbub with plants, trees, rocks and water featured in every view.

She was just tired. That was all. He'd been right about the trip here taking its toll, and everyone else seemed comfortable in following his guidance, so maybe she'd be wise to give herself the reprieve. Feed her curiosity with simple things like wandering outdoors.

Or finding out what she could about the man shadowing her every step.

Reaching the top of the staircase where a catwalk branched left or right, she hesitated.

Priest motioned her to the right. "My room's on this side. Everyone else is to the left, so you'll have privacy and quiet."

"You really don't have to do this. I don't mind sharing with Jade and Nanna."

He inched closer, not quite touching her, but near enough his heat caressed her skin. When he spoke, his voice rumbled with the depth of a storm's distant thunder. "I want you where you belong."

Wanted.

Needed.

Possessed.

The thoughts coalesced all at once and sent a pleasant shiver down her spine. She shouldn't like the idea. Didn't want to. And yet she ached to touch him. "I'm not sure how to take that," she managed barely above a whisper.

"Take it to mean I want you comfortable and protected. The rest we'll figure out together." Not taking his eyes off her, he lifted his chin toward the hallway beyond. "Go, I'll show you where everything is."

Giving her space, he did just that in short order. Like everything else in his home, the design was simple yet spacious and tastefully done. Rich chocolates, grays and taupes offset nature's hues outside the many windows. Even the master bath had ample natural lighting, the wide glass integrated in such a way it afforded privacy even as it made her feel the walls didn't exist.

Exiting the bath, she paused beside the sliding glass door that led to a private deck outside his bedroom. Above the night-shadowed treetops, stars nestled against a blue-black sky, but for once her focus wasn't on the scenery. It was on the man reflected in the glass. In the way he moved and the effortless strength as he hefted her suitcase onto the foot of his king-size bed.

"You can open it if you like," he said as he faced her.

She froze, meeting his gaze in the reflection for at least two heartbeats before she faced him. "How did you know I like the windows open?"

He smiled, a wolfish one that said he was more than a little pleased he'd struck a chord. "I didn't. I only guess because you seemed to enjoy the drive here in your brother's Jeep. That and you're Volán. Most of us are drawn to nature."

He prowled forward, stopping only inches away from her and reaching to the door's handle behind her. The glass whooshed open, and the cool night air swept in, laden with quiet chirps and leaves rustling on a slight wind.

Still, she didn't move. Just stared up at him as he studied her. At five foot five, she wasn't exactly short, but between the near foot he had on her height-wise and the breadth of his muscled torso, she felt positively tiny.

His gaze roved her face, focused on her lips, then traveled lower to her neck. His fingertips whispered along her collarbone, slipping beneath the leather cords that held the charms her grandmother had insisted she wear after her parents' death. He pulled the charms from beneath her shirt, letting them rest between her breasts. "Do you know what these mean?"

Right now she barely knew her name and was doing

good to keep her breaths steady and even. "Not really." She'd done good in those first few days just to keep from losing her mind, let alone ask questions about what she'd always viewed as Nanna's superstitions.

He lightly touched one of the three and her heart kicked as though the connection was skin to skin. "The armadillo is for protection. A shield to hide you from harm." He moved to the next and her pulse accelerated another notch. "The turtle is a protector, too, but more nurturing. A connection to the Earth's energy."

She swallowed as much as her parched mouth would allow, everything inside her poised and eager for his next touch. "What's the bird mean?"

His mouth curled in a crooked smile. "Not just a bird. A raven. To give you courage and insight when you need it." The smile slipped and he rubbed the talisman between his finger and thumb. When he let the charm slip free and straightened, she nearly wept at the loss. As if gravity had suddenly lightened and left her floundering for purchase.

Rather than step away, he reached both hands behind his neck. A second later, he lifted a necklace free. The black leather was nicer than those she wore, pliant, well-worn and shorter in length. Hanging from it was a beautiful medallion—a four-pointed star with a creature etched at its center.

He leaned close before she could study the animal and wrapped the soft leather around her neck. The talisman lay heavy at the hollow of her throat, the heat from his body still present in the smooth metal.

She rubbed her fingers over the top of it, exploring the fine details. "What's this one?"

His gaze fixated on the simple gesture and the gray in

his eyes darkened to that of an impending storm. Only when she dropped her hand did he lift his focus to her face. "Mine."

He stepped away, his breath coming heavier as it had when they'd first met. Like then, she had the sensation that it wasn't just the two of them in the room anymore. As odd as the sensation was, she didn't mind it. If anything, it tempted her to go to him. To comfort him the same as he'd done for her.

Before she could, he turned and strode to the door, pausing only long enough to cast her one last look. "Sleep well, *mihara*."

Chapter Six

Sleep well, her ass.

Katy upped her stride from a casual jog to full-out sprint, her long legs pounding on the edge of the winding asphalt road back toward Priest's house. All night she'd tossed and turned, the driving need for action wrestling with the educated approach of patience and planning.

Oh. And then there was the all-too-consuming awareness that came from lying in Priest's bed. Between the leather and forest scent of him embedded in the sheets and the lingering sensations he'd imprinted on her memory, the only way she'd sleep well any time soon was if she drank or sexed herself into an unconscious state. No way she'd bother with the latter. She'd never met a man who could work her over well enough to take the edge off, let alone sex her into sleep.

Well, not until Priest. Something told her he wouldn't stop with a woman until she was either comatose or purring.

And what the hell had he called her? *Nahina* she'd heard her whole life, an endearment she hadn't realized until recently was a Volán's equivalent of sweetheart or dear, but *mihara*? That was a new one.

Ahead, the growing glow of headlights wavered

against the darkness, paired with the escalating pitch of a car's engine. She slowed and moved well off the street. In another fifteen minutes, the sun would finally make its way into the world for another day and she'd be less of a hit-and-run target for unsuspecting motorists. Until then, she'd have to chance plowing through the winter foliage piled up in the ditch and pray she didn't break her leg instead of burning off frustration.

The car finally passed and Katy loped back up to the road.

Her foot connected with the pavement just as the barest rustle of leaves sounded not twenty feet to her right.

For the third time since she'd snuck out of Priest's house forty-five minutes ago, prickles danced against her neck and shoulders. As if she was being watched. Or followed.

But that couldn't be right. She'd been running at a respectable pace for nearly an hour and, aside from the one rustle of leaves, she'd heard nothing. No footsteps. No voices. Only the soft lure of wind in the trees and soft chirps of cicadas and crickets.

She pushed harder, shoving her concerns aside and putting the last of her flagging energy into a final sprint. Another five minutes and she'd be back at Priest's place, hopefully unwound enough she could enjoy a simple cup of coffee and watch the sun come up without people or her thoughts giving her any trouble.

It was actually more like seven minutes before she stole into the house as quietly as she'd left it, leaving her tennis shoes by the front door and padding to the kitchen on silent, bare feet. Thankfully, whoever organized the kitchen had done so with a mind for common sense, making the coffee brewing process more of the peaceful ritual she craved than a scavenger hunt.

The machine did its thing, the quiet bubble and churn as the water made its way through the reservoir a satisfying soundtrack while she stretched her still-shaking legs. By the time it finished and she'd prepped a mug with a not-so-healthy amount of sugar and half-and-half, the sun was just nudging the horizon.

Now if she could just make her way out to the high balcony off the main living room without waking Priest. The couch was plenty big enough to handle a man his size and was conveniently situated so it faced the mammoth fireplace along the far wall, making it easy for her to sneak by. The tail end of a blanket dangled off one edge, but otherwise, no sounds or movements sounded in the open room.

She eased the sliding glass door open just enough to slip through, closed it behind her and ambled out into the crisp morning air. Even with her cool-down time in the kitchen, her skin was still misted with sweat, but the chill as the wind swept against it felt good. Invigorating.

Alive.

Unlike her parents.

The unwelcome reminder pierced through her. No matter how many times the rational part of herself fought back with arguments of due process and justice, the guilt and shame that came with doing nothing always seemed to find a way back through. A mental ninja that always knew just when to strike.

In the gorge below, something moved.

Katy froze with her coffee halfway to her lips and tried to make out the shape against the morning shadows. Whatever it was was huge. Stealthy and quiet.

A panther.

The same one that had pinned her brother to the gorge's floor the day before.

It prowled closer, every step weighted with intention and its gray eyes focused solely on her. If the darkest night had a form and movement to it, the beast below would be it. Beautiful. Sensual. *Deadly.*

Leaping with a strength that made her gasp, it landed on a low tree branch and deftly navigated up and across other branches until it slowed on one parallel to her on the high porch. It stretched its mighty length out and settled the same as a cat in a window sill, waiting, its tail swishing in what she sensed was irritation.

"Guess that means sneaking past the couch was a wasted effort," she murmured into the quiet. Feeling ten kinds of stupid for having spoken aloud and gawking, she added a little more volume. "Can you understand me when you're like that?"

The swishing tail stopped, and she'd swear the insects singing their last song for the night went silent along with it.

The beast stared at her, motionless. Only after many seconds, did it lift its chin and let out a soft chuff.

She trembled in response, the very palpable memory of how that sound had rumbled against her when they first met blasting white-hot in a second. "I take it you were the one following me on my run?"

Rather than give a verbal response, the cat settled into its pose a little deeper, one huge paw dangling off the branch in a negligent way that said, *"Yeah, and what are you gonna do about it?"*

Maybe that's what prodded her to nudge him a little more. Either that or she had a death wish. "Are you staying where you are because it's not safe to come closer, or because you think you'll scare me away?"

For the longest time, he just stared at her, his heavy-lidded gaze not offering the slightest hint as to his thoughts.

Or did he have thoughts in his cat's form? Maybe she'd misinterpreted his chuff as a valid response and he didn't know *come here* from *sic 'em*.

She sidled toward a lone Adirondack chair positioned just beside the platform's high rail with a bird's-eye view of the gorge. Just as she was about to sit, the cat rose lazily.

Katy froze, her lungs barely doing their job as he silently stalked forward. Every step was cautious. Careful and calculated. And in that second, she wasn't sure if the smarter move was to run like hell, or throw caution to the wind and enjoy the show.

Surprisingly, she opted for the latter. Which just proved how off her game she was. Logic was always placed above passion. Reason above instinct. That was the smart play her father had always taught her.

But logic didn't seem to have much place with Priest. Or with any Volán, for that matter.

Priest paused on the branch directly overhead. Waiting.

For what? Permission? Some sign of fear? For all she knew, he was gauging which part of her to eat for breakfast first.

Well, to heck with that. She'd had enough earth-shattering revelations to prove her mettle the last few weeks. She'd be damned if she let him undermine her confidence this far into Mad Hatterville. She slid into the chair and forced her shoulders to relax.

One exhale was as far as she got.

The next thing she knew, he leapt down to the balcony's protective handrail and paced in front of her.

Amazing.

Where he'd been impressive at a distance, up close, his panther was a wonder. Especially with the way he'd handled the acrobatic feat, the same nimble grace and poise she'd have expected from a much smaller feline. Definitely not from a cat that would easily reach her hip when standing. "You're very sure of yourself."

You couldn't call the sound that eked from his slightly parted mouth a growl. More like a grumble paired with a depth that made the wood platform beneath her feet vibrate. As if to prove her point, he lightly jumped from the rail and landed at her feet.

Logic screamed for her to get up and add distance between them.

Again, she ignored it, sheer fascination overriding every other command and drawing her to the edge of her seat. Unlike the green eyes she'd expect with such an animal, this one's matched Priest's exactly. A mystic gray that seemed to swirl and shift like soft morning fog. She lifted her hand, but hesitated just inches from the top of the cat's head. "Can I touch you?"

Tame as a house cat, the panther dipped its massive head and nudged her palm, guiding it down the back of its neck.

Holy cow, he was soft. A swath of glossy black silk. And he was hot. Not warm like a man when cuddling on a cold winter night, but no-heater-needed hot.

A purr started slow and easy, then grew with each stroke of her hand. His warm breath huffed against her forearm and knees, the open appreciation of each touch echoed in the languid way he lifted and rotated his head.

"You like that?"

Another chuff, only this one had attitude. A very *you have no idea* feel to it that sent a shiver sliding through her.

He shifted closer, his wide chest pushing between her slightly parted knees until he rubbed his temple against hers.

"Oh!" Startled, she started to pull away, but he quickly adjusted, backing off just enough to let her relax before he repeated the gesture on the other side.

Marking you.

Where the thought came from, she had no clue. A stupid idea, really, but one that fired an achy need in her belly. She palmed the space just behind his ears with both hands, softly running the pads of her fingers through his short, thick fur as she whispered, "You're beautiful."

One second she was staring into the cat's beautiful eyes and the next Priest crouched in front of her, only a brilliant silver flash separating the two visions. Unlike yesterday, now he wore only loose gray track pants, his feet and torso bare.

And Lord, what a sight he was.

Like Tate, tattoos marked his collarbone and shoulders, but Priest's were different. Significantly more of them for starters, but more functional in their design. As if the person who'd done them had been focused only on the magic rather than the art. And his muscles...if given the chance and enough daring, she'd spend considerable time giving tactile appreciation for each dip and groove that defined his shoulders and chest.

It wasn't until she flexed and released her fingers that she realized her hands were still cupped around the back of his head. She dropped them to her lap, ruing the lost heat and the slick thickness of his long hair against her knuckles, but thankful the sun peeking from the horizon couldn't spotlight the burning heat in her cheeks. "Sorry."

His voice was dark as midnight. Rough as gravel and yet soothing. "Your touch is nothing to apologize for."

One heartbeat. Then another. His eyes not leaving hers for even a blink.

She broke the stare out of sheer necessity. As hard as her heart was pounding it was either look away, or suffer cardiac arrest. Though, if a woman had to go, being stared down by a nearly naked, insanely alpha male wasn't a bad way to do it.

He splayed one hand atop her thigh, the running shorts she'd picked for her pre-dawn escape leaving her open for skin-to-skin contact. "You weren't afraid of my cat."

Um, yeah, she had been. And still was. It just seemed self-preservation didn't factor where he was concerned. Not that she was going to clue him in on either count. "He's pretty."

His lips quirked, but stopped just shy of a smile. "Pretty." Not a question. Just that universal deadpan quip reserved for men stymied by women everywhere. His gaze slid to the coffee she'd abandoned on the small side table beside her chair, and he stood, snagging the half-empty mug as he straightened to his impressive height. "Come inside. Your skin's chilled and your coffee's colder."

Maybe on the outside her skin was cold. From the

inside out she was roasty-toasty. Still, a little distance seemed like a smart idea, even if it did mean giving up the rest of her sunrise.

Letting him pull her to her feet, she followed him inside. And oh, what a prime opportunity that presented. She'd never really considered herself the type to ogle men, but with Priest it was hard not to. His long black hair hung loose to his shoulder blades covering most of the tattoos that spanned his back, but there were obviously twice what Jade and Tate had. Rougher. Edgier. But what really got her tongue-tied was his ass and the way the soft fabric of his track pants draped over the rounded muscle, practically daring her to touch.

She cleared her throat like that might somehow dislodge the temptation. "Do you drink coffee?"

Rounding into the kitchen, he swirled her mug, studied the contents, then lifted it for a considering sniff. "Live on the stuff."

Interesting. Somehow, she'd expected him to be an herbal tea and organic food type. She slid onto a barstool behind the breakfast counter. "So, was it you?"

"Was what me?"

"Following me. Outside on my run."

Done with pouring her a fresh cup, he scooped out a surprisingly accurate amount of sugar then followed it up with a splash of half-and-half. Only when he'd foraged a spoon from a drawer and started stirring did he turn and answer. "It's not safe for you outside my wards. I heard you leave, so yes. I followed you." He handed over the mug, holding it in such a way the handle was free for her to grab onto, but had to be scalding the heck out of his fingers.

She took it, blew for a second over the top and took a careful sip.

Perfect.

No different than if she'd made it herself. "You're very observant."

"Where you're concerned, absolutely." He pulled out the barstool beside her and positioned it so when he sat his knees bracketed hers. At least four or five other charms rested between his pecs, each on its own black leather cord. Paired with the long hair, tattoos and dark skin, he looked more like a rock star than a magical clan's high priest.

Careful, as though he were afraid to spook her, he traced the space directly beneath one eye. "You didn't sleep."

Oh, yes. Very observant. Unnervingly so. "I have a lot on my mind."

"Tell me." They were blunt words. Clearly a command, but somehow they were comforting. An encouragement to surrender the weight she'd hefted for too long.

"My parents. A heritage I didn't know existed. A race that includes magic and shapeshifting. Kind of messes with a person's subconscious and doesn't play nice at dream time."

"You don't believe in the magic."

She hadn't. Not at first. But it was hard to keep ignoring it after slamming into it like a pinball stuck between two electronic bumpers. "I believe it, I just…" She sipped her coffee then cradled the thick mug between her palms, searching and failing for the right explanation. "I don't know how to process it. I see it. I accept it."

"But you're afraid of it."

Bingo.

The truth rattled her as sure as Priest had grabbed hold of both shoulders and given her a serious rag doll shake. Fear wasn't an attribute she appreciated in anyone. Denial was even worse. Apparently, she was guilty of both. "I don't understand it."

"That's the thing about magic. It's not meant to be understood. It's meant to be accepted. You appreciate and own it. It's about heart, not logic."

"I like logic. I like it when two plus two equals four. Not a butterfly or a pretty bird."

"Hmm." He leaned one elbow on the counter and studied her. "The scientist in you. But nature doesn't always play by the rules either. Surely, you've figured that out with your major."

She fidgeted on her stool, a weird mix of curiosity and self-defense making her squirm under his assessing gaze. "How do you know what I'm studying?"

He grinned. "Because your grandmother is a font of information where you're concerned and I took full advantage."

Figured. While Nanna loved nature as much as Katy did, she never missed an opportunity to point out that Katy's life was far too structured. Too lacking in spontaneity. She took another drink of her coffee and realized he hadn't poured any for himself. She set her mug aside and slid off the barstool. Turnabout was only fitting. Especially if it had been her inability to sleep that had pulled him from his sleep to guard her.

He kept his silence until she slid the carafe back on the burner. "What else kept you up last night?"

Goose bumps lifted up and down her arms and the

muscles in her belly tightened. "Dead parents and magic isn't enough?"

"It's enough, but it isn't all, is it?"

No. Not even close. True the nightmares had invaded what little sleep she'd managed, but it was the vivid dreams that had come later that had left her hot, needy and unable to go back to sleep. She pulled the sugar dispenser closer. "Cream or sugar?"

"Neither."

Bummer. No extras meant she'd have to face him sooner.

"Tell me, Kateri. What kept you awake?"

"Only Nanna calls me Kateri. Everyone else calls me Katy."

"Kateri tastes better on my tongue."

Whoa boy.

Her stomach pitched and swirled at just the idea of anything to do with his tongue and, considering how hard her legs were shaking, the do-or-die sprint she'd finished up her run with had been a serious tactical error. She gripped the countertop ledge with both hands.

His voice registered behind her a second before his hands framed hers on the countertop, caging her in. "I'll tell you what kept me awake." His heat coiled around her and mingled with his manly scent. He inhaled deep beside one ear, the subtle yet sensual sound making her feel as though the beast was right there with him. "I remembered your scent. How soft you felt against me."

She'd thought about that, too. Added onto the memory actually, throwing in a few bonus scenes that involved zero spectators and a lot less clothes.

He nuzzled the back of her neck, his voice a velvet rumble that caressed every nerve ending. "I imagined you touching me the way you petted my cat this morning. Exploring me. Fearless." His lips whispered against the skin at her nape, there and gone like a ghost. "What kept you awake, Kateri?"

"You." How she actually managed to verbalize the admission, she wasn't quite clear on, but the second it slipped past her lips, something in her shifted. A crack slowly edging through the thick ice of her emotions.

He must have sensed the change, because he stilled behind her, keeping her caged, yet not pushing her further. "And that frightens you?"

"Yes."

"Why?"

"Because things are different around you. I've never felt anything like it. It's irrational. Not normal."

"Ah, but you're not normal. You're Volán. A sensual creature born with the promise of magic." He paused and pressed as close as he could without making full contact. "Do you want my touch?"

A shiver wiggled through her, ripping yet another unexpected confession past her lips. "Yes." As soon as she said it, she squeezed her eyes shut and shook her head. "No. I mean…" She huffed out an irritated breath and hung her head. "I don't know what I want. I can't trust anything anymore."

"There is one thing you can trust." Before she could open her mouth to ask what he meant, he slid his hands around her waist and pulled her against him, one palm sliding up to rest above her heart and the other splayed low on her abdomen.

And it felt *fantastic*.

A possessive grasp that urged everything inside her to release the fragile hold she'd fought so hard to maintain and simply surrender. A soft and pleasant vibration radiated against her back, a more subtle version of the purr his cat had offered as she'd stroked its fur.

"Close your eyes, kitten. Breathe and forget everything except what you feel right now."

So tempting. So very tempting. "I'm not a kitten."

"Yes, you are." Spoken right beside her ear, low and daring her to argue otherwise. "Fearless and so ready to grow into your claws you can't hardly stand it, but curious enough to get into trouble."

Okay, the curious part she'd give him. Actually, she'd give him just about anything right now, the heat and energy coming off him as he pulled her deeper and deeper into whatever spell he wove clouding what was left of her judgment. Never in her life had she felt this safe. This anchored and at home in her emotions.

"Are you afraid now?" No superiority. No command. Just a simple question rooted in genuine concern.

"No." Insane or not, there was something about this man her instincts and body trusted. Completely. Which only made her mind want to rebel twice as hard.

Drawing in a slow, deep breath, he slowly rubbed his temple against hers, the action unsurprisingly similar to how his cat had marked her outside. "You'll never be safer than when you're with me, *mihara*. What you feel right now will never fail between us. Will be there even when you're infuriated with me. When you're ready to accept it, I'll give you everything you need." His lips brushed her cheek for the barest second and he stepped away.

The room's chill closed in instantly, marking the loss of his warmth in an almost accusing slap. She turned and opened her mouth, only to realize she hadn't decided if she wanted to demand he come back, or tell him good riddance.

Apparently, she wasn't getting much choice in the matter because he was almost out of the kitchen, his long feline strides taking him God only knew where. "Priest," she said, still not knowing what she'd say if he stopped.

He paused at the massive entrance that marked the boundary of the vaulted living room. "No more running, kitten. Not without me. Tate and Jade know the property's boundaries and can take you out if you need to stretch, but nothing more."

"So, what? I'm grounded? Under lock and key?"

His lips quirked just enough to prove she'd yet again proven her kitten status, but the gray in his eyes deepened. "Protected. Always." His gaze took a leisurely trip down and up her body before meeting her stare head-on. "Take today and rest. Tomorrow we train."

Chapter Seven

When Priest had said he'd put a call out to other families in the area, Katy hadn't thought he'd meant *all* of them. At least sixty people milled inside the house, on the high balcony and the open gorge below, the general mood of the occasion somewhere between a Sunday afternoon family reunion and boot camp. At least half of them were Nanna's age or older—Nanna's age being 125 instead of the seventy-five she'd represented herself as at her last birthday party. Another shocker she'd discovered while taking a lazy trek across Priest's sizable property and dallying along the lake's edge. Apparently, most people in her clan lived to as old as 175, barring untimely deaths. And the usual ailments that brought the singura low, like cancer and heart disease, didn't stand a chance against a Volán magic-imbued body.

Back in the Adirondack chair on the balcony, Katy propped her feet on the rail and traded her open laptop for her phone on the side table. As it had since she'd settled onto her perch, her gaze drifted to Priest striding from the cluster of healers in his garden to the warriors gathering to spar. Learning he was seventy-seven years old and would likely live well into his third century had been the biggest shock of all. Nanna had laughed herself silly after sharing the news, but Katy still couldn't wrap her head around it. He didn't look a day over thirty-five at most. Strong and blisteringly virile. An alpha who not only took what he wanted, but had the confidence and experience to make sure he got it in short order.

At the base of the long wood staircase that led to the open land below, a few of the women gathered in the seer's circle giggled, her Nanna's familiar laugh one of them. As had been the case since they'd set foot in the house, Jade was at her side.

Two peas in a pod.

Actually, everyone here moved with a familiar connectedness. Like a common thread ran through each one of them despite their varied demeanors and appearances.

Everyone but Katy, anyway.

Irritated with the fresh blast of resentment and self-pity, she let the print reader on her phone do its thing and thumbed through her contacts. Maybe she didn't have a place with this group yet, but she wasn't without skills and connections—even if they weren't of the magical variety.

She punched in David's number and shifted her laptop screen so the family names Nanna and Priest had shared the night before were easier to see in the bright midmorning sunshine. Despite only two years between them and similar social circles, David was the only friend Katy shared with her brother—a happy accident borne of Alek begging a fellow criminal justice major to show his little sister around campus when Alek was too busy chasing tail to do it himself.

Only two rings in, David's bold voice cut through the line. "Okay, I know I jacked up, but I got sidetracked with some big tests at school. I swear to God, I'll do it tomorrow."

Katy fought back a smile. She'd told Alek that David was a bad choice as far as apartment sitters went, but they hadn't exactly had a whole lot of choices hauling butt out of town as fast as they had. "Actually, I wasn't calling about the mail, but now that you've confessed, you're screwed."

"Oh." Movement sounded through the line and the moderate background strains of some bizarre funk song disappeared. "Well, now that I've screwed the pooch on that one, what's up? You and Alek find the dude you were looking for?"

As if he'd heard David's question, Priest chose that exact second to look up and lock stares with Katy.

But he couldn't have heard. Could he? Unless he had super duper cat hearing or something. Definitely something she'd need to ping Nanna about later. Preferably when they were well out of earshot. "We found him."

"And?"

"And what?"

"Alek said you needed him to find something, but he never said what."

No, and neither of them ever would. Not that David would believe a thing they said even if they did spill. "Just a family deal. After what happened to Mom and Dad, we needed to track down some relatives and share the news." She absently scrolled to the top of the Word document she'd put together. "Speaking of which, I was wondering if you could reach out to some of your techno-genius contacts and see if they could help us with some online searches."

"What? You can't navigate Google?" His snicker was

cut short with what sounded suspiciously like an apple. Or one giant Kit Kat. With David, the only thing that was a given was that there was food either in his hand or within reaching distance. Funny, considering he was beanpole thin.

"Not that kind of search, smart-ass. I meant like genealogy, maybe. Or however you go about finding people you've lost contact with."

"But I thought you found the guy?"

"We found *this* guy. Turns out there are some other folks who'd want to know about Mom and Dad, but we don't have any contacts for them. I thought you might be able to help."

Another crunch followed, but there was enough silence with it to promise David was working on an angle...because David always had an angle where she was concerned. One she'd fought from the first day she'd met him. "So, if I help you out, will you reconsider a date when you get back?"

In the distance, Priest's head snapped up so fast he nearly got beaned in the head by a man he was training with.

Guess that answered the hearing thing.

For a second, she was tempted to play it up and say yes just to make Priest squirm, but even if she'd been willing to string David along—which she absolutely wasn't—the idea of agreeing sat wrong on her tongue. "I've told you a million times, you don't want to go there with me. I don't know my *Supernatural* from my *Game of Thrones* and you are nothing if not the pop culture guru. You need a woman with a healthy Netflix addiction. I don't even have cable."

David harrumphed. "You *are* a little weird where TV's concerned."

Not really. She just couldn't find any desire to sit still and watch anything. Outside, she could sit for hours. Behind a little box in a stifling room? Not so much. "So, will you do it?"

"Sure, why not?" Typical David. Why stress over anything when you could just shrug things off and tuck them away for assessment later? "Can you email 'em to me?"

Down in the gorge, Priest stepped away from the man he'd easily captured in a choke hold and moved in beside him to demonstrate an alternate move.

"Yep," Katy said. Though the more she watched Priest move, the harder it was to keep her mind on track. "Already have them loaded up in a Word doc. Any idea how long something like this would take?"

"I dunno. A week. Maybe two?"

Not exactly the answer she was after, but better than nothing. "And you'll actually go clean out our mailbox before the day's over?"

"I don't know why you're in such a hurry. The last time you two went out of town, all either of you got was junk mail."

Actually, that wasn't all they got. Until she'd moved into a two-bedroom apartment with her brother, she'd had no clue how many workout and martial arts publications there were in this world. "I like my things where they are. Full mailboxes are a neon sign for burglars."

"Right. Responsible adult behavior. I get it." Clearly, he was done with the call because the music he'd turned down grew in volume. "Shoot me your names and I'll get some people to take a look."

A few more niceties and a little slapstick banter later,

she wrapped up the call, closed her laptop and meandered down the stairs. Much as she'd felt like an outsider with those who'd gathered, sitting all alone and stewing in self-pity wasn't her style. She might not have magic or a house of her own, but she was a scientist. Or would be. Someday. After her parents' killer was dead and she could get back to finishing her degree. In the meantime, she could focus on having an open mind and feed her curiosity with the people around her.

Nanna spied her before she reached the bottom step and waved her over to the seer group. Those who'd gathered in the loosely formed circle were a mix of old and young, but even the older participants had a youthful vitality that defied the norm she'd grown up with. Now that she saw it in such abundance, she couldn't help but wonder why she hadn't questioned Nanna's energy and vigor compared to the other people who lived at her retirement village.

Not bothering to rise from her cross-legged place on the ground, Naomi snagged Katy's hand as soon as she was in reaching distance. "Come sit with us, *nahina*. I want you to meet everyone."

Priest's deep voice sounded behind Katy a second before his hands settled on her waist and stopped her from lowering to the ground. "She can meet everyone after training."

Her heart stuttered then took off at an uncomfortable jog, the surprise of his arrival mingling with the same sensory overload that came anytime he was within ten feet of her.

Every gaze in the group zeroed in on his familiar touch at her hips.

Arms shaking, she squeezed his wrists, intent on

breaking the connection—and hopefully the curious stares that went with it—but he wouldn't budge. "You still haven't explained this whole training business. Hard to engage or remember what you're training for when you don't know why you're doing it to start with."

"Our clan was all but dormant for twenty years," he said. "It took us another twenty to find and start consolidating families nearby and new Volán are coming into their magic every day. You'd be surprised how much clan knowledge has been lost in that time."

"Priest started the training days a few years ago," Jade explained from her place beside Nanna. "The more people moved nearby, the less he could handle training one-on-one on his own. This way the elders we've still got share their knowledge and the clan stays connected."

"Like they used to be." The solemnity in Naomi's voice drew nods from some of the older-looking people in the circle.

"Everyone learns the basics of each house, the advanced skills of their own and then trains for self-defense with the warriors for at least a few hours." As if his touch hadn't seemed possessive enough, he slid one arm around her waist, pulled her back flush against his front and swept those gathered around with a calm but commanding look. "Speaking of which, your trainers are ready. Everyone pair up."

Jade was the fastest to her feet, but no one in the group seemed to dread the physical activity ahead. And gauging from what she'd seen of the sparring in the early hours, any training with the warriors would be *very* physical.

Katy twisted out of his hold, though it took some doing, both logistically and emotionally. No matter how much her brain railed at the idea of his open and familiar touch, once her body got next to his it had zero inclination to let go. "Why does everyone work with the warriors? What if they don't like that kind of thing?"

He noted the extra distance she'd put between them and grinned. "Aside from exercise and self-defense being good for them?"

Well, there was that. But still… "Everyone ought to be able to choose what works for them. And not all self-defense has to be physical." Hence, the reason she had the pepper spray on her key chain.

He stalked toward her. "True. But warriors are meant for protection. Sparring with those they're sworn to protect builds a deeper bond."

Realizing she'd matched his every step forward with a backward one of her own, she forced herself to stand tall and pressed her shoulders back. High priest or not, she wasn't going to take whatever he dished out like everyone else seemed inclined to do. "So, everyone else just does what you say?"

"Healthy bonds work both ways." As if to prove his point, he wrapped his arms low around her waist and her own lifted to clutch his shoulders. An action resulting in a balancing reaction. "Where the warriors feel protectiveness, the others receive safety. Comfort in knowing they're cared for and watched over."

The voices of those gathered remained steady behind them, a mix of laughter and encouraging commands offered by those doing the training. The leaves in the treetops above them whispered on the soft spring breeze and the sun blanketed everything around them in a peaceful glow.

But it all dimmed in the moment. Paled in comparison

to whatever pushed and pulled between them. However they'd started this conversation, she was fairly certain they weren't talking about sparring anymore.

And it scared the ever-loving heck right out of her.

She pushed against his shoulders and stepped out of his arms. "I don't know anything about fighting or self-defense."

"Then it's time you learned."

Oh, no. Making an ass out of herself in front of her brother would be bad enough. Doing it with at least five dozen strangers was an absolute no-go. "I thought you said I'd be safe with you."

"When you're with me, yes. But what about when you're not?" She'd swear it was his cat that smiled back at her, the predator inside him openly pleased its prey had opted to play. "Unless you're saying you want me with you all the time. I'd be fine with that arrangement."

Damn.

So much for appealing to his male ego.

She crossed her arms and studied those that had paired off. Everyone except her brother was engaged in everything from what looked like entry-level explanations to maneuvers more fitting of a dojang. Alek wove in between each couple, carefully examining each move and offering advice like he'd been with these people for years. "I'm not sure I'd be any good at it." And if there was one thing she didn't think her self-confidence could handle it was being anything other than exceptional under Priest's watchful gaze. Not with all the other uncertainties in her life piling up.

He moved in beside her, watching those who practiced even as his voice rumbled in temptation. "I suspect my *mihara* would be good at whatever she sets her mind to."

The statement ripped her attention away from the group and straight to him. "You keep using that word. What's it mean?"

"I'll tell you when it's time."

"I think now's the time."

His gaze dropped to her arms still tightly banded across her chest and his lips curled in a wry smile. "No. Not yet." He stepped back and motioned her toward the lake in the distance. "Come with me. We'll run first and warm you up."

"You know good and well I already ran today." Because he'd followed her as she'd slipped out of the house again this morning, blatantly making it known her attempts at stealth were abysmal.

"I also know you want to join in with everyone else, but don't have a clue where to start. So, we'll run first, take the edge off, then work together. Alone and away from everyone else." He cocked an arrogant eyebrow. "Unless you're afraid?"

That son of a bitch.

As chess plays went it was a brilliant taunt. The one nudge practically guaranteed to make her swan dive into just about any situation. Though, she'd be damned if she didn't get her own dig in before she leapt. "Fine. We'll run." She started toward the path that wound toward the lake, her long strides crunching in the dregs of winter leaves. "But if it's all the same with you, I'd rather spend time with your cat."

She couldn't hear him move behind her, but the nearness of his unruffled voice promised he was no more than a few steps back. "Not many people trust my cat more than they trust me."

"Oh, I don't trust him either," she commented over one shoulder without breaking stride. "I just think he's prettier than you."

Chapter Eight

Watching Kateri in motion was a thing of beauty. Long legs, blond hair shining in the sun, and efficient, graceful movements.

Stunning.

Priest easily kept pace behind her, his panther's paws near silent. No doubt, she'd meant her preference for his cat over him as a taunt to even the emotional balance between them, but he'd actually been grateful. When shifted, the darkness held minimal sway. A definite plus considering the multitude of graphic and animalistic urges he'd fought where she was concerned the last few days.

Ahead, the well-worn path to the lake veered to the right.

Priest bounded ahead of her, welcoming the extra stretch in his shoulders and flanks as he poured on the steam and shot away from the path.

Her rhythm faltered then halted. "Hey, where are you going?"

Turning, Priest kept his place well off the trail and waited.

"The path is this way."

Oh, yes. Naomi was right about her granddaughter. She wanted to follow him. Wanted to explore and color outside the lines, but somewhere along the way had learned that wasn't allowed. That it was either unhealthy or unwise.

A shame, too, because he sensed inside her an astonishing amount of passion. How he'd walked away from her yesterday morning had been nothing short of a miracle, the sheer power of her response to only his arms around her strong enough to silence even the darkness for once.

Whatever the cause for the rigid structure that controlled her life, he was prepared to fight it. To annihilate whatever barriers caged the woman inside and show her how sweet life felt when lived outside any pre-defined paths.

Starting today.

He lifted his chin and urged her to him with an impatient growl.

She studied him, the shin-high foliage between them softly moving on the breeze and the rich landscape behind him. When she glanced back at the clear footpath leading the opposite direction, he thought for sure she'd either head back to the house, or go the trail alone, but instead she nodded and loped forward. "Okay, but do me a favor and don't let me jog through any potholes. If I break my ankle, I can't run. And if I can't run, I get cranky."

He didn't doubt it. In fact, he'd bet by the toned muscles in her legs and the distance she'd covered the last few mornings, running was the sole outlet for all her pent-up frustration and emotions. But he'd give her new outlets. One in particular that had taken up an enormous amount of his own headspace the last few days.

As soon as she was close enough, he darted ahead. The trees on this section of his property were thicker and blocked most of the sunshine, but the soft undulating slopes made for a more challenging run. Something he hoped would pull Kateri further out of her thoughts and focus more on the moment.

He paused at the shallow but wide stream between them and the destination he'd chosen and shifted. With his experience, the snap and burn that always followed the transition was more of an expected nuisance than deep discomfort. A whip across every square inch of his skin he'd come to not only accept, but appreciated as a reminder of his gifts. But with Kateri closing in and the anticipation of time one-on-one together, even the usual tingle was muted.

She slowed as she reached the water and her lips lifted in a soft, appreciative smile. "I love that sound."

So did he, the soft trickle of water streaming over and between the pebbles and larger rocks a comfort he often sought when his dark thoughts threatened to overwhelm him. "The water's still cold, but you'll get across better without your shoes." He motioned to a flat rock jutting alongside the stream's edge. "Leave them there and we'll pick them up on the way back."

"You want me to wade across?"

"If you want to train someplace soft and private with a great view, then yes." He cocked an eyebrow. "Or I can carry you."

While he hoped for the latter, he knew damned well it was a long shot. One she almost immediately quashed by toeing off her tennis shoes. "Is it slippery?"

"In some spots, but I won't let you fall." He leapt onto one of the broader rocks only partially submerged by the cool water and held out his hand. "Better to move quickly when it's this cold, though. Don't overthink it. Just step in and move."

The biggest challenge of all for her. Every action she took was likely precipitated by hours of careful forethought. A behavior that seemed to be the exact opposite of her brother's instinctive approach. "Your brother seems to have a much different approach to life than you," he said to help her detach her over-engaged mind.

She took his hand and carefully dipped her toe in the cold water streaming along the edge. A shiver moved through her and she held on tighter. "Different how?"

"He's driven by his gut. Moves on compulsion and natural insight. Have you always been logical and deliberate in what you do? Or did you learn that through school?"

Her answering frown was quickly replaced by narrowed concentration as she mimicked his path from rock to rock. "Some of it's from school I guess. Cause and effect. Scientific method. Hypothesis grounded on systematic observation, measurement and experimentation provides more stable and reliable output." She shrugged and for a moment a raw vulnerability flickered across her face. "Plus, my approach just seemed easier."

"Easier how?"

She kept her eyes averted, gaze locked on each careful step she took, but Priest had the feeling there was more going on inside her than she could bear to share with eye contact. "Dad and Alek fought a lot growing up. He hated how Alek never planned. Hated how he let his emotions run his life." She paused a second, her brow furrowing as though a few new hypotheses were forging together. "Knowing what I know now, I'm guessing he was afraid Alek's impulsiveness would lead him to accept his gifts when the time came."

No doubt, he would. Alek was a warrior through and through, likely filtering and processing his environment with the natural tendencies of a predator from a very young age.

She paused mid-step and looked up. "What's it like anyway?"

Up until that second, his heart and breath had maintained a steady pace. An even flow not the least bit impacted by the precarious path they navigated. But with that one question, both increased. Of all the conversations they'd had, all had been guarded. Protected by a thin veil of caution. But this one was open. Honest. Free of fear.

It was a start.

A good one he had every intention of cultivating. "The magic itself, or the quest?"

She pursed her lips, judged the distance between her and dry land and let go of his hand. "The quest, I guess." She zigzagged her own path to the damp soil and planted her hands on her hips, waiting for his answer.

Showboating was probably a bad idea under the circumstances, but both man and cat were too excited by the surge in her playful confidence not to engage in a little. He sprung forward, clearing a fallen log and a particularly tricky cluster of rocks before landing beside her, making the same distance she'd made in three bold jumps in one. "You've heard that no snowflake is the same?"

She nodded and, for once, didn't automatically put an extra step between them.

"Soul quests hold the same quality. They're each

unique and suited for the person undertaking the quest." He motioned her toward the lake's loamy inlet in the distance.

"Quest implies it's a search for something. Or a challenge to overcome. Is that really what it is?"

"In a way. But deeper."

"Deeper how?"

He smiled despite his best intentions. Someday, her questions would likely drive him insane, but right now they were cute. Every bit the adorable kitten poking and prodding without fear. "Because you don't face physical challenges. You face emotional ones."

She stopped and faced him, apparently not only disliking that answer, but intent on debating the merits of such an approach.

He splayed his hand low on her back and urged her forward. "It's not as ominous as it sounds. How else can the Keeper fit you with magic and a companion who suits you, without knowing and understanding what drives you?"

She scowled at the ground, so deep in piecing things together she seemed unaware of the beautiful landscape creeping into view. "Who's this Keeper person?"

"Exactly what she sounds like. The guardian of our magic and the one who gives us our companions."

"So, the Keeper's a she?"

"To me she is. To you she might be someone else. Or some*thing* else. She appears to each person in the manner they can best comprehend and appreciate the experience."

She stopped and planted both hands on her hips. "Let me guess. She's beautiful, has perfect curves and in general looks like a goddess."

More emotion. A spark of jealousy barely masking a very real insecurity.

"She has no physical form for me, kitten. She's a comfortable, but unseen presence with a voice that reminds me of my mother." He inched closer and cupped the side of her neck, grazing his thumb along her jaw. "If she wanted to appeal to me sexually, she'd look like you."

Her face softened and her lips parted a near-silent gasp.

Take her, the darkness demanded. *Use your advantage. Force her surrender.*

His cat hissed in response, jumping to the defense of its mate and warning off the unwelcome command. Like Priest, his beast had come to know Kateri in the past few days. Had accepted she wasn't one to be forced into anything. Lured and tempted, maybe. But hell would freeze over before anyone backed her into any corner.

Besides, it was the hunt and seduction that made a female's surrender so much sweeter. In that, he and his cat were in perfect alignment. Ready to do whatever it took to earn her submission.

Rather than take her lips the way he craved, he slid his hand to her shoulder and turned her toward the lake. "Is this private enough for your training?"

Whatever thoughts or response she'd harbored in the emotionally taut seconds between them were wiped clean with one glance at the isolated cove. Tall gray rock etched by years of erosion surrounded them in a deep U, but clusters of determined and hardy trees had taken root in at least five of the natural shelves. In winter, their naked branches left the inlet a more somber, empty feel, but in spring and summer the rich green blended with the lake's deep blue for a natural oasis.

"I've been toying with building a house at the top of the bluff," he said. "The property just to the east of this boundary's been vacant and for sale a while. I could use its access point for a winding driveway."

"Why hasn't it sold?"

"It's older. Not updated the way a lot of the buyers coming to this area want."

She padded forward, stopping as soon as her bare feet hit the small stretch of sandy loam beach to sigh and wiggle her toes. "The soil's softer than the beach."

Soft enough it would mold to her body if he gave her his weight. Cradle her hips and hold her steady while he worked his cock inside her.

He shook off the searing image. "It's not the Caribbean, but more comfortable to practice on than hard-packed earth." He moved in behind her and rested his hands on her hips.

She tried to face him as she spoke. "What are you doing?"

He tightened his grip and held her in place. "Teaching you some basics so you can join the rest of our clan when they train. Now relax and brace your feet hip-width apart."

For the next thirty minutes, he coached her, walking her through the rudimentary self-defense training each of their women learned with a forced detachment he didn't remotely feel. Every brush of her skin against his was both a thrill and absolute torture, and her jasmine scent clung to him even when he gave her space to practice moves he'd shown her. Even more enticing, was how quickly she learned. Whether it was the drive to catch up with those she'd avidly watched this morning, or a natural, physical aptitude, there was little he demonstrated that she didn't properly assimilate by the second or third try.

As with running, watching her was a heady thing. Grace and poise in motion.

And she was his. Open and interacting with him easily. Asking questions with the single-minded focus of a hungry pupil ravenous for information.

She finished a series of blocks, paused as though replaying and evaluating her performance in her own head, then turned to him, her blue-gray eyes bright with excitement. "Okay, I think I've got it. What else?"

What else indeed. He rubbed the flat sandstone he'd picked up off the beach between his fingers and stood, leaving the rock he'd watched her from and the cool water he'd been tempted to douse himself with far behind. "You're ready for more? Something with more contact?"

God knew he was. Not that he was sure he had much resolve left in him.

She eyed him as he strode closer, holding her ground with the same stubborn pride he'd come to appreciate, but a healthy wariness painting her features. "What kind of contact?"

"The kind of contact you should know how to get out of. Frankly, I'm surprised your brother hasn't already taught you this much already."

She scoffed and planted her hands on her hips. "My brother gave up teaching me anything when he was ten. He said I asked too many questions to ever actually learn anything."

"Was he right?"

She scrunched her nose and shrugged. "I was eight and he was trying to teach me Tae Kwon Do forms he learned in class. I didn't see the point and wanted him to explain what the steps were for."

"I bet that went over well."

"Like I said—he gave up."

He circled and moved in behind her. "I won't." Wrapping his arms around her shoulders before she could guess his intent, he squeezed, effectively trapping her arms against her torso.

As expected, she fought, but his grip was too tight, his stance too evenly balanced for her to draw him off center with the methods she chose.

"Relax," he said, forcing calm into the command.

She stilled almost instantly, but her heart pounded heavy against his clasped hands and her chest rose and fell more sharply than even after her sprints.

"First lesson—don't panic. Still your thoughts and find your center. Your instincts can't guide you if your brain's clamoring too loud to receive the input."

Twisting her head enough to glance up and over her shoulder at him, she frowned. "It's not about instinct. It's about steps. Tricks and techniques."

"Those are the foundation, but it's your instincts that tell you when to employ what."

Her brow furrowed deeper. Like he'd just told her the Earth was not only flat, but that two plus two equaled ten.

Not willing to let her dive too deep into analysis mode, he squeezed to get her attention. "Now, I want you to let your weight drop straight down. Bend your knees until you free your arms enough to escape."

God, she was cute, that scientist brain of hers pausing to study his grip while her brain no doubt pieced together the logistics of what he'd asked. Comprehension flashed across her face and she dropped like a rock, though instead of spinning as she would eventually, she ass-planted on the soft sand.

"Good."

"Good?" She twisted and glared up at him. "I just made it so some asshole can pin me to the ground instead of getting away."

"So, if you bungle it in real life, you'll know to roll, scramble upright and get out of reaching distance before they can figure out what's happened." Then, if whoever dared to touch her was smart, they'd cut their own throat before he found them, because the death he'd deliver wouldn't be pretty.

He spun her around and wrapped her up once more. "Faster this time. Think fluid and quick."

She did, surprising him with how quickly she acted compared to the analytical approach of her first round. The drop was still too steep, but this time she caught herself, rolled and leapt out of arm's reach.

Over and over they practiced, each time adding a new element to the routine. Once she'd sufficiently learned how to escape with all manner of obstacles thrown in her path, he moved on to more advanced techniques. Simple takedowns. Strike points.

None of it fazed her. Though, the more they worked, the more her dormant energy sparked, bits and pieces of her careful restraint peeling away to reveal raw, untapped emotion.

And it was powerful. Feminine for sure, but bold and fearless. Yet underneath it was something unexpected. A finely honed anger on par with the darkness inside him. Only hers was on a much tighter, shorter leash.

She sidestepped, swiveled and backed out of a choke

hold with the speed and efficiency of a person who'd trained for months instead of hours. Gripping the back of his neck, she pushed downward with a strength she'd probably never realized she possessed and rammed her knee upward.

Priest caught it, kicked her standing leg out from under her and pinned her to the ground.

Her startled huff gusted against his face and her eyes rounded with surprise. "What was that?"

"A reminder. Everything can shift in a second and overconfidence can get you killed." Without thinking, he swept her sweat-dampened hair away from her cheek and cupped the side of her face.

A simple touch. But with it her demeanor shifted, the shields she'd lowered in their time alone too far gone to mask the need the caress created. The hunger in her gaze. The softening of her mouth.

"I think you've had enough for today." Logic told him to move. To pair his pronouncement with space and time, and leave her wanting. Curious and eager for more.

Instead, he stayed locked in place.

Beneath him, her body trembled. Her chest rose and fell harder than even at the height of her training, and whether she realized it or not, her fingertips dug into his shoulders. As if she couldn't choose between pushing him away or urging him closer.

Both beast and shadow clamored to take her. To maximize the vulnerable moment and claim what was theirs. Consequences didn't matter. Only that the predator hungered for its prey, and the dominant craved her submission. Now. Here. Wild with no trappings of civilization or reality.

But he'd made her a promise. Vowed to give her what

only *he* could when she was ready. When she accepted what burned between them. He inched closer, fingers tightening against her scalp as if that might give him the control he needed to keep himself in check and ghosting his lips along her jawline. "Unless you want more?"

Her breath hitched at the subtle contact and she arched her neck, innocently exposing the vulnerable stretch of flesh.

So easy to take her. To mark her flesh with his teeth and lips. To strip her bare and bury himself inside her. Cover her body with his scent and fill her with his come. He gripped her chin and guided her face to his. "Open your eyes, *mihara.*"

Her eyelids lifted, the usual brightness of her blue-gray gaze darkened by stark need and uncertainty.

"You feel it, don't you? The pull. The demand between us." He skimmed his thumb along her lower lip and all too quickly his mind conjured an image of the plump flesh wrapped around his cock, his hand fisted in her hair while he guided her mouth up and down his length. "You want it even though you don't understand it."

Her gaze dropped to his mouth and she licked along the path he'd traced. Her voice was little more than a whisper, fear and desire threaded through the defenseless response. "I *need* to understand it."

"No, you don't. You need to feel it. Own it."

Surrender to it.

Words he didn't dare utter to her. Not yet. Lowering his head, he skimmed his nose alongside hers and inhaled deep. "You want my mouth as much as I want yours. You want to let go and see what waits on the other side." He eased back only enough to meet her stare, their lips separated only by a thin strip of air. "Take it. Take what's yours and trust me to keep you safe."

The heat in her eyes flashed white-hot and her fingers dug into his muscles as though they were all that kept her from a perilous free fall.

One second.

Two.

And then her lips were on his.

Full. Soft. Hot and demanding. A ravenous woman unaware of her power, yet claiming her due.

He gave it to her, palming the back of her head and taking full control. Licking inside her mouth. Stroking his tongue against hers and savoring her unique taste.

She moaned into his mouth and urged him closer, her hands fisting in his hair. Her teeth grazed his lips as though desperate for more, but frustrated with the uncertainty of how to proceed.

He had more than enough ideas for both of them. An endless stream of carnal images that fueled the escalating fire between them. He nudged her thigh with his and her legs parted, eagerly cradling his hips.

Perfect. Soft flesh welcoming his weight. The hard press of his cock against her sex, only the thin slick glide of her jogging shorts and his track pants to separate them.

She belongs to us.

Take her.

Claim her.

God, he wanted to. Wanted to slick his fingers through her folds. To watch as his shaft sank inside her. To power deep, hear her moans and feel her pussy pulse around him as she came.

He rolled his hips and she flexed in answer. So responsive. Open and void of pretense.

Trust me to keep you safe.

Another promise. One he'd break if he gave in now.

His cat snarled and the darkness wailed as he pulled away.

Until she opened her eyes.

Man, beast and shadow stared down at her, passion-weighted eyelids framing dazed, but dreamy eyes. In that moment, there was nothing between them. Only trust and the beginnings of a fragile bond he'd nearly destroyed with his lust.

For the first time since his brother's betrayal, the darkness inside him stood tame and silent beneath her gaze. Dumbfounded. A belligerent child who'd comprehended an Earth-shattering truth and matured in a split second.

She wasn't just a possession to be taken or tamed. She was a treasure. To be protected at all costs.

She's exactly what you need to find balance.

"Naomi was right," he whispered.

Whether he spoke to Kateri, or to himself he wasn't sure, but it was her who answered, her voice as easy as the wind drifting off the lake beyond. "Right about what?"

He braced his forearms on the soft sand and framed her face, the truth giving him hope for the first time in half a century. There was only one thing capable of eradicating shadows. One cure to lift the darkest veil. "You're my light."

Chapter Nine

Three days Katy had waited. Three very long, awkward days with ample time in Priest's presence and not one more kiss. Although, she had to admit—getting out of the house after almost a solid week away from society was a huge bonus. Even with high-speed internet and a constant stream of clanspeople stopping by to keep her company or teach her more about her heritage, there was only so much she could take of the same scenery.

She shifted on the rolling stool she'd stolen from Tate's section of the tattoo shop and angled her head for a better look at the design Priest painstakingly drew on a burly man's forearm. Every move was confident. Every stroke as if it were guided by a divine hand instead of his own.

Okay, so maybe the last three days had been more awkward for her than him. Where she'd been plagued by a heightened awareness and insecurity to rival a pimply teenage girl since their time at the cove, he'd settled into a surprisingly calm demeanor. As assertive and unruffled as the indelible lines he drew on the man in front of her. Far less intense than their first days together.

No, that wasn't right. The intensity was still there, but something had happened after he'd kissed her. Something that placated the ravenous hunter. At least for the time being.

He watched her, though. Constantly. Even when she didn't catch him in the act—though she did that often because he didn't hide it—she felt it. As if some unseen force reached out from the very air around her and painted her skin with a sparking awareness. And when she did meet his hungry gaze there was always an undercurrent to it. A silent dare to act on the swirling need she couldn't seem to douse no matter what she tried.

Take what's yours and trust me to keep you safe.

She wanted to. Badly. But then what? Something told her stepping into more with Priest would be on par with a cataclysmic event rather than scratching a simple itch.

The customer's voice cut into her brooding thoughts, the sound as gruff as Hank's appearance. "Priest is damned good, ain't he?"

Good was putting it mildly. Artwork aside, just watching him work left her spellbound. As if the process itself was a sacred endeavor. A fluid meditation.

And his hands...

More than once, she'd wished he'd set the iron aside and use them on her the way he had at the lake. Sure, he'd touched her since he'd pulled her to her feet and guided her home that day, often showing casual affection that left her strung out and restless, but nothing strong and possessive like when he'd held her captive for his kiss. The fact that she craved such a repeat was insane. Never once since she'd started dating had she ever gone for the overbearing, controlling type. But with Priest?

Yeah, everything about him said, *Sign me up.*

"He's very gifted," she managed.

Priest paused in his work and lifted his head only

enough to make eye contact, a wry smirk crooking one side of his mouth.

Hank threw back his head and hooted loud enough to rattle the building. "Gifted." He zeroed in on Priest. "I think that's fancy speak for able to charge a small fortune."

Priest shook his head and went back to work in lieu of an answer, which all but confirmed Hank's statement.

That was another thing she'd noticed in the last three days. With most people, Priest was sparing with his words. Not exactly blunt, but frugal in how he went about communicating. Concise and to the point.

Except with her.

With her, he'd opened up. Usually after her run while they drank coffee on his raised back porch and watched the sun come up, a routine she'd come to not only welcome, but craved. Another oddity, considering how much she'd always hoarded that special alone time, but she genuinely enjoyed it. How he not only shared when she asked him about what clan life used to be like before his brother sabotaged their future, but actively listened to bits and pieces of her life. As if he valued everything about her, even the parts she found uninteresting.

The hum of the tattoo iron stopped and Priest's attention shifted to the side, his gaze distant for three or four seconds before he went back to his work.

But there was something different in his focus. The shift was subtle. Definitely not something Hank would have noticed, and likely only something she'd picked up on because she'd studied him so closely.

And it hadn't been the first time he'd done it either.

"Kitten, go ask Jade to come bandage Hank up." Spoken so low and calm, it took Katy an extra heartbeat before his words translated properly in her head.

Of course, rather than do as he asked, she got a better angle on Priest's work. "Wow, I didn't realize how close it was to being done."

"Me either," Hank grumbled, though there was a certain amount of appreciation mingled with the statement.

Priest straightened, studied the finished product a second, then lifted his gaze to her.

Waiting.

"Oh. Right." She hustled out of the private area and found Jade chatting up a couple of young girls at the display case. "Hey, Jade. Priest asked if you could come bandage up Hank."

Frowning, Jade held up a finger to the short-haired blonde considering the jewelry beneath the glass. "Give me a second." She rounded the case and hustled toward Katy. "Something wrong?"

"Not that I know of. Why?"

"Because I can count on one hand how many times Priest didn't finish his own work and still have four fingers left over."

Before Katy could puzzle out what that meant, Jade strode into Priest's private room and planted both hands on her hips. "What's up?"

Despite her bold arrival, Priest kept cleaning up his equipment, his back to the room at large. "Need you to bandage Hank up and clear the rest of the day unless Tate can cover my clients."

"Tate's awesome, but he's not you. We'll have to reschedule."

"Then do it." Finally turning to meet her stare, Priest

gave Jade a look that seemed to say a whole lot more than the words that went with it. "Something's come up."

Yep.

Definitely one of those unspoken, *you get me?* looks. And didn't that just make her want to wade into topics best left untouched?

"All right, Hank." Jade plucked a pair of sterile gloves out of the dispenser mounted on the wall and pried them on with as much efficiency as a neurosurgeon. "Looks like you get beauty instead of talent to finish you up today."

"Aww, I don't know about that." Hank jerked his chin up at Katy and grinned. "The way she's been eyeballin' Priest the last three hours, I'd say he factors as pretty in someone's book."

"Reeeally?" Jade settled onto Priest's stool and waggled her eyebrows at Katy. "Do tell. Did I miss something?"

Priest tossed his gloves in the trash and turned. "Hank, how about you keep quiet and let Jade focus so she can get you finished up and out of here?"

"Do I get a discount on the next round?"

"Do I ever give discounts?"

Hank's pout was instant and rivaled that of a two-year-old deprived a promised candy bar. Or at least it was until his gaze slid to Katy. "She gonna be here next time around?"

Not bothering to give Hank his attention, Priest prowled to Katy, cupped her shoulder and turned her for the door. "Oh, she'll be here."

Hank's ornery chuckle trailed them into the shop's main area.

Despite the light conversation they'd left behind, Katy

couldn't shake her curiosity or the sharp focus coming off Priest. "Is something wrong?"

He slid his hand to the back of her neck and gave a reassuring squeeze. "Nothing wrong. Just my real job taking precedence over this one." He knocked on the door to the room where Tate did his tattoos, giggles from the trio of girls who'd disappeared inside an hour ago answering back.

"What's that supposed to mean?" Katy asked.

Rather than answer, Priest opened the door, scanned the two women off to one side and the third stretched out facedown on the table. Tate sat off to one side, his focus squarely on the tattoo he worked into the skin at the base of her neck. "Hey, what time do you wrap up today?"

The steady buzz stopped and Tate swiped the ink before he looked up. "Got one more after this and any walk-ins we get. Why, what's up?"

The same unspoken communication he'd shared with Jade seemed to move between them, though this time Priest added a little more into the mix. "I've got a job to do at home."

Understanding sharpened Tate's gaze and he glanced at Katy. "You want Katy to stay here?"

"No." As firm as it came out, he might as well have said, *Not a snowball's chance in hell.* "I've got at least an hour. Maybe more. She'll ride home with me."

And that was it. Aside from a few man-to-man chin lifts, no other information was shared.

Katy hustled behind Priest toward the break room, so intent on catching up to him, she nearly plowed into his back when he stopped and gathered his things by the back door. Embarrassed by her clumsiness and the whole puppy dog routine, she backed off and made a show of studying the artwork mounted along one wall, determined to keep her questions to herself.

Unlike the more simplistic designs intended for walk-in customers up front, the ones here were intricate and solely Priest's work. All of them featured either animals, nature, or knots and symbols like those inked on his torso, but their detail was so vivid it seemed as if they were real entities frozen in time. Most were in black, but a few had a single accent color interwoven.

"What did you mean by your real job?"

Way to go, smooth. Very nonchalant.

Priest glanced at her and grinned. "The one where I take care of my clan."

Well, duh. Kind of a hard detail to forget considering the things she'd heard and seen over the last week. She turned her back and went back to studying the artwork, hoping her cheeks weren't as red as they were hot.

"It's a soul quest, kitten."

That got her attention like little else could have. She spun, a host of questions lining up on her tongue. "Someone's having one now?"

"No. Not yet. But soon."

"But how do you know?"

He shrugged and stuffed his billfold in his back pocket. "I just know. I feel it. The same way you sense you left a light on at your house or walked away from something you shouldn't have, only it gets stronger as the person's time comes."

The distance she'd sensed while he was working. That's what he'd been focused on. And while she understood the analogy on a day-to-day level, the concept of being tied to another person by such a mystical connection was harder to wrap her head around. "That's odd."

"Not really. More like necessary. If I had no warning before the Keeper pulled me to the Otherworld, who knows where I'd be or what I'd be doing. The sensation alerts me. Gives me a chance to get somewhere private."

"But what if the person you're supposed to help is a long way away? How do you get to them fast enough?"

He smiled, a full one that hinted of mischief and all manner of dirty deeds intended if given the time and opportunity. He stalked toward her. "I'm not with them physically. Only in the Otherworld. Though, you'll see soon enough." He turned her, motioned to the designs on the wall and rested his hands on her hips. "If I gave you your own, what would you want?"

Mounted low on the wall was a black-and-white depiction of a tropical cove, a full moon reflected on the water's glass-smooth surface with exotic flowers carefully interspersed in the design. A panther padded along the shore's edge. Not the focal point of the picture, but a powerful presence encroaching and ready to take over.

So beautiful and uncannily similar to the feelings churning through her.

"I'm not sure I'm right for a tattoo," she said, but her answer sounded wistful even to her own ears.

His heat blanketed her back and his low voice rumbled through her. A wicked caress that left her wanting. Needing. "What I'd give you wouldn't just be a tattoo. It would be a talisman. A protection." His fingers tightened on her hips and he inhaled deep, the sound as sensual and primitive as the words that followed. "I want to mark you."

A shudder wracked her, and her breath hitched, her hands gripping his corded forearms as if the contact could ground her through the maelstrom he'd created.

Take what you want.

God, she wanted to. To arch her shoulders against his hard chest and guide his hands up to her breasts. To feel his lips and teeth against the tender junction of her neck and shoulders where his warm breath buffeted against her skin, and the press of his cock against her core. Already her sex was ready. Wet, aching and eager to feel him slip inside. For the claiming stretch of his cock.

"I'm right here, *mihara*." He pressed one hand above her abdomen and flexed his hips against hers. And oh, was he *there*. Hard as a rock and ready to give her everything she wanted. "Right here. Whatever you need. Everything you need."

It would be so easy. A simple yes, or maybe even just an answering touch.

But then what?

Three electronic pings sounded in quick succession from across the room, the sound abrupt and irritating in the supercharged silence. Logic urged her to move. To step away while she still could, but another part of her—the one she'd stifled and ignored so much of her life—rallied to ignore the summons. To surrender and simply feel for once in her life.

Priest pressed a firm kiss to her temple and growled, his cat merging with the openly irritated sound before he stepped away. "Get your phone, kitten. I need to get us both home before I push things too far."

The loss of his heat and his solid presence behind her left her adrift, the same drunken sensation she'd experienced after her high school senior cruise, only this time the disorientation originated from deep inside rather than anything to do with balance.

Before she could clear her head enough to retrieve

the device, Priest fetched her purse and handed it over. The ringing stopped before she could answer the call, but her grandmother's number showed as a missed call on the screen.

An ironic chuckle bubbled up as she punched the redial button. If Nanna had any idea what she'd just interrupted, she'd be furious with herself. Especially considering how she'd gone out of her way to put Priest and Katy in the same room alone together the last few days.

Nanna answered on the first ring, her voice more animated than usual and uncustomarily abrupt. "Kateri, is Eerikki with you?"

At first the name wouldn't register. Not until Priest tensed and zeroed in on the phone clutched against Katy's ear.

Why her grandmother insisted on using the name when even the man it belonged to refused to honor it was beyond her. But then, her grandmother had forgone much of her heritage in the last fifty years, choosing to honor her son's choices rather than keep with the ways she'd grown up with. Maybe using Priest's given name was just her way of making up for lost time. "Yeah, Nanna. He's right here. Is something wrong?"

She paused, but movement sounded through the line before she lowered her voice. "Oh, no. Quite the opposite. Let me talk to him."

Quite the opposite, her ass. Very little in this world nudged Naomi Falsen off her calm and cool demeanor. Even in the face of finding her son and his wife gruesomely murdered, she'd kept her head. The tears might have flowed as openly as her grief, but not once had she lost her focus. Her groundedness in the face of the most horrifying upheaval.

"What's wrong?" Katy demanded.

"Just let me talk to Priest. I'll explain when you get home."

The warmth that had blossomed under Priest's touch chilled in a second, and a prickling unease rippled down the back of her neck. She handed the phone to Priest. "She wants to talk to you."

Face blanked of emotion for the first time since she'd met him, Priest took the phone, turned and paced the length of the small space. "Yeah." He paused beside the window that overlooked the small parking lot used only by building tenants and stared out at the cloud-coated sky. "How long has he been out?" Listening, he planted one hand on his hip. "What was he like before that?" Whatever the answer, it made him glance back at Katy before he nodded. "Right. We're on our way home."

Rather than offer a formal goodbye, he punched the end button and handed Katy the phone. "We need to get home."

Yeah, that part she'd figured out the second she'd heard Nanna's voice. The real question was what had everyone tied up in knots. "Is something wrong with Alek?"

"Nothing's wrong with Alek. He just needs my help." He held up the black leather jacket he'd given her to buffer the crisp spring air on their morning ride to the shop. Of all the adventures she'd been on in her life, riding on the back of his bike had been an unexpected and delightful first. Between the engine's power and the wind streaming all around her, she'd never felt more alive. More rooted in the moment.

Until this second, she'd looked forward to the return trip. Had even toyed with asking Priest to take the longest way home possible. But now all she could do was jam her hands in each sleeve and wish she could genie-blink herself back to Priest's house. She faced him and shoved the overlong sleeves up as much as the thick leather would allow, the temper she'd fought to keep tamped down bubbling perilously close to the surface. "Can you elaborate? If my brother's in trouble, I deserve to know."

If he was fazed by her sharp reprimand, he didn't show it. Just opened the back door, splayed his hand low on her back and urged her ahead of him. "Your brother's not in trouble and he's not in any kind of danger."

"Really? Because all the cloak-and-dagger behavior and veiled wording makes it sound like you're trying to cover something up."

Priest slung one leg over his bike, righted it and knocked the kickstand back. The engine roared to life, the deep growl of it eerily similar to the sounds that came from his panther and oddly comforting in light of the unease scampering around her chest. He met her gaze. "We're not covering things up, kitten. We're being mindful of something that might upset you when you're just beginning to learn about your heritage. Now hop on so I can take care of your brother."

"Take care of my brother how? Why does he need you?"

His lips crooked, the confidence of a man about to level an *I told you so* moment. "Because, unless I'm reading it wrong, the soul quest I've been sensing all day is your brother's."

Chapter Ten

Twenty minutes. Normally, the drive from Priest's shop to the lake took a solid thirty, but between his mate's tension whipping him to hurry and her arms urgently banded around his waist, he'd taken the winding curves at breakneck speed.

Kateri hadn't protested in the slightest. Hell, if anything she'd leaned into each turn like her active participation might somehow make the bike go faster. Another indication how anxious she was to be with her brother.

He backed his Harley into its covered spot and killed the engine.

The roar hadn't even died down before Kateri jumped off the back, but he snagged her wrist before she could get away.

She tugged against his hold and stopped just short of snarling, gaze locked on the front porch. "Let me go."

Like hell he would. She'd had enough upheaval in her life the last few weeks. And while a soul quest was something the people in his clan not only expected, but looked forward to, an outsider wouldn't be nearly prepared for how things would look. "Not yet. Not until you understand a few things."

She frowned, but at least she stopped fighting him.

He leaned his bike onto its stand and swung his leg over the back, not daring to release his grip. "One of the things we've fought with the new generation is a lack of awareness. Too many of our race don't know the signs and symptoms of a soul quest and they react to it the way a singura would."

"What signs and symptoms?"

"To you, the early stages would mirror the flu, only without the fever. You don't want to eat and you've got no energy. The only thing you want to do is find a place to lay down and pass out."

"Is that what Nanna told you he was doing?"

"That's what he was doing two hours ago. By now, he'll be much deeper."

Her eyes narrowed. "How deep?"

"Deep enough you'll question if he's breathing, but I promise you, he is. And he's absolutely safe."

Her lips tightened, but she lifted her chin a notch higher. "Anything else?"

So brave. Determined to face whatever life threw her even when it defied the order and logic she'd buried her emotions under. But she was waking up. Unearthing her Volán nature and the rich vitality that came with it bit by bit.

And he couldn't wait to see her in full bloom.

He fanned his thumb along the pulse point at her wrist, drew her flush against him and anchored his hand low on her back. "Only that where he's going is sacred. A gift. Definitely not something to be afraid of. And I'll be with him."

Her answering expression warned of a cutting retort queued up and ready for launch, but something raw and vulnerable chased it away. As if some new and awkward thought had dared to lift its head. She swallowed hard enough it looked painful. "I want to see him."

Inside, everything was quiet, the cloud-covered sky bathing his home in a sleepy, lazy afternoon feel. Though, as soon as the closing door ricocheted through the entry, soft footfalls sounded down the stairs, followed by Naomi's excited voice. "Eerikki?"

He fought the grin that always tried to emerge when Naomi insisted on using his given name. Knowing his luck, Kateri would pick that second to turn, see his response and lash him up one side and down the other for not taking the moment seriously enough. The truth was, a soul quest was reasonable cause for not just smiles, but celebration. "Yeah, we're here."

Kateri beat him into the living room and met her grandmother at the bottom of the stairs. "Where is he?"

Naomi calmly blocked her from heading up, grabbed her by the wrists and met Priest's gaze. "You told her?"

"I won't ever keep anything from her. Besides, she already knew I'd sensed someone's quest was close. Another minute or two and she'd have figured it out anyway." He motioned them both up the stairs, the familiar tug behind his sternum urging him to get a move on. "Let's go."

Tate's room wasn't much. Just a full-size bed, an old couch with a pull out, a dresser and a desk in the corner. Aside from Tate's moody mid-to-late teens stretch, he'd always preferred to spend his time outdoors or with other people, so his space was more about function than personality. A few mementos from NBA games he'd gone to with Priest were tacked up on the wall along with some of the first designs he'd inked on early clients, and a picture of his parents stood alone on the corner of his maplewood dresser, but the rest of his décor consisted of hoodies, T-shirts and jeans tossed over the desk situated in front of the wide window.

Thankfully, Naomi had drawn the curtains wide. If she'd left them closed the way Tate preferred them, Alek would have looked more like a corpse on top of the hastily made bed. Instead, the overcast skies did a decent job of highlighting the fact that his skin tone was that of a healthy man in his prime.

"Alek?" Kateri sat beside him and clasped his hand in hers. When he didn't answer, she twisted to Priest beside her. "Can he hear me?"

Priest shook his head. "Not now. He's too deep. Like a dream." Actually, it was more along the lines of what she'd consider a coma, but he wasn't about to add to her stress level with unnecessary details.

The pull from the Otherworld intensified, the radiating burn deep in his chest warning that Alek was close. If it were anyone else, he'd settle in for the journey in his own room, or at least find someplace quiet and dark, but with Kateri this tense, he couldn't quite force his feet into motion. Not to mention the fact that she'd probably see such isolation as desertion rather than the need for focus.

Naomi must have sensed his turmoil, because she inched in behind Kateri and cupped her shoulders. "Go ahead, Eerikki. I'll stay with her."

"No. I'm fine here." He crouched beside Kateri, squeezed her thigh and lowered his voice. "I need you to promise me something."

She shifted her gaze to his, the confusion and discomfort on her face making both man and beast bristle.

"No matter what happens—no matter what you

think is going on or whatever fears come up while he's asleep—I want your word you will not leave this house. Not for anything."

"Why would my leaving be an issue?"

A good question. And likely not something that would happen considering how tightly she gripped Alek's hand. The harder part was his answer. Especially since he'd yet to share what she was to him. "Because inside this house and on my property my brother can't find you. Away from it and without me to protect you, you're exposed. I need to focus and take care of Alek and I can't do that if I'm worried about you being safe."

And because you will always take precedence over any living soul on this Earth.

Her gaze narrowed as if she'd heard his unspoken thought, but instead of questioning him further, she dipped her head. "I won't leave. Just take care of my brother."

Priest shifted his gaze to Naomi, who gave her own nod, then settled on his ass beside the bed. The heavy nightstand was solid wood and had been a bitch to carry upstairs even with his strength, but it still groaned as he leaned his weight into it.

The burn inside his chest deepened, a fist-like sensation building between his solar plexus. But still he couldn't close his eyes and focus. Couldn't force his thoughts off Kateri and the obvious worry on her face.

You don't have to go, the darkness whispered. *She's more important. There's no law that requires your presence. Let him take care of himself. We take care of her.*

Maybe not a law, he argued back in his thoughts. *But it is my responsibility. My right and honor. And nothing would piss our mate off more than to leave someone she loved alone and unguided.*

The counter argument won, his shadow-self curling in upon itself and stilling enough that its constant drone was little more than background noise.

His eyelids grew heavy and the real world began to blur, Kateri's still form beside the bed misting with layers of gray. He tightened the grip he'd kept on her thigh and she laid her free hand over it a second before he saw nothing at all. Could only feel her palm against his as his spirit slipped away.

Seconds later, his destination came into view. Why he was surprised by the environment the Keeper had chosen for Alek he couldn't say, but Alek was clearly confused. Standing in the middle of a traditional Korean dojang, Alek scanned the two stories of black sliding doors with their ivory paper panes as if both fascinated and stymied.

He must have felt more than heard Priest's presence, because he spun and braced on the balls of his feet, prepared for a fight.

"Relax," Priest said. "You'll probably get a fight before this is over. Or several, from the looks of things. But not from me."

Alek straightened and lowered his hands to his side. "I don't get it. What's going on?"

"What's going on is your soul quest."

Behind Alek, the center door slid silently open and a man with short-cropped black hair and a lethal focus strode through it. The Keeper.

Priest dipped his head to indicate the newest arrival and grinned. "Welcome to the Otherworld."

Chapter Eleven

Seven hours Katy had waited—every minute except for two insanely fast bio-breaks—spent in Tate's tiny bedroom either holding Alek's and Priest's hands or pacing a path around the bottom half of Tate's bed.

Oh, and straightening clothes.

Whether Tate appreciated it or not, every article of clothing he owned was now not only neatly put away but fanatically organized. Odds were good he'd read her the riot act the way Alek did whenever she encroached on his sacred space, but by the time she'd given in and slipped into OCD mode, she'd been desperate for something to do. Surely, he'd cut her some slack considering the circumstances.

Now, she was cooling her jets all over again. Only this time her brother was very much awake, and she didn't want to move because what she was seeing was nothing short of fascinating. With Nanna seated on the ground and watching beside her, Katy stretched her legs out in front of her and braced her hands on the soft soil behind her back as Priest and Alek battled it out.

If you could call it a battle. More like two super humans exploring their hyped up skills and showing off all rolled into one while the Tiki torches Priest had lit with only a thought accented every move against the night skies. From the time Alek was six, she'd watched her brother spar with people, but what he was capable of now boggled the mind. It was like watching the Matrix minus the leather, hair gel and sunglasses.

But his speed, skills and agility hadn't been the only things to change.

Alek was different.

Focused. Centered and grounded like she'd never seen him before. Gone was the wildness he'd fought in recent weeks, replaced with an easygoing peace. As if in the time he'd been asleep he'd matured by a decade instead of hours.

Ironic, because by the time he'd woken up, she'd been strung tight enough to launch straight through the ceiling.

Alek landed a punch to Priest's jaw that sent his head whipping to one side, the jarring thud that went with the contact almost sickening.

Priest shook his head and laughed, which of course only made Alek laugh, too.

"Men," Katy muttered. "They're idiots."

Naomi grinned, but kept her gaze riveted on the action. "Yes, but you have to admit, for idiots, they're fun to watch."

When Katy didn't answer, Naomi broke her rapt stare and lifted both eyebrows at Katy. "What? You can't tell me you're not impressed."

Oh, she was impressed all right. The first time she'd watched Priest go head-to-head with her brother, her stomach muscles had contracted so hard she'd barely been able to breathe. But this time Priest held nothing back, pushing Alek in a way that said he had nothing but confidence for her brother and was intent on teaching him even more.

Plus, Priest had ditched every stitch of clothes save the track pants he favored when lounging at home or outside, this pair dark as his panther's fur. Working with Priest alone every morning the last several days had been an exercise in temptation, but watching his slick, graceful moves with firelight glinting off his sweat-slickened, muscled torso seemed downright sinful.

When they finally took a break from their ninja slug-fest, Priest glanced at Kateri over his shoulder then muttered something to Alek she couldn't quite make out with the distance between them.

A strange look moved across Alek's face. Surprise maybe? No, more like uncertainty. Which explained why it was so strange, because it was an expression she seldom saw on her brother. Still, he nodded and trudged up the slight slope to the raised ridge where she and Nanna had watched the show.

"Well? What do you think?" Alek asked as they drew close. Like Priest, he was drenched in sweat, but smiling like a ten-year-old boy who'd just scored his first bike.

He might not have asked the question in an arrogant way, but he was still her brother and had an ego the size of Texas. A fair amount of sibling ribbing was not only allowed, but a little sister's guilty pleasure. "I think all those years you wanted to be the Black Power Ranger have finally paid off."

Priest barked out a laugh and gave Alek one of those manly backslaps that would have knocked her face-first to the ground. "A punch to the gut and she didn't even lift a finger."

Surprisingly, Alek just grinned and rolled with her

playful comment—another glaring indicator something big had happened to her brother in the Otherworld. Something special, just as Priest had predicted. "Hey, don't knock Zack Taylor. He could fight *and* dance."

Happy to see the laid-back brother she'd grown up with back among them, Katy cocked her head and smiled up at him. "I'm only teasing you. You looked great. How do you feel?"

"Fantastic." He rolled his shoulders and pumped his fists a few times as though checking his fatigue level and finding it nonexistent. "It's weird. Even after all that, I don't feel tired. More like I'm warmed up and ready for the main round."

"Good, because the main round is coming up," Priest said.

Naomi pushed to her feet and dusted the loose soil off her coral cotton pants. Funny. Katy had always thought the loose styles Nanna favored were just a hip coincidence to match her vibrant personality. Turned out most of the people in their clan favored unrestricted clothing whenever possible with jeans being about the tightest fashion form she'd seen.

"Come on, Kateri," Nanna said. "That's our cue."

"What cue?"

Naomi waved Katy toward the house. "To skedaddle so Priest can help Alek shift for the first time. The first time is always private. Special. Not to mention your brother will need all the focus he can get."

"Actually, I want Kateri to stay." Priest's words might have been couched casually, but there was a strong undercurrent that said he not only had a reason for his request, but didn't want it questioned. "Alek agreed."

A wry gleam sparked in Nanna's eyes and her soft

smile was one of happy secrets. She nodded, patted Katy's shoulder and turned toward the house. "Well, then, I'll see if I can wrangle up some food before Tate and Jade get home from closing down the shop and leave the three of you to it."

Priest settled on the ground next to Katy, and a second later all but one of the Tiki torches staked along the wide clearing went dark.

Katy glanced back at Naomi steadily making her way up the wood stairs. "I don't get it. Why can't Nanna stay, too?"

"Because she was right about a person's first shift being private," Priest said. "Partly because it's difficult and requires focus, but also because it's emotional."

Alek's wary expression said he didn't care for that development in the slightest. Happiness, anger and laugher her brother had no problem with, but anything that dug into deeper, more vulnerable feelings made him itchy at best. A flight risk at worst. God knew, she'd seen his flight instinct with more than one poor woman who'd had the misfortune of falling for him.

"Then maybe Nanna's right." Katy started to stand. "I can help with the food and give you two time to do your thing."

Priest snatched her wrist before she could fully gain her feet and tugged her backward.

Not expecting the action, she lost her balance and would have tumbled in an ugly sprawl, but Priest caught her by the waist and guided her ass square between his thighs. No doubt exactly where he'd intended her to be all along.

Knees bent and braced on either side of hers with his hot torso blanketing her back, his voice was a gentle yet stern demand near her ear. "You need this, kitten. Every bit as much as he does. Stay and share the gift he's giving you."

As dirty plays went, it was a doozy. He'd intentionally phrased his command in such a way her curiosity was thoroughly piqued, and her mind was too scrambled by his presence to argue. The latter, of which, was outrageous considering if anyone else had manhandled or taken a heavy hand to her like he just had, she'd have physically or verbally lashed out and immediately gained some distance.

"It's okay, Katy." Alek's voice cut through her daze, the tone of it that of a man determined to mask his fear, but not at all sure of the overall game plan. "I really don't mind. I just don't have a clue what I'm doing."

"None of us do the first time out," Priest said, "but you'll figure it out." He motioned to the space in front of them then casually banded one arm around Katy's waist and pulled her against him. He draped his other forearm loosely over one bent knee. "Now have a seat."

Have a seat.

Relax.

Focus.

Katy tried to focus on Priest's guidance as he coached Alek, but her body wasn't nearly as cooperative about paying attention. It was too fixated on the man behind her. On the possessive arm he kept around her waist. How confidence emanated from him even when sitting still. Of the deep rumble in his voice and how it rippled pleasantly across her skin.

"Now, remember your time in the Otherworld," Priest said to Alek, though with his mouth so close to her ear it felt like an intimate caress. "You remember how it felt to merge with your companion?"

He'd merged with his companion? As in it became one with him? So, did that mean Alek already knew what his animal was? And why hadn't he told her as much? She almost asked the questions out loud, but Priest tightened his hold around her and softly kissed her temple. A gentle, but firm unspoken reminder that this wasn't the time for questions.

Seated across from her with his back resting against a moderate-size dogwood tree with his eyes closed, Alek's lips curved in a crooked boyish smile. "Oh, yeah. I remember."

"Good. Focus on that," Priest said. "It's the path to your animal, and the same one you'll use to shift back. All you need to do is let your companion know he's not only welcome, but needed."

Alek frowned, but kept his eyes shut tight. "How do I do that?"

"Do you want to shift?"

"Yeah."

"Why?"

"Because I need to learn how."

"Why do you need to learn?"

Hesitating, Alek cocked his head. Almost as if there were more voices and data streaming through his head than Priest's steady coaching. "Because he's part of me. He deserves the time to roam."

As soon as the words were out of his mouth, Alek's jaw dropped and his eyes popped open. "What the fuck?"

Priest chuckled. "That's your companion. They hear what we hear. Feel what we feel. Just by you thinking through how you felt, it learned alongside you and responded."

Alek smiled huge and locked stares with Katy, the excitement in his gaze like so many of the other firsts they'd shared growing up—only magnified by at least twenty. "He talked to me." The smile disappeared and his eyes narrowed. "I mean, he kind of talked to me. Not with words, but somehow I heard it all the same. He liked my answer."

"The Keeper picks our companions specifically for us," Priest said. "That's part of the soul quest's purpose— to learn who you are and pick the animal best suited for our nature. Right now, you're new to each other, but you're perfectly suited. They're called companions because that's what they are. An extra set of eyes and ears to guide you, and a tie to our magic. Over time you won't be able to imagine a you without them."

"So, why didn't he shift?" As soon as Katy asked the question, she clamped her mouth shut, worried she'd inadvertently trampled somewhere she shouldn't.

Fortunately, Priest just gazed down at her, the barest hint of amusement and what looked like hope lighting his eyes. "What he felt was just a start. The first words in a new language. It takes time to gain confidence and make a whole sentence. That's what shifting is like."

As analogies went it was brilliant, apparently registering with Alek just as strongly, because he shut his eyes and stilled, obviously eager to try again.

Over and over, Alek followed Priest's instructions. How he kept after it with so many false starts, Katy couldn't comprehend. If it were her, she'd have thrown in the towel after the third attempt. But Alek swore the connection he built with each pass grew stronger and more amazing, so what did she know? The last thing she could ever accuse her brother of being was overly dramatic, and if he said it was a sensation to be reckoned with, then she'd be the last one to short-change the process.

Alek closed his eyes again, a little of the vigor he'd woken with ebbing and fatigue weighting his shoulders.

Katy covered Priest's forearm with her own and laced her fingers with his. The touch was intimate. Familiar in a way she couldn't believe she'd initiated, but was helpless to fight. It was as if she'd been wrapped up in a sacred moment. Included in some rare and revered event her soul recognized even if her mind was too slow to comprehend.

"He's getting tired," she whispered low enough she hoped it wouldn't distract Alek.

Priest rubbed his temple against hers, a familiar touch that not only soothed her creeping anxiety but made her want to reach for more. "He's fine. A few more tries and he'll have it. It's human nature to try and retain control. The fatigue wears down his resistance."

The last of his words still hung on the cold spring night around them when a brilliant light fanned across them, the rich garnet color there and gone so fast she halfway wondered if it hadn't been an illusion.

Until her mind fully registered the sight in front of her.

In the spot where her brother had patiently reached for his companion time and again sat one of the most beautiful creatures she'd ever seen.

"He's a wolf," Katy said. Though, how she'd managed to put words around her thoughts was a miracle in and of itself.

"A gray wolf," Priest said. "The largest of its kind and revered in our clan. A powerful choice for our warrior primo."

Katy gasped and twisted. "He's the primo?"

Priest nodded, obviously pleased with the development. "I would have been surprised if he wasn't. He's a natural fit. Skilled and more balanced now that he has his gifts."

More balanced. Yes, that was the perfect way to explain it. As if the magic had evened out his demeanor.

She turned back to the wolf. On height alone, the animal would nearly reach her hips. The same deep blue eyes as Alek's stared back at her, but their shape was more slanted and focused in a way that said the animal in front of her missed absolutely nothing. His coat was a mix of gray, white and tawny, the latter unsurprisingly similar to Alek's dirty-blond hair, and his chest was broad enough to promise astounding power behind any attack.

And he was part of Alek's life now. A protector. A confidant.

A friend.

Why the realization rattled so profoundly through her, she couldn't say, but her throat constricted to the point it was hard to breathe and her eyes burned. "He's beautiful."

Priest hugged her tight, his voice a comfort. "He is. But no more so than your companion will be."

Her companion.

For the first time since Nanna had shared their clan's existence, something inside her clicked. A revelation solidifying at the most fundamental level. Despite how many times she'd seen Nanna or Priest shift, it had seemed more the stuff of fantasy than reality. But this wasn't a hoax. Wasn't a figment of her imagination running wild and untended. This was real. Her future if she chose to accept it. "What's it like?"

Priest kept his silence for thoughtful seconds, his fingers drawing idle patterns against her shoulder. As if he realized how sincere her question was compared to her usual cataloging queries and wanted to find the best response possible. "Freedom."

One word and yet it conveyed so much. When was the last time she'd really felt such a thing? Truly unwound her relentless grip on control and simply allowed herself to just *be*?

In answer, her mind offered up the kiss she'd shared with Priest in the cove. True, a part of her had stayed locked away, tethered by fear and uncertainty, but in that tiny space of time he'd given her a taste of liberation. A sampling of another way of life.

The wolf shook his massive body, startling Katy out of her rumination. The action drew an image in her head of Alek doing the same in human form and she laughed, the sound lighter and freer than any other she'd produced in years. "Takes some settling in, does it?"

Lifting its chin, the wolf huffed out a sound that seemed suspiciously like a laugh.

"His wolf will help him," Priest said. "Once the shift happens, the animal's instincts take precedence. Alek's thoughts are still his own and his companion will ultimately cede to his direction, but right now the animal is smarter. Wiser." Priest held out his hand and motioned the beast over. "Come say hello."

The wolf hesitated, studied Priest and Katy one at a time, then scented the air.

"You know who I am," Priest said to the wolf. "And she belongs to Alek. Come."

It answered with a low, almost petulant grumble, but padded cautiously toward them. The closer he drew, the more his head and body lowered, a mix of submission and preparedness for flight.

Without the least amount of fear, but mindful of the wolf's open reticent, Priest rubbed the animal's neck. "You see? Not so much different here, is it?"

The wolf grunted in answer and closed his eyes, openly appreciating Priest's attention.

"Touch him," Priest murmured beside her ear. "Let him know he's safe."

"He's afraid?"

"Not afraid. Just wary. It's his first time in our world, so his senses are on overload. The touch will help ground him."

Katy hesitated, resting her fisted hand on her thigh rather than reaching out. Part of her trusted that her brother was the one driving the massive animal, but another far more primitive side of herself insisted that cozying up to a predator was a monumentally bad idea.

The wolf shifted its massive head, nudged her fist with its muzzle and whined.

Okay, maybe it was a predator, but right now it appeared to not only need, but want her affection. Slowly, she lifted her hand and the wolf ducked its head beneath it, effectively guiding her palm to the back of its neck.

Katy chuckled and relented, rubbing both sides of his head. "Well, all right then." Unlike the sleek feel of Priest's panther, Alek's wolf was snuggly and warm, her fingers easily disappearing in his dense coat as she scratched behind his ears.

The wolf sniffed her, inched closer and licked her jawline.

Priest growled. Or maybe it was his panther surfacing with a warning. Whatever or whoever it was, the wolf eased back, but not so much as to disengage from her touch. Or Priest's for that matter.

"He wasn't scaring me, if that's what you're worried about," Katy said quietly.

"I wasn't worried. My cat just didn't like him that close."

"Why not? He's my brother."

"He's your brother, but his wolf was moving in to mark you. That's my right. Not his."

Her fingers stilled and she twisted. "You've known me six days. He's known me my whole life. How can it be your right over his?"

Not missing a beat, Priest maintained the slow and steady strokes along the lower stretch of the wolf's neck, but the easiness in his gaze sharpened. He shifted his attention to the wolf. "Go for a run. I'll catch up after I talk to your sister, but stay within the wards and remember to conserve energy for your shift back. Listen to your companion and he'll keep you safe."

The wolf looked from Priest to Katy, the understanding behind his azure gaze a little surprising. Rather than take off as Katy had expected, he stepped in close, butted his head against her chest, then rubbed the side of his body against hers.

"She'll be fine." The remark was dry, but there was humor in Priest's words, too. "Stop worrying and run."

Alek backed up, studied her for one last second, then loped away.

Her brother had his own wolf. A beautiful and powerful creature who could explore without a single light to guide him on a nearly moonless night. How freaking cool was that?

But it still didn't answer her question. And if there was one thing she hated it was untidy threads. Particularly with a man as powerful and commanding as Priest. "Why won't you answer me?"

For the first time since he'd settled her next to him, his touch was curiously absent, his fists braced against the Earth behind him. "Stand up."

"I'd rather talk."

"Then you need to stand up. Now. Otherwise, I'll have you naked and under me before you can ask another question."

Pleasure, pure and sharp, speared straight between her legs, the image her mind paired with his words snatching the breath right out of her lungs. Talk about the wrong incentive to get her moving. Especially after how many times she'd replayed the feel of his lips and his weight above her.

"Kateri."

It was the plea in his voice that did it, the struggle mingled with his panther's growl that spurred her to her feet and urged her out of reaching distance while he stood as well. "Are you okay?"

He gauged the distance she'd put between them and crooked a cockeyed grin. "I said stand, not run." He prowled closer. "Running only makes me want to chase you."

For some stupid reason, that idea thrilled her almost as much as the first one had. So much so, she shifted her feet and considered the direction Alek had disappeared into.

"Don't even think it." His arm snaked around her back, pinning her to him. "I'm trying to go slow. To give you time and not overwhelm you all at once, but there's a part of me…"

"Your cat, you mean."

He frowned, the action more pronounced with the firelight's shadows. "No. It's something else. Something dark."

As in his brother's black magic. It had taken some doing over dinner prep one night with Jade and Tate while Priest was still at his shop, but she and Alek had finally gotten all the gory details. By the time the story was over, Katy wasn't sure if she wanted to run and not look back, or redouble her efforts to track down Draven and gut him herself. "Jade said it doesn't control you anymore. That it hasn't for a long time."

"Not until you, no." He inhaled long and deep and cupped the side of her face. "It doesn't want to play nice. Doesn't want to give you time. It just wants you. Now."

A shiver moved through her, one she suspected was more centered with agreement than the healthy fear her brain said was smart. "And what do you want?"

His gaze dropped to her mouth and he traced her lower lip with his thumb. "Oh, I want the same. Only I want it with you knowing what you're getting going in."

There it was. The carrot dangling just out of reach. She forced her lips to move, though she wasn't completely sure she wanted the question to take flight. "What am I to you?"

His arm tightened around her and the expression on his face looked as if a heated battle warred inside his head. "You're my *mihara*." He paused for one heart-stopping beat and met her gaze head-on. "My mate."

Chapter Twelve

It was a beautiful spring evening, Katy was finally getting another trip out of Priest's house and her brother was happy. Heck, *everyone* was happy, the news that a new warrior primo had been named and a celebration imminent making visitors at Priest's house a nonstop event. In fact, the only two people who seemed miserable were her and Priest.

Katy glared out the back of Alek's Jeep as they drove to the bar, Tate, Jade and Nanna's excited chatter mingling with the wind. The lack of doors and windows did a number on her hair, but she didn't care. Sure, it was a party, but it wasn't the first time she'd celebrated one of her brother's accomplishments and it wouldn't be the last. Not to mention, dressing up would only give Priest the wrong impression.

Right. Because the complete shift in wardrobe doesn't say something else entirely.

Okay, maybe she'd spent a *little* extra time getting ready. But the jeans and cobalt blue cotton wraparound shirt with its dolman sleeves was more about exploring and fitting in with the people she was slowly getting to know than appealing to Priest. So what if the soft cotton and faded denim molded her curves more than her normal skirts?

Besides, her time prepping had nothing on Jade. She'd primped for over an hour, and while she'd stuck to black jeans and girly combat boots, she'd paired them with a light cedar-green sweater tunic that accented her striking eyes. Unlike the simple French braid she normally wore to the shop and around the house, she'd left her soft black hair loose with at least four or five delicate charms braided into strands on one side.

Tate hadn't gone to nearly the trouble Jade had, though he definitely had the look of a man ready to work his mojo on any and all women who caught his eye. Not to mention, the way his jeans and T-shirt showcased his muscled body, he wouldn't have to bring his A game.

Nanna leaned forward enough to make sure Tate could hear from the driver's seat. "Do you think Priest and Alek will be finished by the time we get there?"

Tate downshifted and took the last curve into downtown Eureka Springs like the Jeep was his instead of someone else's. The fact that Alek had actually volunteered his Jeep for carting everyone around while Priest finished the last of Alek's new tattoo only solidified his change in demeanor. He never let anyone drive his Jeep. Ever. "I checked in before we left. He'll be at least a half hour behind us. Maybe a little more. But they're close."

Nanna nodded and eased back in her seat. Even she'd taken a little extra care in her outfit, choosing a breezy taupe skirt and a winter-white gypsy-styled blouse for their night out. She openly gave Katy the once-over, her gaze zeroing in on the base of Katy's neck before she crooked her mouth in a smug grin. "You took it off."

Without thinking better of it, Katy smoothed her fingers along the hollow of her neck. She'd grown so accustomed to the weight of Priest's medallion in the time since he'd put it on her, it had taken her a full day of all but hiding from her so-called mate before she realized she still wore it. Ever since she'd mustered her mini-rebellion and taken it off this morning, she'd felt off. Adrift. As if the slightest wind could throw her off course. "I didn't realize what it meant. It's better I don't give him any more mixed signals."

Nanna rolled her lips inward and averted her face, but the humor Katy glimpsed in her eyes as she did so almost made Katy think her grandmother had a direct line to her thoughts. "I take it he told you," she said once she'd schooled her expression.

"You knew?"

The sudden silence from the front seat and the smirk Tate unsuccessfully tried to hide in the rearview mirror said they'd not only overhead the conversation, but had also been in on the secret.

Katy scooted forward and peeked around for a good look at Jade's face. "You all knew?"

Well, of course, they knew. Tate all but told you as much that first day. Remember?

"It's a bit hard to miss when a Volán finds his mate," Naomi said calmly beside her. "It's also a treat for the rest of us. Nothing more entertaining than watching the fireworks."

"Why didn't you tell me?"

Naomi shrugged it off. "What? And give you reason to run? Why would I do that? Besides, Eerikki would have only chased you." Her gaze dropped to the empty space at the base of Katy's throat and she grinned. "Although, you're giving him ample reasons on your own."

"Yeah, I caught that, too." Jade giggled from the front seat. "This is gonna be fun."

Unsure if she was pissed off or just stymied by the fact that she'd been the last to know, Katy slid back in her seat and clamped her mouth tight.

If the rest of the crew realized they'd just thrown her for an extra spin on her already out of control merry-go-round, they didn't show it. Just shifted into a rapid-fire discussion on the events planned for tonight and who was expected.

Tate whipped into a parking lot behind a yellow building with green trim and killed the engine. "Rogue's Manner, ladies. Who's ready to party?"

"Hell, yeah!" Jade cheered as she hopped out of the front seat.

Naomi laughed and let Tate help her climb out of the backseat, though Katy knew damned good and well she could probably hop out as easy as anyone despite her age.

"Do you think we'll hear anything from the other seers while we're here?" Katy said as she jumped to the cracked asphalt. She'd hounded David with as many voicemails as she dared, hovered around the seers gathered trying to gain information and crammed as much Volán knowledge as she could the last several days, but the lack of information and growing helplessness grated what was left of her patience.

As one, Jade, Tate and Nanna all swiveled their heads her direction, their expressions similar to what they'd have had if she'd grown three heads and sprouted a forked tail.

"What? I just thought if everyone was going to be here, we might learn if anyone's seen or learned something on their own." Not to mention she needed something else to think about besides Priest.

Naomi motioned Jade and Tate ahead. "You two go on in. Kateri and I will be along in a minute."

For a second, Katy gave serious consideration to snatching Alek's keys from Tate's fingers and hightailing it back to Priest's place. Or a hotel, for that matter. Because *Kateri and I will be along in a minute* was likely code speak for *I need to pull my granddaughter's head out of her ass.*

Jade must've figured the same thing because she shot Katy a semi-sympathetic look and shrugged her shoulders before disappearing in the bar. Tate studied Katy, scanned the street, and circled the key fob like an old west gunslinger. "How about if I hang out here while you talk? Priest put wards up, but he'd kick my ass if I left Katy unguarded."

He'd put wards up? When? Because he'd spent the better part of the last two days working on Alek's marks, meeting with the clan's seers and dealing with visitors in general. Not that she was bitter with the lack of attention, because she wasn't. At least that was the line she was sticking to until she actually believed it. Fake it till you make it and all that.

With a firm grip on her arm, Naomi guided her to a metal park bench braced along the sidewalk for tourists. "I know your goals where your parents are concerned, *nahina*. I also know sitting idle is the hardest thing anyone could ever ask you to do. But what you don't realize is that Eerikki is doing quite the opposite. Apparently you don't see it, but he's working every outlet he can to find the remaining primo families and, in turn, Draven."

Katy dropped to the park bench, the shock of what

Nanna had shared adding extra weight to gravity as she did so. "He is?"

"He is. And you'd see that if you weren't so caught up in either avoiding him or refusing to look at things beyond the lens you're used to." Nanna rested easy against the bench's high back, crossed her legs and stared out at what was left of the sunset. Only a thin slice of deep mango peeked between the store fronts and the deep green leaves from the trees around them wavered against the night's darkening skies. "Your mother wasn't your father's mate."

The sharp shift in topic captured Katy's attention as little else could have. "She wasn't?"

"No. Volán males can only see the aura that surrounds their mate once they've accepted their powers. Since he shunned his quest, he never received that guidance." Sadness filled her gaze, the look of a mother who knew all too well that their child had not only missed an opportunity but suffered unknowingly for it. "As couples went, they did well. Well balanced and peaceful. But it was nothing compared to the life I had with my mate. To the deep relationship any Volán woman shares with her man."

"Are you trying to tell me this whole mystical arranged marriage hocus-pocus is all unicorns and sunshine?"

"No, I'm trying to tell you you're uniquely paired. For God's sake, Kateri, look how many people today sign up for those online dating sites and try to match based on compatibility. This is no different, only the algorithm is unbeatable because it's designed by fate. Don't tell me you don't feel it."

"Feel what?"

Nanna scowled at her. "Don't play dumb, *nahina*. It doesn't become you. I've watched you avoiding him the last few days. I see the pain it causes you. The pain it causes *him*. That urge to be with him—the pull you feel when you're away from him—is natural because he's part of you."

It hadn't been pain at first. More like the discomfort you felt when you walked out of your house and worried you'd accidentally locked your keys inside. Or left water running that was sure to overflow. Every time she put more distance between them, it had been all she could do not to turn around and cut the space in half.

Today, though...today had been worse. A growing unease and gnawing pressure behind her sternum. Still, the idea of giving in to that sensation battered against the life she'd built for herself. "I don't want to be dependent on a man. I can take care of myself."

Surprising the heck right out of Katy, Naomi let loose with a sharp bark of laughter.

Katy folded her arms across her chest. "It's not funny."

"Actually, it is, because you're looking at it the wrong way. Understandable, given the way you've grown up, but your vantage point is slanted. Colored by the everyday mindset of the singura instead of your true race."

"So, what? I should just happily jump into his arms, simper around and rely on him?"

"I know you never met my mate, but can you actually envision me simpering at any time in my life?" Not waiting for an answer, Naomi kept going. "No. I didn't. I wouldn't. That's not what Volán women do. The problem is you're seeing Eerikki as a separate part of yourself. But in truth, he's no different than an extension of your body."

Stymied, Katy just blinked back at her grandmother. As if the repeated effort to clear her eyesight might somehow unscramble her brain in the process.

"Think about it this way," Naomi said. "How much more difficult would your life be if you didn't have your hands? Your feet? Your eyes? Eerikki is just another part of you. Without him, life is harder. Not impossible, but more complicated. Uncomfortable. With him, things flow. Feel good."

"But I did fine before I met him."

Naomi smiled softly and her voice lowered, the gentleness of her tone a stark contrast to the power of her words. "Because until you met him, you didn't know what you were missing."

Lightning piercing through her chest couldn't have been more appropriate. That was *exactly* the difference. The truth she'd tried to avoid but grew more and more incapable of distancing herself from with each look from Priest. Each deep, rumbling comment and confident touch.

She tried to swallow, but the realization left a boulder-sized knot wedged in the base of her throat. "So, I have no choice?"

"You have a choice. He knows you're his mate, but you are the one who seals the bond when you accept him."

A shiver that had nothing to do with the cooling temperatures snaked down her back.

Take what's yours.

Priest had repeated the phrase ample times since their first day at the cove. Had insisted he wouldn't push her until she was ready. But maybe he'd meant something else altogether. "You mean sex?"

"No, *nahina*. I mean when you accept him with your heart."

Across the street, a couple she recognized from visits to Priest's house ambled toward the bar. Neither looked much older than Katy, maybe nearing their late twenties to early thirties at most. Though, with the way Voláns aged, they could be closer to fifty or sixty for all she knew. They walked with their arms comfortably banded around each other's waist, an easy synchronicity in their relaxed gait that looked like something from one of those epic love stories. Were they mates? Just dating? Finding their way? And how did a woman go about giving her heart to a man? Or, maybe the more important question was how to avoid it until they were absolutely sure.

"What's that look like?" Katy asked still eyeing the couple.

Naomi sighed and patted Katy's thigh. "My poor girl. Always trying to put a description on the indescribable or logic to emotion." Like Katy, she watched the couple disappear inside then turned her gaze on Katy. "It's not what things look like where your mate is concerned that matters, but how it feels."

That.

That right there was the most terrifying proposition of all. To feel meant to lose control. To relinquish sound reasoning and planning. To take unnecessary and potentially painful risks. "I'm not sure I know how to do that."

Grinning, Naomi stood, clasped Katy's wrist and pulled her to her feet. "You'll learn. And quickly I'd imagine with a man like Eerikki." Her gaze dropped to the empty space at the base of Katy's throat and the grin shifted to more of a smirk. "But just know...the more you run, the more heated the game will be."

Chapter Thirteen

Priest was exhausted. The last two days had been non-stop, the biggest chunk of it spent giving Alek a mark worthy of a primo and imbuing it with his magic. The rest he'd spent building wards around Rogue's Manner and guiding Alek as fellow warriors visited to offer their vows. Having the party at his house would've been a hell of a lot easier, but Kateri was obviously itching for a change of venue. Considering she'd spent the time since learning she was his mate diving into all things Volán and avoiding him like the plague, it was the only way he knew to give her some relief.

So, he'd slipped out of the house while everyone else was asleep to get the job done. He sure as hell wasn't getting any sleep anyway.

He stalked across the parking lot toward the bar's main entrance, Alek quiet yet focused beside him. Which was the exact opposite of the one-on-one time they'd spent at the shop. Alek might have only learned of their race three weeks ago, but now he seemed bound and determined to make up for lost time in short order.

Hard not to blame the guy for being tight-lipped and nervous tonight, though. Nothing slapped a man to attention more than realizing the extent of responsibility they'd been saddled with.

Priest pulled open the door for Alek and waved him through. "Relax. It's a celebration. Not your first presect. The goal's for you to have a good time and get to know people."

"Says the man who looks like he'd gladly take on every MMA contender at once just to take the edge off." Alek hesitated halfway through the doorway and lowered his voice. "Speaking of which, how much longer are you going to be able to fight back..." He motioned toward Priest and shrugged like he wasn't sure how to address the black elephant. "You know. Your thing. If you two being apart makes you both pissed off, aren't you just begging for trouble if you don't do something?"

"Oh, I'm going to do something. How much and when is the only matter in question. Just remember what I said about not getting between me and your sister. I don't care how much new mojo you've got. If you interfere, I'll rip your guts up through your throat and hang you with them."

Alek froze, a whole bevy of emotions flashing across his face, not the least of which was indecision about letting Priest through the door.

"Relax, big brother. I'm yanking your chain." Priest put a hand to Alek's shoulder, urged him forward and muttered. "Mostly."

Before Alek could dig in his heels and follow up on the quip, the crowd caught sight of him and sent up a chorus of welcomes. Calling the place a manor was pushing it, but the maroon-painted walls, stained woodwork and old-English tapestries gave the place a ton of character.

And it was crowded. Packed with enough clans people they had to have come from as far as a hundred miles out. Not surprising considering their network and the importance of a primo being named. Also not surprising was, while he and Alek might have been well over an hour late to the party, the clan hadn't wasted time getting things rolling. At least a third of them filled the dance floor while the rest ignored the tables and meandered from group to group.

Standing with Alek, Priest shook hands, hugged and high-fived those who approached, but it still only took him three seconds to lock sights on his mate. Standing with a cluster of men and women Jade often ran with, Kateri sipped what he'd bet was one of those fruity cocktails Jade always ordered and watched as everyone crowded around Alek.

Interesting. Normally Kateri stayed near the fringes of the clan's social circles. Watching versus talking. And while he hadn't actually caught her in conversation this time, she was still a part of the fray and even smiling a little bit.

Or she was until she met his gaze and her smile slipped.

He braced for the sharp scowl he'd gotten irritatingly familiar with, only to be greeted by something else. Not an open welcome, but not a rejection either. More of an alertness mingled with confusion. As if a war was going on inside her head and who the winner would be was a toss-up.

One of his oldest warrior elders, Garrett, turned from greeting Alek and held out his hand to Priest. At 163, his hair had finally turned silver and his skin reflected the amount of time he spent outside, but his eyes were still as sharp as Alek's. "You must be happy."

Just as Garrett's words trailed off, Priest's gaze locked on the base of Kateri's neck.

No medallion.

A flash fire ignited beneath his skin. His cat bristled and the darkness surged with a nearly overwhelming push to take action. To mark her any and every way he could.

Priest forced his attention back to his elder. "Hard to question the Keeper's choices, but yeah. Alek's a strong pick, the same as his grandfather." He glanced at Alek practically wedged between two younger women who'd yet to take their soul quests. From the coy looks they were giving him, they were both interested in offering more than simple congratulations. "Do me a favor. Stick with Alek while I handle something."

Garrett chuckled and his gaze slid to Kateri. "Don't suppose what needs handling is standing over there with Jade and dressed for her high priest's attention, is it?"

Whether or not her sexy attire was for him, was up for debate. But the shirt she'd picked was a wraparound style that made a sharp V at the neck and all but cast a spotlight on his missing mark. Although, the fact that she'd gone with a clinging fabric and faded but stylish jeans that molded her body was another shock. While he'd had ample time to appreciate her curves in her running gear, not once had he seen her dress to accentuate her body the way she had tonight.

Dressed to attract.

Blending in with and participating with the clan.

Making a statement.

She wants the hunt.

The thought came from his cat. More a feeling than actual words, yet confident and sure.

And his cat was right. She *did* want it. Though, she likely didn't realize it. Or didn't want to acknowledge it. But it was there. The thrill and anticipation rippling just beneath the surface, trapped beneath the crumbling control she fought to maintain.

"She needs handling all right," Priest said, not taking his eyes off her. The brass chandeliers overhead were dimmed enough to give a relaxed pub vibe, but were bright enough to highlight she'd slept for shit the same as he had. He hoped like hell she was ready for the reaction she'd earned, because his fatigue was gone. Obliterated in a handful of seconds by a fresh surge of adrenaline.

He wove through the crowd, taking his time and only breaking his stare when unknowing clansmen stopped to greet him. Those who stopped him didn't stay unknowing long, though. Not with the way his attention kept drifting back to Kateri and the electric charge that pulsed between them. No one mentioned the lack of his medallion, but there was no doubt they'd all noted it. And those that hadn't would've heard through their rampant grapevine. Priest's mate—the woman who'd walked for days among them with his medallion around her neck for all to see and who always sat on his left, closest to his heart—had thrown down the gauntlet.

The band shifted to a slow and sultry blues tune just as Priest rounded a couple locked in a heated discussion. He slipped up behind Kateri and palmed her hips. "You haven't been sleeping."

She startled at his voice and tried to face him, but he tightened his fingers and held her in place. Even then, she craned her head enough to shoot him a sharp "I'm fine," then snapped her attention back to the dance floor.

"You're not fine. Far from it." He dipped his head and smoothed his temple against hers. Her jasmine scent whispered through him, soothing his tension even as it urged him for more. To have it imprinted on his skin. "You're miserable and I'm done letting you suffer."

Gripping one of his wrists with more strength than he'd expected, she shoved his hand away and jerked out of his grip—an act he allowed, but only barely. The only other option was to yank her against him, devour her mouth and give everyone watching the show they wanted. "You're done *letting* me?"

"That's what I said." He prowled closer, snatched her wrist before she could gain further ground. "You're edgy. Tired. Ready to lash out."

She tried to yank her hand free, but quickly realized it was a fruitless task unless she wanted to gain more attention. "We haven't talked to each other in two days. What makes you think you know what I'm feeling?"

"Because I feel the same." He plucked her drink from her free hand, set it on a nearby table and guided her to the dance floor.

At first, she followed, but as soon as she figured out where they were headed she dug in her heels.

He went with the action, using the counterweight to spin her around and off balance so she landed flush against his front. He banded one arm around her waist and the other around her shoulders, guiding her head so it rested against his chest. "You need my touch," he murmured beside her ear. "Literally. Mates stay close for a reason, namely because distance is painful. Now wrap your arms around me and let me give you some relief."

The hands she'd braced against his chest fisted and a shaky desperation threaded her voice. "I can't. People are watching."

They were. The weight of their stares pressed him on all sides, but he didn't give a damn. He cupped the back of her neck and fought the need to fist his hands in her soft hair and tug her head back for a blistering kiss. "They're watching because my mate decided to take a stand and give me a challenge. One I'm happy to answer. But not until you're more grounded and ready to do battle. Now wrap me up and take what you need."

Slowly, she slid her arms around his neck, her body tense against his. As if she desperately wanted what he offered, but didn't trust either of them enough to let go and accept it. Only when the muscles in her back and shoulders began to relax did he move, gently swaying them with the music.

Her response was uncertain. Timid, the same as her kiss had been before she'd come to life beneath him and eagerly opened for his mouth.

He smoothed his hand along her spine and pressed her hips more firmly against his. "Relax, kitten."

"Easy for you to say," she grumbled against his chest. "You're not the one winging it with everyone watching."

The comment brought his thoughts up short. "Winging what?"

"Nothing. Forget I said it."

Like hell he'd forget it. He cupped the side of her face and urged her to look at him. "Have you never danced with a man?"

The glare she shot him answered almost as effectively as a sharp *no* would've, yet instead of confirming it vocally, she went another route. "I'm not sure what we're doing is dancing."

So, she *hadn't* danced with anyone else. As firsts went, it was an innocent one, but immensely pleasing. A simple pleasure to help lure his kitten out of her dark cave. "Oh, we're dancing. A long, seductive dance that I have no intention of ending."

Her lips parted and she ducked her chin, but not before he caught the flash of excitement in her eyes.

His chest expanded, a lightness that was nearly uncontainable pushing his shoulders back from the inside. His beast paced and growled with anticipation. "Look at me."

She shook her head.

"I need your eyes, Kateri. Give them to me. Show me what's burning behind them."

Her chest rose and fell. Once. Twice. A third time. Then, slowly, she looked up.

And the space behind his sternum swelled.

Pure desire. It filled her blue-gray eyes, mingled with a guilelessness that nearly knocked him over. His arms tightened instinctively around her. As though part of him sensed the need to shield her even as another sought to horde her for himself. "You've never danced with a man."

"That doesn't mean anything. I've just focused on school more than socializing. And before you ask, no, I'm not a virgin, so don't think about adding that to your list of firsts."

There was his kitten, doing her best to claw through the intimate moment, even when it only made her that much more adorable. "No, I don't imagine you are. You're too curious. Have too much passion locked inside you to avoid experimenting." He grinned even as his cat considered tracking down those who'd taken her and whittling their spines with its teeth. "But you didn't like it."

She scowled and pursed her mouth like it was all she could do to hold back a long string of profanities.

So. Fucking. Cute.

He probably should have backed off. Should have simply eased her deeper into the dance and pet his kitten back to a playful mood. Instead he set the chuckle building inside him free and nuzzled her neck. "You'll like it with me. Love it. Even crave it."

Her fingers dug into his shoulders and a delicate shudder that had nothing to do with another escape attempt worked through her torso. When she spoke, it was obvious she tried to inject displeasure in her voice, but there was too much rasp behind it to hide another far more tangible, telling response. "Contrary to what you think, me hopping in bed with you isn't a forgone conclusion."

"Yes, it is." He pulled away only enough to run his nose alongside hers and traced his fingers from her collarbone to the hollow of her throat. "You can refuse my mark, but it doesn't change anything. You're my mate. Nothing ranks higher for me than winning you and I won't quit until you accept me."

Oh, yes. She wanted the pursuit. The need and hunger radiating off her licked against his skin. Potent. Addictive. Dangerous. Fighting its way free and fully grasping the attention of man, darkness and beast.

He smiled against her lips. "By all means, though. Take all the time you need getting there. Make me work for it however you see fit." He ghosted a teasing kiss across her mouth, drawing her shaky exhale into his lungs like the prize it was. "I love a good hunt."

Chapter Fourteen

Take what's yours and trust me to keep you safe.

You didn't know what you were missing.

I won't quit until you accept me.

I love a good hunt.

Four phrases. All of them swirling in an endless loop through her head, buffeted nonstop by more emotions than she could process. Her whole life, she'd stayed on track. Focused on her studies. Her career. Always put responsibility and logic over whims and instinct.

And now look at her.

Planted on the back of Priest's bike with the wind in her hair and a pleasant buzz humming beneath her skin. Granted the cocktails she'd nursed throughout the night contributed to part of the latter, but Priest had already proven he was capable of making her drunk without a drop of alcohol. It was like her mind switched to off and her body took over in his presence.

But if she was honest, there was more going on than just Priest and the very carnal response he created when he put his mind to it.

Her control was slipping.

Several times tonight, she'd gone with her gut and acted impulsively. The first being when she'd taken his medallion off. At the time, she'd thought it was a statement. A declaration and a refusal to be pushed into something she didn't want. But maybe it had been something else. Maybe Nanna was right and it was just a subconscious ploy to prod him into action.

If so, her instincts might not be highly experienced, but they'd been deadly accurate. The second he'd laid eyes on her and noted the missing medallion, his whole demeanor had shifted.

And she'd nearly come just by watching it. By the time he'd circled the bar and moved in behind her, her sex was not only damp, but throbbing. How she'd managed to keep from grinding her hips against his when they danced, she still couldn't fathom, but those instincts had kicked in again and she'd held herself back. As if her body knew what to do even when her head was clueless.

She'd also danced with Jade and her girlfriends. Had given way to her inhibitions, closed her eyes and surrendered to the music, moving without any worry of who watched her.

Of course, Priest had watched. About five minutes after she'd cleared the dance floor, he'd stood and all but dragged her from the bar, then promptly informed her he was taking her home.

The Harley's insistent rumble ebbed and Priest leaned them into a sharp curve.

No, not a curve. His driveway.

A thirty-minute drive that had passed in the blink of an eye.

She smiled into the night, the sharp spring chill leaving her cheeks tight and tingly. If Priest had any clue how close to the edge she'd been at the bar, he'd have driven her home hours ago.

He killed the engine, and Katy hopped off the back, the loss of the bike's vibrations, his heat and his summer storm scent a cruel punishment. She tucked her hands back in the pockets of his thick leather jacket and ducked her face partially beneath the collar. True the air was nippy and her cheeks were cold, but the action was more about affording her some semblance of cover while she watched him lean the bike to rest and dismount.

That was the thing about Priest. Everything he did, he did with grace, his feline side guiding everything from the way he walked—or more like stalked—to the way he chewed his food. She could watch him for hours. Actually she'd done exactly that and too often got caught in the act.

He grinned as if he'd heard her thoughts and splayed his hand low on her back. "Let's get you inside and warm."

Warm. Right. Because she wasn't already running about a thousand degrees hotter than normal, the bulk of her overloaded temperature centered between her legs.

Inside, only one lamp in the vaulted living room and a hallway light had been left on, the soft glow a comfortable welcome after a rollercoaster night. Although, just about the time she neared the stairs, the quiet pressed in and reminded her she wasn't just home for the night. She was home *with Priest*.

Alone.

She paused at the bottom of the stairs, clenched the banister in a death grip and glanced over her shoulder at Priest. Given his languid strides as he moved toward her and the devilish glint in his eyes, the lack of other occupants in the house was a tactical advantage he'd counted on.

Her heart kicked, each beat growing heavier the closer he got. "So…" She cleared her throat and forced a smile that was probably as shaky as her voice. "Thank you for bringing me home. It was a good night."

Priest moved in as her words trailed off, unzipped his jacket and slid it off her shoulders. "It's about to get better." Not giving her time to process the remark, he tossed the jacket on the couch behind him, palmed her hip and guided her up the stairs.

Oh, boy.

Her stomach swooped and her breath caught, but her traitorous feet fell right in line. Though how she managed any coordination at all with the onslaught of adrenaline flooding her bloodstream was the miracle to end all miracles. God knew, her brain wasn't working right. Where her thoughts were usually ordered and logical, it seemed like a swarm of drunken trolls had taken over the controls and were scrambling fifty different directions without a clue on how to operate the machinery.

Before she knew it, they'd reached the landing, the door to Priest's room closing in too fast. And what was she supposed to do when she got there?

Priest answered the question before her mind could, loosely grasping her wrist, pulling her to a stop and crowding her against the wall just beside the bedroom door. "Breathe, kitten."

"I am breathing."

Liar.

The quick grin he shot her said he agreed with her conscience, but rather than press the point, he gripped her hips and obliterated all but inches between them. His heat was all-consuming. His presence pure temptation licking against her skin. "We need more reasons for you to dance."

What? He wanted to talk about dancing? Now? Because with the way his hard pecs felt underneath her palms all she really wanted to do was find a way to ditch his T-shirt and explore every ridge and valley underneath skin to skin. "Why would we need that?" she whispered.

"Because it makes me want to feel you move the same way against me." He dipped his face close enough his exhalation gently brushed her face and skimmed his nose alongside hers. "Or better yet, beneath me."

He seized her mouth, capturing her gasp even as his arms stole around her torso and crushed her to him. This wasn't the same kiss as the one they'd shared in the cove. This was a possession. A claiming that plundered and demanded her submission. An unrelenting storm that battered and bombarded her defenses, wiping all but the last of her shields out of his path and leaving her raw and exposed.

This was the something she'd missed in other encounters. The chemistry and connection she'd craved. The burn and sweet abandon that made the world around her utterly irrelevant.

And his taste...it had been addictive before, but accented by the lingering bite of Scotch he'd nursed all night it was bolder. Richer and pure male. So delicious she groaned in frustration when he relinquished her mouth and painted wicked kisses along her jawline.

His voice rolled low and dark as rumbling thunder. "Are you ready, *mihara*?" He palmed her ass and ground his hips against hers, the insistent press of his formidable cock driving home exactly what he meant. "Do you want what I can give you?"

What he could give her physically? Absolutely. It was what came after that scared the hell out of her. She tilted her head, giving his questing lips and teeth more room to work along the column of her neck. "I'm afraid of what you'll give me."

He stilled for only a second, then lifted his head. "But you want it."

God, yes, she did. So bad every nerve ending practically screamed for her to throw herself at him. To rub herself against him like a desperate cat in heat. "Wanting something and something being good for you are two very different things. What you're offering comes with a price I'm not sure I'm ready to pay."

"There's no price with me. Only pleasure. And your heart won't allow our bond until you're ready." He fisted her hair and slowly tugged her head back. He nipped her lower lip. "Maybe you need a taste." He licked the spot and soothed the sting. "To explore without the risk."

"I don't think that's possible."

His lips curved in a roguish grin. "Oh, it's possible." He loosened his grip and kissed her again, this time softer. Coaxing. A promise and a temptation all rolled into one. When he lifted his head, he traced the space where his medallion had lain at the base of her throat. "Put it on before you go to bed. Let me show you what you're missing."

"Show me how?"

"You're a scientist. Put it on and find out. I dare you." Another kiss. This one a soft goodbye that nearly drew a whimper. "Sweet dreams."

Chapter Fifteen

Priest lay on his couch, his house utterly silent save the sounds of nature filtering in through the open sliding glass door behind him. The light blanket draped over his naked body was an irritation to his skin, and his cock was a painful weight against his belly, long, thick and throbbing. Even if Katy took the dare he'd thrown her—wearing his pendant and allowing him to meet her in her dreams—he wouldn't find the release he needed. Not tonight. Not until he was inside her.

Kateri though... Kateri he'd take care of thoroughly and enjoy every second of it. Her sweet body was strung tight, poised on the edge of something she couldn't yet comprehend. All he needed was an opening. A chance to reach her emotions and free her from the inside out.

If she'd just take the risk and let him in.

Fuck, but he needed her. Wanted to bury his face between her legs and inhale the arousal that had driven his cat wild all night. Wanted to lap her slit and suck her clit until she ground her pussy against his mouth and came against his tongue. Wanted to sink his shaft inside her wet cunt and claim what was his.

He fisted himself at the root and squeezed. Hard. He waited, letting his thoughts drift and ideas of what he'd show her in her dreams percolate. Time did nothing to ease his aching dick or the tension in his muscles.

Only when enough time had passed to let her settle in and find sleep did he dare close his eyes and find his center. Imagined his mate stretched out on his bed. Dreaming. Waiting.

The room's quiet buzzed louder and bit by bit, his muscles uncoiled until his body lay tomb-heavy on the couch's thick cushions. But his spirit was light. Ready to travel and give his mate what she needed. He homed in on his mark, the ancient metal and magic imbued in it drawing him steadily toward his room and hopefully to the woman who wore it.

The sounds around his spirit shifted, crickets and rustling leaves registering in his sightless form from a different source than the room he'd left behind.

The balcony.

Like him, she always opened it when she slept. But it wasn't just the sounds that were different. The scent had changed, too. Jasmine, crisp cotton and his own scent mingled together.

Kateri.

In his bed.

She'd worn it. Had taken the dare and put his mark back where it belonged. Was giving him the chance to show her how good it could be between them. How freeing despite her fears.

He stilled his spirit. Centered it. Then reached for her dreams.

Chapter Sixteen

"Kateri."

The voice came from the gray mist, whatever dream or vision that had played out in Katy's head moments before erased and forgotten in a second. She knew that voice. Loved hearing it as much as she loved snuggling in a warm bed on a cold winter morning. So deep. Comforting.

Arousing.

The voice came again, this time carried on a pleased chuckle. "I like the sound of your voice, too, kitten. Very much."

"Priest," she whispered into the swirling nothingness.

"You expecting someone else in your dreams, *mihara*?" Though she couldn't see him, his presence solidified behind her and his hand settled on her hip. He swept her hair off the back of her neck and coasted his lips against the bared skin, his hot breath a beautiful caress that trickled down her spine. "You took the dare."

She had. Though, it had taken her fifteen minutes staring at the pendant and another ten cradling it in her palms before she'd fastened it around her neck. "So, I'm dreaming?"

"More or less. Only I'm your tour guide instead of

your subconscious, and I've got a very specific outcome in mind." His arms encircled her, one slanted across her belly and the other across her shoulders, his hand a possessive brand above his medallion. "You're safe here. No strings. No repercussions. Only pleasure."

Well, it was *her* dream. Where could a woman let go and set all her worries and rules aside if not in the unscripted realm of sleep?

"Exactly that," he said, answering her thoughts. "It's freedom. Only what feels good. What you want instead of what you think you should do." His voice dropped a notch, his lips a whisper behind her ear. "Are you ready?"

Ready? She'd been ready days ago. Had imagined countless interludes between them despite the backlash reason kept throwing at her. But right and wrong didn't matter here. Nor did rules or expectations. "Yes."

As soon as the word was out of her mouth, the endless gray disappeared, replaced with the peaceful splendor of the cove where Priest had first kissed her. Only inches from her toes, the water gently lapped the loamy beach, and while her skin didn't make direct contact with the water, its cold temperature still registered in the squishy sand beneath her feet. An easy breeze lifted her hair off her shoulders and sent the sun flickering through the thickening green canopy of trees overhead.

An exact replica of that day. Except where was Priest? "Here."

She spun toward his voice and found him perched on a boulder as high as her waist, one knee cocked so his bare foot rested on the rock's edge while his other leg stretched to the soft grass below. Like the day they'd trained, his torso was bare, only his fierce tattoos and the charms he always wore hanging just above his sternum. Only his gray track pants kept the rest of his prime body a secret. "What are we doing here?"

"We only share so many memories together to work from, *mihara*. And besides, I thought I'd give us a chance to finish what we started here."

Sure as if the memory had just been waiting beneath the surface, the feel of his hard body pressed against hers that day flashed bold and beautiful. She wanted that. Wanted to see and feel him without their clothes between them. Although, she hated the fact that such an interlude would start with her in running gear. Talk about your un-sexy propositions. "Which one of us is guiding this dream? You, or me?"

"Oh, I'm guiding it, but it's your dream. The nuances are yours to add. Your mind completely your own." He draped one arm over his bent knee and twirled a long blade of grass between his fingers. His hair spilled like soft black silk over his deep tan skin. A dark god idly waiting to indulge in his wicked ways. "If you don't like what you're wearing, change it."

"It's weird you're in my head."

"But I *am* in your head. Hard not to hear your thoughts when we're quite literally in the same mental space."

Well, that made sense. In an altogether disconcerting way. "Why can't I hear your thoughts?"

"Because it's not my dream. It's yours."

Not exactly the answer she'd hoped for. A little tit for tat in this scenario would have been nice. "So, how do I change?" Or more importantly, *what* should she change?

He grinned. "How about what you wore to bed?"

She shouldn't be pushing him, not with such a mischievous glint burning in his eyes, but she couldn't help it. "What if I slept naked?"

His smile slipped. "Then I'd be disappointed."

He would? "Why?"

"Because you'd rob me of the chance to unwrap you." His gaze slipped down the length of her, the languid glide an intimate caress. "Think of what you wore. Show me what's covering you while you sleep in my bed."

The image was easy to conjure. God knew, she'd stood in front of the mirror long enough, fascinated with how the lace V of her sapphire blue slip nightie had framed his medallion.

A light breeze drifted through the cove and the silk slicked against her skin, the barest hint of air slipping between her thighs. "I did it."

So thrilled with the simple feat, it took an extra beat before she realized Priest had gone eerily still, his covetous gaze taking her in inch by inch. Only when his stare met hers did he flick the blade of grass aside, lower his leg and straighten. "Come here, little kitten. Your big cat wants to play."

Oh, she liked that idea. A lot. Rather like ditching the cake and enjoying the guilty pleasure of licking homemade cream cheese frosting right off the spoon.

"The only one doing the licking is me," he said. "And I can damned well guarantee I won't feel the least bit guilty about it. Now get your sweet ass over here so I can give you what you need."

"So bossy," she teased, the lighthearted retort unlike any of the other banter they'd shared. More playful and fun than their usual tentative conversations or intricate verbal dances. Like a couple who'd been together years and still found inordinate joy in each other's presence.

She obeyed, but took her time in getting there. Beneath her feet, the sand transitioned to spongy, soft grass, a natural pallet she could all too easily imagine cushioning her body as his pressed into hers.

"You never know," he said, openly appreciating the sway of her hips. "You might like bossy."

"I've never liked it before."

The quick and dirty grin she'd grown to crave snapped into place and his voice dropped sinfully low. With only five feet left between them, the depth of it vibrated perfectly against her skin. "Ah, but you've never had it from me." As soon as his last word hit air, he struck, grasping her by the hips and hauling her straight between his thighs.

She couldn't have hidden her gasp if she'd tried, the heady cocktail of surprise and his demanding grasp deliciously intoxicating. Beneath her palms, his hot skin stretched taut over unforgiving muscle. If she had her way, he'd give her ample time to touch and savor every inch with her hands and mouth. She traced the intricate lines of one mark along his collarbone. "I think that falls under manhandling, not bossy."

"And I think you like them both."

"You don't know me well enough to say that, yet."

His hands at her hips drifted up her sides, taking the silk beneath them with it and stroking her skin even as the hem of her nightie tickled her upper thighs. "I know you're petting me like you pet my cat." Fanning his thumbs inward, he teased the underside of each breast. "I know your eyes are dilated and your voice is breathy." He coasted the backs of his fingers up along the lower swell and circled her distended nipples. "And I can smell your arousal."

Her breath eked out on a shaky exhale and her shoulders pushed back, encouraging him for more. "Okay," she managed, proud of the fact she'd managed that much. "You might have one or two clues."

"One or two." He held her gaze, a watchful, waiting predator marking her every reaction. "But I'll have more before we're done." He scraped his nails along each tip and pinched.

Her eyes slipped shut and her hips flexed, the insistent tug and pressure spearing straight to her sex. The needy groan that rolled up her throat was foreign to her own ears, raspy and demanding to match her death grip on his shoulders.

"More?"

Yes. Absolutely. Or at least that's what she meant to say, though she was pretty sure it came out more of a whimper. Regardless, he must have gotten the point, because his big strong hands got in on the action, kneading and plumping her breasts until she threw her head back and arched into his touch.

His breath whispered warm just beneath where his medallion rested, his lips teasing her skin as he spoke. "I think my mate craves an edge when she plays."

Crave was an excellent word, though the edge part was a hell of a surprise. "I don't know what to call it, but I'd be sorely disappointed if you stopped."

"Oh, there's no stopping. Not until you've come hard enough for both of us."

Thank God. Because the way he was touching her right now she was counting down for one hell of an explosion.

As soon as she had the thought, he released her breasts and slicked one possessive hand down her belly.

When he paused and held it still just over her abdomen, she snapped her head up. "Don't stop."

He grinned at that, and while part of her wanted to do something to wipe the pleased-with-himself smirk off his face, another far more practical part of her just wanted to get him back on track.

Back in motion, his fingers dipped toward her mound, the mix of his teasing touch and the silk rasping against the tight curls beneath. "I'm not stopping. I just want to see your eyes."

Another dip and another swirl, but not quite reaching her clit.

"You're teasing me," she said.

"No, kitten. I'm learning you." Reversing his path, he slowly skimmed both hands up her sides and over her breasts, then hooked his fingers beneath the thin straps of her nightie. "Cataloging every single moan and twitch and planning for how I'll take you outside of your dreams."

Despite the weight of her eyelids, she held his gaze. No way could she look away. Not with the intensity burning in his mystic gray gaze.

Inch by inch, he tugged the straps over her shoulders.

Her breasts, already insanely sensitized by his attention, grew heavier. Weighted and tight to the point they ached. "Priest." Why she said it, she couldn't say. Only knew that she'd never in her life felt more intimate with a man and he hadn't even seen her yet.

"Feel it, *mihara.*" The straps fell loose and the silk slipped an inch, kept from whispering to the ground only by the tight press of her arms against her torso. Still he didn't break their stare. Only traced the upper swell of one breast with his fingertip as if he had all the patience in the world. His touch shifted to her sternum and nudged the silk. "Own it. Relax and bare yourself to me."

Own it.

He was right. It was *her* dream. Her incredibly passionate dream with a skilled and patient partner.

Her mate.

Something sparked inside her and the tension in her arms eased.

The silk whooshed against her skin and pooled at her feet, leaving her heightened skin exposed to the wind's decadent touch. She gasped at the unusual caress and closed her eyes, offering herself not just to Priest, but to the moment. To the truth.

The rough, calloused scrape of Priest's hands smoothed against her belly, and the low and guttural growl of his cat reverberated against her bared flesh. "Oh, kitten. If this is how you see yourself, I can't wait to see you with my own eyes."

"What?" She forced her eyes open, the languid yet bold exploration of his hands along her hips, her thighs and ass leaving her thought processes trudging in slow motion.

"Your body," he said, not taking his gaze off his work. "This is your dream. What I see is how you see yourself. Knowing what I do of you, your perspective is a downplayed version of the truth, so I can't wait to see reality."

The scientist in her marveled at the distinction and struggled to formulate clarifying questions, but the woman in her was too alive and focused. Too eager to feel more of what he offered. Curiosity was for later. Right now was for feeling. For assuaging the building pulse his touch stoked deep inside her sex.

"Then say what you want." He lifted his eyes to hers,

cupped her breasts and leaned in, nuzzling the inner slope of one mound with his beard.

"Why? If you can hear my thoughts, you already know what I want."

He shifted to the other side, rolling and pinching her nipples as he ghosted his lips against her tight skin. "Because I want my mate to be able to tell me what she wants. To put words to it. No matter how delicate or dirty."

Delicate wasn't on the table. And she'd had plenty of dirty occupy her thoughts and dreams the last few days. More so than she'd had in her whole life. So much so it left her shaken, more than a little afraid of the change. "I want to feel your mouth on me."

He smiled against her flesh then scraped his teeth along the lower swell of one breast. "And?"

And what? Just saying that much had been a huge feat.

"Tell me what you really want." He shifted his attention to her other breast. "What's missing for you? What am I not giving you that you crave?" Another nip, this one more demanding. Prodding her to jump. "Say it, kitten." He licked the spot and growled against her. "I want it, too. Say it."

"You're being too gentle." It was only a whisper, but his response was instant, his touch more commanding. Demanding and strong. He tugged one nipple, not so hard it hurt but bold enough her sex convulsed. He licked around the other nipple and locked his eyes on her. "And?"

Oh, God. He wanted her to say it. Out loud. Something she'd never thought in a million years she'd utter. Not even in her dreams. She speared her fingers through his thick hair, her whole body shaking with a mix of thrill and terror. "I don't want to be in control."

"No, you don't." He scraped his beard against her nipple, never taking his gaze from hers, then licked the distended tip. "But I do."

The wet heat of his mouth surrounded her, the incessant pull as he suckled deep spearing right to her core. Gone was the careful hunter, replaced with the predator consuming his prey.

And she loved it. Welcomed it. Arched deeper into his mouth and surrendered to his tight hold. She was safe. Physically and emotionally. How she knew both to be true, she couldn't say and frankly didn't care. Only knew that this was the single most defining and enjoyable sexual experience of her life and it wasn't even real.

A ferocious snarl filled her ears and the landscape changed, Priest's wicked touch disappearing with it.

No, not a change in landscape, but her placement in it. The soft grass that had welcomed her cautious footsteps now cushioned her back and the brilliant blue sky flickered through thick treetops, her knees cocked to one side as though she were lazing in bed on a Saturday morning.

And Priest towered above her. "Don't think for a second this isn't real, *mihara*." He looked his fill, his slow perusal as powerful as his physical touch. "Everything you feel here, your body experiences with you."

"Yours, too?"

His hand went to the sizable bulge behind his pants and stroked the impressive length. God, how she wished she'd seen him. Wished her mind could properly visualize what lay beneath. "Everything. Now spread your legs for me, kitten. Show me where you want my mouth."

Another push against her control. One even more terrifying than admitting her truth. But she'd found release in her admission. Intense pleasure. What harm was there in reaching for more? She straightened her knees, heels planted on the soft grass beneath her.

Priest waited. No sign of impatience, only an implacable command on his face.

It was all her. Her choice. Her pleasure. Her acceptance.

Legs quivering, she let her knees fall wide, opening her to his hungry gaze.

Man and beast growled together. "Mine."

Holy hell, that was hot. Insanely possessive and ridiculously primitive. So much so, her hips undulated as if to agree. To welcome his claim.

He slowly dropped to his knees and palmed the back of her thighs, exposing her farther. "You're going to come for me, Kateri. Hard. And when you wake up in the morning, you'll feel it. Your skin will be pink from my beard. Your nipples will ache, and your sex will be drenched in your release."

Another flex from her hips, this time paired with a desperate moan.

"Hmmm." He splayed his hand on top of her mound, the heel of his hand insanely close to her clit. "My kitten wants to be petted." He teased his fingers through her curls then dipped lower, boldly stroking his blunt fingers through her slit. "This is what I want. Your juices on my tongue. Sliding down my throat until it's all I can taste. All I can smell."

"Yes." It was more plea than agreement, her hips rolling encouragingly against each tormenting stroke.

He chuckled and slipped his hands beneath her ass.

"Then open your eyes, *mihara*. If you want my mouth, you have to watch. I want you to know who's pleasuring you. Whose tongue is fucking your sweet pussy."

A tremor rocked her, the filthy words coming from his mouth nearly enough to push her over the edge. But she did as he asked, the sight that greeted her exquisitely erotic. Priest's dark hair and skin contrasting against her pale complexion. His warm breath wafting against her damp and swollen folds. And his gray eyes locked on hers. "I can't believe how much I like the way that sounds."

"I can. My kitten has a dark side I can't wait to explore." He grinned and nuzzled the top of her sex with his nose, inhaling deep. "But you'll like this better." He licked through her sex, a blatant swipe that promised he'd see her dark side and raise it by a thousand.

She rocked against his mouth and fisted her hands in his hair, shocked at her boldness even as she reveled in it. "Priest."

He growled and tongued her deeper, the vibrations paired with the carnal image pushing her release that much closer. "That's it, kitten," he muttered against her flesh. "Let go and come for your mate."

It was too soon. Waaay too soon to relinquish such an exquisite buildup. And yet it barreled toward her. Implacably demanding her surrender.

"Not too soon." He lifted her hips higher and slid his thumbs up, parting her folds for his attention. "Just the first."

He thrust his tongue inside her, and she came apart. Splintered into a thousand shards she had no hope of putting back together. At least not as she had been before. The woman who'd dared to enter this dream was different than the one now open and vulnerable to the predator consuming her. Unfinished and sleeping. Waiting for this man to wake her and color in the missing pieces.

Humming against her sex, he eagerly lapped her release, his dark head between her thighs the most beautifully wanton thing she'd ever seen. Yes, he was the hunter, but in that second, he was also supplicant. A devoted recipient of her release.

Only when the powerful spasms ebbed to a slow and easy pulse, did he shift his attention. His tongue flicked her swollen clit. "That one was for you." He circled the tight nub and raised his gaze to hers. "The next one is for me."

His lips closed around her and he suckled. Gently at first then building in intensity.

The grip she'd loosened in his hair as her release left her, retightened. Part of her wanted to drag him away, to inform him any repeated attempts to orgasm would be utterly wasted. Especially since she'd done well in the past to find one, let alone multiples. But another, far more confident part of herself, held him in place. Encouraged him to work his dirty magic and let the encroaching storm have its way.

But something was missing. Something she craved at the most primitive level. "I want you inside me."

With the odd, yet magic fluidness of dreams, he stretched out beside her, braced on one forearm and smoothing his hand along her upper thigh. "You're only riding my fingers tonight, kitten. You'll only earn my cock in the flesh."

She started to protest, but he hooked his hand behind her knee and guided her leg over his, opening her to the skies above. The sun warmed her core even as the air cooled her sweat-misted skin.

"It feels good, doesn't it?" he said, slicking his fingers through her slit. "Someday, I'll bring you back here. Will toy with your pussy until you weep then pin you on your hands and knees and take you from behind."

The image came all too clearly and ripped a whimper past her lips.

He answered by sliding a single finger inside.

But it wasn't enough. Not nearly the impact she craved. So, she covered his hand with her own and ground her hips against their hands. "More."

The loss of his languid smile was the only warning she got. In a blink, he pinned her hands above her head and the weight of his body anchored one leg high and wide. "You ask for what you want, Kateri. You don't take."

She opened her mouth to dispute his claim, but closed it just as fast when he thrust two fingers inside her, eradicating what little arguments she could muster. And the way he worked her sex, she was inclined to agree that he was right. It was animalistic. Almost barbaric. But it was also freeing. A confounding concept her muddled brain couldn't quite comprehend.

"Because outside our play, you are your own woman. An alpha female in your own right." He pumped deeper. Harder. His voice thundered above her to match the building tempest inside her. "But here, I'm stronger. Dominate. And most importantly, you're mine."

As if to prove his point, his thumb circled her clit, the remnants of her release and his mouth creating a sumptuous glide for his rough touch. He angled his wrist and his fingertips brushed along the front wall of her sex.

"Come for me, *mihara*." Again, this time more purposeful. Demanding her physical response with each stroke. "Come and show me how hard your sweet cunt will milk my cock when I claim it for my own."

Release.

Instant and magnificent.

Over and over, her core fisted around his unrelenting fingers, pulsing in time to her thrashing heart. With each thrust, she ground her hips up to meet his hand. Reveled in the heel of his palm against her clit.

How the hell had she lived without this? Or more importantly, why had she avoided it?

This was bliss.

Liberation in the most literal sense.

Yes, she was complete on her own, but in this moment, the two of them together were *more*. Something bigger than they could ever be apart.

And she wanted it.

Needed to explore the new terrain he'd shown her even if she didn't have a clue how to go about it.

"I'll show you," he murmured against her lips, slowly drawing her back to her dream body with his soft, questing kiss. His fingers glided in and out, guided by the softening rhythm of her hips. "Everything you want. Whatever you want."

Needing his strength as much as his warmth, she wrapped her freed arms around him, letting her hands play against the honed muscles of his broad shoulders. It was odd, this mix of vulnerability and newness. A strength borne from the deepest intimacy. "Now what do we do?"

His smile was a sweet comfort. A soft and patient welcome from a man looking forward to the days ahead of

him. "My logical mate. Always planning her next steps."
He framed one side of her face and traced her cheek-
bone with his thumb. "For now, you sleep. Deep." He
pressed a lingering kiss to her lips and muttered, "And
in the morning, you remember."

Chapter Seventeen

As views went, the one off Priest's raised back porch was second only to the one off his bedroom. But for the first time since he'd built the modernized cabin on stilts, it wasn't the view that held his attention, but the subtle rush of running water from the master bath upstairs.

He kicked his bare feet up on the middle rung of the rail that surrounded the porch, set his nearly empty cup of coffee aside and checked the time on his phone.

12:21p.m.

He grinned and set the device aside. Good thing he had a big hot water tank and no one in the house to hog the water, because with Kateri nearing the thirty-minute mark, she seemed determined to bleed the damned thing dry. Though, he had to admit…imagining what could be taking her so long had definitely spurred him to pencil in a tankless unit to his list of home improvements.

Three minutes later, the water shut off, followed by the steady drone of her blow dryer ten minutes after that. Since getting the darkness under control all those years ago, he'd spent countless mornings just like this. Alone and quiet. Either roaming the woods in his panther form, or sitting in this exact spot, letting his mind wander where it wanted. Not once had the practice been difficult. If anything, the stillness helped keep him balanced. The same as when he inked a talisman into someone's skin.

But today had been an exercise in restraint. He'd lost count of the times he'd nearly stood and given up all pretense of waiting in favor of waking Kateri up the same way he'd helped her fall asleep.

The whole damned dream had been phenomenal, every detail as vivid as if it had happened in real life only seconds ago. But it was those last few seconds—the unguarded softness in her eyes as she'd sleepily smiled up at him, caressed the side of his face and let her eyelids slip shut—that had moved him the most. She'd been happy. At peace with what she'd experienced and easily trusting him to guide her back from her dream.

And now he waited. Waited to see if the woman who walked out of his bedroom was the one who'd soared as she'd come apart, or the one determined to keep every emotion bound and locked down tight.

A muted *thunk* sounded from upstairs and his cat stirred, his beast's heightened hearing instantly zeroing in on the soft footfalls rounding the top of the stairs.

Finally.

He forced himself to stay in place, covering his need to move by finishing off what was left of his lukewarm coffee. He'd shown her what he could last night. The next step was hers and he'd be damned if he pressured her one way or another with his actions.

A wood plank at the bottom of the stairs creaked and the electric awareness that always came when Kateri grew near prickled along his shoulder blades. And yet, she didn't come out.

She was there, though. Watching him. Probably over-thinking way too much while she did it, but there all the same. He knew it the same way he sensed an imminent soul quest. Felt her stare as sure as a hand wrapped around the back of his neck. And she was nervous. Even without looking at her he could feel it. The aggravated emotion rippled through the open sliding glass door out into the still air in tiny waves, the same as a shock wave moving across a glass-topped lake.

Giving her space to make the next move was one thing. Making her suffer with nerves was something else altogether. "You finally slept," he said, breaking the silence, but keeping his gaze on the swath of trees ahead.

She hesitated only a beat, then stepped out onto the wood porch. "Apparently well enough I missed everyone leaving the house."

Yeah, definitely nervous, the tremor in her voice holding more uncertainty than he'd heard from her in the whole time they'd known each other. Which was saying something considering how many new and strange things she'd seen.

He stood, stuffed his phone in his back pocket and snatched his mug off the side table, still forcing himself to maintain some semblance of casual when all he really wanted was to wrap her up and hold her until she settled. "Naomi and Jade are working with the other seers in town. Tate is covering the shop."

"What about you? Don't you have clients?"

He turned and met her gaze. One second, and his plans for calm and casual were soundly wiped right off the table. *This* was the woman he'd loved in her dreams last night. Uncertain, yes, but ready to face him in the real world all the same. She'd left her feet bare and dressed in the same hip-hugging jeans as the night before, but paired them with a form-fitting tank. And from the tight points peaking beneath the white cotton, there wasn't a damned thing else underneath.

He prowled toward her. "My *mihara* needed sleep and my protection while she got it. Nothing is more important than that." He cupped the side of her neck and fanned his thumb along her hummingbird pulse.

Her eyes dilated and her lips parted, her breath coming just a notch faster than it had a moment before.

Beautiful.

A woman awake, alive and ready to explore. She just hadn't quite figured out how to take that first step. But he'd help her. Just like he promised her last night.

Slipping his hand up to frame her face, he tilted it for an easy, yet lingering good morning kiss.

She sighed into it, a mix of relief and want as her hands tentatively rested against his bare chest.

"Do you want your coffee, kitten?" he murmured against her mouth. The same intimate contact reserved for languid mornings in bed after an intensely carnal night. "Or would you rather run first?"

She backed away only enough to meet his gaze beneath her lashes, a light pink creeping along her cheeks. "I think I'll skip my run today."

He couldn't help the smile that split his face, the unspoken *I got plenty of exercise last night and feel like playing hooky today* undercurrent too hard to ignore. "Then let's get you coffee and figure out how to tackle the rest of the day."

Stepping away, he steered her into the kitchen and into the same quiet routine they'd developed over the last week. Since that first day when she'd tried to slip out of the house unnoticed, their mornings had always

ended here. Her perched on a barstool behind the breakfast counter. Him making her coffee the way she liked it
before he poured his own. Only then would they settle
into her endless questions about what his clan had been
like before Draven.

Except today, she didn't wait. "Are we going to talk
about it?"

With his back to her, she couldn't see the tiny falter
as he poured the cream into her mug. He shouldn't have
been surprised by her head-on approach. Still, today was
about her accepting not only what happened, but who
she was underneath all that control, and anything worth
owning was worth working for. "Talk about what?"

The quiet stretched bold and charged between them,
broken only by a few intermittent raps of the spoon
against the ceramic as he stirred. "I dreamed about you
last night."

He set the spoon in the sink and went about pouring
his own cup, keeping his silence.

"Only it wasn't an ordinary dream." So breathless.
Less from nerves now and more on par with the sounds
she'd made as he'd explored her body. "It was you guiding the whole thing, wasn't it?"

Mugs in hand, he ambled to her, slid her mug in front
of her fisted hands and settled on the empty stool beside
her. "What do you think?"

"I think I've never had a dream like that."

"Like what?"

"That real."

Talk about your revealing moments. The words themselves might have been innocent, but the sheer vulnerability behind them spoke volumes. As if in uttering her
thoughts out loud, she'd finally dared to step outside her

comfort zone and truly considered her heritage in the full light of day. He sipped his coffee. It was either that or haul her between his thighs and dive into a replay of last night until the rawness in her gaze spawned from another emotion entirely.

"I felt it," she said. "All of it. My body…" Her eyes widened as though she'd realized too late where she was headed, but then narrowed again with the same soft determination he'd grown to appreciate. "In my dream, you told me I'd feel it all today."

From deep inside, his cat paced, tail twitching with irritation at Priest's inactivity. As far as his beast was concerned, she'd done enough. Said enough to earn his comfort. And surprisingly, the darkness agreed.

He couldn't blame either of them. More than anything, he'd wanted to be there when she woke up. To see the marks he'd left behind and tend to every tender ache. "And the things that happened in your dream… how did that make you feel?"

Heat blossomed in an instant. So fast and powerful he felt it like a flame against his bare torso. Lower than before, she voiced her confession in a sultry rasp. "I liked it."

Fuck it.

He thunked his mug to the counter and stood. "That's good, kitten. Because you're right. It wasn't an ordinary dream." He pulled her off her stool, slipped his hands around her lithe waist and smoothed them along her spine, one ending low and the other loosely fisting her hair. Where he'd managed a steady tone before, now the undercurrent of his beast was in every word. "It *was* me guiding you. Showing you what it will be like between us."

Her gaze dropped to his mouth and she licked her lip, an invitation he took a second later, tracing the path with his own tongue before delving deeper. And damned if her taste wasn't sweeter today than when he'd left her at his bedroom door last night. Richer and more addictive. A flavor heightened by her growing emotions.

He forced himself to ease the kiss. To focus on the slow burn instead of the flash fire she offered. Resting his forehead on hers, he traced her jawline, her neck, his medallion back where it belonged at the base of her throat. "This is what it means to have a mate. To feel what you're feeling now, only deeper. Stronger. To be protected. Always." He skimmed his lips against hers, remembering all too vividly how she'd arched and cried his name as she'd come around his fingers. "And, Kateri, it's good you enjoyed what I gave you last night. Because your dream will be nothing compared to when I take you in the flesh."

The front door opened then closed with a resounding thud, and quick footsteps clipped down the hallway. More than one set and lighter than Alek or Tate's heavy strides, which meant Naomi and Jade were about to intrude at a seriously inopportune time.

Sure enough, Kateri tried to push away, but he held her fast. "This isn't over, *mihara*. You're mine. You know it. You *felt* it. Your fear is the only thing keeping you from claiming what's yours."

His last word hadn't even died off when the troublesome seer duo rounded the corner, Naomi in the lead. Though she came to such an abrupt halt that Jade nearly plowed into her from behind. "Oh." Her hand went to her throat, and in the two seconds that followed, she assessed Priest's possessive hold, the scowl he made no pretense of hiding and Kateri's dumbfounded expression.

Another woman might have scampered right back out of the room. But not Naomi. She smiled huge, then sauntered into the breakfast nook. "I'd ask if we're interrupting, but I think that's a forgone conclusion."

This time when Kateri pushed against his chest, he gave way and let her face them, but kept her anchored at his side. "We were just talking."

Jade snickered, but caught Priest's answering scowl, rolled her lips inward like that might better fight back the growing laughter and averted her face.

"Mmm." Naomi paused at the kitchen table and cocked her head. "Should we let you finish your...talk? Or are you up for a new development with the primos?"

Not surprisingly, Kateri lurched forward and pulled out a chair. "What developments?"

If Priest hadn't already zeroed in on Kateri's thirst for vengeance against Draven, his ego might have taken a hit at the sudden change in focus. As if their kiss and talk of dreams had never existed. Instead, he chalked the shift up to her giving her emotions more room to flow.

Naomi met his gaze, a silent check-in to make sure he was on board with the interruption.

He moved in behind Kateri's chair and squeezed her shoulder. "Go ahead. Pretty sure my mate could use the distraction."

Whether the scowl Kateri shot him was based on the go-ahead coming from him instead of her, or the fact that he'd driven home her place as his mate in front of the other two women, he couldn't say. What he could say was he liked the fire behind it.

"Right." Naomi dug in her purse, pulled out a journal and slid into her own chair. "The last few days our group has broken up into three teams, one for each of the primo families we need to find. Up until today, everything's been limited to images too hard to narrow down outside of regional generalities. For instance, with the descriptions those focused on the seer family have described, I'm inclined to think they relocated to Colorado, or someplace similar, like our family did."

"It could be southern Wyoming, too," Jade said as she circled the table to point at one page over Naomi's shoulder. "I'll swear this sketch Rada made from her vision looks right out of a paper I did in high school on Medicine Bow National Forest."

Naomi nodded. "Maybe. Both would be a good place to target going forward."

"But no cities or more distinct clues to go on?" Kateri prompted.

Naomi shook her head. "No. Not for the seer family. Not yet. But we did get a lead on the healer family."

She flipped a few pages, turned the book around and tapped just above a rough sketch of what looked like a mom-and-pop cafe, or an old-time convenience store. A tall sign stretched across the top of it with the name *Mary's on Butte La Rose* painted in easy cursive. On either side was a seagull and a patch of cattails and tall grass. "For days, all we've been able to glean from the healer medallion has been shallow water, an old, but unique-looking bridge and a street sign with the name Yellow Street on it. But today one of the ladies saw this."

"Butte La Rose is in Louisiana," Priest said.

"Exactly!" Naomi said clearly on a roll. "Which is just south of the Atchafalaya Wildlife Refuge. A perfect place for a shifter family to pick if they wanted to hide."

"Is there a Yellow Street in Butte La Rose?" Kateri asked.

Jade chuckled and ambled toward the fridge. "According to Google, there is. Yellow Street, plus about ten others and that's it." She pulled out a grape Gatorade and cracked the lid. "Not exactly a big network to work through."

"Still, it's a lead," Kateri said. "And if you think about it, a smaller population ought to make tracking families in the area easier." She swiveled in her chair and locked gazes with Priest. "I'll call David and see if his contacts can come up with any names. If they can find something that fits, Louisiana's close enough we could drive there and scout them out."

"I thought we'd established my brother's looking for the primos."

"Right. So, we have to find them before he does."

"No, *I* have to find them. You have to stay the hell away from him."

Her frown whipped into place, a ready argument obviously cuing up behind her blue-gray eyes.

So, he cut her off at the pass and zeroed in on Naomi. "Anything on the sorcerer family?"

He sensed more than witnessed Jade's apprehension behind him, but the concern that clouded Naomi's expression confirmed he'd unintentionally struck a nerve with his ward. By the time he turned to assess Jade, she'd paced into the kitchen, intentionally avoiding his study by making far too big a deal out of selecting a glass from the cabinet. "Jade?"

She kept her silence.

Naomi's soft voice drifted from behind him. "You

should tell him, Jade. You may not trust your gifts yet, but the rest of us do. Especially Eerikki."

Shit.

Another vision. As if she hadn't already been indoctrinated to her magic in the worst way possible. "What did you see?"

She huffed, turned and braced her hands on her hips. "It was probably a fluke. Bad timing with memories."

"A memory or a vision?"

"A vision," Naomi said the same time Jade answered, "A memory."

Priest leveled the same don't-fuck-with-me glare on Jade that he'd used to keep her and Tate out of all kinds of trouble through their teenage years. "I thought you were working with the seer team. What happened?"

"I was." Jade sucked in a long breath, shot a glower at Naomi that said she wasn't at all thrilled with what she'd been cornered into sharing, then refocused on Priest. "But one of the girls asked me to hand her the sorcerer medallion. When I did, I remembered the vision I had before. The first one."

Fuck.

As news went, the development wasn't just bad, but worst case. Especially with the sorcerer house.

"It wasn't a memory," Naomi said, clearly on the same page as Priest. "Visions don't work that way. Yes, we can mine for them as we've been doing, but usually they're triggered. Either by objects or events. I saw you, Jade. We all did. That was a vision."

Kateri stood and padded to the breakfast counter, meeting Jade's stare head-on. "I don't get it. What was the vision about?"

Jade went back to pouring her drink, but her hand was

nowhere near as steady as it normally was. "It started in a house. There were people, but the images were too blurred to make out. Kind of like a hazy filter on a slow-motion action flick. But the blood was crystal clear. And I heard them, too. Screaming." She set the Gatorade aside, but the plastic crinkled from the brutal grip she kept on the bottle. "It ended with a mist. Or maybe a fog. Someone was running. Panting really heavy." She turned and faced them all. "I'm pretty sure whoever was in the vision was being hunted."

One beat.

Then another.

"You touched the medallion," Kateri muttered, quickly putting the same pieces together the rest of them already had. The quiet grew thick and supercharged, the deeply buried anger he'd sensed in his mate blossoming fast and furious. She looked to Priest. "Tell me that doesn't mean what I think it does."

"I can't," he answered, but wished like hell he could. "With what Jade's seen, especially with the connection to the medallion, odds are good Draven's already found the sorcerer family."

Chapter Eighteen

*SARATOGA, Wyo. (AP)—Authorities are search-
ing for suspects in the death of a 65-year-old
woman. Evidence at the scene indicates the cause
of death as blunt force trauma to the head, but in-
vestigators are not yet releasing any details found
at the scene or persons of interest.*

Not exactly the MO Draven had used with her parents
or anything similar to the vision Jade had described, but
Katy flagged the location on the map she'd printed, jot-
ted down a few notes and punched the back button on her
browser session. As research options went, Google probably wasn't the most sophisticated method out there, but
at least she was doing something. Which was more than
what she could say about how she'd spent the last week.

Some daughter you are.

She clicked the next link down in her search results
and scanned the news article for any nuance that might
resemble her mom and dad's murder. After what Jade
had shared, she'd been shocked she managed to talk
Priest into her leaving the house, but she'd needed a
new environment even more than she needed to blow
off steam. Finding out Priest had the whole floor above

his shop tricked out as an office and art space? Well, that was just an added bonus. Especially with a birds-eye view of the main drag on a Friday night and unfettered high-speed internet access.

"Did you get ahold of David?"

Startled at the sound of Alek's booming voice, Katy jolted a good two inches out of her chair and nearly knocked over the mega Starbucks she'd never finish. "Jesus, Alek. You're as bad as Priest."

He grinned, clearly taking the comment as a compliment, and sauntered toward her. "So? You give David the info the seers found?"

"I gave it to him, but he said tracking the kind of data we're after would take at least a week." Not seeing anything worth capturing on the current search result, she backtracked again and went to the next one on the list.

Alek peeked out the open window beside the desk and scanned the street below. "It takes whatever it takes, but we'll get what we need when we need it."

"Says the once irritable and fight-ready guy who's suddenly found his inner Zen." The next article wasn't even a homicide. More of a homicide report for Wyoming as a whole. "What are you doing here anyway? I thought you were running down some possible leads with some of the other guys."

"Katy, it's ten o'clock. I left six hours ago."

The clock at the top corner of Priest's laptop confirmed it. Although, now that she thought about it, it had been a while since Jade and Nanna had been by with dinner. "Shoot. Is Priest still downstairs?"

"It's Friday night on Main Street in a town known to be a biker hangout and Priest owns a tattoo shop. So, yeah. He's downstairs." He cocked one hip on the edge of Priest's desk and crossed his arms. "A better question is what the hell you've been doing up here all afternoon and most of tonight."

She shrugged and scrolled down on the page. "I thought I'd see if I could come up with something."

"Come up with what?"

"I don't know. Anything."

Before she could track what he was up to, Alek shifted the laptop to face him and toggled the cursor. "You're searching homicides?"

"In Wyoming." She pulled the map of Colorado she'd put together after her talk with David out from underneath the new one for Wyoming and handed it over to Alek. "It's probably not the most scientific way to go about it, but I thought if I mapped out other violent murders, something might pop out at me."

Alek shut the laptop, took the map and tossed it aside. "You know we're already working on this stuff. Several of us actually."

"So, what? One more won't hurt. It's better than me sitting around doing nothing." She shoved to her feet and paced to the wide art table set up at the far end of the room. Like Priest's desk, it was anchored near the window with loads of natural light and ample inspiration from the comings and goings of people below. Given the number of pencil sketches tacked on the wall around it, he'd spent considerable time there.

"You're not doing nothing. You're learning. And considering how little we knew about who we are less than two weeks ago, I'd say that's pretty damned important."

"I didn't come here to learn about who we are. I came here to find the man who killed our parents."

"You can't do one without the other. And has it occurred to you we might *need* the things you're learning about our clan once we get a solid lead?"

She had. But the logic didn't do much to ease her guilty conscience. And why the hell was she so antsy? Like a living current had been piped into every muscle and circled her body in an endless loop. She braced her hands on the window sill and leaned out. The temps had dropped since she'd ridden to the shop with Priest, easily hovering in the lower fifties with the promise of even colder temps before the night was through. A stubborn reminder of winter on the last day of March. "Something's wrong with me."

The confession slipped out as little more than a whisper, but perceptive as ever, Alek caught it. "Something's wrong with you, or something's changing?"

On the street below, a trio of men ambled down the street, their deep laughter bouncing off the old buildings. They reached the pub just catty-corner to Priest's building, pushed the door open and let the live music underway inside filter out into the night. The answer to Alek's question was as elusive as knowing anything about the strangers she watched. "I don't know."

"I think you do know. You're just not ready to admit it yet."

She pushed back from the window and met his steady gaze. "What's that supposed to mean?"

He hung his head, scratched his jaw and studied the floor for a handful of heartbeats before he sighed and lifted his head. "Look, the only person I can speak for is me. But I can tell you that—pre-soul quest funk aside—I've processed more emotions in the last month than I know what to do with. Losing Mom and Dad was brutal. It still is. But I'm mad as hell, too. Every day I wake up pissed off that Dad stole our heritage from us. Then I remember he's gone and feel like a giant ass for getting pissed. It's like an out of control emotional Tilt-A-Whirl."

That was *exactly* what it felt like. Only for her, the onslaught of feelings had her mired in a swampy place so thick it gripped and sucked her in like quicksand, and the only response that felt right was to fight. "I don't like how it feels."

"Of course, you don't. I don't either. But here's the thing, Katy. I can either let that guilt rule me, or I can own it and let it go. Because once you get through the shitty part of feeling, you get to the good part. The part that makes you feel alive and makes all the mundane bullshit worthwhile. I *like* this new life. I dig the hell out of our heritage and I'm proud of the things I can do. But most importantly, I'm embracing who I am. Not what someone told me I'm supposed to be."

"I'm not afraid to be who I am."

"Really? Because, I watched you with Dad growing up. I heard the lectures about leading with your head and not your heart. About responsibility and logic being the wiser course. But for the life of me, I never understood why you listened to it. I remember what you were like when you were little and the things you wanted. Do you?"

For some stupid reason the injured bird she'd found walking home from the bus stop when she was eight came to mind. The weather had been horrible, the front line of a predicted blizzard just starting to dump fat snowflakes on their small suburb and making the temperatures miserable. She'd shucked her coat anyway, cradled the poor thing in the center of it and carried it all the way home—only to get the mother of all lectures about the diseases she could have contracted through such an act. Whatever happened to the bird, she never knew and had been too terrified to ask. "He just wanted me to have a career that would support me."

"You mean he wanted your life to be predictable. Not something where you flew by the seat of your pants like your big brother."

"He was being practical."

"No, Katy. He was scared." Alek stood, his expression compassionate despite the sternness behind his words. "Following your gut or your emotions isn't a bad thing. It's just something he wasn't comfortable doing and he pushed that belief off on you."

Had he?

She'd always thought the way things had changed was more a case of growing up. Of accepting reality, and stowing away all her flighty ideas the way every other responsible person did.

And yet, looking back, Alek had never compromised on what he'd wanted. Not once. He'd had exceptional aptitude for the career he'd chosen in criminal justice, but he'd ditched it in favor of starting his own dojang and never once looked back—no matter how much her parents had taken him to task for what they'd deemed a foolish decision.

So, who was she? The woman who only weeks ago had been close enough to landing the coveted environmental internship she'd fought so hard to get? Or the passionate, deeply feeling woman she'd glimpsed in her dreams last night?

"What do *you* want, Katy? If you can figure that out, you'll have a helluva better shot at navigating all the shit life throws at you—the good and the bad. More importantly, you'll have a good time doing it. Which, if you ask me, beats taking everyone else's marching orders hands down."

She turned, drawn to the sketches mounted on the wall, those closest to the window lifting in a subtle flutter on the night's soft breeze. One by one, she studied them. Such detail. And the subjects ranged from people to symbols she didn't stand a prayer of recognizing.

Over six hours she'd spent in this room, but not once had she taken the time to appreciate Priest's talent. To explore and learn more about the man who'd kept her captivated even at a distance.

All because of guilt.

Because she'd dared to feel and explore something that didn't fit neatly in the realm of logic. Worse, she'd done it in the wake of her parents' death, setting aside what her conscience deemed was right in favor of what she wanted.

Outside the window, the live music from the pub swelled as new patrons made their way in or out, then died once more. Although, the throbbing bass was still there. Muted, but persistent. Rather like the pulse growing inside her.

She faced her brother and took a deep breath, the muscles in her torso trembling as if it had been years since they'd had such room to do so. "Was Priest busy with a client when you came up?"

The grin that split her brother's face was pure mischief. All male and one-hundred percent locked on the direction her thoughts had taken. "Gonna jump in the deep end, huh?"

Jump wasn't exactly the word she'd have used. More

like *swan dive* or *bungee jump*. "I don't have a clue what I'm doing."

Alek chuckled and rubbed the back of his hand against his chin. "Yeah, not sure that's gonna matter with Priest. Once you say go, my guess is you won't need to steer anymore." He jerked his head toward the hallway and the stairs that led down to the shop. "Come on."

"But if he's busy with a client, I don't want to bother him."

"Who gives a shit? Live a little." He wrapped one arm around her, hugged her tight to his side in the grizzly bear way he'd used since they were little and led her to the door. "Besides, watching you two circle each other last night was funny as hell. I'm looking forward to an encore."

Chapter Nineteen

A funny thing about curveballs and life—any time a man thought he'd hit his daily quota and imagined shit couldn't go any more sideways he was pretty much guaranteed of at least earning one more.

Priest's theory proved true the second his mate ventured out of the cave she'd created of his office. For all of a second, he spied the same soft hope and curiosity she'd looked at him with this morning. Then she clocked the busty blonde perched in front of him—or more importantly the way the blonde thrust her barely covered tits out while he finished up the bandage on her chest—and Kateri's softness morphed to lethal fury.

Hard not to blame her. If he'd walked in and found Kateri this close to a man, he'd have slaughtered first and asked questions later. But dealing with people like the woman in front of him was part of the job. A very unpleasant part he'd have happily pawned off on Tate if his ward hadn't already been two hours into a full sleeve when the blonde had sauntered in with a wad of cash.

Priest rolled away, tossed the adhesive to the table and peeled off his gloves. "All done. Follow your aftercare instructions and call the main number if you have any problems."

"Don't you have a personal number I could call?"

Kateri's cheeks flamed red-hot and her gaze narrowed with an intent that said she was ready to gut the woman.

Yep. Definitely a job that would've been better for Tate to handle. Honest to God, Priest couldn't decide if he owed Alek for getting Kateri back downstairs, or if he wanted to kick fate in the balls for its shitty timing. "Afraid not."

Alek chuckled and settled on the black leather couch with a prime view of the show playing out in front of him. Just for that, Priest had half a mind to bloody the fucker when they sparred tomorrow. And there would absolutely be sparring tomorrow. Especially, if Kateri's jealous spurt ended up playing against Priest instead of for him.

Standing, he braced his hands on his hips and gave the blonde a look he hoped quashed any last hopes. "Any questions?"

The blonde glanced over her shoulder at Kateri, finally cluing in to the death glare aimed her way. "Um, I guess not."

"Good call. Get dressed." He jerked his head in Alek's direction. "The goofy lughead over there will walk you to your car."

Not waiting for a reply, he stalked toward Kateri, taking his gaze off her only long enough to say to Alek, "You good to stay with Tate?"

He'd said it as a question, but he'd put a healthy amount of demand behind it. Enough so that Alek's attention only volleyed between Kateri and Priest once before understanding materialized behind his eyes and he cleared his throat. "Yeah. Sure."

He turned his sights on Kateri and closed in.

She matched it with a few steps backward, the furrow between her brows digging deeper. "Don't even think about it."

"I'm not thinking." He kept going, the display case where Jade housed all her charms and piercing supplies leaving Kateri nowhere else to retreat. He snaked one arm around her hips, yanked her against him and cupped the back of her head none too gently. "I'm doing."

And then he took.

Consumed her mouth as man, cat and darkness commanded.

Not surprisingly, she moaned into his mouth and sunk her nails into his shoulders. Whether it was a primal female instinct to mark him in front of another woman, or sheer fury at how close an intruder had come to her mate, he hadn't a clue, but his T-shirt was likely the only thing that kept her from drawing blood.

He didn't care. He'd take whatever she dished out if it meant wiping away whatever ugliness had settled in her head. If it grounded her in the truth that was them.

Her mouth opened on a protest and he thrust his tongue inside.

The sweet trace of chocolate, coffee and a spice he'd swear was spurred from her anger greeted him. Only when her muscles uncoiled beneath him and she slid her hands to the back of his neck, did he ease the kiss, assuring her with every languid nip and lick exactly who he wanted.

Murmured voices sounded in the background, followed by the bell's jingle over the main entrance and the heavy clunk of the door falling shut.

Then silence, broken only by the muted buzz of Tate's iron behind closed doors and the escalating breaths between him and his mate. He broke the kiss and ran his nose alongside hers. "Talk to me."

Her nails dug into his skin and the sweetest growl slipped past her lips. "I didn't like her touching you."

Her touching him. Not him touching her. A minor distinction, but a promising one. "You've watched me working on other women."

She pulled back enough to meet his eyes and snapped, "On their ankle and their back. And neither one of them looked like they were about to throw themselves at you."

Damn, but she was beautiful. Furious and afraid, but fully embracing her emotions and absolutely gorgeous doing it. "It's never sexual for me, Kateri. Especially, not with a stranger and some random, clichéd tattoo off the internet." He tightened his grip on the back of her head and held her steady, his voice dropping for the rest of his words. "But I guarantee you, when I mark you it will be very sexual. The magic, the ink, the pain and my touch…by the time I'm done, you'll beg me to take you every way a man can take a woman. And make no mistake, *mihara*. I'll take you up on every one of them."

She swallowed, and the way her eyes dilated gave a decent hunch at the images her mind had conjured to accompany his statement.

"Now," he said before she could claw herself up from her stupor, "we're going to get on my bike, and you'll get the time it takes between here and home to figure out if you want more space, or if you're going to put us both out of our misery and take what you need."

He pulled away and snagged her wrist in a firm grip, eager to get her alone and away from the reminder of what she'd seen.

"I don't need the ride home to know what I want."

Her bold words stopped him cold before he'd gotten a full stride toward the door, and the warning hum that had hit him only minutes before his brother had wrecked their clan with his dark magic danced along every inch of his skin. Only this time there was something different to it. A lightness similar to walking out into the sun after being in the dark. Nothing like the weighted dread he'd felt that day.

He turned, met her fathomless stare and braced for the worst.

"If there was any uncertainty before, it turned crystal clear when I came down here and saw that woman close to you." She stepped forward, closing what distance he'd created, threading her fingers with his and squeezing tight. "I'm done with waiting. I want what's mine."

Chapter Twenty

Whoever penned the expression *tugged the tiger's tail* had obviously never tugged a panther's. If they had, the latter would have been the ultimate adage for pushing the limits of bravery, because Katy had done exactly that. In fact, the way Priest had stared down at her in the seconds following her confession, she'd halfway expected him to shove her against the wall and take her right then and there.

Instead, his frown had shifted to a devilish smirk, and his whole demeanor had taken on the languorous movements of a predator who'd just been presented with its favorite dessert and was intent on savoring every succulent bite.

And oh, how he'd savored. Rather than take her right to his bike, he'd taken them on a detour along Main Street, neither of them speaking except when he stopped and insisted they indulge in ice cream. But what he didn't share with words, he shared with touch and heated looks that made her heart race and her breath hitch.

Even the eventual ride on his bike had been a seduction. As if he knew that each drawn-out second as they neared his home ramped her desire that much higher. By the time he pulled into his drive, killed the engine and walked her to the door, she'd have willingly taken him on the front lawn if he'd asked.

Now here she was, in lockstep beside him taking one step after the other, his open bedroom door across the catwalk a gateway she was both terrified and thrilled to cross. Twenty-four hours since she'd followed this same path. Where yesterday she'd been a riotous mess, muddled by so many conflicting thoughts and feelings it was impossible to tell one from the other, today there was stillness. A certainty she wasn't sure she'd ever felt before.

But Priest was hers.

She'd known it the second she'd laid eyes on the blonde offering herself to Priest and had nearly launched herself across the room in a frenzied rage. How she'd managed not to do exactly that was still a mystery she couldn't unravel, but there was no way she was letting what she wanted slip through her fingers.

Not this time.

Reaching the bedroom door, he guided her through ahead of him. Her gaze landed on the bed and the full impact of what she'd agreed to reverberated clear to her bones. This was it. Full intimacy with a man who wouldn't balk in his dominance. Who'd demand her submission and not stop until she gave it.

Moving in behind her, he turned her to face him then gently framed her face. "Breathe, *mihara*." As he had at the shop, he stole her kiss before she could speak, taking full advantage of her surprise and slicking his tongue past her lips.

It was exactly what she'd needed. As if his lips and tongue gliding wet and warm against her own had the power to unplug every thought save those tied to sensation.

She sighed, tilted her head back for more of his addictive taste and pressed closer to his heat. Savored the slab of warm, hard muscle beneath his T-shirt and the way her heavy breasts gave way to his strength. She wanted more. Wanted to feel his heat without their clothes between them. The rasp of her straining nipples against his bare flesh.

But he only kissed her, lazily drawing her deeper and deeper and taking his sweet, frustrating time.

She moaned and rubbed herself against him, tilting her neck to give him better access as he blazed a drugging trail with his mouth along her jawline. It was beautiful. Relaxed and unhurried, but so far from what she'd expected her thoughts slipped out without censor. "Why are you being so tender?"

His lips curved against her skin and he nipped the spot right where her neck and shoulders met. He licked the same spot and chuckled, the warmth of his breath teasing the wet path he'd left behind. "This isn't tender, kitten." Slowly, he lifted his head and began working free the hasty braid she'd fashioned for their ride home. "This is me keeping a choke hold on my beast and the darkness so I don't throw you down and fuck you until all you know in this world is the feel of my cock inside you."

Holy hell.

Her body mirrored the thought with a tremor she couldn't have hidden if she'd tried.

And he felt it, tightening the arm he kept around her waist as he lazily combed his fingers higher and higher, studying her every response. "You like that." Not a question, but an observation spoken aloud.

Still, she answered, the admission on her lips fascinatingly erotic. "Yes."

He hummed at that, the approving tone of the low rumble stroking her much the way she'd petted his cat. "That's good. Because sooner or later, I won't be able to hold it back, and the darkness is going to get its turn." He speared his fingers in her hair and fisted the thick strands, giving her just a taste of what he'd promised. "Until that happens, I plan to build you up and make sure you're ready for it."

Ready for it? She was already strung so tight she could likely power half the electricity needed for his house. Worse, she didn't have a clue how to manage it all. Only knew that the growing current needed an outlet. A place to unleash and purge the burgeoning surplus before it consumed her entirely. "Priest—"

He captured her protest with another kiss, the press of his mouth more insistent than the last. A vow and an order all rolled up into one. When he finally pulled away again, it was only enough to murmur against her lips. "Now, you're going to stay right here and do exactly what I tell you."

He shifted as though to move away, but she dug fingertips into his broad shoulders, practically clawing to keep him in place. "I don't like the way that sounds."

"You may not like the way it sounds, but you'll like how it feels." He pried her hands free and eased back, a salacious grin on his face that said whatever came next would either break her, or send her into a whole different stratosphere.

He ambled to the oversized club chair near the bed.

Compared to the rest of his manly furnishings, the sub-tle gold damask design had seemed slightly out of place when she'd first seen it. Though, watching him settle in it now, splaying his big body on the deep cushions and resting his head against the raised, yet slightly reclined back, it made perfect sense. A chair meant for a king... or a high priest. "Take off your clothes."

It was the last thing she'd expected. A blunt order with zero give that whipped her thinking brain to life and urged her to run. But her body rebelled and stayed locked in place, her thighs quivering in anticipation. Be-neath her ribbed tank, her nipples strained harder against the cotton, eager for his gaze. And since she'd pushed the limits of her courage and gone sans bra this morn-ing, they'd jetted right to feature presentation.

She smoothed her hands across the jeans covering her hips, her palms damp where her mouth could barely muster any moisture at all. At the back of her mind, the question Alek had posed whispered and nudged her to jump.

What do you want, Katy?

She wanted *this*. Right here. Right now. Nothing but pleasure and what felt good. Curling her fingers around the hem of her tank, she sucked in a bracing breath and peeled it up and over her head.

The room's cool air rushed to greet her, sinfully ca-ressing her skin and making her breasts grow taut and heavy. Priest's pendant hung heavy at the hollow of her throat, the weight somehow accenting just how much she'd bared.

Priest rubbed his hands along the chair's thick arm-rest and gripped the edge, his covetous gaze locked on her breasts. Despite his outward appearance of control, his voice was deep. Almost broken. "More."

She'd done that. Drawn a confident and powerful man to the edge. Made his voice crack with the same desire that pulsed at her core. The effect was staggering. Intoxicating and strangely addictive.

With shaking fingers, she loosened her jeans, the muted rasp of the zipper as she drew it down and her shaky breaths strangely erotic against the room's silence. But rather than peel the denim back, she dipped her fingertips beneath her waistband and teasingly skimmed the flesh underneath.

His gaze flicked to hers, a warning to match his words burning behind his predatory stare. "You're dancing a dangerous line, kitten. Your claws may not be very sharp, but mine are lethally accurate. If you value those jeans, you'll get them off your body before they're in shreds."

Another dirty lash against her senses, this one leaving no doubt that when she peeled her panties down her legs they'd be soaked in the center. And if he'd meant to hurry her along...well, he'd pushed the wrong button. More like stoked her newfound courage and built a raging blaze.

Slowly, she shimmied her jeans past her hips, but made sure to leave her simple white hipster panties in place. From the front, the silky lace wasn't all that revealing, but from the back they were cheeky as hell. A fact she couldn't wait for him to discover. She straightened as she spoke, stepped out of her jeans and kicked them aside. "What about your teeth? Will you use them on me, too?"

A growl rumbled up his throat, part panther, part

man. Though, both seemed to be fighting for the upper hand. "Oh, you'll get my bite. Right about the time your pussy clamps down on my cock. Now lose the panties."

A sassy *Yes, sir. Anything you say, sir* almost slipped past her lips, but the greedy woman who relished the reins nestled in her grip quashed the smart-ass quip before it could air and peeled the lacy fabric down her thighs.

Oh, yes. She was slick and ready for him. Drenched. A fact driven home by the glistening wetness in her discarded panties.

Apparently, her mate didn't need the visual, because he gripped the armrests hard enough they groaned and his nostrils flared. He licked his lower lip and practically snarled, "I can smell you."

It shouldn't have turned her on. Wouldn't have with anyone else. But with Priest it was glorious. A primitive testament to her impact on the beast eyeing its next conquest. "You'd smell it better if you were closer."

His gaze snapped to hers. "I'll do more than smell it. I'm going to eat it. Lick every damned drop and tongue you until you come and give me more."

"Okay," she whispered, the precursor to what promised to be an earthquake-sized release rippling between her legs.

He grinned and cocked his head, his expression far too perceptive. "Did you touch yourself this morning?"

Boy, had she. Both when she'd woken up and again in the shower. Though nothing she'd done had sparked the same response he manifested in her dreams. "Yes."

"Show me."

Another rung on the ladder. The next flight up on the death-defying swan dive he seemed hell-bent on facilitating. But she'd done this much. Had pushed him to the point he looked as if he might launch himself at her any second. And more, she'd found a level of confidence she'd never dreamed of owning. A stunning and self-assured sexuality that burned hot as an August sun. What better way to own what she felt and who she was than right now? Here, with her own two hands.

Fingers trembling, she started at her hips, the touch cool despite the fire licking beneath her skin. She let her eyes slip shut and her head drop back, the delicate caress of her hands along her rib cage and then cupping her breasts leaving goose bumps in their wake.

"Is that really what you want?" he said. "How you want me to touch them?"

"No," she groaned, the answer the easiest one he'd asked of her all night. She forced her heavy eyelids open. "It's not the same." She lifted and gently squeezed each mound, remembering how his touch had felt in her dreams. Wondered how reality would be in comparison. "My hands are too small. Not as strong or as rough as yours." Or as confident, though she refused to admit as much out loud.

He rose and prowled toward her, the power contained in every step that of a man not only close to the edge, but eager to cross it. His big hands splayed along the upper curve of her hips, the heat branding her as sure as his words. "Are you ready for that, *mihara*? Ready to be claimed?"

God, that word. It should have made her run. At least generated a host of arguments. Instead, a tremor wiggled down her spine and her shoulders pressed back in invitation as the traitorous truth slipped free. "Yes."

One second. Maybe not even that long, and he cupped

her breasts, molding and shaping the taut mounds the way he had in her dreams. Only this was *so* much better. Hotter. Harder. The difference between sunshine slanting through a closed, dust-covered window and standing unobstructed beneath a brilliant afternoon sun.

And his mouth. Thought wasn't possible with this kiss. This battle he waged with his lips and tongue. Expelling what little tie she had to reality and laying to waste the last fragments of her fears. The only play left to make was surrender, and she gave it. Willingly. Eagerly.

She slipped her fingers beneath his shirt and moaned at the hard, hot flesh underneath. Over a week, she'd watched him sauntering shirtless and barefoot around his home and *finally* she had unfettered access. An open opportunity to explore every plane and indentation. She shoved the offensive cotton higher only to be road blocked by his broad chest and the fact that he was too busy using his hands on her to lift them up and let her pull the fabric free. "Priest. Shirt."

The way he devoured her mouth, she was lucky to get that much out, but he did as she demanded, snarling as he tore his lips away from hers and ripped the shirt over his head. "Need you under me. Now." Hands back at her hips, he hoisted her up like she weighed a whopping five pounds and palmed her ass in a possessive grip. "Wrap me up."

Her legs obeyed. God knew, her brain hadn't sent the order because when he'd pulled her flush against his bare torso her mind had come completely unhinged. But before she could fully appreciate the blistering sensation of his skin against hers and the erotic feel of his charms pressed against her sternum, she was on her back, his massive body braced above her and his mouth relent-lessly drawing one nipple deep.

With something between a sigh and a groan, she speared her fingers into his thick hair, the heavy length of it spilling against her torso a stark contrast to the rough rasp of his jeans against her bare thighs.

She rolled her hips, torn between pulling him away from the wicked suction he kept on her breast so she could see his eyes and holding him exactly where he was. "Your jeans."

Apparently, talking in minimal sentences wasn't working anymore, because all she got in return was a grunt worthy of a caveman. He shifted to her other breast, nipped the puckered tip, then enveloped it in his scalding mouth.

And holy crap, it felt good. An erotic tug tied straight to her sex that would only get about a thousand times better if she could get him to let up long enough to shuck his jeans and let her grind against the hard length un-derneath.

She fumbled for his waistband and got the top but-ton undone before he jerked her hands away and pinned them over her head.

"Don't even think about it," he growled, clearly irri-tated she'd interrupted his plans.

"I'm way past thinking about it. I'm doing."

"Not yet, you're not." He lifted his weight and took his sweet time perusing her body. Despite the purpose-ful action, his chest pumped in and out like a man who'd sprinted a marathon. "I took you with my mouth last night, but dreams aren't reality." He met her stare and re-leased her hands, the conviction behind his gaze enough to hold her without physical restraints. "I want the real deal and I'm getting it tonight." Sliding his hands beneath her ass, he tilted her for his mouth and openly inhaled her scent, his cat chuffing in pure delight. "Every last fucking drop."

He licked straight through her slit and she cried out, the velvet rasp of his tongue against her sensitive folds demanding not just her surrender, but her pleasure. Amping the slow-building fire to a raging inferno until there was nothing but sensation. It was overwhelming. Startling in its intensity. So much so, she writhed beneath his mouth, part of her desperate for more of what he offered and another desperate to escape and catch her breath.

Instead, she dared to open her eyes. To feast on the insanely carnal image of her mate devouring her sex— and nearly came when he met her gaze.

He circled her clit with his tongue, the leisurely glide sending fresh ripples out in all directions. "That's it, kitten," he growled against her flesh as he teased one finger at her entrance. "Enjoy how it looks." Another circle, this one tighter and faster. "How it feels when your male devours your cunt."

And she was gone.

Completely outer limits and soaring through a whole different stratosphere where right, wrong and reason didn't even compute. Where it didn't matter what words he'd used to push her over the edge, or the judgments she'd once attributed to them. Only the press of his fingers filling her, pushing her higher with every pulse. The sweet draw of his lips around her clit and the decadent vibration of his hungry groan.

She rolled her hips and savored each wave, riding his steady fingers with a wanton, yet freeing openness and shamelessly holding him to her with both hands. Or maybe it was just her holding on. God knew, the reality she'd known before had been completely rearranged. Every color, every truth, every assumption turned on its head and new possibilities uncovered.

Lazily feeding from her release, he lifted his gaze to hers, a heavy dose of male arrogance adding an extra spark to his gray eyes.

Spearing her hands through his hair, she urged him toward her. "You look awfully proud of yourself."

"My mate just came for the first time in my mouth and she did it hard." He kissed the top of her cleft and slowly shifted so he braced himself above her. Between her legs, his fingers pumped slow but steady, stoking the embers he'd left behind. "Not a man alive who won't smirk when his woman's taste is on his tongue and her moans are rattling around in his head."

He kissed her, deep and thorough. As if he needed to drive home how intimately he now knew her and how much more they had yet to go.

Except there was one thing she wasn't skipping on the trip. One thing she'd yet to indulge in, even in dreams. She pushed against his chest, gaining only enough room to cant her head and leave her jaw and neck exposed to his devious lips. "I want to see you. Want you to show yourself the way I did."

She felt more than heard his low growl rumbling against her chest, then the slow bristle of his beard against her collarbone as he seemed to consider her request. When he lifted his head, his gaze burned with an edge she'd never seen before. A glint that warned the darkness was closer than she'd realized.

For a second, she expected him to speak. To utter another of those jaw-dropping statements he'd floored her with since they'd begun their sexual dance all those days ago. Instead he slowly eased his fingers from inside her as he sat back on his heels, smoothed his calloused palms along her splayed inner thighs and unhurriedly drank her in.

"Priest?"

"I want you to stay just like this. Open and ready for me. Understand?"

Oh, boy. She was definitely dancing with the dark side. If the tension woven within his voice didn't prove it, then the otherworldly edge around it did.

And yet she wasn't afraid. Not even a little. Excited, yes. Drunk on endorphins, absolutely. But not afraid. Not of Priest or any part of him. She swallowed hard, but fisted the comforter at her sides and eked out a broken "Yes."

He growled in approval and eased to the foot of the bed. Running the heel of his hand along the thick length behind his jeans, he cocked his head to one side, considering. "How does it feel to wait for me like that, kitten?"

Sinful.

Indecent.

Dirty.

"Exposed," she said instead, opting for the one that hit the closest to home.

"Hmmm." He tugged his zipper down and peeled the denim back. To her surprise, his cock sprung free, long, thick and heavily veined. Enough so, his hesitation at giving her a show made a lot more sense. Heck, the thing was as intimidating as he'd been the first day they'd met.

Not breaking his stare, he shoved his jeans free, crawled back on the bed and stood tall on his knees between her splayed thighs. A hunter. A warrior. A protector.

And he was hers. Every dark, deliciously muscled inch of him.

"I guess that answers if you're a boxers or a briefs man," she managed, though her attempt at humor was quickly sidetracked when she spied the pre-come seeping from his cock.

She licked her lower lip and he growled, swiping his thumb through the pearly white substance and slicking it along his shaft. "I tolerate clothes on a good day. Less so when all I can think about is fucking and coming inside my mate."

The muscles in her sex quivered, the combination of his voice, his wicked words and the image of him working himself making it almost impossible to keep her knees wide as he'd asked. Though, now that she thought about it, he hadn't said anything about keeping her hands to herself. If he was free to put on a show, then so was she. Especially, if she could nudge things further along in the process.

She snaked one hand between her legs and fingered her slick folds. "That's a little dangerous don't you think? You have no clue who I've been with, and I doubt you've been celibate. Not with blonde bimbos sticking their boobs in your face all the time."

His mouth crooked in a devious grin, apparently not only pleased with the initiative she'd shown, but eager to watch the show. "Kitten, the worst diseases in the world don't impact our race. That includes sexual ones."

A nice perk, but still, not a full get out of jail card. She slid one finger inside and circled her hips, her voice just a little bit threadier than before. "But I'm not on the pill."

The grin grew to a full-on smile and he released his cock. "And you're not in heat." His hand covered hers, his strong fingers adding more pressure to her own. "If you were, I'd have carted you off and fucked you days ago."

Oh, yes. His touch was *much* better than hers. Bolder. Bigger. Stronger. She ground her hips against their joined hands, only the curious part of her clinging to the conversation with dogged determination. "What's that supposed to mean?"

"It means you're my mate. When it's time, we'll both know it. Either you'll welcome me, or I'll die trying to change your mind, but we'll figure that out later." He punctuated his statement by gripping her knee, pressing it up and wide and replacing the path their fingers had taken with the wide crest of his cock.

Later was good. Very good. Because right now all she wanted was to feel him inside her. To check the rest of their conversation and get down to something far more primitive.

Up and down, he teased her, coating himself in her wetness. "You wanted to see me, *mihara*. Well, here I am." He notched the tip inside her and paused long enough to grasp her hips in each hand and growl, "Watch while I claim my mate."

Watch? Good God, it was so much more than watching. More like being reborn. Resurrected from the half-life she'd known and plunged into one blindingly bright. Inch by inch, he took her. Tunneled his thick, beautiful length inside her with an aching slowness that reeked of possession.

And it was *amazing*. Liberating. The stretch and full-ness as he invaded ricocheting out in all directions. His dark, taut skin disappearing inside her with each slick pump deliciously explicit. The pinnacle of intimacy.

Fascinated, she trailed her fingers across his abdomen and savored the powerful flex and release of each thrust. The thin layer of sweat building against his hot skin.

"Priest." It came out reverent. As awestruck and dazed as the connection deepening between them.

"That's right, kitten. Feel it." He tightened his grip at her hips and adjusted his angle, driving up so the tip of him raked perfectly inside her. "Take what I give you. Own it."

He was out of his mind. No one could own sensations like this. No more than they could own a violent storm or a raging ocean. But she could ride it. Ride it and let it sweep her into this new reality with both hands held high.

Matching each thrust of his hips with her own, she wrapped her legs around him and dug her heels into his flanks, urging him deeper. "How about if you give me more?"

The sound that came out of him was part dirty chuckle, part snarl and his gray eyes darkened to that of an encroaching thundercloud. "There she is. My naughty mate dancing closer to the edge."

Lord, but his voice was wicked. A sultry stroke to her already overloaded senses. "I'm not naughty."

"Oh, yes you are. You may not see it, but I do." He upped his thrusts, rolling his hips with each stab in the most sinfully beautiful display of masculinity she'd ever seen. Smoothing his hands up her sides and beneath her shoulder blades, a resonant purr rumbled from his chest. "And I'm going to prove it."

One second he was above her, and the next she was

upright, her legs wrapped around his waist and her pussy impaled on his glorious cock. Gone was the man who'd carefully watched his every step, replaced with an animal driven by base instinct. One determined to sweep her up in the frenzy and erase all the tidy ideas she'd thought to be true.

Over and over his pelvis slapped against hers, her breasts jiggling against his solid, sweat-slick chest with each buck and her hair softly teasing the delicate skin along her shoulders. She'd never felt more alive. More connected than in this moment.

With one hand splayed just above her ass and the other fisted in her hair, he tilted her head to one side and scraped his teeth along her neck. "You like that."

She did. All of it. Everything. So much a fresh release swelled inside her, burgeoning up from her toes and crouching low in her belly, ready to leap. She whimpered and clutched his shoulders, hanging on for the merciless ride.

"I know you do, because you were made for me." He held her hips in place, grinding his pelvis against her clit on each upward advance. "We were made for each other."

He slipped the hand above her ass lower, curving it around and running his fingers alongside where they were joined. "There is nothing I won't give you. No boundary I won't cross, because you belong to me." Fingers coated in her wetness, he slicked them backwards. "All of you."

He circled her anus and she jerked against him, digging her nails deep in his skin. "You wouldn't."

"Oh, I would." Back to her sex he delved, gathering

more of her juices and heading right back to her ass for another teasing touch. "I will."

A violent tremor racked her body and the building release inside her ratcheted higher. A tension poised with the ferocity of a spring stretched to the peak of its limits. "Priest!"

Over and over, he primed her, steadily coating her in her essence. When she finally relaxed and welcomed him with a fresh stroke by lifting her hips, he hummed and murmured against her skin. "That's it." He circled again, this time harder, barely breaching the surface. "Let it out."

As soon as he said it, he backed away. A slight respite that made her fists clench in frustration and her groan rip up her throat.

He nipped her neck and resumed the pressure she'd begun to crave. "Welcome it." He pushed past the barrier and drove his cock to the hilt. "Come for your mate."

On demand, her body obeyed. Filled and possessed in ways she'd never believed she'd welcome, the whole world opened up. Blossomed bold and beautiful while her sex convulsed around his shaft. She *was* his. The missing link that hitched together the empty spaces inside her and made the overall plan make sense. A safe place where what she wanted was not only accepted but championed.

He growled against her shoulder, still pumping his finger inside her ass in alternating strokes with his thick shaft, wringing one contraction after another from her sex. "Fuck, yes. My woman." He licked and sucked the spot where her shoulder and neck met and stabbed deeper. "My. Fucking. Mate."

He drove to the hilt, wrenched her down and sunk

his teeth into her flesh, the triumphant roar as his cock jerked inside her setting off powerful aftershocks.

She held on tight, arms trembling as wave after wave rippled through her gobsmacked body and the room's chilled air danced against her damp skin. Earth-shattering physicality aside, this was more than sex. More than chemistry and compatibility.

It was magic. Sensual. Carnal. And yes, maybe a little dirty, but still absolutely beautiful. And for once she didn't care to understand how or why it worked. Only that it did and that it was hers. That this man was the one who'd not only guided her to it, but vowed to give her more.

She smoothed her hands along the back of his neck and rubbed her cheek against his temple. "That was…" God, what could she say? As much as she wanted to say something, no words felt right. None worthy of what he'd given her.

"As it should be." He kissed the tender spot he'd bitten and stroked his hands along her spine, lazily petting her the way she'd stroked his panther that first morning. "What it will always be."

It was perfect. A summation she'd never have found on her own that cast a spotlight on the vast world they'd just opened up. One that both excited and scared her silly.

Holding her to him with one arm, he leaned forward, laid her on her back and pressed a reverent kiss to her lips. "Thank you, *mihara*." The next kiss he placed just below his pendant and another above her heart.

She savored the thick fall of his hair between her fingers and the velvet glide of his lips as he moved farther down her torso. "I'm not sure why you're thanking me."

His shaft slipped free and she whimpered, the loss more tangible than on a purely physical level.

"Because you took the risk." As if to prove his point, he ran his fingertips through their joined release seeping from her sex. "You were afraid and you still jumped."

She swallowed huge, reality rushing in faster than she cared to welcome it. "I'm still afraid." The honest admission slipped out, bolstered by his nearness and the utter certainty that, no matter what she faced, he'd be there. Rock solid and ready to help her through it. "This feels huge. Bigger than anything I know how to deal with."

He inhaled deep and rubbed his coated fingers atop her mound. As if he were marking her in a far more primitive fashion. Leaving tangible proof of his claim behind.

Slowly, he lifted his gaze to hers and shifted so he lay beside her, propped on one elbow. He fingered the pendant at her throat. "Maybe it seems too big because you're looking at it from the wrong angle."

Of all the things he could have said, a logical slant was the last thing she'd expected. Especially in such a poignant moment. "Well, it *feels* like I'm looking at it dead on."

He smiled at that, a soft one only shared by those who were intimate, and wrapped his arm around her waist. "You're looking at it backward, *mihara*. This isn't the end. Not a shackle to endure." Tangling his legs with hers, he rolled to his back, pulled her with him and hugged her close. When his lips grazed the top of her head, she felt it everywhere. A benediction and a promise all rolled up into one. "This is the beginning."

Chapter Twenty-One

It was too early. Even hovering beneath the upper veil of sleep, Priest's humming mind insisted it wasn't yet time to rise and face the day. Though, to be fair, his brain might be biased by the soft, welcoming press of Kateri next to him and her breath whispering against his chest.

He stroked her bare back and palmed her pert ass, every spectacular detail of last night rising to the top of his consciousness like a cloudless sunrise. Taking her again was tempting. Disturbingly so. But between their first wild joining and the two more tender ones through the night, she had to be sore. Not to mention exhausted.

Hugging her tight, he nuzzled the top of her head and tried to slip back into sleep, hoping the tangible contact would ease whatever had woken him and left his cat on edge.

But the mental nudge came again, even more insistent—and this time the source was unmistakable.

His eyes snapped open to the pre-dawn darkened room and the inner compass he'd come to rely on homed in on the tugging sensation.

A soul quest.

Damn it.

As shitty timing went, this was the worst. Yeah, Kateri was a reasonable woman. More so than many he'd known. But last night had been huge for her. A step into something completely foreign. Reasonable or not, odds were good she'd be pissed if she woke up the morning after and found herself alone. Hell, *he* was pissed and he wasn't even gone yet.

He rolled to his back and fisted his hair on the top of his head. Whoever's quest it was, they were reaching the Otherworld fast. Far faster than normal. Either that, or he'd simply been so preoccupied with his mate, he'd subconsciously turned a blind eye to reality.

Beside him, Kateri lay perfectly still, sleeping so deeply his movement hadn't seemed to faze her. It was odd seeing her like this. He'd grown so used to the non-stop intellectual fire burning behind her blue gaze that studying her in repose was like spying on an intimate moment.

He liked it, though. Loved how innocent she looked. How even in the shadows her pert nose, cupid lips and high cheekbones made him think of a sleeping yet mischievous pixie.

Yeah, definitely shitty timing. The first time since the Keeper named him high priest that he'd regretted his responsibility.

He propped himself up on one elbow and skimmed his lips across hers.

They parted only a fraction and a soft sigh slipped free, but otherwise she kept sleeping. Interesting, because every other kiss he'd given her she'd woken in an instant, eyes flashing with awareness to find him not only close but naked against her.

Chuckling low, he pulled the covers up around her shoulders and eased from the bed. His poor kitten.

Clearly, he'd worked her harder than he'd thought. He snatched his jeans from the floor near the foot of the bed and tugged them on, the rough denim offensive compared to Kateri's warm, silky skin.

Screw the soul quest, the darkness prodded. *Stay with her. We've earned it. She deserves it.*

He hesitated at the door to his room, fisting the knob nearly hard enough to do damage.

Bundled under the blanket, she looked so tiny. Engulfed by the size of his bed and achingly alone. Giving in was tempting. Painfully so. But it was the wrong choice. One even Kateri wouldn't ask him to make.

Forcing himself into motion, he strode across the catwalk that separated his suite from the rest of the bedrooms toward Tate's room. With every step the urgency lashed harder. As if the distance he put between him and his mate drove the quester closer to the Otherworld.

But that couldn't be right. Kateri might have accepted him physically, but she hadn't accepted their bond yet. He'd have felt it. Every male he'd spoken with who'd ever earned their mate's bond insisted the merging was unmistakable. A welcome tether even beyond what they'd experienced when gaining their companion animal. And even if Kateri *had* accepted their bond last night, a soul quest wouldn't involve her.

Unless the quest was hers.

He paused at Tate's door, both hands braced on the frame at either side as the thought rattled through him.

Surely not. She'd not shown any signs. Definitely none as prominent as Alek's. But then women seldom did. They were better at navigating emotion. Better at rolling with shifting physical changes that often marked an impending quest.

Except Kateri wasn't an average woman. And she'd been highly emotional yesterday. Conflicted. Wrestling with not only the idea of a fated mate and the over-whelming physical response that went with it, but the death of her parents, too.

And she'd been almost still as death beside him. Not responding to his kiss.

Fuck.

Not bothering with a knock, he barged into Tate's room. "Alek, get up."

Splayed in the center of Tate's pullout and barely covered with a single sheet, Alek grunted and covered his eyes with his forearm.

Always a light sleeper, Tate propped himself up on one forearm in the queen bed along the opposite wall and rubbed one eye with the heel of his hand. "Something wrong?"

"Not wrong, no. But if I'm reading things right, I'm about to have a hell of a challenge on my hands." He shook Alek none too gently by one shoulder. "Need you up, primo. Now."

"What the hell?" Alek pushed up on his elbows, squinted into the shadows and fumbled for his phone beside the pullout. "Man, it's not even six o'clock yet. We only got home three hours ago."

"The Keeper doesn't care what time it is, and your grandmother won't either. You're Kateri's brother. It's your job to wake Naomi up and be with her while you wait."

"Holy shit," Tate grumbled, quickly putting two and two together, sliding out of bed and flipping on the light.

Either the urgency in Tate's tone or the speed with which he'd started yanking on clothes must have penetrated Alek's sleep-hazed mind, because his whole body finally went on full alert. "Wait with her for what?"

"Kateri's soul quest," Tate answered before Priest could.

Alek hesitated only long enough to gauge Priest's expression then shot out of bed. "Holy shit. She's gonna freak."

Satisfied, both men were on track, Priest gave way to the need to get back to Kateri and stalked toward the door. "Like I said, I'm about to have a challenge on my hands."

"You don't think she'll refuse them, do you?"

Alek's question stopped Priest in his tracks, the fear behind it echoing his own. Yeah, she'd opened up. Had begun to embrace the woman she'd kept deeply buried growing up. But the Keeper wasn't known for subtleties. More like a ringmaster comfortable with parading a person's every deep, dark secret out into a three-ring spotlight and addressing it head-on. As a method for matching magic and companion to the quester, it was perfect. For Kateri it could easily backfire. "For her sake, let's hope she doesn't."

The path back to his bedroom went by in a blur, the single intention of caring for his mate and the escalating tug from the Otherworld the only thing his mind could process. By the time he got there, she still hadn't moved. Not even an inch. But the sun had risen just enough outside to show how pale her skin had become and the light sheen of perspiration dampening her hairline.

He shucked his jeans and dragged on his loosest pair of track pants, wishing like hell he could crawl between the covers and hold her skin to skin as he guided her through her quest.

It wasn't an option, though. Naomi would no doubt park herself bedside through the whole thing, as was her right, and Alek, for all the level-headedness he'd shown the last many days, would likely pace like a caged beast. Their clan might be immodest by nature, but baring his mate in any way was out of the question. Not to mention, Kateri would kill him if she found out he'd allowed such a thing.

Moving fast before anyone else descended, he dug out his biggest, softest T-shirt and gently dressed her in it. No easy task considering her body was complete dead weight. He'd just tugged the hem to her hips when a host of footsteps and hushed voices sounded from the hallway.

Out of breath and smiling ear to ear, Naomi rounded the doorway first, trailed by Tate, Alek and Jade. "How close is she? Do you need anything before you join her? Water? Food?"

Priest grinned despite the insistent pull growing stronger and stronger by the second. Leave it to Naomi to not only assume her granddaughter would readily accept her gifts, but was likely already planning Kateri's celebration in her head. "No time for that. She's moving too fast."

He piled the pillows up on his side of the bed, but paused before climbing in and pegged Alek and Tate with a harsh stare. "No one comes in this house until I'm awake. No one. No clan and definitely no strangers no matter what they say or who they are."

Both dipped short nods, but where Tate was all business, Alek was clearly distracted, the worry etched on his face echoing his own concerns. "I should have told her more about what our magic was like. How it feels. I don't want her to pass this up."

"You shared your first shift. She saw what it was like, but the choice is hers to make." Careful not to jostle her too much, Priest lifted Kateri into his arms, settled with his back against the mound of pillows and cradled her against him.

"You're not giving her enough credit," Naomi said. "Neither of you." Not the least bit uncomfortable with whose room she was in, Naomi sat on the bed and smoothed the stray, sweat-dampened hairs off Kateri's cheek. "Our girl might have been slow to wake up, but she's not stupid. She'll be too curious to bypass this chance. No matter what nonsense my son put in her head."

She was right on that score. Kateri was nothing if not inquisitive. It was her level of willingness to face the next few hours he was worried about. Still, Naomi was right. If he didn't go into this quest believing in her, he wouldn't do her justice. Not as her high priest or her mate.

Forcing his breaths to slow and deepen, he focused on the light jasmine scent that clung to her skin and each exhalation that fluttered against his chest. "She'll make whatever choice she needs to make." He closed his eyes and the gray of the Otherworld rushed up to meet him. "And whatever that looks like I'll stand beside her."

Chapter Twenty-Two

It had been years since Katy had been to a circus, let alone dreamed of one, but she loved them. Always had. The spotlights. The colorful costumes and majestic animals. The laughter from the crowd and the booming ringmaster's voice resonating through the sound system. All of it in a cocoon of black while hundreds of people looked on.

From her place high in the stands she took it in. The bench she sat on was empty as were several rows below it, but the rest of the venue was packed, every eye trained on the performers warming up for the show.

Priest's amused voice rumbled behind her, close and far more distinct than the sounds coming from below. "Now this is an interesting venue."

Her heart lurched with a mix of surprise and delight, and she spun on her bench. "You're here."

Perched on the bench behind her with his elbows planted on his knees and his hands clasped loosely between them, he cocked his head. "Of course, I'm here. Where else would I be?"

"Well, considering I was twelve the last time I dreamed of the circus, you're not exactly a participant I'd expect my subconscious to drag into the picture."

As soon as she said it, her mind offered up the memory of the last dream they'd spent together, drawing an entirely different manner of smile to her lips. "Unless this is one of *those* dreams. Though, I gotta say—recently uncovered naughty side or not—a circus venue may be a little weird for me."

The lightness in his expression sobered and he skimmed his fingers across her cheek. When he spoke, his voice was gentle. A careful delivery that sent warning prickles along her skin. "It's not a dream, kitten."

She scanned the crowds. The three rings and the performers inside them. The air was thick with the scents of animal, dirt and popcorn. Had her sense of smell ever been this strong in dreams before? She had with Priest, but that dream had been different. Guided by him rather than her sleeping mind. "But it can't be real. I mean, I don't know Eureka Springs too well, but I haven't seen a venue that could house a circus. And we were at your house last night."

He pressed his fingers to her shoulder, urging her to face him. Only when she dragged her gaze away from the activity below did he speak. "It's not reality either. At least not as you know it." He studied her face, a wise man calculating how well the rest of what he had to say would be accepted. "We're in the Otherworld, and this is your soul quest."

Despite the warmth generated by the crowd and the spotlights below, an eerie cold whispered across her skin and the muscles along her spine and belly clenched tight. She swiveled on the bench's hard, metal surface. There were no exits. No people milling around the rings or milling anywhere near the sides of the tent.

No escape.

Standing, she squeezed Priest's forearm. "We have to go back. You have to help me. I'm not ready."

"The Keeper thinks you are." He pried her hand free, stood and descended to her row with a feline grace loaded with confidence. Cupping her face with both hands, he leaned in close and declared, "I think you are, too."

He did? Because right now she felt about as prepared as a right-handed person faced with penning a thesis with only their left hand. "Well, you clearly have a much higher opinion of me than I do. I need more time. Preferably with a study course and a practice session."

"It doesn't work that way. You get one shot. One chance to face who you are and claim your birthright." Something behind her caught his attention and his fingers tightened, preventing her from turning. Whatever it was, though, brought the lightheartedness back to his face before he gazed gently down at her and said, "You wanted to know how the Keeper would come to you." Sliding his hands to her shoulders, he guided her around. "I think it's time you got your answer."

A woman.

A beautiful one, dressed in an acrobatic version of a woman's horse riding outfit with sleek black riding pants that shimmered in the light and a brilliantly fitted periwinkle coat that came to her thighs with black piping along the edges and lapel to match her pants and knee-high boots. Her hair was dark and glossy, arranged in one of those sleek styles worn by screen goddesses of the twenties. Atop her head was one of those old-fashioned silk top hats affixed at a jaunty angle and her makeup was that of a seasoned performer, the rich color of her eyeshadow accenting her coat and blended with deep liner to give her a sultry appearance.

Kateri spoke without conscious thought, the memory surging in tandem with her voice. "I remember you."

"Do you? From where?" Her voice was as divine as her appearance, warm with the compassion of a mother and yet resonating with a power too complex to describe.

"You were here." Dragging her gaze from the woman, Katy focused on the blonde woman galloping on a white horse around the left ring's perimeter. "You were down there. I talked my dad into waiting in line to meet the performers after the show."

He'd regretted agreeing later. Had called it bad judgment on his part to expose her agile mind to such a spoiled breeding ground.

Katy shook the ugly reminder free and let the Otherworld grow hazy, focusing instead on that day so long ago. On how lovingly the woman had looked down on her and the way her black horse had eagerly lowered its head for Katy to pet its muzzle. "I was ten. You smiled at me and told me I was beautiful. That my hair was the stuff of sunshine and stars."

"I don't believe that's all I told you."

The memory fell away and the real world—or whatever the Otherworld was—came back into focus. For the life of her, she couldn't remember the rest of their conversation that day. Only being moved by her dazzling smile. "Maybe not. But it was at least thirteen years ago. That's a long time to remember the details."

"Do you want to remember them?"

There it was again. The whispered foreboding cold against her skin. A crossroads reached with a simple question. The same deciding point she'd run across too many times to count in her life, but never once crossed.

Priest lightly squeezed her shoulder, a subtle prompt confirming the magnitude of the question at hand.

You get one shot. One chance to face who you are and claim your birthright.

Her whole life she'd turned back. Taken the known road over the unknown. But her brother hadn't. Neither had her grandmother. Or Priest. They'd all taken a chance and seemed not only happy with the outcome, but reveled in it.

She covered Priest's hand with her own, hanging on as though she might somehow siphon his strength with the desperate contact. "I want to remember."

A second later she was there, watching her ten-year-old self stare up in complete admiration at the woman.

"I want to be just like you," her younger self said, complete certainty coating every word. "I'll ride bareback and wear pretty costumes, too. Only I want my horse to be a gray one. Shiny gray with a black tail and mane."

The woman leaned down and tucked her hair behind her ear. "You can be whatever you want to be, sweet girl. Hug your dreams tight and let them take you wherever you want to go." She opened her arms to give Katy a hug, but her father jerked her away and ushered her through the crowd toward the exit.

Katy struggled to keep the woman in sight, but as small as she was the crowd prevented it, the press of bodies on all sides engulfing the beautiful woman in only seconds.

And then she was home. The late afternoon sun slanted across the tufted ivory comforter she was tucked under, her arm propped on a pillow beside her and covered in a cast. A low throb pulsed from her shoulders to her fingertips in time with her tired heartbeat, but her father seemed clueless to the pain. Or her fatigue.

He paced the length of her bed, her mother sitting silently beside her as if she too were too afraid to interject. "Are you out of your mind? You could have done much worse. Could have killed yourself."

"It was an accident, Daddy. I was just practicing. The lady said—"

"Not another word, Katy." Pinning her with an unmerciful stare, he stopped beside the bed. "That lady was a circus performer. A *circus performer*. Do you understand? It means she lives paycheck to paycheck. Means she'll never be able to plan more than a few weeks at best for her future. I expect better from you. Now you will let this stupid idea of yours go and move on." He spun and stalked out of the room, but not before uttering, "I wish I'd never taken you."

Over and over, the scenes kept coming. For each one, Priest and the dark-headed lady stood beside her, witnessing each head-to-head and consequent surrender of her dreams. Of her passion.

The day she'd had to witness her mom and dad fighting because her mother had caved and taken her to her first gymnastics class. And two years later when the coach had asked her to join the gymnastics team—only to have her father insist she focus on the science and mathematics group he'd signed her up for instead. Even the opening night to the high school musical when she'd scored the leading role and only Alek and her mother showed up.

Every memory she watched. A shadowed spectator

as the ugly truth she'd buried deep pushed its way free, spurred by a consuming, burgeoning fury.

She'd given up her dreams. Repeatedly. Altered herself for the sake of peace and conformity.

The landscape changed once more, shifting back to her room. The walls were no longer the cherry-blossom pink she'd begged for as a child, but a softer more acceptable version. A pale tea rose color that only whispered of the imaginings she'd left behind. She sat alone beside her desk, but her brother and father's heated argument drifting from the living room through her open door was enough to crowd the room.

She turned the pages on the well-worn hardback in her lap, the escalating shouts making her hand tremble as she fingered the title at the top of one page.

Tarzan of the Apes.

It wasn't the most fantastical story she'd ever read, but it had painted all kinds of beautiful images. The animals. The jungle. The wildness and the understated promise of romance. She'd lost count of the times she'd read it, picturing herself as Jane and learning the ways of the beasts Tarzan so easily interacted with.

Tucked inside one page was one of many travel brochures she'd saved over the years. Safaris. Cruises. Sites and experiences. She'd collected at least a dozen, each of them a reminder of where she wanted to go. Just a week ago she'd graduated from high school. Her enrollment at the University of Colorado was complete, but what she really wanted was to join two friends who'd invited her to work their way across Europe and Africa over the next year. One year to explore. To live and see all the things she'd read about. To put real life images to all the pictures she'd drawn in her mind.

Her father's voice cut through the room, nearly as clear as if he were beside her rather than down the hall. "Goddamn it, Alek! You can't just throw away two years of college. Your mother and I saved for that. The least you can do is finish what you started and be reasonable for once."

"You call it reasonable," Alek fired back. "I call it safe. And no offense, but criminal law is what *you* want for me. I want something else. Something that fits me."

It kept going. Back and forth like it always did.

She smiled down at the book, though it lacked the usual pride she felt for her brother. He never backed down. Always stood up for who he was and what he wanted.

She pulled the brochures free of the book, the tiny fragment of hope she'd anchored with each one slipping free as she did so. She closed the book and stared at her nightstand. For years, she'd kept it close. Tucked inside reaching distance.

This time she stood, padded to the bookcase and slid it next to the textbooks she'd kept on hand for reference. She skimmed her fingertip along the side. A sad goodbye that broke something inside her spectator-self.

"No." Her incorporeal self stepped forward and tried to stop her. "No. Put it back."

But her remembered self didn't respond. Only turned away, dropped the brochures in the small wastebasket beside her desk and paced down the long hallway.

"No!" Katy stormed after herself. "You don't want to do that. You wanted to go. You *should* go."

As she had in real life, the old Katy kept going, grabbed her purse and quietly slipped out the front door.

In the living room, the argument raged on, her father

now outlining every foolish decision and perceived irresponsible behavior Alek had ever taken.

"Stop it!" Katy yelled, all the rage and pain she'd stuffed while growing up breaking free with the force of a fearless gale. She stomped so she stood between them, and while neither of them acknowledged her presence the words poured forth in a torrent. "He doesn't *want* to do what you want. *I* don't want to. It's our life. Not yours. You had your chance and you didn't take it. You stole from us all because you were afraid and I *hate* you for it!"

Unrelenting, the words rushed out of her. Uncensored. Honest and full of all the pent-up anguish that had festered until it hardened and lodged in her gut like a merciless thorn. With it, tears streamed down her face. Her throat burned with the emotion clawing its way free.

How long it went on, she didn't know. Only knew that she needed to free every thought. Every burden until it was gone.

She welcomed it. Let even the memories she hadn't been shown bubble up and dissipate in the light of truth until there was nothing left.

Nothing but the comfort of Priest's arms around her. His solid chest beneath her cheek and his strong hands smoothing up and down her spine while she openly wept for the dreams she'd lost.

"Not lost, *mihara*." He palmed the back of her head and smoothed his temple against hers. "Just tucked away. A reference for you to build new ones. Whatever they might look like."

She sniffled and a hiccup rattled her torso, an ugly sound that matched what had clearly turned into the ugliest cry of the century. Not daring to lift her head for fear of how splotched her face likely was, or how red and swollen her eyes were, she dashed the back of her hand along her cheek to clear what tears she could. "You're in my head again."

"I like being in your head. It's a complex and beautiful landscape."

"One now free of the weeds that once choked its glory."

The Keeper.

She was still here. Waiting.

And now that Katy had paused in her crying jag long enough to assess her surroundings, she wasn't in her parents' living room anymore. The air was thick. Redolent of rich soil and flora with the sweet lure of some untouched habitat.

Cautiously, she lifted her head from Priest's chest.

The jungle.

Every bit of it unspoiled and painted in every variation of green possible. Beneath their feet, the soil was the color of dark chocolate and littered with fallen leaves, bark and vines.

Waiting patiently on a fallen tree with a trunk as big around as her first compact car, the Keeper watched her.

"You brought me here."

"It seems only fitting that a woman who faces her darkest truth be rewarded for the effort."

Dear God, she'd come unwound. Unleashed everything without the least regard for what came out. And not alone either. Priest and the Keeper had witnessed it all. "I loved my dad."

"I know you did," the Keeper said.

The silence stretched long and stoic between them. As if even the trees and brush waited to hear her pained confession. "But I hated him, too. Hated how he wouldn't let us be who we were."

Still, no one spoke.

Katy swallowed, what should have been a simple process complicated by the barbed knot in her throat. When she spoke, it came out as a whisper. "But I hated myself for giving him what he wanted even more."

With the arm Priest had kept around her shoulders, he hugged her tight, showing without a single word spoken how proud he was of her honesty.

"There is no peace in being who others want us to be," the Keeper said, "and no greater injustice to ourselves." She stood and ambled toward them, her circus clothing bizarrely out of place and yet somehow perfect considering the ride she'd taken Katy on. With the same motherly kindness she'd sensed that day when she was ten, the Keeper wiped what remained of Katy's tears away.

The gentle touch cleansed her. Left her feeling like she was ten years old again. A blank slate ready to draw whatever she wanted on it.

"Not a blank slate," the Keeper said. "Life has simply given you more colors to fill in the finer details. How you change the design is up to you." She looked to Priest. "Fate blessed you with a bright and compassionate mate. A worthy partner for a high priest. Are you prepared to teach her what she's gifted with today?"

Clearly more comfortable in the Keeper's presence than Katy was, Priest moved in squarely behind her and wrapped an unyielding arm around her waist. With his height and the form the Keeper had chosen, he easily towered over them both. "I would give her anything. Everything she needs."

"I don't doubt that." The Keeper cocked her head,

considering. "Though, you should have a care your vow doesn't make you take a step too far one day."

Before Katy or Priest could question what she meant, the Keeper crowded closer to Katy and cupped her face with both hands. Her voice whispered through Katy full of untold mysteries and fathomless power. "Will you accept the gifts I'm willing to give you?"

She'd thought when this moment came, she'd falter. That stepping into the unusual world she would have once said couldn't possibly exist would take more courage. But after all she'd seen—all she'd felt and set free—it was easy. As if by letting the past go, she'd made room for belief, the spark of hope dusted off and bright again. "Yes."

"Then remember this," the Keeper said. "Those open to their emotions—flexible in their approach to life—are the strongest. Use the tools you're given and let life flow through you."

The Keeper leaned in, her mouth on track for Katy's.

Priest's arm tightened around her, holding her steady for what was most assuredly going to be a kiss.

The contact registered for all of a second, the plush wonder of her glossy lips there and gone faster than she could draw breath. Replaced with a riptide of color and sensation. She didn't have a body. Only had a pulse. A heartbeat alive with every shade of purple and shimmering with the delicate wink of moonlight on a softly undulating lake. It swirled and coalesced all at once, tossing her back to the surface of reality...or the Otherworld.

Her eyes snapped open and she gasped, air surging into her lungs as though she'd been underwater for hours. In front of her, the jungle stretched lush and quiet in all directions. Behind her, Priest held steady and firm.

But the Keeper was gone.

"What just happened?"

Checking every tree, every shrub and the fallen log where she'd seen her guide before, Kateri waited for Priest to answer. Only after several seconds did he answer, a quiet awe marking his rumbling voice. "What just happened...the rush and the color...that was your magic."

Fisting and stretching her fingers over and over, she slipped from Priest's strong hold and paced forward, turning her hands this way and that as if she might find some explanation for the soft-spun hum that danced beneath her skin. "It feels amazing. Like a night of twelve-hours uninterrupted sleep and a triple shot of B12."

She turned, bounced a little on her toes to see if her body was as buoyant as it felt and grinned up at Priest. "I know I don't have anywhere near the skills Alek does, but do you think you could at least teach me to give him a run for his money? I mean, I'd never do anything to make him look bad in front of the other warriors, but let's face it. Every little sister wants to get a whack in on her big brother every now and then."

One corner of Priest's mouth quirked to a wry smirk. "Oh, I think you'll be able to get a few in on him now, no problem."

Stilling at the mysterious undercurrent to his words, she studied him. Rather than looking directly at her, his focus seemed to drift from the top of her head to her shoulders. As if he were outlining her body with his gaze. "What? You think he'll be afraid to hurt me?"

He chuckled at that, finally meeting her stare head-on. "He won't hurt you, kitten. He doesn't stand a chance against you."

"But he's a primo. I thought the only one who could outfight him was you."

"Me," he said stalking forward, "or a sorcerer with your strength."

She froze. Iced to her very core despite the jungle's humid warmth and trembling beneath an onslaught of fear. "My family is warrior house."

"Your family is *predominately* warrior house. But your grandmother is a seer, and now they have a sorcerer. A powerful one given the depth of your aura."

She swallowed hard and forced her fear to the surface, her voice little more than a rasp. "Draven is a sorcerer."

"And the only one I've ever known who's embraced the darkness." As his words trailed off, he reached her, firmly cupped one shoulder and angled her face to his with the other. "You are light, Kateri. Caring. Thoughtful. Smart. Nothing like my brother was before or after he twisted his gifts. To receive the magic you've been given is not only an honor, but a testament to the Keeper's belief in you. Take it as the blessing and compliment it was intended to be."

A blessing? Based on what Jade and Tate had shared with her, sorcerers were the most revered and most powerful house of their clan. "But you saw me. Saw how angry I was. What if I let it… I can't be the person who abuses their gifts like he did."

"And that's exactly why you won't. You've faced your past. You've owned it. And now you're in a position to help us right the havoc my brother created."

A growl sounded behind her, the depth of it more of a greeting or polite interruption than anything ominous.

Katy dug her fingers into Priest's forearms, but Priest merely shifted his gaze to the space directly behind her, a flicker of annoyance shifting across his face before his mouth curved in a delighted smile.

Okay, so not a bad development. Which was good, because as out-of-body experiences and unexpected gifts went, she'd had more than enough. Slowly, she pivoted toward the sound, careful to keep her body close to Priest's.

Not twenty feet away, a lioness slowly padded their direction, her coat nearly matching the wheat-colored tones of her own hair and her eyes eerily close to the blue-gray Katy and Naomi shared. And she was huge. Not quite as big as Priest's panther, but enough the two of them could easily walk side by side.

"Oh my God," she whispered. "Is that what I think it is?"

"I guess calling you kitten was more apt than I thought." Priest chuckled, settled his hands on her shoulders and pressed a soft kiss to her temple. "Kateri Falsen, say hello to your companion."

Chapter Twenty-Three

Not one visible difference. Not in her face or her body.
Yet no matter how long Katy stared at her reflection in
the mirror, she couldn't reconcile the woman staring
back at her with the person she'd seen every other day
of her life. As if the last twenty-four hours of her life
had altered so much beneath the surface and offloaded
so much internal junk, she was actually seeing herself
for the first time. The *real* Katy. Not the flaws. Not the
limitations, but the true woman along with all her hopes
and dreams.

She braced her trembling hands on the vanity's mar-
ble surface and leaned closer, studying the outline of
her head and shoulders for the aura Priest assured her
was there.

"You won't see it." Priest moved into the reflection behind her, set a glass of water on the counter and
cupped her shoulders. Like hers, his dark hair was still
slightly damp from the shower they'd shared after waking up. Rather than mill about bare-chested as was his
norm at home, he'd donned a tight T-shirt along with his
track pants. "Mirrors do a good job with objects. Not
so much with magic." He kissed the top of her head and
smiled. "But it's beautiful."

If it was anything close to the luminescent silver surrounding Priest, she believed it, but she still wanted to see it for herself. "It's purple?"

"Purple doesn't do it justice. It's deep. Thick but soft like the color just before the sun surrenders to the night."

And dark meant powerful.

Which, in her case, was kind of like handing a lit blowtorch to a two-year-old. She straightened and pumped her fists as she had repeatedly since waking in Priest's arms. No matter how many times she did it, the pulsing vibrancy beneath her skin persisted. As if the only thing she'd ingested for the last twenty-four hours was enough double-fudge chocolate cake to feed a classroom full of six-year-olds and a case of energy drink.

Priest chuckled, covered one of her hands with his own, and gently squeezed. "You need to get out of this room and move. Your cat wants out and is going to pester you until you let her, but until you burn off some of the jitters that will never happen."

Translation—no more hiding from her family. Although, she'd studied the drop from Priest's balcony a few times and considered if she could make the leap in human form and bypass their reactions and consequent questions altogether. At least for a little while longer. "Did you tell them?"

He turned her, cupped the side of her face in a strong grip and forced her face to his. "You're a sorcerer, Kateri. Not an abomination. Not something to be feared. Certainly, not by your family."

Right.

Not a curse, but a blessing. A really freaking strong one without an instruction manual or warning labels attached.

"But no," he said matter-of-factly. "I didn't tell them. Not them or the other fifty or sixty people who caught wind my mate had her soul quest and are camped out in the backyard waiting to see you."

She jerked herself free of his hold and stormed to the sliding glass door that led out to the balcony. "They're here? And why in the backyard?"

"Yes, here," he said following behind her at a much slower pace and a boatload of humor in his voice. "It's a big deal when a primo's sister has her soul quest. A bigger deal when it's the high priest's mate. And they're in the backyard because I threatened Alek and Tate with their nuts if they let anyone in the house before I was back from the Otherworld." He shrugged and grinned. "By the time that happened, the crowd was big enough that outside made more sense room-wise and it turned into a party."

She gave up peeking through the curtains and rose on her tiptoes for a better look, but between the depth of his balcony and the height his room had on the gorge below, the best she could catch were a few straggling men talking in the distance. Both had beers in hand and were apparently settled in for the long haul. "I can't do this."

"Sure, you can." Priest pried the heavy chocolate curtain from her hand and it fell back into place, blocking out the soft evening light. "There's not a soul out there who doesn't know what you've just gone through. They understand you need to take the edge off and give your companion time in this world. None of them will stop you or expect more than a brief appearance."

He frowned as if a thought had just occurred to him. "What?"

His lips quirked as though he couldn't decide if he

wanted to smile or grimace. "Okay, *one* person expects more. Naomi cornered me when I went for your water and made me swear I'd talk you into showing her your companion after you shift."

"Did you tell her about my cat?"

That time he did smile, a huge one full of beautiful white teeth and a ton of pride. "Not gonna ruin that surprise, kitten." He eased in close and pulled her flush against him, his voice dropping to an easy rumble. "She's perfect for you."

"You're not going to comment on claws again are you? Because I'm pretty sure the ones I've got now will do more damage than the curious ones you're used to."

He chuckled at that and nuzzled his nose alongside hers. "No. I meant it. A lioness is a fierce hunter, but her real skill is taking care of the pack. Nurturing and providing for the people she calls her own."

A pleasant flutter whispered beneath her sternum, and she'd swear a contented purr rolled through her head. "Holy crap." She stilled and focused on the broad expanse of Priest's chest, listening for the sound again. "I think…" Surely not. But Priest had said their companions heard and felt what they did. And Alek had said he'd heard his wolf. She refocused on Priest. "I think I heard her."

"All the more reason to get you moving. She deserves a reward and there's no better one than letting her run in our world."

She wanted that. Wanted to experience the world through her companion's eyes and feel the unique connection she'd experienced when her lion had merged with her spirit. Enough, it was worth facing her whole clan if that's what it took.

She sucked in a deep breath and nodded her head. "Okay, let's do it."

Five minutes later, she neared the foot of the stairs, Priest's fingers laced tightly with hers as he led her forward. Inside, the house was strangely quiet, but beyond the open sliding glass door the happy chatter and laughter of those who'd gathered billowed up from the open expanse below.

Priest slid the screen door aside. "Breathe, *mihara*. All you have to do is walk outside and let them see you're safe and happy. Then we'll go for a nice long run to even you out."

God, yes. A run sounded perfect. And if the vibration beneath her sternum was any indication, her cat thought so, too.

The swish of the screen door opening almost instantly quieted the voices below, and Priest squeezed her hand encouragingly.

Step by step, the crowd came into view below, every eye trained on her. For a second, she thought about running. Ducking back inside or at least out the front door and going for a run solo.

But then the rainbow of auras around those who waited stole her attention. Reds for the warriors, gold for the seers and green for the healers. "I'm the only one." Not one spec of purple emanated from the crowd. Priest had said he knew of no living sorcerers, but until that second, it hadn't really clicked. Didn't fully register how very important her gift could be for their clan. And if she could see their auras, then they could most assuredly see hers.

"Like I said. A blessing, not a curse." He steered her down the wooden staircase to the waiting crowd below.

Not surprising, Naomi beat her to the foot of the stairs, though along the way she nearly knocked down two men and one unsuspecting woman. "Look at you!" Before Katy could offer a response, Nanna wrapped her up in a fierce embrace and rocked her back and forth. "I knew you'd accept your gifts. And a sorcerer, too!"

"She's gonna be a dead sorcerer if you don't ease that choke hold, Nanna." Planting a firm hand on Naomi's shoulder, Alek somehow managed to pry her away and pulled Katy in for his own hug. Unlike her grandmother's happy and unapologetically bold voice, Alek's was low and only for her. "Leave it to you to find a way to one-up your brother being primo."

Typical Alek. Always leveraging his humor to unwind the tension. And neither Nanna or Alek seemed afraid of her. Weren't worried or even remotely hesitant about her house or the strength of her untried gifts. Even as she made her way through the crowd, accepting hugs, a few wildflowers from some of the children and well-wishes all around, not once did anyone look on her with anything other than happiness.

Through it all, Priest stayed silent, yet supportive by her side. When someone made attempts to draw him into the conversation, he subtly redirected, ensuring the focus stayed on her and her happy moment. The only exception was when they neared the silver-haired man waiting at the edge of the crowd. A warrior she'd seen Alek spend considerable time with since he'd earned his place as primo, but couldn't for the life of her remember his name.

Priest wrapped one arm around Katy and held out his hand to the warrior. "Garrett."

Now she remembered. He'd been one of the first to

relocate to the area after learning Priest had settled there as a show of support. One of the last living warriors from her grandmother's generation.

Shaking the hand offered, Garrett slapped Priest on the shoulder and grinned in a way that spoke of experience only two men would understand. "Not sure which one of you deserves a pat on the back more. You for finally cornering your mate, or your mate for making such an impression on the Keeper."

He turned his shrewd eyes on Katy and the warmth in their pale green depths thawed what was left of her worries. He'd been there the night Draven had worked his dark magic. Had seen firsthand the devastation a sorcerer gone rogue could wreak. And yet there was not only genuine happiness for her in his expression, but hope as well. "It's good to see another one of our clan find their way back into the fold. Even better to see our sorcerer house getting some life in it."

"I'm not sure how comfortable I am being the first one to wade back in, but Priest says he'll help me figure it out."

"We'll all help you," Garrett said. "That's what clan does. All you have to do is ask."

"Speaking of asking…" Priest jerked his head at the milling crowd behind them that showed no signs of breaking up anytime soon. "You mind hanging around and helping out if Alek or Naomi need it?"

Garrett grinned and shook his head. "You're kidding, right? Either one of them could lead a whole damned battalion and not bat an eye. But yeah, I'll hang." He winked at Katy. "Besides, I heard rumor there might be some new mystery animal making rounds in the woods soon. Wouldn't want to miss out on the big reveal."

God, her grandmother was going to be the death of her. Barely an hour and a half back from the Otherworld and she was already building an audience for her first time out in animal form. Given enough time, she'd probably turn the whole thing into a parade. No pressure or anything.

"Yeah, well, let's cross one bridge at a time," Katy said. "I've got to figure out how things work first. Then we'll see about taking my new-and-improved half out for a spin."

"You'll figure it out," Garrett said with the confidence of a man who'd seen more than his share of celebrations. "Go. Have fun. We'll make sure everyone gives you a wide berth."

Before he could amble away, Katy blurted, "A wide berth for what?"

He stopped, shot a knowing smirk at Priest, then turned back for the crowd, his voice loaded with amusement when it floated back to them. "I think I'll leave that one for your mate to answer."

Chapter Twenty-Four

This was what peace felt like. Surrounded by good people, their laughter sparking through the open air like the flames on the torches around them, and his mate happily exploring her newfound companion among his people.

Priest had had glimpses of this kind of contentment in the last fifty years. Simple experiences with Jade and Tate growing up, or when he lingered in his panther form, but they were just snippets compared to tonight. Nowhere near the quiet stillness that rested behind his sternum right now.

Beside him, Garrett popped the top on his cooler, pilfered a fresh longneck from the slowly melting ice and resumed his lazy sprawl against the thick tree trunk where the two of them had taken to watching Kateri interact with the clan. "She shifted easy, I take it?"

"One of the fastest I've ever seen. But then she watched Alek's first shift, so it could just be she had a leg up."

Garrett nodded, but kept his gaze on Kateri in lion form, stretched out on her belly between two ten-year-old little girls who'd made it their personal mission to pet her into a trance. "Could be?"

As if Garrett had to ask what the other cause might

be. He'd seen his share of alpha companions over the many years he'd been alive and knew the challenge they presented. Nothing was more important than establishing human control over the animal in those first shifts, and as ready as Kateri's had been to enter this world, there was a high probability Kateri's lion would give her a run for her money. "All right, so odds are good her cat's an alpha."

"Yeah, the Keeper's not gonna give a beta to a sorcerer with Kateri's power." Garrett chuckled and tossed his bottle cap into the bag where he'd stowed his empties. "Gotta say, I'm a little bummed I can't be a fly on the wall when it's time for her to shift back."

Meaning Priest would likely have to use his powers as high priest to force her transition—an act that would no doubt piss off both females. He hadn't liked it when the outgoing high priest had forced it on him and he'd actually known what was happening.

Still, if it came to him forcing things, he was counting on the aftereffects of her first shift to help cushion the blow. Honest to God, until he'd seen how fast Kateri had welcomed her cat, he'd looked forward to her transition back to her human self and the very carnal rush that came with it. Now, it would be a crapshoot if she took her frustration out in physical form, or just tried to unman him with her bare hands.

"Speaking of, I've gotta get things moving." Priest stood, finished off his own beer and added the empty bottle to Garrett's nearly full bag. "Wish me luck."

"No need for that. The Keeper wouldn't have given her to you if you couldn't handle it." He grinned and raised his bottle in salute. "I'll mourn for you, though, if you end up back on the couch tonight."

Right. More like his love life would retain its place at the top of everyone's gossip sheet. One thing about a growing clan—everyone knew everyone else's business. A fact he'd hate if it wasn't so damned nice to see everyone coming together again.

He wandered across the clearing, pausing here and there to offer thanks to those who'd brought food and helped.

On either side of Kateri, the two little girls animatedly exchanged the pros and cons of Ever After High dolls versus Littlest Pet Shop figurines. Personally, he didn't have a clue what either reference meant, but every now and then they'd aim questions toward Kateri and wait as if she might chime in with an opinion as well.

While she might not have given the appearance to knowing where he was as he made his way toward her, Kateri lifted her head and blinked sleepy eyes as soon as he drew within ten feet. He crouched in front of her and the two little girls and balanced his forearms on his knees. "Time to go, *mihara*."

With somewhere between a grumble and a groan, Kateri yawned then rested her chin on her big paws.

The dark-headed girl giggled and scratched Kateri behind one ear as though she could absolutely sympathize. The blonde, however, took it upon herself to champion Kateri with a more direct approach. "She's happy with us."

Priest couldn't help it. He'd given Kateri space and watched while everyone fawned over her for the last half hour, but now it was his turn to pet and play with his mate. He smoothed his thumb along the sweet spot his panther loved just above and between Kateri's eyes. "I see that. But her companion's had enough time. I want my mate back."

Kateri's eyes drifted open and this time it was more of an irritated growl that rumbled up the back of her throat.

"See?" the dark-haired girl said. "Now you've made her all cranky."

Oh, he hadn't even begun to make her cranky. That part would come later. Especially once he pushed the envelope and finagled her into using her magic for the first time.

Fortunately, before he was forced to come up with some reasoning that might make sense to little girls, Naomi's unflinching voice sounded behind him. "Shara. Annie. You two come help me and your mothers hand out dessert. Kateri's had a long day and needs to shift back so she can rest."

Both did as she asked, but not before giving Kateri warm goodbyes and aiming a few displeased frowns at Priest.

Apparently, Kateri was disgruntled, too, because her tail swished hard enough to send a handful of fallen leaves sideways.

He couldn't blame her. With an animal's form came an emotional respite unlike anything available to humans. A temporary pause button that allowed a person's spirit to just *be* and find balance. Given all she'd been through since finding her parents murdered, the mental quiet was undoubtedly a potent drug. "You're cute, kitten, but you forget I've been doing this awhile. I know it feels good, but you're setting a bad precedent for your cat."

She opened her mouth and let out an angry huff. Not quite a hiss, but close enough his panther bristled.

Seriously cute. So much so, his chuckle slipped out before he could check it. "Keep acting like that and I'll let my panther out. I guarantee he'd give your kitten's sass a run for her money."

Pairing an indelicate snort with another snap of her tail, she pushed to her feet and padded toward the clearing, her chin lifted with the same universal defiance of pissed off females everywhere.

Oh, yeah. Totally cute. And chock full of attitude, to boot.

Still, she paused once out of the sight of their visitors and waited for him to lead the way through the woods. He leveraged his warrior strength and speed and took the most challenging route possible in human form. By the time they reached their private cove, both of them were breathing hard. A good thing considering he'd need her energy as low as possible if he had to force her transition. Not many things were tougher in the world than a man going head-to-head with a pissed off lioness.

He stripped his T-shirt off, tossed it to a nearby boulder and paced toward her. "All right. Just like last time. Focus on the connection between the two of you. It's as simple as trading places. Show her your intent and assure her you'll call on her again."

As tired as she was from the run, the best she managed was a huff, but it was still a refusal.

Priest crouched in front of her and gentled his voice. "You can't hide anymore, *mihara*. I know your cat feels safe. And she'll be there for you whenever you need her, but now it's time for you to come back to me."

She looked away and sighed.

Fuck, but he wanted her to do this on her own. She'd already had too much forced on her too fast. Death. Her whole world turned on its head and a fated mate on top of it. Taking yet another thing from her control rubbed his sense of justice the wrong way.

"Do this for me, Kateri. Look me in the eye. I'm waiting for you." He cupped her nape and rubbed his fingers through her thick pelt. The touch was comforting now, but if she kept refusing he'd have no choice but to hold her scruff and keep her in place for his magic. "Come back to me and let me show you how proud I am to have you as my mate."

He waited, every second stretching with a weighted tension that made him itch to pace. He was just about to firm his grip and draw the Keeper's influence to him when Kateri swiveled her massive head and met his gaze.

There she was. Shining from the depths of the lion's eyes was his mate's intelligence. Fear was there, too. Mingled with confusion and what looked like a plea.

"You can do this." Taking his chances with the lion's prickly attitude, he rubbed his temple against hers and murmured low, "I need you, Kateri. We all do."

He felt it before he saw it—the crackling energy beneath the lion's skin and the supercharged shift in the air around them. A second later, a soft lavender glow rippled to life. A pulsing vibration that deepened in color bit by bit.

"That's it." He backed away enough to meet her eyes. "Feel it. Take control and push through. Come to me."

Deep purple flashed against the darkness followed by a muted clap of significant, yet untamed power.

And then she was standing in front of him, gloriously naked with nothing but the moon above to paint her flawless skin. She shivered and wrapped her arms around her torso. "Wh-wh-where are my cl-clothes?"

Conveniently missing in action.

Though that probably wasn't the smartest answer to go with. Not after what it had taken for her to push through her cat's stubborn will. He stood and snatched his shirt from the boulder. "Remembering your clothes on the return trip takes some time."

"You mean they're gone?"

Tempting as it was to use his own body heat to warm her, he guided his T over her head. Besides, in another minute or so, the backlash would hit and she'd have all the heat she needed. "I have no idea where they go. I have a secret suspicion the Keeper has the mother of all lost and founds from first-time shifters."

Surprisingly, she let him guide her hands into each armhole and simply stared up at him with a mix of wonder and delight. "That's why you wore a shirt today."

He pulled the hem down, the size of it reaching half-way down her thighs, and cupped the side of her face. "I've never seen a shifter come back in anything more than their skin the first time. There's no way I'd risk you walking home without something to cover you."

Her gaze roved his face for all of two seconds, searching for what, he couldn't guess.

And then she kissed him.

No finesse. No prelude or coy looks. Just the full-on, eager kiss of a woman at the height of a sexual surge.

He wanted to go with it. To take full advantage and finish the fantasy they'd started in her dreams that first night. To take her from behind and tease and prime her body until she screamed her release to the star-studded heavens.

But he couldn't. Not yet. Yes, she was his mate and she needed release, but she needed her high priest more.

To face her gifts and experience the wonder of their magic before her fears could wrangle more reasons to avoid her destiny.

Dragging his lips from hers, he gripped her forearms and unwound them from around his neck. "Easy, kitten. I know what you want and I'll give it to you."

She fought him and tried to regain what little distance he'd created. "Don't tease me. Not right now."

"No teasing." He turned her around and banded his arms around her waist, keeping her back tight against his front. "Just postponing until we can cover one last thing."

She wiggled her pert ass against his dick, every bit a cat in heat—right up until the word *postpone* finally registered. She tried to break free enough to turn, but he held her in place. "I've covered enough today. I shifted back. For you."

Damn, but that stung. He'd earned it, though, and would likely earn even more before he gave her what she craved. "You did, and it was beautiful. But this will be, too. Just trust me."

Groaning, she dropped her head against his shoulder and writhed as if the contact might somehow ease her ache. "Priest, you don't understand. I *need* you. *Please.*"

Oh, he understood. The first shift back to human form always came with a nearly overriding heat, and not taking what she offered was tantamount to a starving man refusing a full buffet.

Holding her wrists firm at her waist, he pressed his aching cock against her ass. "I need you, too. Your scent is everywhere. Rich and thick." He nuzzled the back of her neck, man, beast and darkness all clamoring for more. "I want to taste it. Lick and toy with you until you come on my tongue, then bury my cock inside your tight cunt."

"Yes." Desperate for relief, she tried to slip her hands between her thighs. "Let's do that first. Then I'll try."

"No, *mihara*. You try first and then I'll give you what you need."

"I can't."

"You can. Just focus your thoughts." Big words from a man who could barely think straight, especially with her sweet musk growing stronger by the second. "You want me to let you go? Then make me. Reach for your magic. Force it to happen."

A low, guttural moan ripped up the back of her throat. She arched, pressing her pebbled nipples tight against the thin cotton that covered them. Her eyes were screwed shut and what looked like pain marked every feature on her face.

"Do it, Kateri. The magic is there. Use it. Free yourself. Make it happen."

The sound that came from her mouth was somewhere between a plea and a shout, but an awesome surge of magic fired bold and bright, the power behind it so intense he nearly lost his grip from sheer surprise alone.

"That's it. Feel it. Use it. Now."

Her magic coalesced in one unstoppable shove and sent him hurling through the air. He slammed against an old oak at the cove's edge before he could cushion the blow with his own powers. A second later he was facedown on the ground and aching from head to toe.

"Oh, my God." Kateri crouched beside him and her trembling fingers stroked his back. "I didn't mean to do that. I mean… I did, but I didn't mean to hurt you."

Funny. She'd just rattled him more thoroughly than

anyone in the last fifty years and all he could think about was her scent. How his cock was still hard and willing to service her any and every way she wanted. For as long as she wanted.

"I'm not doing that again," she whispered.

"Oh, yes you are." He pushed to his knees and snatched her wrist. "In fact, now that you know how things work, I think some rough play is in order."

"No."

"Yes." He tugged her off balance, caught her torso and rolled her to the ground, his hips cradled between her soft thighs. "Again. Now. Don't overthink it."

"I hurt you."

He ground his pelvis against hers. "Does it feel like I'm hurt?"

She hissed and dug her nails into his shoulders, her words coming between heavy pants. "But it's dangerous."

"No, it's not." He pinned her hands to the ground and nipped her lower lip. "Trust me, kitten. You caught me off guard once. It won't happen again and I can take everything you can dish out."

She whimpered, but her face was flush, the need to fight or fuck escalating near the breaking point.

He skimmed his lips along the delicate place where her neck and shoulders met. "Play with me, Kateri. Let it out. Own who you are." With that, he gave his panther what it wanted and bit the sensitive flesh beneath his lips.

Her shout was part human, part lion, but the purple force that jolted against him was pure sorcerer. One pushed and prodded to the edge of her control.

His body flew upward, but this time he was ready, counterbalancing the thrust with a flip that left him poised on the balls of his feet and ready to engage. "Again."

Seamlessly, she surged upright, the force of her magic so strong she nearly lost her balance. Rather than hesitate, she threw a strike that would have knocked him out had he not dodged at the last second, a pulsing stream of power that singed the air as it streamed past him and blasted a hole in a wide tree trunk not three feet behind him. "There it is."

Her voice was as soft and fragile as the smoke wafting around the point of impact. "Oh, my God."

"Impressive, isn't it?" He stalked toward her, taking full advantage of her dumbstruck wonder and the temporary sexual reprieve her release of power had created to move in close.

Despite the predator prowling toward her, her gaze never wavered from the damage she'd created. "I can't believe I did that."

"I can." With a speed he'd never used with her before, he wrapped her up and tumbled her to the ground, catching the back of her head just before it made contact. "And I do believe it's time I gave you that reward."

Chapter Twenty-Five

Two feet. That was all that kept Katy from completing Priest's latest challenge of piling ten moderate-sized rocks into one tidy mound. With her hands, it would have taken seconds.

Not so with magic.

For the last hour she'd painstakingly lifted, guided and carefully stacked each stone—a task she'd quickly learned was on par with lighting a candle with a blowtorch. When Priest had first given her the challenge five days ago, she'd laughed in his face. After all, she'd lasered a hole through a two-foot-thick tree trunk with barely a thought. Then she'd tried doing as he asked and realized the hardest part of being a sorcerer wasn't calling the power, but *controlling* it.

A single bead of sweat trickled down her spine and sent shivers rippling along her skin.

The rock hovering midair shook as though her physical response had manifested through her magic.

"No," she whispered, and the rock stilled.

Sprawled behind her in the Adirondack chair he'd easily levitated from the balcony to the ground in way of demonstration, Priest chuckled. "You know that was more about your mental thoughts than words actually saving your ass, right?"

Ignore him. Just focus on the freaking rock.

She slowly exhaled through her mouth and carefully guided the stone toward the others. No way was she blowing it when she was this close.

Two inches from the top of the pile, she opened her mental fingers—and the rock shot across the clearing. "Ugh!" She spun to Priest and stopped just short of stomping her foot. "You did that on purpose."

To his credit, he at least tried to cover his grin by rubbing his fingers across his lips, but he kept his gray gaze locked to hers. "It's my job to teach you, kitten. The real world won't stay silent."

"No, but you could at least let me finish *once*."

He stood and stalked toward her. "You're right."

The admission alone was enough to leave her speechless. Paired with his bare torso on prime display and the way his pants accented the V at his hips all thoughts save getting him alone and feeling all of him next to her scattered. Which was utterly insane given how intimate they'd been since their first night together. But soft and sweet, or hard and fast, she couldn't get enough of him. Her power and how it felt to run and experience the world in lion form was addictive. But being with Priest? It was *everything*. And as much as it terrified her, she'd begun to understand what her grandmother meant by a mate being an extension of oneself. Except instead of going with the need to give in, she was fighting it. As if she desperately needed to run, but refused to use her legs. Or was parched for a drink of water, but turned her mouth away from the fountain.

"I'm pushing you harder than I would anyone else,

but it's because I see the potential in you." He pulled her to him and cupped the side of her face. "You shifted in no time. Your power is massive, and your companion is nearly as dominant as my panther. You may not be a primo, but you will lead this clan beside me."

Her magic prickled beneath her skin. A featherlight tickle that whispered of something more left unspoken. "That's not the only reason you're pushing me, is it?"

For the barest moment, fear flickered in his eyes. He banked it nearly as fast, but the vulnerability rocked her. "Until you let me mark you, Draven could track you. If you won't let me do that much, then I want you to be able to hold your own against him."

A flutter winged beneath her sternum and goose bumps lifted across her skin despite the warm noonday sun overhead. Since the day after her soul quest he'd been after her to let him work his magic into her skin. Part of her wanted it. Badly. But that last shred of independence saw it as the final link. A final step toward accepting their bond.

She smoothed her hands up his chest. "It's not that I don't want to. I just—"

"I need you safe, Kateri. Of all the people my brother could use against me, you're the ultimate weapon. You have no idea how far I'd go to keep you safe. The depths the darkness inside me would sink to. Nothing would stop me. Nothing and no one."

Heavy footsteps on the wood balcony above broke the tense moment. "Priest." Alek poked his head over the ledge, hands gripping the rail tight and an urgency on his face Katy hadn't seen since the day they'd found their parents murdered. "You need to come up here."

Despite his calm exterior, Priest's arms tightened around her. "What's wrong?"

"My friend from college just called."

"David," Katy said, prying herself from Priest's hold. "He said he'd call when he found something."

Inside the house, Tate and Jade were ambling down the staircase just as Priest and Katy came through the backdoor. Garrett, who'd become a nearly daily visitor since Katy's soul quest, stood with his back against the far wall with his arms crossed. As it had been on several occasions the last few days, his position in the room was directly behind Naomi, who was seated in Priest's oversized club chair. More than once, Katy had considered asking Priest if he'd noted how much time the two of them were spending together, but somehow sex or practicing her new gifts always ended up a conversational distraction.

"What's up?" Jade sprawled on the couch and Tate leaned one hip on the arm beside her.

Alek waited until Katy sat at the other end of the couch and Priest mirrored Garrett's protective stance behind her. "So, you know Katy called David and shared the lead the seers found about Butte La Rose."

"Please say he found someone," Katy said.

He glanced at Priest first, then met Katy's stare. "He found a lead, yeah. A family by the last name of Ralston that ties with some of the historical information we gave him from the old primo families."

"The old healer primo family went by Rallion," Garrett said.

Katy felt more than saw Priest move in closer behind her. "Close to their old name, but still different enough to hide."

"Exactly," Alek said. "And honestly, we're lucky, because the only offspring born to the last generation was a woman. Records show she had a kid twenty-three years ago. A daughter named Elise, but the parents don't appear to have gotten married. Both the mother's parents are deceased."

Twisting to face Priest, Katy found him scowling at Alek. "So, we go talk to her. Introduce ourselves and see if she knows anything about us."

"What else did your friend turn up?" Priest said without breaking eye contact with Alek.

One simple question. But with it the energy in the room shifted. A heightened awareness or alertness that stirred her magic.

Still standing in the center of the room, Alek held Priest's stare, the intensity that moved between them thick with unspoken danger and dread. "David went to our house to pick up the mail today." His gaze slid to Katy. "Our place is trashed."

"Draven," Jade murmured.

Naomi nodded her head. "He's looking for something to track you with. Something personal."

"Well, he can't find Alek even if wanted to," Tate said. "Not with Priest's marks."

"No, but he can find Kateri." As if he needed the contact to ground him, Priest clamped a firm hand on her shoulder. "When was the last time your friend was there?"

"Sunday," Alek said.

Ever the pragmatic one, Garrett threw the obvious right out in the open. "Four days to track her."

The magic inside Katy prickled. Or maybe it was the bond she'd sensed building between her and Priest.

Whatever it was, it strained toward Priest with a magnetic pull she couldn't have ignored even if she'd wanted to. She stood and turned to him, smoothing her hands up along his bunched biceps and tension-riddled shoulders. "He can't get me here. I'm safe."

"I hate to point it out," Jade said, "but Draven's not the only one with tracking skills anymore. Katy can just as easily use Draven's charm to find him as he can use something personal to track her. Let's just see where he's at and deal with it."

"No."

The resounding response came from Garrett, Naomi and Priest simultaneously, but it was Priest who followed up on it. "She's too new. Too susceptible to his tricks."

"Then teach me." Katy squeezed his shoulders. "I can learn. I'll work harder."

A sadness that pierced her deeper than any physical wound could ever reach moved across his face. "You're *good*, Kateri. My light. The Keeper knew that. It's why she trusted you with so much magic. The last thing I want is to teach you anything remotely close to what stole my brother's soul."

"Sorcerers are bound to the law of ultimate good." Garrett's voice was low and respectful, but loaded with the wisdom of years and experience. A man who'd seen firsthand what happened to sorcerers who crossed forbidden lines. "Any act taken not in the best interest of life or the universe—with a genuine heart—draws the person closer to darkness."

"Even if you tried," Naomi added, "there's a strong possibility Draven bespelled the charm. It's why I never dared touch it. Without direct contact, you can't track him."

"Fine." She focused on Priest. "Then we stick with our plan and go visit Elise. If Draven's this determined, she's at risk, too. She deserves to know what's going on. Especially, if she's like Alek and me and doesn't know anything about our race."

"She hasn't had her soul quest," Priest said. "I'd know if she had. That means Draven can't find her as easy as he can find you. Do you actually think I'd let you leave protected ground knowing he can find you anywhere?"

And there it was again. The mark. The single act her instincts insisted would solidify their bond. That would make them one cohesive unit instead of two independently beating hearts.

And what's wrong with that?

The thought was whisper soft, but resonated with the impact of a sledgehammer to the gut. For the last five days, she'd felt more balanced than at any other time in her life. Complete and supported in a way that surpassed anything she'd imagined possible.

The only thing missing was acceptance.

He's part of you.

Naomi's words. Guidance from a woman who'd experienced what it was like to have a destined mate. Who truly understood the connection. And of all the people in her life, Alek and Naomi were the two who'd always seen *her*. Who'd always taken time to ask her what *she* wanted.

I want my mate.

"Then mark me," she blurted on a rush of adrenaline. "He can't find me if you mark me."

He lowered his voice. "Kateri, I'd never offer my magic as anything more than a gift. If you take my mark, I want it to be because you want it. Not because my brother forced it."

So much pain in his voice. An uncertainty she'd never felt in him before.

She'd put that there. All because she feared what her instincts had told her from day one. He was hers. She'd felt it in one touch. Known it on the most fundamental level of her being with one look.

She smoothed her hand above his heart, her fingers tangling in the black leather that held his charms. "I'm not asking because of Draven. I'm asking because I want you." Her magic pulsed beneath her palm. A living, breathing current searching for its other half. "I want all of you."

Chapter Twenty-Six

This was it. Whether it was minutes, or mere seconds before Priest walked back through the master bathroom door, Katy's life was about to irrevocably change.

She lifted one leg above the water's surface and traced the curved edge of the porcelain tub with her toe. The lodge décor from the rest of the house was just as present here with rustic stone work accenting the rich wood details. Unlike the standard-size tub she'd had in her room at her parents' house, or the one in the apartment she shared with Alek, this one was huge. Built to comfortably let a man of Priest's size stretch and linger when the mood suited him. Or better yet, when he had a mind to linger with someone.

After tonight, that someone would only be her. From now until who knew when. Oddly, the more she sat with the idea, the less it rattled her. And Priest being who he was, he'd made her wait a full twenty-four hours to give her plenty of time to change her mind.

But that wasn't going to happen. Even with her heart thumping like a panicked rabbit, she wouldn't divert from the path she'd set for herself. Or more aptly, the path fate had put her on. Priest was hers. Already, the bond was thickening. From the second she'd spoken her truth she'd felt it. Threads that went soul deep weaving impenetrably between them.

Muted movement sounded through the closed bathroom door, a gentle reminder that her mate would be coming for her. Learning he planned to tattoo her here rather than the shop had been a shock. A testament that tonight meant just as much to him as it did to her.

He'd run her a bath, scented the water with an exotic oil she couldn't quite place and then slowly undressed her in reverent silence. The water's warm embrace had been just what she'd needed. A welcome relief to tight muscles earned through a long day of strenuous training. Although, today she'd been her own taskmaster. Priest had been right to push her. With Draven hunting their primos, they needed every advantage they could get. But more than that, she couldn't shake his vow.

You will lead this clan beside me.

He'd meant it. The truth and want behind his words resonated with a depth that went beyond description. Powerful and yet soft and welcoming.

The doorknob twisted, the soft metallic click as the latch disengaged almost symbolic in the otherwise silent room.

And then he was there.

Prowling toward her with a feline yet masculine grace that made her sex clench. With every move, the candlelight licked his dark skin and the shadows lovingly caressed each defined muscle. "How do you feel?"

Breathless.

Weightless.

Drawn tight and ready to snap.

And he hadn't even touched her yet.

He crouched beside the tub and traced the line of her jaw. "You don't have to do this. Not if you're not ready."

She covered his hand with hers and tiny droplets sluiced off her hand, trickling a soft song against the water's surface. "I'm nervous, but I'm not changing my mind. I'm ready."

He threaded his fingers with hers and studied her for long seconds. Not that she minded. With other men, such concentrated study might have made her uncomfortable, but with Priest it felt special.

Whatever answers or insight he sought, he must have found it, because he nodded once, straightened and grabbed the thick towel he'd laid near the edge of the tub. He shook it out and held out one hand. "Then let's get you ready."

Taking his hand was easier than she'd expected. But then, no woman in her right mind would turn away a man like Priest. Least of all her.

He dried her with painstaking care, wrapped her in the fluffy towel and released the clip that held her hair piled on her head. Before she knew it, he was guiding her to the bedroom.

The masculine comforter that had once covered his bed was gone, replaced with a single black silk sheet. The nightstands on either side had been cleared of all but a much smaller tattoo machine than what he used at the shop and the inks and other supplies he'd need to work. Candles filled the room and a mix of scents from patchouli to vanilla assailed her senses.

She paused at the foot of the bed and clenched the towel gathered just above her breasts. "Don't you need more light?"

He swept her hair off the back of her neck and kissed

the spot she loved at the top of her spine. "What I'm giving you won't come from my eyes. It's an extension of me. Everything I want for us. Everything I feel for you." He covered her hand with his and tugged the towel from her grip. "Nothing about tonight will be like what you've seen before because I've never given this much to anyone else."

The fluffy fabric slipped free and pooled around her feet. With the sliding glass door open to the fading light outside, the room's temperature was comfortable. Free of the manufactured coolness that came with air-conditioning and yet still crisp enough her nipples pebbled when the air swept across her breasts. "Will it hurt?"

It was the one question she'd been afraid of asking. Which was insane given the intimacies they'd shared already. But the last thing she wanted to be in his eyes was fragile. Wimpy or fearful.

He smoothed his hands up her arms. "I can take your pain if that's what you want." He skimmed his lips from her shoulder to her neck. "But the more you feel—the more you embrace the pain—the more potent the magic will be."

"Then I'll take it." Brave words considering she had no clue what she was signing up for, but with his hands and lips lulling her and the heat of his body, she would have agreed to anything. Would have committed murder if he asked.

"We'll work you up to it," he said. "You don't have to take it all at first. Only as much as you want." He nipped her earlobe and his warm breath tickled the skin on her neck. "But you might find you like the pain."

A shiver snaked through her, anticipation and the dark

thrill that always came with his touch and his words heightening every sensation. The soft sounds from nature outside. The candlelight. The warmth of his skin and his intoxicating, manly scent.

He slipped one hand around her throat and murmured against her ear. "Are you ready?"

More than ready. And yet terrified as well. Still, she swallowed and managed a shaky, "Yes."

He released her, but the lingering touch as his hands slipped away was a temptation in and of itself. "Then lay down on the bed. Facedown."

Facedown. Right. Easy enough to do as a starting point. Except that as she crawled across the bed, it felt a bit as if she was laying herself on an altar with nothing but the unknown stretched out before her.

The silk sheet slicked across her skin in a welcoming stroke, the coolness of it a stark contrast to the fire building inside her.

Priest gathered his things from the nightstand onto a small stainless steel tray, slid them on the bed beside her head, then moved out of sight. Rustling sounded behind her and the bed dipped. "You're not breathing, *mihara*."

As if they realized they'd been caught falling down on the job, her lungs expanded on a huge inhale. "It's not because I don't want this."

He braced his knees on either side of her hips and gently gave her some of his weight, sitting astride her ass. Not enough to cause any discomfort. Only enough to make it one hundred percent clear he was naked. His skin was a hot brand. The heavy press of his sac along the seam of her ass and the hint of his hard cock an erotic promise of what would come after the pain.

"I understand you're nervous." Leaning forward, he

carefully gathered her hair and twisted it out of his way. The angle gave her more of his thick shaft low on her spine and her cat urged her to lift her hips and offer herself. "Just talk to me. Breathe and tell me if it's too much." Rather than reach for the machine, he traced a pattern with his finger along her nape and lowered his voice. "Focus on my touch. On me and what you're feeling. Nothing else."

For long, quiet minutes, the simple contact was all he gave her. A slow, hypnotic path that unwound her tension and lulled her toward a deep and peaceful place.

And then Priest shifted. Metal clicked against metal, but the safe and soft cocoon he'd helped her build in her mind stayed strangely detached. Disconnected and yet still present on a level thick with an almost spiritual awareness.

"Take what I offer. Accept my gift. All that I am." The tattoo machine buzzed once. Twice. And then a pressure registered at the base of her neck. Nothing painful. Just a presence.

She went with it, hovering in the pleasant subspace. Back and forth, the pattern built. The steady buzz of the tattoo iron and murmured words from Priest she couldn't understand but sounded like some kind of chant.

Slowly, the pain crept in. A delicate pinprick at first, then increasing to a fiery sting. But she took it. Breathed through the rapid stabs from the needles and surrendered to the process. To the mix of pleasure and pain that zigzagged through her body. By the time the buzz ceased and Priest set his iron aside, a wide swath at least two inches wide scorched along the base of her neck and shoulders, and she'd entirely lost contact with time.

With gentle swipes, Priest wiped away the excess ink

then leaned in and kissed her tender flesh. "Talk to me, *mihara*. Tell me how you feel."

Raw.

Exposed.

Teetering on the edge of something so big it was well past her understanding.

She pulled in a long, slow breath, the adrenaline coursing through her body adding a subtle tremor to the soft sound. "It hurts, but…" How could she describe it? Every word that came to mind, came up short. Lacking the power of the experience. "But it's arousing, too."

And that was the part her brain couldn't wrap itself around. How anything that produced pain could equally build a pulsing need with no relief in sight.

As if he understood even without her thoughts spoken aloud, he planted both fists on either side of her head and traced the line of her jaw with his lips. "Turn over, kitten. Let me take you the rest of the way there."

One second stretched to another. And another.

He waited, seemingly content to let her take all the time she needed. Which was good because she needed this moment. This tiny pause to savor and remember it. To etch it deep inside her memory and call on it in the days and years to come.

Finally, she shifted, rolling beneath him until she stared up into his stern face.

Mine.

Whether it was her own mind staking the claim, or the projection of his own thoughts through sheer will, the word was all consuming in her head. Calming even as it consumed her.

He kissed her. While the contact was light, it seethed with a barely banked compulsion that crackled and snapped with delicious sparks. His hair fell around them in a dark curtain, blanketing them both from everything but the moment. When he lifted his head, his gray eyes sparked with the same splendor as the Otherworld. Mystical and riddled with power.

Skimming his fingers up her sternum, he sat upright.

A dark god. That's what he looked like. Tan and muscled, sitting astride her with his thick cock straining against his belly. A wicked and utterly primal deity about to indulge with his latest conquest. "Can you take more?"

She'd take anything he asked her to. As much as he wanted for however long it took so long as it ended with him inside her. Filling her and driving her to release as only he could. She dipped her chin, the knot of emotion in her throat too thick to speak.

Iron in hand, the buzz kicked in once more.

And so it went.

More pain interwoven with a mounting pleasure that made no sense. Murmured words and a tingling throb that built along each line he drew. One hour after another, she soaked it all in.

But this time she had the benefit of watching him. Of seeing his silver aura pulse as he worked and the stark concentration on his face. And through it all, the design he worked into her skin became a part of her. Thrummed like a living current.

By the time the buzz stopped, nothing in the world existed but the two of them. He set the iron aside and gazed down at her. Fatigue and bare need etched every line on his face.

He loves me.

To the logical mind, it made no sense. Couldn't be possible between two people who'd known each other little more than two weeks. But her heart said otherwise. Saw the devotion and care behind each action. The determination to see to her needs. For days, the tightness behind her sternum had swelled. Grown larger and thicker. As if her heart couldn't stay contained within her chest much longer.

But in that second, it unfurled, reaching for the heart of the man above her. Beneath her skin, her magic sung and her heartbeat echoed another.

His heartbeat.

"Kateri." Her name on his lips was like a prayer. A man teetering with the loss of control and desperate for the abandon beyond the edge. Behind his gray gaze was a primal hunger barely leashed and every muscle was drawn tight.

"The bond." Even before her whispered words trailed off, she knew it was true. He'd felt it as strongly as she had. An invisible connection forged with impenetrable finality. The light dusting of hair along his muscled thighs tickled her palms as she stroked toward his hips, eager to urge him closer. "You felt it, too."

"I feel *everything*. Your pain. Your fear. Your need." He manacled her wrists with his fingers and squeezed them tight. His chest rose and fell as though an escalating war raged inside him. For a moment, he seemed disoriented. Then his gaze landed on the unforgiving grip he held on her and he rolled from the bed. "I need to shift."

Shift? Now?

She scrambled to her feet and clutched his arm.

"Don't." He tried to pull away.

But her magic was too strong, binding him to her and opening her eyes to unimaginable truths. She saw it all.

Felt the raw emotion battering through him. The worry for his clan's future. The gut-wrenching shame he'd carried for his failure. The darkness and how it dogged his every thought. The insatiable compulsion to take her without restraint.

So much pain. Years of it.

You're good, Kateri. My light.

"You don't need to shift." Pure instinct drove her closer, smoothing one hand up his chest as her power banded around them both. "You need to give in."

He fisted his hand in her hair and his cat's deep growl rumbled up the back of his throat. "You don't know what you're doing."

"No, I don't. But my heart does." Relying on her magic to keep him close, she loosened her grip on his forearm and slowly lowered to her knees. His cock strained tall and heavily veined before her, his earthy scent stirring the beast inside her. She understood it now. What he'd meant when he'd shared what tonight meant to him. Because now it was her turn to give. To expose and surrender herself completely.

"Whatever you want, I want." Meeting his gaze, she gripped his hips, leaned close enough her breath whispered against the base of his cock and gave him the same words. "Take what I offer. Accept my gift. All that I am."

Chapter Twenty-Seven

Priest was trapped. Immobilized not by his mate's magic, but by her warm breath and soft lips teasing the base of his shaft.

Yes. Take her. She's ours. Freely given.

He should fight it. Should put Kateri first and keep her safe.

She flicked her tongue against his flesh and traced one vein from base to tip, a soft moan laced with wonder and appreciation filling the tense silence. "I need you, too, Priest." Leisurely licking along the ridge, she met his stare beneath weighted eyelids. "Trust me to know what I want. Trust what's between us."

Yes, the darkness crooned. *Trust us.*

His panther purred in agreement, and the next thing he knew his palm was at the back of her head, the thick silk of her hair wound between his fingers. "Kateri." It was the only warning he could offer. The only word his lips could form.

Lips wet and shiny from her ministrations, she guided his glans along her lower lip. "I'm not afraid. Not of you, or any part of you." Her tongue swept across the pre-come at the tip and her words whispered against the slick wake she'd created. "Take your mate. Make us whole."

My mate.
All mine.
Strong enough. Ready for what you need.

He growled and thrust his cockhead past her full lips. Claimed her eager mouth and the wet heat inside. "Take it." He pumped deeper. "Show me you can handle what I give you."

She moaned and straightened taller on her knees, taking him nearly to the root. Her accelerated breaths huffed against his skin and her tongue swept a decadent cadence up and down the side of his shaft with each bob of her head.

The potent scent of her arousal thickened, the rich musk that had teased him over the many hours he'd marked her now saturating the air around them. At his hip, her nails bit into his skin where she braced for balance, but the other cupped and fondled his tight, heavy sac with devoted urgency.

She wasn't afraid. Wanted him. Needed him. Exactly as he was.

His cock swelled thicker and harder, the ache he'd fought for hours surging to a demanding beat. "Touch yourself."

Ignoring him, she tightened her hold on his nuts and sank deeper on his shaft. Around him, her powers thrummed with challenge. A dare spoken without a single word.

His magic answered, surging up and around him and freeing him from the sensual bonds she'd caged him with. He molded it. Shaped it into a vibrating stream of plum and silver and encircled her wrists with it. "You have no idea what you've just bought yourself."

In one fluid motion, he pulled free of her delectable

mouth and bound her hands behind her back with their combined magic. His cock jerked and his cat snarled at the loss of her hot mouth, but her startled gasp and parted lips, plump and glossy from her efforts, made the darkness in him purr.

"Priest." She wriggled against his bonds, the sudden movement making her breasts sway enticingly. Then she tried to stand and realized he'd weighted her in place as well. "Damn it!" She fought harder, the muscles in her shoulders and arms straining even as she tossed her head in frustration. "Let me go."

"Oh no, kitten. I gave you a chance. Told you to let me go and let me find my balance, but you pushed me." He crouched beside her and used his magic to force her knees further apart.

The scent of her arousal coiled around him. Licked along his skin and made his cock throb with an unrelenting pulse.

He traced his fingers along the inside of one thigh. "You said you trusted me. You can tell me to stop, or you can take it. No in-between." He shifted so his torso blanketed her back, cradled one breast in his palm and teased the tight curls at the top of her mound with the other. "Tell me to stop, *mihara*. Say it, and I'll move away."

"No." Sharp. Not a beat of hesitation. If anything, it was a plea for more. She dropped her head against his shoulder and undulated her hips up toward his fingers. "Please, don't stop."

The sliver of control he'd maintain fractured further and he slicked his fingers lower. Stirred the ready wetness waiting for him in slow, deliberate strokes. "Mmm. Already primed and ready." He circled her swollen nub, stopping just shy of the firm pressure he'd learned she preferred. "I think you like being bound. Is that it? You wanted to poke and prod your mate until he lost control and fucked you like the animal he is?"

"Oh, my God. Priest!" Her back bowed, chasing more of his wicked touch, but he pulled his fingers away and she whimpered. "Please." She rolled her head enough to nuzzle his neck with her forehead. "Please, don't stop."

"Admit it. This isn't a sacrifice, is it? You want it. Want the beast."

"Nothing with you is a sacrifice." Such sweet, desperate words whispered against his neck. "I want you. All of you."

Yes. Do it. Take her. Now.

Impulsive thoughts mirrored by his cat. But he held back and gripped her hips.

She groaned and wriggled against him.

Fast, before she could gauge his intent, he smacked her pussy, the wetness coating her labia adding a decadent tenor to the sharp crack. "Still."

She settled instantly, but her gasp was the ultimate invitation. The luring sound of a woman reveling in a delicious surprise.

"You liked that, didn't you? The same way you liked the pain."

Her answer was a shaky whimper. A sound so needy he felt it like a fist around his dick.

He smoothed his hands across her flesh to ease the sting and grazed his teeth along her neck. The need to bite burned through him. A fundamental urge older than time.

But he couldn't go there. Her flesh was too raw from his mark. Too vulnerable. The rest of her, though...the rest of her was his to claim. "Don't worry. I'll give you more." He stroked one hand up along her spine. "Make your skin burn and your body come apart." He gripped her by the back of the neck, guided her to her hands, then further so her cheek rested against the plush rug. Shifting his magic, he manacled her in place, her knees wide and hips lifted for his languid perusal.

He felt more than heard her increased breathing, the ragged rhythm of it and the subtle tremor that moved through her fueling man, beast and darkness with primal pleasure. Coasting his hand along the back of one thigh, he used the callouses on his palm to tease her flesh. "You should see what I do. Your sweet pussy exposed for me. Pink and swollen. Wet and ready."

"Then take it." A shout and a groan all rolled into one. Her hands fisted in the soft sheepskin and her hips lifted higher. "Please, Priest."

Nothing sounded better than the word *please* on her lips. Nothing save his name filling the room while she came around him. "I intend to." He stood and circled her, letting the distance and the knowledge that he watched her drive her higher. "There won't be anywhere you don't feel me. Where you don't crave my touch."

When he finished a full circuit and moved out of her sight, she wriggled her perfect ass, every bit the needy cat in heat.

He gathered the oil he'd prepared for her off the night-stand and silently kneeled beside her.

"Priest?"

"Mmm?"

"What are you doing?"

Hands oiled and ready, he palmed either side of her sex and slicked his thumbs along her folds, opening her wider. "I'm going to lick my mate's cunt and fuck her with my tongue."

Before his eyes, her muscles contracted, a visual demand for more even as a tiny sob slipped past her lips.

It took everything he had to go slow. To trace every inch of her with purposeful intent rather than devour what was his. But he'd give her fast soon enough. Would take her completely. Claim and consume her the way she'd consumed him.

At the taste of her, he moaned and flicked her clit with his tongue. "Ask me what I'm going to do next, *mihara*. Ask me what dark things I'll do to you while you're bound and helpless."

She bucked against his mouth and for a second he thought she was too far gone to have even registered his words. "Wh-what?"

He speared his tongue inside her, fucked her the way he wanted to with his fingers. With his cock. Only when she fell into a rhythm with him did he guide one slick finger to her ass and circle her rim. "I'm going to take you here. Fill you and stretch you like you've never been filled before."

"Oh, my God." She rolled her head, her forehead pressed square to the ground and her breath coming in sharp, frantic pants. "Priest, I haven't…"

"Tell me to stop. Tell me to stop, or take it."

Her hips lifted. Barely noticeable had his hand not been placed where it was or his mouth greedily feasting on her sex. "I'll take it."

Slowly, he breached her, pressing one finger past the tight ring and easing inside bit by bit. "My gift. My sweet light who loves the darkness." Desperate to feel the flutters teasing his tongue on his cock, he straightened, never breaking the building rhythm of his finger pumping in and out of her ass. He nudged her opening with his dick, notching just the head inside her, and hissed at the scalding heat. "So ready and eager to give me what I need."

He filled her. One merciless thrust that took him to the root and made his shaft jerk inside her, the release he'd craved from the moment she'd stretched out on the bed tightening his balls.

"Yes!" Undulating her pelvis, she tried to spur him on. To gain the sweet friction she needed.

The need to pound himself inside her ripped at every instinct and muscle, but he held himself motionless save the steady cadence of his finger in her ass. "Do you want more, kitten?"

The muscles in her shoulders and back flexed as she tried to lever herself against him and her answer came twined with a snarl. "You know I do. Let me move."

He drizzled more oil along her crevice and added another finger.

She shuddered and moaned, the sound so low and broken he'd have thought the pain was too intense had her sex not convulsed around his shaft.

"You want to move?" He gripped her hip hard and let his magic fall away. "Then do it. Fuck yourself on my cock and fingers exactly how you want it. Show me your dark side."

No hesitation. The second his magic slipped free, she rocked against him. Tentative at first, then building. Long, powerful drives that left her cheeks slapping against his pelvis. With every beat he flexed into her, giving her the subtle slap of his sac against her clit.

Releasing the viselike hold on her hip, he smoothed

a barely there touch along her spine. "It's not enough, is it?"

"No!"

He eased one more finger in her ass, priming her. Teasing her. "You want my cock here, don't you? Stretching you the way I'm filling your cunt."

One hitch. One tiny hesitation before her head whipped back and her low confession filled the room. "Yes."

Her hair spilled around her shoulders, gold and shimmering in the candlelight. She arched her back and surrendered all she was in the most beautiful offering. Even knowing how tight and decadent the feel of her untried ass around him would be, pulling free of her hot sheath nearly killed him.

Until she widened her stance further and peeked over one shoulder. Gone was the driven, yet lost soul he'd met weeks ago, replaced with pure temptress. A wanton goddess ready and willing to savor all life had to offer. Sweat dotted her brow and her eyelids hung heavy over her beautiful blue eyes, her gaze riveted to him fisting his cock as he coated it with oil. Not one ounce of fear marked her expression. Only lust and open curiosity.

The last of his control wavered, pure instinct wiping everything aside save the need to cover and dominate. "Cheek to the rug."

She opened her mouth as if to argue.

"Now." His cat chased his command with a low and deadly sounding rumble and his magic bristled along his skin, a push from his beast for release.

Holding his gaze, she closed her mouth and lowered her head.

His cat purred and the darkness murmured its approval, but both were background noise against the sight of his shaft sliding along her crevice. Of feeling his skin slick across hers and how her rim flexed at the first nudge from his cock.

Just a little more. A few precious minutes' worth of self-control to acclimate her. To ease her dark descent. Then he could let go. For once, be who he was. "My naughty mate." He inched forward and she whimpered, the tight ring he'd stretched and prepared quivering at his invasion. Holding her firm with one hand on her hip, he reached around and strummed her clit. "Surrender. Let me take you under."

Eyes locked with his, she let out a shaky breath and her muscles unfurled around him. Welcomed him.

He sank deeper, gaining ground bit by bit with shallow, easy pumps that slowly frayed what was left of his control. By the time his hips pressed flush to her ass, his arms shook from his viselike grip on her hips and sweat misted his torso.

"Kateri." It was little more than a groaned whisper. One last attempt to let her pull away before the primal drive eating him alive took over.

A growl was the last thing he'd expected. Her shimmering magic even less. But both billowed up as she levered herself up on her hands, her power lashing across his skin in the most erotic whip. "Now, Priest. Do what you promised and fuck me."

Mine.

A roar filled the room. Hers, his or both, he wasn't sure. Only knew that conscience, concerns and doubt no longer existed. Nothing mattered save the tight fist of her ass around his cock. The intoxicating scent of jasmine and sex. The slap of flesh against flesh and the oil's wet sounds as he pumped inside her.

Only when the tips of her fingers grazed his tight sac as he thrust forward did he lift from his rutting haze enough to realize she'd shifted and toyed with her clit. Fisting one hand in her hair, he yanked her upright and seized her fingers. "Oh, no you don't. This pussy is mine." Bypassing her clit, he drove two fingers inside her drenched sex, alternating each stab with his plundering shaft. "You take what I give you. Submit and come by *my* hand."

The sound that slipped past her lips was a thing of beauty. Relief and frustration coiled together in a grated moan as she undulated between his hand and hips. "More. I need more."

"You want release, kitten?" A threat would have sounded less intimidating, but he was too far gone to soften his words. Pure wickedness and untamed instinct driving every thought and action. "Want to come with my cock in your ass?"

"Yes! Harder. Please. It's so close." Body bowed, her breasts jutted outward and jiggled as he pounded into her. Her nails scored his flanks as she held on with all she had, and every place her skin came into contact with his burned like a white-hot brand.

His own release threatened. Drew his nuts up tight and throbbed at the base of his shaft. But there was only one way he was giving in. One sensation he'd allow to pull him over the edge. "Then come for me, *mihara*. Come and take me with you."

Pulling his fingers free, he smacked her sex. Once. Twice. Then drove his fingers back inside, grinding the heel of his hand against her clit.

She bucked and cried out, her muscles clenching around his fingers and cock in a merciless grip. "Priest!"

"Fuck, yes. My mate. All. Fucking. *Mine*." He stabbed to the hilt and let himself go, his release jetting free with a force that made his shaft jerk inside her.

Fifty years he'd waited. Wanted and worried anyone could ever accept all that he'd become. The good as well as the ugliness locked inside him.

But Kateri hadn't just accepted him, she'd welcomed him. Laid herself out and embraced his darkness with a bright abandon that left him free and whole.

Releasing the brutal grip he'd kept fisted in her hair, he circled the front of her throat and sank back on his heels, keeping her flush against his hips as he eased them down from the peak. With his lips, he savored the thrumming pulse at her neck. Reveled in the tiny aftershocks of her sex around his fingers and shaft.

Aside from each languid roll of her hips as she rode the last of her release, his mate sat soft and pliant against him. Utterly replete with the back of her head lolling on his shoulder, eyes closed and every feature that of a woman at peace.

No fear.

No remorse.

No doubt.

He eased his fingers free, but kept his hand cupped possessively over her mound, his other hand still banded around her neck. "It wasn't supposed to happen like that."

Her lips curved in a slow almost sly smile, but her eyes stayed closed. "Which part? The fact that we ended up on the floor, or that I'm officially no longer a virgin in *any* capacity."

Oh, he'd planned on the latter. Just not as savagely with no semblance of control. He skimmed his lips along her shoulder. "I wanted to be gentler with you."

Rolling her head, she opened her eyes. The sincerity behind her gaze was as startling as her blue-gray gaze in the candlelight. "I just wanted you to be you." She covered his hands with hers, the action somehow demonstrating that she understood more than even he did the trichotomy within him. "I love all of you, Priest. Even the parts you're afraid to set free. You might be new to my reality, but inside, I think my soul has always known you. Always waited for you. It just took a while for my mind to catch up."

Everything inside him stilled. No agitation. No unease. Just quiet contentedness.

Even from the darkness.

"You tamed it." Even as he spoke the words, the truth of it resonated deep. "My brother's magic has never been this quiet. This calm."

Her mischievous smile warmed him, scattering what was left of his worry and concern. "It's probably basking in the afterglow like we are."

So light. After years of shame's murky ugliness weighting him down, his spirit soared. A freedom he hadn't felt since the days before he'd earned his magic taking flight behind his sternum. "No. It's not the afterglow." Holding her tight, he shifted forward, gently laid her on her belly and eased free of her heat.

She groaned and rolled to her back, gazing up at him with an adorable mix of playful and sleepy that shouldn't be possible after the fierce way he'd taken her. "So, what? You're saying it's just a case of me wearing out your ugly side? I'm not sure if that's a compliment or—"

"The darkness loves you, *mihara*." He braced himself on one forearm above her and brushed a stray tendril away from her sweat-dampened temple, his hand shaking with the simple act. "Deeply. But still not as much as I do."

Tears filled her eyes, but her tender smile whispered through him like a benediction.

"I knew you were my light," he said, "but I didn't realize you'd be my redemption, too."

She pressed her lips together tight, but they still trembled. A tear slipped down her temple and her voice when she spoke was little more than a whisper. "That's pretty heavy stuff after a seriously intense night."

"Not heavy. A blessing. One I never thought I'd have." He kissed her. A soft press of lips he prayed conveyed even a tenth of the gratitude and awe moving through him.

"I've never seen you sweet and gentle," she murmured against his lips.

He shouldn't have chuckled, but he couldn't help it. After all, it'd been forever since he'd *felt* sweet or gentle. Let alone acted on such an impulse. "Then maybe I should stop pinning you to the floor and get you into bed where I can tend to your body."

"Oh, I don't know. I kind of liked the pinned-in-place part." She wrapped her legs around his hips, cradled each side of his face and grinned. "And I'm only agreeing to a snuggle in bed if I get to see my mark first."

So perfect. Everything he'd ever dreamed of in a mate and so much more. He nuzzled his nose alongside hers and gave her his vow. "Anything for you, Kateri. Anything and everything."

Chapter Twenty-Eight

As appealing settings went, the view in front of Priest was something off a Deep South postcard—an old, but well-kept white cottage house with green shutters set far back from the gravel road. A thick swath of willows and cypress trees laden with moss ran behind it. On the edges of the property, tall grass dotted by small white and gold flowers swayed on the breeze, the heavy, damp scent of the nearby bayou carried on it. The only other house they'd seen on the drive in was a blue single story in need of a paint job with three cars suited for the salvage yard parked in the drive, but this one was a thing of beauty. Peaceful. Homey. A downright welcoming sight on a lazy Saturday afternoon.

And he'd still never wanted to leave a place more.

From his place in the backseat of Priest's Tahoe, Alek sat forward and leaned his forearms on the two front seats. "Isn't this the right place?"

According to the number on the weathered white mailbox it was, but something wasn't right. He just couldn't put his finger on what it was.

"Priest?"

One word from his mate and a layer of his hesitation scattered, just the sound of her voice drawing him back to a grounded center. For the fifth time since they'd pulled in front of the property, Priest studied the road ahead of them, the field opposite Elise's home, then twisted to check the stretch behind them. "Something's off."

Alek took the time to echo Priest's survey of their surroundings, but the expression on his face said he wasn't picking up on whatever had Priest tweaked.

"Off how?" Kateri said.

Damned if he knew. None of the scents coming through the open windows indicated a threat or anything suspicious, and every visual sweep assured him there was nothing to be uptight about, but the darkness inside him was restless. "Not a clue. It just feels like I'm missing something."

"You want to backtrack and scope things out first?" Alek said.

Priest eyeballed the white Honda sedan and sporty electric-blue Nissan in the driveway. Both were older models and covered in a thin layer of dust from the road, but otherwise in good shape. He shook his head. "I sense people inside. Better to do what we came here for while we can. Just stay sharp and be ready for anything."

He parked and rounded the front of his truck for Kateri's door, wishing like hell he'd given more consideration to bringing reinforcements. At the time, coming with fewer numbers had made the most sense—less of an overwhelming impression in an unknown situation. Now, he'd give a lot for Garrett's experience and Tate's muscle to back them up.

Like the shutters, the old wood-framed screen door was painted hunter green and shielded a white-washed door with a stained glass upper section with a host of wildlife in a forest setting. Priest rapped on the screen door's edge and the sound ricocheted around the wide front porch.

Kateri sidled closer and lowered her voice. "You're sure someone's inside?"

"Two," Alek answered from where he stood braced behind them. "Females."

Glaring at her brother over her shoulder, Kateri grumbled, "I don't even want to know how you know that."

"It's a wolf thing."

"Or an arrogant brother thing."

Before Alek could volley back with a smart-ass retort, the door opened just enough to show a woman who looked to be in her early to mid-forties.

Compared to Priest, Kateri and Alek, she was a tiny thing—five feet tall at most and that was probably pushing it. Once upon a time, her chin-length hair had likely been a deep chocolate, but with the amount of gray taking over, what color was left seemed washed out. Her eyes were startling, though, big and wide-set on a classically oval-shaped face and loaded with the wisdom of many hard years.

She scanned the three of them and offered an uncertain but welcoming smile. "Can I help you?"

"We're looking for the Ralston family," Priest said. "I think they once went by Rallion?"

Her expression blanked, but a wariness crept into her expressive eyes. "And you are?"

Unwinding his arm from around Kateri's waist, Priest offered his hand. "I go by Priest, but where I grew up I went by Eerikki Rahandras."

Her gaze dropped to the high priest medallion lying above his sternum and her lips parted on a near silent gasp. "Oh, my God. It's *you*." She covered her mouth as though the act might somehow pull the words back then realized he was still waiting for her to shake his hand. While small, the force of her grip was almost desperate. "I didn't think…" She glanced over her shoulder to the small entryway behind her, then lowered her voice to a near whisper. "Are you here for Elise? I didn't accept my quest, but my father assured me you'd help her when the time came. I just always thought you met them in the Otherworld. Is it time? I've been watching for signs, but she's seemed fine."

Behind Priest, Alek coughed and muttered, "Guess that answers that question."

Priest ignored Alek and concentrated on Elise's mom. "I do meet them in the Otherworld. And I help anyone who answers their quest, but it's not Elise's time yet. Not today, anyway. We're here for something else." Priest released her hand and motioned to Kateri beside him. "This is my *mihara*, Kateri, and her brother, Alek Falsen."

She shook each of their hands, but kept her voice low and peppered each greeting with quick checks of the hallway behind her. "I'm Jenny Ralston. My family hasn't gone by Rallion since I was a baby." As she stepped away from Alek, her gaze locked onto the medallion around his neck and her lips curled in a shaky smile. "That's the warrior medallion, isn't it? I mean, I'm rusty on all the things my dad taught me but I think that's the right one."

"Alek is our warrior primo, yes." Considering no one had yet to show behind her, Priest took a chance at getting them off the front porch. "I know we're springing this on you, but would you mind if we talked to you and your daughter?"

The smile on her face slipped.

Kateri stiffened beside him. "Is something wrong?"

Jenny wiped one palm on her jean-clad hip and tried to cover her hesitation with an unconvincing laugh. She stepped onto the porch and shut the door behind her. "No. Not wrong. Just awkward." She glanced behind her again. "Elise doesn't believe in our clan, or our magic. My dad was the only one alive when Elise was born, but she was still too little to remember him shifting. Since I never accepted my gifts I can't prove it."

"She thinks you're making it up?" Alek asked.

A rawness borne of deep pain flashed behind her hazel eyes. "Worse. She blames my insistence of our magic on why her dad and I aren't together. I was young when I met Tommy. Stupid. He laughed at my story when I told him about my clan. Told me it was a bunch of nonsense."

"You refused your quest because he didn't believe you," Priest finished for her. It wasn't the first time a human had drawn a Volán off their path and it wouldn't be the last. Priest just hated like hell it had happened to their healer line.

"I was in love with him. Wanted to spend my life with him." She peeked at Priest with such regret he could almost feel the emotion himself. "It was the worst decision I've ever made in my life."

"Where's Tommy now?" Kateri said.

"He lives in Lafayette, but talks to Elise on a regular basis." A warmth crept back into her eyes and her smile softened her features. "My daughter might not believe in magic, but she's a classic Volán in her love for nature.

No matter how many times Tommy's tried to convince her to move closer to him, she won't budge."

"Would you be open to us talking to her?" Kateri offered. "You might not be able to prove our clan exists, but between the three of us, I'll bet we can get the job done."

For a second, Jenny considered it, then frowned and focused on Priest. "If you didn't come for Elise's soul quest, then why are you here?"

A tricky question he still hadn't devised an answer for. At least not one that didn't sound as far-fetched as a magical clan would likely sound to Elise. "How much of our history from your parents' generation do you know?"

Her gaze slid to the side, unfocused as though she were trolling through long-buried memories. "That my family used to live somewhere in Colorado. They moved here when I was still a baby." She trained her sights on him again. "Why?"

"Did your father ever tell you why he started going by a different last name? Or how your mother died?"

She shook her head. "He told me lots about Mom. How she was a healer and that her companion was a rare white falcon. But talking about her death was off-limits." She shrugged, a little of the confused child she must have been growing up flashing to the surface. "Whatever took her hurt him, so I never pushed it."

Great. And he'd thought being the one to tell her his brother was on the loose and gunning for the primo lines was a shit task to tackle. Now he got the honor of sharing her mom's death, too. "Elise is home?"

Jenny nodded, but furrowed her brow in the process, a flicker of understanding settling in her gaze. "You know how my mother died, don't you?"

Kateri moved in tight beside Priest and squeezed his biceps.

Priest let the silent encouragement sink deep and steeled himself for the minutes ahead. "I know how she died. More importantly, I know how she lived." He nodded to the door. "If you'll let me, I'll share what I know along with what brought us here today."

Chapter Twenty-Nine

Kateri knew that look. Had felt the roiling confusion and utter shock reflected on Elise's face. That thick, insistent sludge that twisted and spun in your veins while years and years of everything you'd thought to be true got squarely turned on its head and shaken with the force of a major earthquake.

Jaw slack, Elise held absolutely still, her startled gaze locked on Alek's gray wolf not ten feet away. Like her mother, she was petite, but her hair was a sandy gold that spilled in soft waves to her shoulders. The wolf's size alone would have held anyone firmly rooted in place, but paired with the bold garnet flash that came with his transition, the wolf's proximity and the sheer intensity behind his amber gaze, even Katy was hesitant to move.

Two weeks since she'd been where Elise was now and so much had changed. An inauthentic life surrendered to truth and new possibilities. A sense of belonging beyond anything she'd ever imagined possible and a mate to call her own. One who shouldered the weight of his responsibilities and past decisions without letting the burden show.

She saw those burdens now, though. Saw the tension gripping his torso and his jawline as he stood beside

Katy and gauged Elise's response. Heard it in the carefully modulated tone of his voice as he'd shared their clan's truth. Felt the throbbing ache of regret through their bond.

And he still hadn't told them the ugly reality of why they were there.

Fisting her hands at her sides, Elise finally spoke, her voice a harsh rasp. "You weren't making it up."

"No, sweetheart." A soft response from a mother who clearly not only ached for her daughter, but regretted unalterable choices made too young in life. Inching closer to her daughter, Jenny laid a tentative hand on Elise's shoulder. "Our clan is real. Powerful and beautiful."

"It's your heritage," Priest said. "One you'll be given the choice to claim for your own, or surrender the way your mother did. No one will judge you if you choose to walk away, but I hope you'll wait and make that decision after you learn more about us. More about your family and their role in our clan."

"You just…" Elise slowly shook her head. "It still doesn't make sense. It can't be possible."

"I thought that, too," Katy said. "Our father never told us about our clan. He was too afraid of our magic and our history. But our grandmother intervened and showed us who we are."

Finally breaking her gaze from Alek, Elise took a shaky step back and turned her big eyes on Katy. "If he's a warrior and a wolf, what are you?"

Not once since Katy's lion had padded toward her in the Otherworld had she wished for a different companion. But staring back at Elise's fear-stricken face, she'd have given a lot to be something more innocent. Less threatening. "My companion is a lion. She's strong and beautifully protective." She smiled at the memory of the girls who'd preened over her after her first shift. "There are two little girls in our clan who told me they wanted to take me home with them, but didn't think their father's bear would appreciate cat hair in their house."

Elise frowned and glanced at Priest like he might have some explanation. "Their father has a bear?"

"Their father *is* a bear," Priest said with a low chuckle. "To the girls, shifting is normal. An everyday part of their life."

Shifting her gaze back to Katy, Elise swallowed and dipped her head Katy's direction. "And your magic?"

Logic insisted she answer with words, but the still foreign push from her instincts prodded her to go with action instead. Considering the power behind her magic, it was a bit of a risk. Though, with all the work she'd put in the last few days, she'd at least managed to keep herself in check more than half the time. The other times… well, eventually the trees she'd topple in the clearing behind Priest's house would grow back.

Holding her hand palm up in front of her, she concentrated on her magic and slowly gathered it in the palm of her hand. Tendrils with an almost smokelike quality swirled and thickened in her hand, the rich plum color of it mingling with bright sparks of energy as the power leaped from one fingertip to another. She molded the power. Forced it into a tight ball and guided it higher and higher into the air.

"When my Nanna first told me, I kept thinking there had to be a trick behind it all," she said, keeping her eyes focused on the rising power. "That it was a dream I'd wake up from. Or a prank instigated by my family. Even after I realized that wasn't the case, I was still too stubborn to admit there might be truth to it all." She dared to meet Elise's wide-eyed gaze. "But I assure you, it's *very* real."

With that, she loosened her mental hold on the tightly coiled energy and let it zing toward the trees in the distance. It slammed against a smaller tree along the front line and rocked the clearing between them with a sound on par with a gunshot. By the time the ricocheting sound settled, a solid plume of black smoke drifted up into the cloudless blue sky and the top half of the tree was missing.

"Oh, my God." Mindless of Alek still in her path, Elise took a handful of steps toward the woods, then staggered to a stop. "How did you do that?"

"I'm a sorcerer. My grandmother is a seer and my grandfather was the warrior primo before Alek."

Elise studied Katy for a beat, then Alek, then turned her sights on Priest. "So, what do you do?"

With far less of a light show than when he'd shifted into his wolf, Alek changed back to human form, thankfully with all of his clothes in place. "He's our clan's high priest. He can do everything any of the houses can do."

"I hold the same magic," Priest clarified, "but not always as powerfully as my primos. My job is to teach and guide the clan, but I'm strongest in warfare. I'll be the one to guide you when you're called on your soul quest."

"You shift, too?"

"We all shift," Priest said. "The Keeper gives us each a companion best suited for who we are. A partner to face our destinies with us."

"Your grandmother was a falcon," Jenny offered quietly. Almost as if she were afraid her foray into the conversation might jinx the progress they'd made in reaching Elise. "My dad said she loved to fly. That most of her body was a snowy white with soft mink-colored specs scattered down her back and wings."

Elise frowned and zeroed in on her mother. "I don't get it. Why would you walk away from who you are?"

A sad smile tipped Jenny's lips, the pain and remorse behind the action reflected equally in her beautiful eyes. "Because your father didn't believe me either. I thought the only way I could be with him was to give my heritage up. To be like him."

"And you still didn't end up together."

"No." She paused long enough to suck in a bracing breath. "I realized too late that we were vastly different people. But I don't regret my decision, Elise. I can't. If I'd walked away from him after he ridiculed my stories about our clan—if I'd not surrendered my gifts and stayed with him—I wouldn't have you. No companion or power would ever be more precious than having you in my life."

They stood in silence, Priest, Alek and Katy respectfully motionless on the sidelines while something both beautiful and fragile blossomed between Elise and her mother. Understanding. Hope. Forgiveness. Even surrounded by vast beauty, the three emotions pulsed as if the rest of the world had ceased to exist.

"I should have listened to you," Elise whispered, a fragile request for forgiveness woven in the careful words.

"You did the best you could with what I had to show you, sweetheart. I don't blame you for your response any more than I blame your father."

Elise's eyes welled with tears, the shine making the hazel color so like her mother's glisten in the sunlight before they gently spilled down her cheeks. "Will you tell me about them? Your parents and what you know about our heritage?"

"I can tell you what I know," Jenny said. "But honestly, these people will be able to tell you more than I can. They took the path I didn't. They know our clan in a way I could never describe."

One by one, Elise scanned the rest of them, ending with Priest. "Whatever you can tell me, I want to know. All of it. This time I'll listen."

It was all the opening Priest needed. With the same unwavering confidence he'd shown Katy and Alek those first few days, he motioned everyone to the comfy patio furniture on the shaded back porch and dug into the basics. The houses. The age spans most common for a soul quest to happen. How every quest and every person's magic had its own nuances. Every detail—every unique aspect of their nature—he covered with both pride and patience.

Nearly an hour and endless questions from Elise later, the sun kissed the treetops along the edge of the property, beginning its soft descent into night. The strain and awkwardness that had come with their arrival and subsequent show-and-tell was long gone, replaced with a tentative, yet open curiosity from both Elise and Jenny that flowed as soft and comforting as the evening breeze across the clearing.

"So, the primos for each house are leaders," Elise said with a quick glance at Alek. "Like a council that works with you to lead the clan."

"Exactly like that." Priest set the now empty glass of lemonade Jenny had made for him on the wicker and glass coffee table, anchored his elbows on his wide knees and clasped his hands between them. Had Katy not felt the creeping dread through their bond, the way his thumb subtly shuttled back and forth would have been her only clue to where the conversation was headed. He focused on Jenny. "Your mother was our healer prima."

The shock on Jenny's face said the information was the last thing she'd expected. "My dad said she was powerful. More powerful than he was, but he never said she was the prima."

"She was," Priest said. "She'd led the healer house for at least ten years before the Keeper named me high priest, but the whole clan loved her. Respected her magic and her sense of fairness and goodwill." He paused a beat and tightened his clasped hands. "Her loss is one I blame myself for."

"You were there when she died?"

More than anything, Katy wanted to intervene. To interrupt the conversation and divert what he was about to share even if it would only delay the inevitable.

But Priest being who he was, he pushed forward. "Yes, I was there. More than that, it was my lack of attentiveness that caused her death."

"Oh, no," Katy stood and blurted before he could say more. She might not be able to convince him to let go of the responsibility he felt, but she'd be damned if she let him set himself up to take the blame with everyone else. "You're high priest. Even with some seer magic, you're not omnipotent. You learned what you were supposed to learn when the Keeper wanted you to. You acted as fast as you could. The only one to blame for those deaths was your *brother*."

"Deaths?" Elise asked, volleying her attention between Katy and Priest.

Priest frowned up at her. "Let me handle this, Kateri."

"You're not handling it, you're taking the blame for it. Again." She spun to Jenny. "Priest has an older brother named Draven. A sorcerer like me. Only apparently, he's a greedy ass and the Keeper knew that, so she named my mate high priest instead of him. That pissed Draven off enough to go against the law of ultimate good and started twisting his magic. Doing things with it he shouldn't."

"Kateri—"

"He wanted to overthrow Priest," Alek cut in, "but the primos wouldn't go against him. So, at presect when everyone was gathered in one place, Draven tried to steal their magic from them. Priest diverted things before Draven could finish the deal, but the primos died in the process. Priest almost died, too, and probably would have if some of the clan members hadn't healed and protected him."

Mouth tight as though he couldn't decide whether he should thank Alek or rip out his tongue, Priest paused long enough to take a few breaths before continuing in a low, steady voice. A confession wrought with regret. "I knew my brother was angry. I knew he hated my plans to modernize our race and intermingle with the singura, but I thought I could work him through it." He sucked in a long breath. "Your mother and the other primos paid the price for my overconfidence."

Still stunned, Jenny said nothing. Just sat beside Elise on the wicker couch with her daughter's hand gripped tightly inside hers.

Elise didn't miss a beat. "What happened to your brother?"

"Up until a few weeks ago, I thought I killed him."

She looked to Alek and Katy. "You said you found out about our race two weeks ago."

And there it was. The slow pitch that would lead to an even bigger strike against life as they knew it.

Priest opened his mouth to speak, but froze before any words came out, his head cocked to one side as though he'd heard something nearby.

Alek forged ahead. "About a month ago, Katy and I found our parents murdered. My grandmother was with us, too, and found one of the medallions Draven used to wear beside my dad's body."

"He's still alive," Elise said.

"Alive and trying to finish what he started," Priest said, but the tone behind it was as distracted as his attention. He stood and paced to the edge of the wood porch, scrutinizing the woods in the distance.

Kateri followed him, studying the tree line for any clue as to what had caught his attention. "Priest?" She laid her arm on his shoulder and nearly winced at the tension straining the muscles beneath her palm.

She heard more than saw Alek stand and move in fast behind them. "Male. Somewhere just to the south."

"What?" Katy twisted to her brother, then up at Priest. "Who?"

"Get them out of here," Priest said to Alek, ignoring her questions completely. "Take Kateri, too. All the way back to my house, if you have to. Don't stop until you know they're within protective wards."

Alek didn't so much as blink before he went into motion, gripping Kateri's shoulder and steering her toward the house.

But Kateri wasn't so easy to stop anymore. Particularly when the bond between her and her mate pulsed with a dark and disturbing buzz. Using her magic, she broke from Alek's hold and hurried after Priest, striding toward the woods. "I'm not going anywhere. Not until you tell me what's going on."

He stopped so short, she nearly plowed into his back, but the pain and wildness etched on his face made her take two startled steps back.

"He followed us. Probably found you before I'd marked you and trailed us all the way here. It doesn't smell like him. Doesn't feel like him. But the darkness is awake and one way or another, I'm bringing this to an end."

Chapter Thirty

In panther form and moving faster than any normal cat could run, Priest gave his beast free rein and prayed Alek had somehow managed to wrangle Kateri to safety. The darkness stirred and prickled inside him, agitated to a degree he'd not felt since the night of his brother's betrayal. An almost magnetic tug that insisted on finding whatever or whoever had awakened it.

One thing was without question. If he made it through the next few minutes, hours, or however long it took him to track whatever stirred his darkness, he'd be kissing ass a good long while where Kateri was concerned. The look on her face as he'd used his powers to temporarily stun her gifts and tethered her to the earth had been nothing short of raw feminine fury. One that promised she'd not only flay him alive the second she caught up with him, but would likely commandeer reinforcements to help.

But taking her with him on this hunt wasn't an option. If Draven ever captured her, there'd be no limit to what Priest would do to earn her safety. Even sacrifice his life and every living member of his clan.

The vibrant terrain of Bayou La Rose blurred on either side of him. Where the cypress trees thick with moss had seemed welcoming before, now they were nothing more than a swath of rich green. On the bayou, the cypress knees that peeked just above the water's surface flew by like dotted lines on the highway at high speed. But the scent that held his beast's focus was the one floating just above the moist, muddy scent that encompassed the land. The same acrid bite that had overtaken all his senses the night he'd taken Draven's black magic inside him.

Within seconds, the compulsion dragging him forward circled, shifted directions, then came to an abrupt halt.

Priest stopped, lungs heaving from the open sprint he'd put his beast through. A misshapen clearing stretched directly in front of him, no more than twenty-five feet in circumference. To his left, the bayou's soft trickle barely registered above the sound of his labored breathing, and only the wind whispered through the willows and cypress on his right.

A trap?

Maybe. Though, if it meant dealing with his brother once and for all and ensuring the safety of his mate and clan, he'd happily walk into it.

Overhead a deep squawk rang out, the mere challenge of it making his panther's hair bristle from shoulder blades to tail. All too easily, his beast locked onto the source. A great horned owl large enough its wingspan would reach well over six feet. Unlike the standard coloring of most, the one staring down at him strayed more toward black than whites and browns. A deep purple aura surrounded it, one as thick with magic as Kateri's though marred with a black halo. The same black halo that had surrounded his brother.

The owl watched him. Taunted his cat with its calm stillness.

It didn't make sense. Draven was a cougar and companions didn't change. Not only that, the scent his beast detected from the owl was all wrong. Definitely not his brother's, but tainted by the same caustic scent of his brother's black magic.

Gaze locked on the owl and braced for action, Priest shifted and paced to the edge of the clearing. "You've got my attention, so shift and tell me what you want."

No movement. Not even a blink of its golden eyes.

The darkness strained beneath his skin, a compulsive reach toward the owl that nearly pulled Priest off center. But why? Unless the person they'd been chasing all along was a completely different sorcerer gone rogue.

No, that didn't make sense either. Their clan had no living sorcerers save Kateri. He'd have known it when they were called to their soul quest. Would have been there when they earned their magic.

The unexpected summons to the Otherworld.

The darkness.

The unfound soul.

Maybe he *had* been called, but someone else had beaten him to whoever waited. How, he couldn't fathom. No one but the high priest was ever allowed into another person's soul quest.

Unless Draven had found a way to intervene, or even force a Volán's quest. Given Jade's vision of someone from the sorcerer quest being hunted, it made sense.

He pooled his magic, drawing from the Otherworld's pure source and mingling it with the unique gifts granted him as high priest. He might not get answers from an owl, but he'd get them from a human—no matter what it took.

Out across the clearing and up the thick cypress trunk the owl had chosen for its perch, Priest carefully cast his magic, its presence hidden by the wind and guided by his command. "Who guided you with your quest?" While he was almost certain he knew the answer, his question was more for distraction than confirmation.

The owl quirked its head. More of a flinch than anything based in comprehension. As if it wanted to answer, but was held within too tight of a mental grip to do otherwise.

Priest's magic resonated up through the top of the tree, whispering through the leaves and up above the owl.

The bird rustled its feathers and stretched out its wings, either instinctively sensing danger or feeling the subtle prickle of power around it. It leaped upward, ready to flee, just as Priest's magic coiled around it, the inescapable power wrenching around the owl's body like an iron talon.

Careful not to injure the bird, Priest levitated the creature closer.

Its frantic squawks rang out against the deepening evening sky. The nearer it drew to Priest the more desperate its struggles to break free.

"Easy," Priest crooned as he inched closer to the agitated animal. Fighting past the furious swirl of the darkness inside him, he filled his magic with what little calm he had left. Urged the owl to settle and surrender to his power. "I don't want to hurt you. I want to help you."

The second he clutched the bird's torso in both hands the darkness in him surged and burned beneath his skin.

The owl shrieked at this touch and tried to take a chunk out of his forearm with its beak, but Priest's grip was too low and his magic too strong. Its only defense was the ear-splitting cries it spilled into the night, each one of them whipping the ugliness inside him to an untamed fury.

Kateri.

The bond he shared with her pulsed in answer and the rage inside him hesitated. She was his light. His foundation. So long as the connection stayed strong—his soul connected to her goodness—the stain of his brother's magic couldn't take over.

Mind and heart rooted on the connection to his mate, Priest focused on his magic. On the owl struggling within his hold and the soul nestled inside it. "Don't fight it. The more you do, the more it will hurt."

Another squawk. This one filled with pain and desperation, but also laced with that of the tortured man underneath.

Priest tightened his hold and speared his powers deep, digging his silver light into the very heart of the owl. His panther hissed at the burning backlash from the darkness, but Priest pushed through it and put all he had into the connection. "Surrender. Face your priest."

A deep and murky amethyst light exploded around them, and the owl shifted to man.

Definitely not his brother, but no one he'd ever laid eyes on either. Dressed only in beat-up jeans, the stranger's torso bore the dangerous and forbidden marks he'd found in his brother's research too late, each of them drawn in what looked like dried blood. Deep bruises dotted his belly, arms and shoulders, some of them fresh and others the putrid green that came days after injury.

Priest tightened his grip on the man's throat and filled his voice with every ounce of compulsion he could muster. "Your name."

The man's eyes widened, confusion and an almost palpable fear marking his brown gaze. His dark hair was even longer than Priest's and hung loose on either side of his sweat-coated face. "Jerrik."

As soon as the answer was out of his mouth, Jerrik's whole body tensed, his back and neck bowed as though a bolt of lightning had shot from the ground and through his flesh. His tortured shout rang loud and long against the bayou's stillness. Pure pain and agony. Only when the cry died off, did he straighten his head, his body shaking as though filled with more energy than it could stand. A wildness filled his eyes and the brown that had once colored his irises was pure black.

One second.

One stark, debilitating second and the darkness overwhelmed Priest. Choked and held him frozen in place, every muscle rigid and unforgiving as stone.

Jerrik rolled his head and circled his shoulders, the languid act of a man waking from a long, deep sleep. When he locked his black gaze on Priest and spoke, the voice was no longer the man he'd heard moments before, but one Priest knew all too well. "Hello, brother."

Chapter Thirty-One

Stupid, short-sighted, dick-headed men! Katy thrashed against her brother's unforgiving hold and kicked where she prayed to God it hurt like hell, adding what little magic had begun to resurface along with the attack. Thrown over his shoulder as she was, leverage was hell, but her powers were streaming back online and he wouldn't be able to hold her much longer.

Alek all but sprinted toward the car, Elise and Jenny running dead ahead of them. "Goddamn it, Katy, if I don't get you out of here, Priest is gonna kill me."

"He won't be able to kill you because I'm going to kill him first." Punching a sharp blast from her palms, she aimed for Alek's feet.

He stumbled mid-stride and loosened his grip just enough she was able to move with the momentum and rolled from his shoulder to an ugly heap on the ground.

Unfortunately, Alek recovered faster than she did and darted toward her.

She acted without thinking, directing a sharp shock just in front of his feet.

Alek jumped back just before he slammed into the electrical wall. "Jesus, Katy. Would you think for a minute? Priest needs you safe."

"I *am* thinking. I'm also feeling. He needs me. Now. There's no way in hell you're getting me in that car."

"You can't be serious. You haven't trained."

"I'm deadly serious." Straightening from her fighting stance, she fisted her hand against her sternum. "I feel it, Alek. He's in trouble."

Alek hesitated long enough to study Elise and Jenny by Priest's Tahoe, then grimaced and turned his conflicted gaze back on her. "Fine. Then you take them. I'll go after Priest."

"He doesn't need you, he needs me." With that she strode toward the back of the house and the tree line where Priest had disappeared.

"Katy, you don't know what you're doing."

"I'll know what I need when I need to," she shot back over her shoulder. Or at least she hoped she would. For the first time in her life, the only thing driving her were instincts. Instincts that insisted she haul ass before it was too late.

Alek clamped one hand on her shoulder, wrenching her to a halt and spinning her with such force she nearly lost her balance. "I don't think you get it. You could die."

Certainty even beyond what she'd felt surrendering to Priest's bond filled her in a rush, and her voice dropped to a ragged rasp. "If anything happens to him, I'm as good as dead anyway."

With that, she took off running, following the incessant demand that thrummed through their bond. Alek's curse and the lack of footsteps behind her was the only indication he'd finally ceded to her wishes.

Her cat paced and growled, demanding release. Logically, shifting made sense, but fear kept the door to her other self closed tight. Too many times since her soul quest Priest had had to coax her back to human form. If Priest needed her as badly as her instincts insisted, the last thing she'd need would be a fight for control with her companion.

You control your beast. Not the other way around.

Her beast let out a sharp grunt at the memory of Priest's words, an agreement and a promise for support all rolled up into one.

Right. *She* was in control. Not her cat. Not her father, or anyone else.

The shift happened in an instant, her human form giving way to the tight compacted muscles of her lion mid-stride and her companion's senses taking over completely. Like a compass, the bond still led them both, but now there was more. A mix of Priest's scent, the muddy bayou and something uncomfortably pungent. Beneath her cat's massive paws, a foreign energy hummed through the moist soil. Something dangerous. Unnatural.

Evil.

She raced forward, fully surrendering control to her companion even as she reached for Priest through their connection. For a second, she felt his grip. A feeble yet desperate mental touch.

An agonizing scream cut through the air. A deep, gut-wrenching sound that could only be male, but sounded nothing like Priest.

The thick cypress trees flashed by in a blur, her beast laser focused and drawn to a single point somewhere dead ahead.

In the distance, a clearing came into view. At its center two men faced off not ten feet apart.

No, not just two men. Priest and a man she'd never seen before. Where the stranger seemed almost ragged and dazed, Priest was straight and still as stone. Trapped and lifeless. Between them an inky black cloud swirled and twisted, its snakelike form coiled and reared back, ready to strike.

Now.

One simple, all-encompassing direction from her beast, but it was all she needed. She shifted, channeled all her magic into a tight, unmerciful fireball and let it fly.

It crashed into the blackness mere inches from Priest's mouth, but rather than annihilating her target, the substance scattered into ash-like particles, swirled on the air, then streamed through the mouth of the dazed stranger.

Gasping as though he'd surfaced from too long underwater, the once stunned and unfocused man scanned the terrain and trained his black, malevolent gaze on Katy. His smile was pure evil and his voice thick with menace. "Ah, my brother's mate. Come to join the fun."

So, it *was* Draven. Odd because while they had similar coloring and long hair, the man's face looked nothing like Priest. Where Priest was all hard angles and ruggedness, this man had more classic features. Definitely not someone she'd consider Priest's flesh and blood.

"Possessed." Not so much a clear word spoken in her head, but a whispered thought. A feeling not unlike when her companion communicated its desires, but with a different source. *"Brother."*

Their bond. Priest was using it. Fighting whatever it was that held him immobile and using it to guide her.

Desperate to keep Draven's attention off Priest, she filled both palms with more energy and circled away from her mate. "What have you done to Priest?"

"Done to him?" Draven turned with her, leaving his

back exposed to Priest. Which meant whatever means he'd used to hold Priest locked in place was something he was confident of maintaining. It wasn't much in the way of knowledge, but it was something. "I'm merely taking back what he took from me. My clan. My magic. All of it."

The magic cradled in her palms grew heavier. Hotter. Tingling along her fingertips and burning up her forearms, eager to do what she'd summoned it for. But if the man in front of her was truly only a shell for Draven, then she couldn't strike without hurting an innocent.

Draven's gaze flicked to the dark energy swirling in her hands and he chuckled. "Throw it. There's no way you'll beat me on your own, but you'll see how good it feels."

"Darkness."

A warning from Priest. Or maybe a clue. More than anything she wanted to look at him. To glean what she could from his eyes and offer whatever non-verbal assurance she could, but she didn't dare take her eyes off Draven. "I don't need to hurt other people to feel good. I don't need to steal something that's not mine to feel worthy."

Draven's grin slipped, the disgust on his face evidence she'd plucked a sore spot. "You're a self-righteous little bitch, aren't you? Just like my brother." He cocked his head. "I wonder. Once I use my darkness to take him over, will that make you *my* bitch? Or will you just suffer knowing your mate is trapped as my puppet?"

With barely any telegraphing to clue her in, he struck, an ugly bolt of magic darting straight for her head.

Katy ducked, rolled and countered the attack with her own jolt, but Draven knocked it aside with a negligent, backhanded swipe. Inside her, the bond between her and Priest wavered, the light that had beat within it dimming to a pale gray.

Darkness.

Possession.

Puppet.

That was it. If Draven could possess Priest, he wouldn't need the primos. He'd have all the high priest's gifts at his disposal. And with the darkness already in Priest, God only knew what kind of thrall he could hold Priest under.

Finding her feet, she braced and surrounded herself in a protective wall of shimmering magic. "You won't take my mate and I damned sure won't be your bitch." She fired. One short, inconsequential blast after another. None aimed to injure the poor man who'd fallen prey to Draven's possession, but enough to keep him occupied.

After all, Draven wasn't the only one with sway against the darkness.

The darkness loves you, mihara. Deeply.

She hoped that was true, because she was banking on that love. Counting on it to make a choice and save them all.

Channeling all the love she could through their bond, she reached for his shadow self. *"He said you loved me, too. That you wanted me. If you want me you have to fight him. Stay with me. Fight for me."*

Draven laughed, the sinister edge to it leaving her iced to the core even though sweat coated her skin. He prowled forward. "You think it would choose you over me?" He swept her next strike aside and whipped a vicious bolt straight for her solar plexus.

In the split second her shield wavered, a black tendril snaked through the cracks and cinched around her neck.

Behind Draven, Priest's eyes flared wide. His face was a fierce red and the visible muscles along his neck and arms strained against the invisible force that held him locked in place.

Her lungs burned with the need for air and her temples throbbed a demanding beat, but the bond inside her strengthened. Cast off the dark pall that had begun to intertwine the strands and began to glow. *"Help me. Choose me."*

Draven smirked, circled behind her and wrapped one arm around her head. The perfect stance to snap her neck. His vile voice was a nasty gurgle at her ear. "Hard for it to choose you if you're dead."

She braced, blackness overtaking her vision even as her gaze locked on Priest.

And then she was free.

Flat on her back, but free and staring up at the early night sky. Fresh air tainted by Draven's acrid magic flooded her lungs, and her ears rang with the beat of a thousand bass drums.

No.

Not drums.

Fighting.

Forcing her quivering muscles into action, she rolled to one side.

In the center of the clearing, Priest and Draven went head-to-head. A formidable sight. Two tightly matched predators intent on winning.

Except Priest was at a disadvantage. Where Draven wouldn't hesitate to kill his brother, Priest wouldn't risk Draven's host if he could avoid it. Especially not if he was the sorcerer primo they needed to balance the Earth's magic.

Instinct prickled and pushed her up on shaking feet. Priest might not be willing to hurt an innocent man, but he could absolutely purge his brother's spirit if she could give him enough time to work.

Slowly, she straightened. Grounded herself in the earth and air around her. Drew her power inward and fueled it with all the emotion of the last few weeks. The pain of losing her parents. The shock of learning her heritage. The freedom in finding who she was and the love granted her by fate. Every bit of it filled her. Whipped her magic into a fearsome frenzy.

Priest dodged an attack from Draven and spun.

Draven followed, but glanced over his shoulder as he turned.

One second. One heart-stopping beat of realization in Draven's eyes.

Her magic shot forward.

But it was too late.

In a burst of color, Draven—or whoever his host was—disappeared, and an owl as big as her lion surged into the sky, a purple aura tinged with black surrounding it.

And then it was gone.

Swallowed whole by the darkening night as if it never existed.

Not taking her eyes off the sky, Katy stumbled toward Priest. "Where'd he go?"

He caught her with hands at her shoulders barely two steps in, spun her and yanked her against him. "He's gone." His arms shook with fatigue and his labored breaths huffed beside one ear, but he was alive. Exhausted and covered with sweat, but with his strong heart pounding an affirming rhythm. "He felt your power. Knew he couldn't fight us both. He won't be back. Not until he has a chance to regroup."

She drew back only enough to meet his eyes. "What do you mean he felt it?"

His hand at the back of her head tightened. A telltale sign that even the marginal distance she'd created went against his protective instincts. "You haven't even learned a tenth of what you're capable of. Let alone how to hide it. I knew what you were doing. Tried to set him up and keep him distracted, but your magic was too intense. Too big for him not to notice."

A weight far more potent than fatigue or disappointment settled on her shoulders and her voice cracked when she spoke. "I screwed up."

His face softened, genuine concern and pride marking his stern features despite her missteps. Keeping one hand anchored firmly low on her back, he cradled the side of her face and dipped close, his rough yet gentle words a comforting caress. "No, *mihara*. You freed me. Saved me when absolutely no one else could have and bought us the time we need to regroup."

"But now he's free." All the emotion she'd held in check rolled up from the pit of her belly and sent tears spilling down her cheeks. "He's already possessed that poor man. What if he kills him? Or hurts someone else?"

"My brother won't risk his host. He's too powerful. Probably our sorcerer primo. Draven needs that strength. Whoever he is, we'll find him and the rest of our primos and we'll deal with Draven." He swept his thumb along her cheek and wiped away her tears. "We'll do it together."

She stiffened in his arms, the remembered anger as she'd watched him run into the woods without her catching up with all the other turmoil surging free. "You left me."

He pulled her close enough to rest his forehead on hers, but the action wasn't fast enough to hide the smile he fought in the process. "I did."

"You needed me."

"I did." The hand he'd cupped her nape with, gave a gentle squeeze and he drew in a long, shaky breath. "I'll train you. Everything you need to know."

"And next time you won't leave me behind."

He lifted his head. Behind his dark eyes burned the reverence and solemnness she'd grown not just to appreciate, but to rely on and love. A vow from one mate to another. "The next time we face my brother, you'll be right where you're meant to be. Beside me in everything I do. Every step of the way."

Chapter Thirty-Two

A lot could happen in a week. Or two. Or three. If anyone knew how quickly life's twists and turns could rearrange things these days it was Katy, but Elise and Jenny were getting their own crash course all the same.

Manning one corner of the outdated, but quaint kitchen, Katy dug into one of the cardboard boxes and carefully unwrapped the last of Jenny's hastily packed dishes. "You know, Priest said he worked a clause in the rental that allows you to fix the place up however you want. The clan's not exactly busting at the seams with people nearby yet, but I'm sure everyone would chip in if you want to update some things before we get the closing documents ready."

If Elise registered Katy's offer she didn't show it, just stared out the dining room's bay window overlooking the front yard and watched the men systematically unload the U-Haul of their furniture. The melancholy was understandable, especially with the stack of photo albums she'd uncovered from the box in front of her. An all-too-stark reminder of just how one-sided her viewpoint of history had been.

Jenny, on the other hand, didn't miss a beat. "Oh, I don't know." She hefted the stack of plain white ceramic plates off the dove-gray Formica countertops and neatly slid them into the cabinet closest to the kitchen sink. "I kind of like some of the old stuff. Reminds me of our cottage when Dad and I first moved in. It was nice taking our time and doing projects together. Though I wouldn't mind losing the avocado green in the master bath sooner rather than later."

"I'll volunteer for that job." Naomi sliced through the packing tape on the bottom of the box she'd just finished emptying, flattened the box for storage and set it along the long wall that separated the dining area from the cozy living room with its raw stone fireplace. "The taping and caulking is a chore, but the painting is a joy. A chance to turn my brain off and just let my thoughts coast wherever they want."

Quick paint jobs or longer projects, Elise and Jenny would have all the time they'd need, that was for sure. The payments on the lease-to-own deal Priest had negotiated with the seller were something he'd already adamantly insisted on covering until Jenny's home sold and she could make the property her own. Of course, he'd also finagled access to the cottage he planned to build in their cove—a concession Jenny had been more than happy to make in exchange for their new and considerably more protected life.

Priest strode in with two boxes stacked on top of each other and Jade on his heels with her own box, both of them navigating the packing paper and cardboard obstacle course without the slightest hesitation. "These are the last of the ones marked kitchen." He slid his boxes on the weathered farmhouse table they'd unloaded off the truck then hefted Jade's out of her arms. "Elise, the men are ready to haul your bedroom stuff in. You pick which room you want yet?"

The question finally managed to yank Elise out of her funk, though the way she blinked at Priest's question it was evident she'd missed the content behind his words.

"Your room," Jade said in way of clarification. "I know the one with the forest view is bigger, but I'd go with the lake view."

Checking with her mom first for guidance, but getting nothing more than an encouraging smile, Elise nodded and went back to looking out the window. "The lake view's good, I guess." She frowned and cocked her head. "Hey, who's that with Alek?"

Priest rounded the table and comfortably slid his arm around Katy's waist just as Jade leaned over the table for a better look at the window.

"Finally!" Jade said. "Leave it to Tate to miss all but the last hours of a move." She spun to head outside, but paused long enough to shoot a grin at Elise. "Tate's like my brother. A total pain in my ass, but a decent guy for everyone else." With that, she was out the door and striding across the lawn only seconds later.

The timing *had* been convenient. Though in fairness, he and Garrett had taken off to follow a lead in Wyoming before Priest, Alek and Katy had gotten Elise and Jenny across the Louisiana state lines. Leads that had unfortunately turned up more questions than answers on their missing seer family.

"Is he a warrior like Alek?" Elise asked. Not surprisingly, categorizing each person's house and companion had been at the top of her priorities in the last several days. That and spending inordinate amounts of time with Jade and Naomi and quizzing them on all things Volán.

"He is," Priest said almost distractedly as he studied her watching Tate. "His companion's a mountain coyote." His gaze shuttled to the window and Tate walking with one arm slung around Jade's shoulder toward the house.

Despite Tate's casual posture, his expression was pure focus. A look shared by Alek who kept pace beside Tate and Jade with a plain manila folder clutched in one hand.

Katy leaned in close to Priest and murmured, "Why do I get the feeling they're not here to help finish unloading?"

Shaking off whatever had given him pause, Priest reassuringly squeezed her hip and brushed a soft kiss across her temple. "If they've got news, I don't care if they never lift a finger."

That was the biggest change in the last week. While she doubted anyone would ever categorize her mate as anything other than the fierce and intimidating predator he was, there was a stillness to him now. A serenity that had woven together all the once incongruent parts of him and made him whole. Stronger and more formidable because of the nuances that made him who he was instead of hindered by them.

Nanna must have caught the tender action, because she cast Katy a quick smirk, then ducked her head and cut open a new box. She'd insisted it was Katy that had rendered the change in Priest. That her simply accepting him for all that he was had welded the fractured parts into one impenetrable shield. One that would make their clan stronger for it.

Maybe it was her acceptance.

Or maybe it was just the byproduct of two people

coming together and supporting each other as they faced the most difficult parts of their pasts.

Whatever it was, she felt *right* for the first time in her life. As if her hopes and dreams had finally become a part of her reality instead of the far-off stuff of childhood memories. A woman living fully in the present instead of merely existing and trekking from one life goal to another.

The sound of footsteps sounded only seconds before Alek strolled through the wide archway. "Hey, Priest, you got a minute?"

Jade rounded behind Alek and smacked him good-naturedly on the shoulder on her way to the outdated fridge. "Geez, say hello first. Maybe grab a beer and say hi to Jenny and Elise."

Priest chuckled. "Where'd Tate go?"

"Got sidetracked helping the guys maneuver a headboard up the stairs," Jade said. "He'll be here in a sec. Anyone else need a cold one?"

"We all deserve one," Alek said. "David called with a lead on the sorcerer family." He tossed the folder on the dining room table and opened it up. "This look like the guy you guys saw at Elise's place?"

Unwinding his arm from around Katy, Priest sidled to the table and angled the folder for a better view. "That's him."

It was him. Though the candid man in the picture was a whole lot healthier and happier looking than the man they'd faced in the clearing. "Who is he?"

"Jerrik Aucourte. David found a story about an older couple that was murdered around the time of Priest's weird summons to the Otherworld. Blacksburg, West

Virginia. This guy's their son, but he's been MIA since the murder. Cops are looking at him as a suspect."

"Blacksburg makes sense." Priest dragged one finger along the edge of the photograph. "Appalachian range and lots of forest."

Naomi moved in for a look at the picture. "Any chance David found clues on where Jerrik is now?"

"No. And I doubt Draven would stay anywhere near West Virginia. Not with the cops looking for his host." Alek took the beer Jade handed to him and motioned toward Priest. "We're gonna have to get another source for information, though. A PI or something. David's asking way too many questions for us to explain away anymore."

"It sucks Tate didn't find at least something to go on with the seer family," Katy said. "Finding them would make this hunt a whole lot easier."

"We'll find them," Priest said. "Both of them."

Tate strode around the corner and ground to a halt right in the middle of the kitchen entry, openly bewildered by the mess strung out in front of him. "Damn, I need to stick to heavy lifting. This place is a mess."

Jenny laughed and slid a few vivid yellow ceramic mugs into the cabinet. "The kitchen's always the slowest part, but we're working on it." She shut the cabinet door and held out her hand. "You must be Tate."

The new voice and the direct comment yanked Tate out of his stymied study of the mess enough to sidestep a pile of yet-to-be-broken-down boxes and shake the hand she'd offered. "Sorry. Yeah. Tate Allen."

With a smile that seemed not only easy, but genuine, Jenny released his hand and nodded toward Elise.

"Priest's told us a lot about you. I'm Jenny Ralston and this is my daughter, Elise."

Since she'd arrived in Eureka Springs, Elise had met introductions to the rest of her clansmen with everything from shyness to awkwardness, but this time she stood, set aside the photo album she'd cradled in her lap and wiped her hands on her jean-clad hips. Her lips lifted in a tentative smile. "Hey."

It was a sweet greeting. The stuff of high school crushes, innocence and hope.

So, Katy had a hard time covering her shock when Tate's eyes met Elise's and his easygoing demeanor slipped. Rather than offer the same warm welcome he'd given her mother, or at least wave, he just stood there, a dumbfounded expression on his face.

"Hey, dumbass." Jade punched him a lot harder in the shoulder than she had Alek and motioned with the beer she'd just cracked open to Elise. "Don't be a dick and say hello."

Flinching, Tate dragged his gaze from Elise, frowned at Jade like he wasn't exactly sure what she was doing in punching distance, then locked stares with Priest.

Confusion.

Terror.

Hope.

Determination.

How so many different emotions could meld together at once, Katy couldn't fathom, but they were right there for everyone to see. Or at least they were until he took two huge steps back, cleared his throat and all but growled, "I gotta go."

Priest dipped his head to hide a grin and nodded. "Yeah. I get that." He rubbed the back of his hand along his chin long enough to compose himself, then looked up. "You go. I'll come find you."

"Right."

And with that he was gone, dodging boxes and the crinkled paper strewn on the floor like a barefoot man quickstepping it through hell.

Jade stared at the empty opening he'd disappeared through, then swiveled to Elise. "Oh, boy."

"What?" Elise scanned everyone in the room. "Did I do something wrong?"

Suddenly, Naomi was all business and digging into the box she'd abandoned with single-minded focus.

Alek clearly didn't know what to think and cast a *what was that about* look at Priest.

Oh, no.

Surely not.

Katy twisted to Priest. "Was that—"

Naomi popped up from her box and threw up her hands, all too eagerly interrupting before Katy could give voice to her suspicions. "You know what we need?" She dusted off her hands, not waiting for an answer. "Pizza! There's a great place in town we tried a few days ago, and pizza means we won't have to finish the kitchen as fast." She waved Katy toward the entrance. "Come on, Kateri. We'll take Garrett and Alek with us and let Priest take care of business."

Wow. It was *exactly* what she thought it was. Nothing else in the world got her Nanna into matchmaking mode like witnessing a dumbstruck Volán male finding their mate. She grinned up at Priest. "Take care of business, indeed."

Not the least bit shy of sharing affection in front of those watching, he moved in close and pressed a lingering kiss to her lips. "Hurry up with the food, *mihara*. All of a sudden I'm feeling reminiscent." He smacked her on the butt and strolled after Tate, but not before giving her a wink and a parting comment. "I've got a mind to take care of something else as soon as I get home."

* * * * *

To read more by Rhenna Morgan and
find out about upcoming titles,
visit www.RhennaMorgan.com.

Acknowledgments

Getting through this book was a rough and bumpy ride. Not because of the book, mind you. My characters are often a source of comfort through both good and bad times. But life while the story worked its way free was…well, life. There were several people, though, who not only held me steady through it all, but lifted me up and kept reminding me of everything good in this world. To Lucy Beshara, Duane Magnauck and Jennifer Mathews—thank you so much for your unwavering support.

As always, I owe Angela James big-time for not only coaching me in ways I can relate to, but keeping me focused on the big picture. Not many people can be a solid teacher and tireless cheerleader at the same time, but she makes it look easy. There isn't one day that goes by that I don't thank God and every lucky star out there to have her in my corner.

And of course, a huge shout-out to Cori Deyoe, Juliette Cross, Kyra Jacobs, Audrey Carlan, Dena Garson and my *amazing* daughters. Doing this gig without you wouldn't be nearly as much fun.

*Love your heroes a lot on the protective side
and totally in love with their women?
Meet the MEN OF HAVEN
Jace will go to any lengths to protect
and care for Vivian in
ROUGH & TUMBLE by Rhenna Morgan*

*"Rough & Tumble by Rhenna Morgan will
warm your heart and melt your panties."
—#1 New York Times bestselling author
Audrey Carlan (Calendar Girl series)*

Chapter One

Nothing like a New Year's Eve drunk-sister-search-and-rescue to top off a chaos-laden twelve-hour work-day. Vivienne dialed Shinedown's newest release from full blast to almost nothing and whipped her Honda hybrid into a pay-by-the-hour lot in the heart of Dallas's Deep Ellum. Five freaking weekends in a row Callie had pulled this crap, with way too many random SOS calls before her current streak.

At least this place was in a decent part of town. Across the street, men and women milled outside a new bar styled like an old-fashioned pub called The Den, with patrons dressed in everything from T-shirts and faded jeans, to leather riding gear and motorcycle boots. Not one of them looked like they were calling the party quits anytime soon.

Viv tucked her purse beneath the seat, stashed her key fob in her pocket, and strode into the humid January night. Her knockoff Jimmy Choos clicked against the aged blacktop, and cool fog misted her cheeks.

Off to one side, an appreciative whistle sounded between low, masculine voices.

She kept her head down, hustled through the dark double doors and into a cramped, black-walled foyer. A crazy-big bouncer with mocha skin and dreads leaned against the doorjamb between her and the main bar, his attention centered on a stunning brunette in a soft pink wifebeater, jeans, and stilettos.

The doors behind her clanged shut.

Pushing to full height, the bouncer warily scanned Viv head to toe. Hard to blame the guy. Outside of health inspectors and liquor licensing agents, they probably didn't get many suits in here, and she'd bet none of them showed in silk shirts.

"ID," he said.

"I'm not here to stay. I just need to find someone."

He smirked and crossed his arms. "Can't break the rules, momma. No ID, no party."

"I don't want a party, I want to pick up my sister and then I'm out. She said she'd be up front. About my height, light brown, curly hair and three sheets to the wind?"

"You must mean Callie," the brunette said. "She was up here about an hour ago mumbling something about *sissy*, so I'm guessing you're her." She leaned into Scary Bouncer Dude's formidable chest, grinned up at him, and stroked his biceps with an almost absentminded reverence. "May as well let her in. If you don't, Trev will spend closing time hearing his waitresses bitch about cleaning up puke."

Too bad Viv didn't have someone to bitch to about getting puke detail. Callie sure as heck never listened.

Bouncer dude stared Viv down and slid his mammoth hand far enough south he palmed the brunette's ass. He jerked his head toward the room beyond the opening. "Make it quick. You might be old enough, but the cops have been in three times tonight chomping to bust our balls on any write-up they can find."

Finally, something in her night that didn't require extra time and trouble. Though if she'd been smart, she'd have grabbed her ID before she came in.

"Smart move, chief." The woman tagged him with a fast but none-too-innocent kiss, winked, and motioned for Viv to follow. "Come on. I'll show you where she is."

An even better break. The last search and rescue had taken over thirty minutes in a techno dance bar. She'd finally found Callie passed out under a set of stairs not far from the main speakers, but the ringing in Viv's ears had lasted for days. At least this time she'd have a tour guide and an extra pair of hands.

The place was as eclectic on the inside as it was out. Rock and movie collectibles hung on exposed brick walls and made the place look like it'd been around for years even though it reeked of new. Every table was packed. Waitresses navigated overflowing trays between the bustling crowd, and Five Finger Death Punch vibrated loud enough to make conversation a challenge.

The brunette smiled and semi-yelled over one shoulder, never breaking her hip-slinging stride. "Nice turnout for an opening week, yeah?"

Well, that explained the new smell. "I don't do crowds." At least not this kind. Signing her dad's Do Not Resuscitate after a barroom brawl had pretty much cured her of smoky, dark and wild. "It looks like a great place though."

The woman paused where the bar opened to a whole different area and scanned Viv's outfit. "From the looks of things, you could use a crowd to loosen up." She shrugged and motioned toward the rear of the room. "Corner booth. Last I saw your girl she was propped up between two airheads almost as hammered as she was.

And don't mind Ivan. The cops are only hounding the owner, not the customers. My name's Lily if you need anything." And then she was gone, sauntering off to a pack of women whooping it up at the opposite end of the club.

So much for an extra set of hands. At least this part of the bar was less crowded, scattered sitting areas with every kind of mismatched chair and sofa you could think of making it a whole lot easier to case the place.

She wove her way across the stained black concrete floors toward the randomly decorated booths along the back. Overhead, high-end mini sparkle lights cast the room in a muted, sexy glow. Great for ambience, but horrid for picking drunk sisters out of a crowd. Still, Viv loved the look. She'd try the same thing in her own place if it wouldn't ruin the tasteful uptown vibe in her new townhouse. Funky might be fun, but it wouldn't help with resale.

Laughter and a choking cloud of smoke mushroomed out from the corner booth.

The instant Viv reached the table, the chatter died. Three guys, two girls and the stench of Acapulco Red—but no sister. "You guys see Callie?"

A lanky man with messy curly blond hair eyed her beneath thirty-pound eyelids and grinned, not even bothering to hide the still smoldering joint. "'Sup."

The redhead cozied next to him smacked him on the shoulder and glowered. "She's after Callie, Mac. Not stopping in for a late-night chat." She reached across the table and handed Viv an unpaid bar tab. "She headed to the bathroom about ten minutes ago, but be sure you take this with you. She stuck me with the bill last night."

Seventy-eight bucks. A light night for New Year's

Eve, which was a damn good thing considering Viv's bank balance. She tucked the tab in her pocket. "Which way to the bathroom?"

The girl pointed toward a dark corridor. "Down that hall and on your left."

Viv strode that direction, not bothering with any follow-up niceties. Odds were good they wouldn't remember her in the morning, let alone five minutes from now.

Inside the hallway, the steady drone of music and laughter plunged to background noise. Two scowling women pranced past her headed back into the bar. One glanced over her shoulder and shook her head at Viv. "May as well head to the one up front. Someone's in that one and isn't coming out anytime soon from the sound of things."

Well, shit. This was going to be fun. She wiggled the knob. "Callie?"

God, she hoped it was her sister in there. Knowing her luck, she was interrupting a New Year's booty call. Although, if that were the case, they were doing it wrong because it was way too quiet. She tried the knob again and knocked on the door. "Callie, it's Viv. Open up."

Still no answer.

Oh, to hell with it. She banged on the door and gave it the good old pissed-off-sister yell. "Callie, for the love of God, open the damned door! I want to go home."

A not so promising groan sounded from inside a second before the door marked Office at her right swung wide. A tall Adonis in jeans and a club T-shirt emblazoned with The Den's edgy logo blocked the doorway, his sky blue eyes alert in a way that shouldn't be possible past 1:00 a.m.

Two men filled the space behind him, one shirtless with arms braced on the top of a desk, and another leaning close, studying the shirtless guy's shoulder. No wait, he wasn't studying it, he was stitching it, which explained the seriously bloody shirt on the floor.

"Got more bathrooms up front. No need to break down the damned door." Adonis Man ambled toward her, zigzagging his attention between her and the bathroom. "There a problem?"

Dear God in heaven, now that the Adonis had moved out of the way, the shirtless guy was on full, mouthwatering display, and he was every book boyfriend and indecent fantasy rolled up into one. A wrestler's body, not too big and not too lean, but one hundred percent solid. A huge tattoo covered his back, a gnarled and aged tree with a compass worked into the gothic design. And his ass. Oh hell, that ass was worth every torturous hour in front of her tonight. The only thing better than seeing it in seriously faded Levi's would be seeing it naked.

"Hey," Adonis said. "You gonna ogle my brother all night, or tell me why you're banging down one of my doors?"

They were brothers? No way. Adonis was all...well, Adonis. The other guy was tall, dark and dirty.

Fantasy Man peered over his injured shoulder. Shrewd, almost angry eyes lasered on her, just as dark as his near-black hair. A chunk of the inky locks had escaped his ponytail and fell over his forehead. His closely cropped beard gave him a sinister and deadly edge that probably kept most people at a distance, but his lips could lull half the women in Texas through hell if it meant they'd get a taste.

Viv shook her head and coughed while her mind clambered its way up from Smuttville. "Um..." Her heart thrummed to the point she thought her head would float off her shoulders, and her tongue was so dry it wouldn't work right. "I think my sister's passed out in there. I just want to get her home."

Adonis knocked on the door and gave the knob a much firmer twist than Viv had. "Zeke, toss me the keys off the desk."

Before either of the men could move, the lock on the door popped and the door creaked open a few inches. "Vivie?" Callie's mascara-streaked face flashed a second before the door slipped shut again.

Months of training kicked in and Viv lurched forward, easing open the door and slipping inside. "I've got it now. Give me a minute to get her cleaned up and gather her stuff."

Adonis blocked the door with his foot. The black, fancy cowboy boots probably cost more than a month's mortgage payment, which seemed a shame considering it didn't look like she'd be able to pay her next one. "You sure you don't need help?"

"Nope." She snatched a few towels out of the dispenser and wetted them, keeping one eye on Callie where she semi-dozed against the wall. "We've done this before. I just need a few minutes and a clear path."

"All right. My name's Trevor if you need me. You know where we are if you change your mind." He eased his foot away, grinned and shook his head.

"Oh!" Viv caught the door before it could close all the way and pulled the bar tab out of her pocket. "My sister ran up a tab. Could you hold this at the bar for me and let me pay it after I get her out to the car? I need to grab my purse first."

He backtracked, eyeballed Callie behind her, and

crumpled the receipt. "I'd say you've already covered tonight." He turned for the office. "We'll call it even."

Fantasy Man was still locked in place and glaring over one shoulder, the power behind his gaze as potent as the crackle and hum after a nearby lightning strike.

She ducked back into the bathroom and locked the door, her heart jackrabbiting right back up where it had been the first time he'd looked at her. She seriously needed to get a grip on her taste in men. Suits and education were a much safer choice. Manners and meaningful conversation. Not bloody T-shirts, smoky bars and panty-melting grins.

Snatching Callie's purse off the counter, she let out a serrated breath, shook out the wadded wet towel, and started wiping the black streaks off her sister's cheek. A man like him wouldn't be interested in her anyway. At least, not the new and improved her. And the odds of them running into each other again in a city like Dallas were slim to none, so she may as well wrangle up her naughty thoughts and keep them in perspective.

On the bright side, she didn't have to worry about the tab. Plus, she had a fresh new imaginary star for her next late-night rendezvous with BOB.

Damn if this hadn't been the most problematic New Year's Eve in history. It wasn't Jace's first knife wound, but getting it while pulling apart two high-powered, hot-headed drug dealers promised future complications he didn't need. Add to that, two more customers arrested at his own club, Crossroads, in less than three days, and nonstop visits from the cops at The Den, and his New Year wasn't exactly top-notch.

Thank God his brother Zeke wasn't working trauma

tonight or he'd have had to have Trev stitch him up. That motherfucker would've hacked the shit out of his tat.

"You 'bout done?" Jace said.

Zeke layered one last strip of tape in place and tossed the roll to the desk. "I am now."

"Took you long enough." Jace straightened up, tucked the toothpick he'd had pinched between his fingers into his mouth and rolled his shoulder. It was tight and throbbing like a son of a bitch, but not bad enough to keep him from day-to-day shit—assuming he didn't have any more drug dealer run-ins.

"I don't know. Our straitlaced partygoer didn't seem to mind me taking my time." Zeke packed his supplies into one of the locked cabinets, the same triage kit they kept at every residence or business they owned. It might have been overkill, but it sure as hell beat emergency rooms and sketchy conversations with police. "Thought for a minute there the sweet little thing was going to combust."

"Sweet little thing my ass." Trevor dropped into his desk chair, propped his booted feet on the corner of his desk, and fisted the remote control for the security vids mounted on the wall. "I'd bet my new G6 that woman's got a titanium backbone and a mind that would whip both your asses into knots."

Jace snatched a fresh white club T-shirt from Trev's grand opening inventory and yanked it over his head, the wound in his shoulder screaming the whole time. "Based on what? Her courtroom getup or her uptight hairdo?"

"Like I judge by what people wear. You know me better than that." Trev punched a few buttons, paused long enough to eyeball the new bartender he'd just hired ringing in an order on the register, then dropped the remote on the desk. "You ask me, you're the one judging. Which is kind of the pot calling the kettle black."

The setback hit its mark, the Haven tags he wore weighting his neck a little heavier, a reminder of their brotherhood and the code they lived by.

It's not where a man comes from, or what he wears, that matters. It's what he does with his life that counts.

Twenty-seven years he and Axel had lived by that mantra, dragging themselves out of the trailer park and into a brotherhood nothing but death would breach.

"He's right," Zeke said. "You're letting Paul's campaign crawl up your ass and it's knockin' you off course."

Damn, but he hated it when his own mantras got tossed back at him. More so when he deserved it. He let out an exhausted huff and dropped down on the leather couch facing the string of monitors. "Play it again."

Trevor shook his head but navigated the menu on the center screen anyway.

"Not sure why you're doing this to yourself, man." Zeke pulled three Modelos out of the stainless mini-fridge under the wet bar and popped the tops faster than any bartender. God knew he'd gotten enough experience working as one through med school. "Paul's a politician with a grudge, nothing else. Watching this again is just self-inflicted pain. Focus on the real problem."

Jace took the beer Zeke offered as the ten o'clock news story flashed on the screen. The third-string reporter's too-bright smile and pageant hairdo screamed of a woman with zero experience but eager for a shot at a seat behind the anchor desk.

"Dallas's popular club, Crossroads, is in the news again this New Year's Eve as two additional patrons were arrested on charges of drug possession with intent

to distribute. Undercover police are withholding names at this time, but allege both are part of a ring lead by Hugo Moreno, a dealer notorious in many Northeast Texas counties for peddling some of the most dangerous products on the street."

"She's not wrong on that score." Zeke plopped on the other end of the couch and motioned to the screen with his bottle. "The number of ODs coming in at Baylor and Methodist the last six months have been through the roof. The guys from DPD swear most are tied to some designer shit coming out of Moreno's labs."

Trevor leaned in and planted his elbows on the desk, eyes to Jace. "You think Otter's going to hold out long enough to waylay Moreno?"

If Jace knew the answer to that one, he'd be a lot less jumpy and minus one slash to his shoulder. Pushing one pharmaceutical genius out of his club by strongarming him with another was a risky move at best, but it sure as shit beat ousting Moreno on his own. "Otter's a good man with a calm head on his shoulders and a strong team. If he says he'll only let weed in the place and keep Hugo at bay, I'm gonna give him all the backing he needs. DPD's sure as hell not going to help. Not the ones in Paul's pockets, anyway."

"Paul doesn't have any pockets," Trev said. "Only his daddy does."

Right on cue, the camera cut to an interview with Paul Renner as reporters intercepted him leaving another political fundraiser.

"Councilman Renner, you've been very vocal in your run for U.S. Representative in supporting the Dallas Police Department's efforts to crack down on drug crime, and have called out establishments such as Crossroads

in midtown Dallas. Have you heard about the additional drug arrests there tonight, and do you have any comments?"

Renner frowned at the ground, a picture-perfect image of disappointment and concern. Like that dickhead hadn't been trying to screw people since his first foray from the cradle.

"I continue to grow more concerned with establishments like those run by Jace Kennedy and his counterparts," Renner said. *"It seems they continually skirt justice and keep their seedy establishments open for business. It's innocent citizens who end up paying the price, courted by heinous individuals peddling dangerous substances and amoral behavior. My primary goal, if elected to the House of Representatives, will be to promote legislation that makes it difficult for men like Mr. Kennedy and Mr. Moreno to escape justice."*

The toothpick between Jace's teeth snapped in half. He tossed it to the coffee table in front of him and pulled another one of many stashed in the pocket of his jacket.

"It's official, now." Trevor raised his beer in salute and tipped his head. "You're an amoral son of a bitch leading innocent citizens to ruin."

Motion registered in one of the smaller security screens, the bathroom door outside Trevor's office swinging open enough to let Little Miss and her seriously drunken sister ping-pong down the hallway. The two were about the same height, but you couldn't have dressed two women more differently. Next to Little Miss, her sister was best suited for a biker bar, all tits, ass and wobbling heels. Not that she was bad to look at. She just lacked the natural, earthy grace of the sober one.

Damn it, he needed to pace. Or get laid. Just looking at the ass on Little Miss in tailored pants made him want to rut like a madman. Never mind the puzzle she presented. Trev wasn't wrong—she had a shitload of backbone blazing through those doe-shaped eyes. The combination didn't jive with her image. Nothing like a paradox to get his head spinning.

"Guess we found one way to get his head off Renner." Zeke knocked back another gulp of his beer.

"What?" He back and forthed a glare between his brothers.

Trevor chuckled low and shifted the videos so Little Miss's trek to the front of the bar sat center stage. "Zeke said the only thing you've done amoral was that freak show you put on with Kat and Darcy at last month's barbecue."

"Fuck you, Trev."

"Fuck her, you mean," Trev said. "No shame there, brother. You didn't even see her up close. If you did, you sure as shit wouldn't be sitting here rerunning sound bites of asshole Renner."

"Hell, no," Jace said. "A woman that uptight is the last thing I need. Or did you miss her casing not just Zeke patching up my shoulder, but the bloody shirt on the floor, too? You'll be lucky if the cops don't show from an anonymous tip called in."

Little Miss and her sister stumbled into the front section of the bar, the sister's arm curled around Little Miss's neck in a way he'd bet would still hurt tomorrow morning.

Nope. Sweet hips, fiery eyes and a good dose of mystery or not, she was the last thing he needed right now.

Two men blocked Little Miss's path.

The women stopped, and the drunk sister swayed

enough it was a wonder she didn't topple onto the table beside her.

One of the men palmed the back of Little Miss's neck, and she jerked away.

Jace surged to his feet, grabbing his leather jacket off the table. "I'm headed to Haven. You hear more from Axel at Crossroads or get any more grief from the cops, let me know."

Both men let out hardy guffaws and waved him off.

"Twenty bucks says our buttoned-up guest gets some help on the way out the door," Trev said.

Zeke chimed in behind him. "Yeah, let us know if Sweet Cheeks tastes as good as she looks."

Bastards. The sad thing was, Trev was about to score a twenty from Zeke, because Jace might not be willing to curl up with Little Miss, but he wasn't watching men paw her either.

Chapter Two

Viv tightened her arm around Callie's waist and shook off the not-so-shy behemoth of a man gripping the back of her neck. His height alone was enough to make him intimidating, but paired with his shaved head and leathers, the scary vibe packed an extra punch. "I appreciate the offer, but we'll be fine."

"Ah, come on, darlin'." He stepped closer and shot a quick, conspiratorial grin at his cohort in crime, a much smaller guy who more than made up in the shaggy hair department what Cue Ball was missing. "Just trying to help out. Can't have a pretty thing like you out on the streets alone this time of night."

Stupid, stubborn men. One thing about guys who lived and breathed a hard life, they seemed to think the word *no* was a coy version of *maybe*. She feigned an innocent smile as best she could with Callie wrenching her neck. "Well, before I take you up on that, I should warn you, Callie's probably about five minutes from puking on anything or anyone within a twenty-foot radius. Seeing as how I'm right next to her, that would include me. You still up for helping?"

The mood killer worked even better than she expected, dousing the naughty gleam in both men's eyes faster than the people at the table behind them downed their shots. The big guy stepped back and waved her through without another word.

Viv half laughed and half scoffed, leaning into her first few steps to get some extra forward momentum.

Callie staggered closer and nuzzled next to Viv, her words coming out in a drunken, sleepy slur. "Thanks for coming to get me, Vivie." The scent of tequila and other things Viv didn't want to contemplate blasted across her nose and riled what little was left of the snack she'd pilfered at the New Year's Eve party. "You're a good sister. I can always count on you."

An uncomfortable pang rattled in her chest, memories of coming home to an empty apartment when Mom and Dad should've been there clanging together all at once. Family was supposed to be there for one another. To love each other and have their backs, not leave them to grapple with life all alone. "Yeah, Callie. I'm here. Always."

The bouncer who'd let her in took one look at her sister and stepped out of hurling range. "See you found your girl."

"I did, thanks." She shouldered the main door open and braced when Callie stumble-stepped down to the sidewalk. A little farther and she'd be home free, or at least in a place where she could battle the rest of the night barefoot in a comfy pair of sweats.

Behind her, the bar door chunked open, and a few of the people crowded in front of the bar called out goodnights and wishes for a happy new year to whoever had come out.

Viv stepped out onto Elm Street, Callie pinned to her hip.

Mid-stride, Callie lurched and waved to someone

across the street. "Stephanie!" The unexpected happy dance knocked them both off center. Callie fisted Viv's hair in a last-ditch grasp to stay upright, but wrenched Viv's neck before she went sideways.

Viv stumbled, heels teetering on the blacktop and arms flailing for purchase.

Callie smacked her head on the curb.

Viv braced for her own impact, but strong arms caught her, her back connecting with a warm solid chest instead of the painful concrete she'd expected.

A deep, rumbling voice rang out behind her. "Get Zeke and Trevor out here. See if Danny's still around, too."

She clenched the leather-clad arms around her waist and fought to catch a steady breath.

The bouncer hurried into the street and kneeled beside Callie, gently lifting her so her head rested on his lap.

This fucking night. This horrid, embarrassing, fucking night. Behind her, murmurs and giggles from bystanders grew by the second. Her mind pushed for her to get up, deal with Callie, and get home where it was safe, but her body wouldn't move, mortification and the flood of adrenaline rooting her in place.

The man behind her tightened his hold as though he sensed her self-consciousness. "We got this, sugar." The tiny movement made the leather of his jacket groan. His scent permeated her haze, a sea-meets-sun combination that made her think of Mediterranean islands and lazy days on the beach, not at all what she'd expect from a man coming out of the dive behind her. He sifted his fingers through her freed hair, moving it to one side of her neck, and a stray bobby pin clattered to the asphalt. "Your neck all right? Your sister gave it a hell of a snap."

That voice. Every word radiated through her, grated and deep like the rumbling bass of a stereo cranked up too loud.

He stroked her nape, the touch confident and not the least bit platonic.

Her senses leaped to attention, eager for more of the delicious contact. It was all she could do to hold back the moan lodged in the back of her throat. She swallowed and blew out a slow breath instead. "Yeah, I'm fine."

He lifted her upright, and the muscles in his arms and chest flexed around her, tangling what was left of her reasonable thoughts into a hopeless knot.

A man jogged up, hunkered down beside her sister, and opened up a leather duffel. Not just any man, the guy who'd stitched up the hottie in the office.

She surged forward to intervene, but firm hands gripped her shoulders and pulled her back. "Give Zeke a minute to check her out."

Viv twisted, ready to shout at whoever dared to hold her back—and froze. Her breath whooshed out of her like she'd hit the pavement after all.

Fantasy Man grinned down at her, a toothpick anchored at the corner of his mouth. His tan spoke of far more hours in the sun than the surgeon general recommended, and his almost black eyes burned with a wicked gleam that promised loads of trouble. And not necessarily the good kind, judging by the vicious scar marking the corner of one eye.

"Zeke's a trauma doc," he said. "Perks up like a bloodhound if anyone so much as stubs a toe."

Callie moaned, and Viv spun back around to find the doc prodding the back of her sister's neck.

"I know it hurts," Zeke said. "Can you tell me your name?"

"I don't feel so good," Callie said.

Zeke carefully moved Callie's head back and forth and side to side. "I imagine you don't. Still want to know your name though."

"Callie."

"That's a pretty name." Zeke dug into his duffel and pulled out a penlight. "You know what day it is, Callie?"

Callie's eyes stayed shut, but she smiled like a kid at Christmas and threw her arms out to the side, damn near whacking Trevor as he sat on the curb beside her. "Happy New Year!"

Trevor chuckled and shifted Callie away from the bouncer so she rested against his own chest. "I got her, Ivan. See if you can't find the crowd something else to gawk at."

"You know where you're at, Callie?" Zeke checked her sister's pupils for responsiveness.

As soon as Zeke pulled the light away, Callie blinked and focused on Viv. "I'm with Vivie."

Fantasy Man's voice resonated beside Viv's ear, the tone low enough it zinged from her neck to the base of her spine. "Vivie, huh?"

A shudder racked her and she crossed her arms to combat the goose bumps popping up under her suit jacket.

His arm slipped around her waist from behind and pulled her against his chest, his heat blasting straight through to her skin. "You okay?"

Hell, no she wasn't okay. Her sister was hurt and bystanders lined both sides of the street waiting to see what happened next, but all Viv could think about was how his voice would sound up close and in the dark. Preferably between heavy breaths with lots and lots of skin involved. She'd chalk it up to exhaustion, but her nonexistent sex life was probably the real culprit.

"I'm fine. Just tired." She forced herself to step away and faced him, holding out her hand. "And it's Vivienne. Vivienne Moore. Or Viv. Callie's the only one that calls me Vivie."

He studied her outstretched palm, scanning her with languid assessment, then clasped her hand in his and pierced her with a look that jolted straight between her legs. "Jace Kennedy."

Figured that Fantasy Man would have a fantasy name to match. It sounded familiar, too, though with all the pheromones jetting through her body she couldn't quite place where. Maybe wishful thinking or one too many romance novels. She tugged her hand free and stuffed her fists into her pockets. "Thanks for not letting me bust my ass in front of everyone."

He matched her posture and shuttled his toothpick from one side of his mouth to the other with his tongue. "Pretty sure I got the best end of the deal."

Zeke's voice cut in from behind her. "I think she's fine. Just a nasty goose egg and too much booze."

Viv turned in time to see the two men guide Callie to her feet. She weaved a little and looked like she'd fall asleep any second, but the pain seemed to have knocked off a little of her drunken haze. Her floral bohemian top was wrinkled and askew on her curvy frame, and her golden-brown hair was mussed like she'd just had monkey sex. Otherwise, she fit the rest of the crowd a whole lot better than Viv.

Pegging Zeke with a pointed look, Jace cupped the back of Viv's neck. "Check Little Miss out, too. Didn't like the angle her neck took when her girl went down." He focused on Viv and held out his hand, palm up. "Keys."

"What?"

"Keys," he said. "Give 'em to me and we'll bring your car around."

"You don't need to do that." She pointed at the lot across the street. "I'm just over there, and Callie looks—"

"It's almost two in the morning, your sister's hammered, and you both took a fall. Fork over the keys, we'll get your car, pull it around and load your girl up."

Four unyielding stares locked onto her—Zeke, Trevor and Jace, plus a new guy with black hair and a ponytail nearly down to his ass. The way the new guy trimmed his goatee gave him a Ming the Merciless vibe. She shouldn't let any one of these guys near her, let alone surrender the keys to her car. "I think it's better if Callie and I handle it ourselves."

The muscle at the back of Jace's jaw twitched and his eyes darkened.

"I don't mean to sound ungrateful," Viv added. "I appreciate everyone jumping in to help. It's way more than you needed to do. I just don't know you guys. Have you watched the news lately?"

"That's fair." Trevor's focus was locked on Jace when he spoke, but then slid his gaze to Viv. "But this is my bar, your sister drank too much while she was in it, and hurt herself on the way out. It's in my best interest to make sure you make it home safe. Anything bad goes down between here and there, you could give me and my new business a whole lot of heartache I don't need, right?"

Trevor had a point.

"Give me the keys, sugar." Jace crooked the fingers on his outstretched hand. "You've done enough solo tonight."

She handed them over and Zeke stepped in, gently prodding the muscles along the back of her neck. "Any soreness?"

Viv shook her head as much as she could with Zeke's big hands wrapped around her throat.

Behind Zeke, Jace handed off the keys to Ivan. A second later, jogging boot heels rang against the asphalt followed by the chirp of a disengaging car alarm.

Zeke tested her movement side-to-side and front and back as he'd done for Callie and checked her pupils. "I doubt you'd feel it until tomorrow anyway. Probably wouldn't hurt to take a few ibuprofens before you go to bed." He jerked his head toward Callie, still swaying next to Trevor. "Same goes for her. You'll have a hard time keeping her awake and not puking with as much as she's had to drink, but if she starts to act confused, can't remember things, or complains of ringing in her ears, get her to an ER."

"You got anyone that can help you tonight?" Jace asked.

Trevor piped up. "I can ask one of the girls to stay with you if you want."

"No, I can handle it."

Zeke gave her a knowing look, pulled a card out of his billfold, and handed it over. "You need help, call. We'll get her where she needs to be."

As in to an ER, or a place that had a minimum thirty-day stay? God knew, she'd begged her sister to at least try an AA meeting, but Callie and their dad had cornered all the stubborn genes for the family.

Her hybrid hummed up beside them and Zeke stepped away. "Lay her down in the back, Trev."

The bouncer hopped out of the driver's seat and opened up the back door for Trevor, who'd given up steering Callie and opted for carrying her to the car.

Jace moved in close and lowered his voice. "She get like this a lot?"

The men situated her sister in the backseat.

"Yeah." God, she was tired of this routine. She'd give just about anything to surrender, curl up into a little ball and let someone else handle Callie's tricks for a day or two.

Jace splayed his hand along the small of her back and urged her forward as a big, mean-looking bike with even nastier sounding pipes rolled up behind her car. "Danny's gonna follow you home and help you get Sleeping Beauty settled in for the night."

"I don't think—"

"If your sister passes out, can you get her in the house on your own?"

"No."

"Then stop thinking and let us handle this," Jace said. "Danny so much as breathes funny, you call the number on Zeke's card and we'll deal with it."

Another good point. After everything they'd done for her tonight, the odds of any of them having bad intentions were pretty slim. And her dog would leave even a big guy like Danny a heaping bloody mess if Viv so much as snapped a finger.

He opened the car door and she slid behind the wheel, fastening her seat belt in a bit of a daze. "Thank you. For everything."

"Just doing what decent people do." He started to shut her door and stopped. Leaning slightly into her space, he seemed to listen for something, glanced at the stereo display, then eased back. He studied her car, Callie curled up in the backseat, then Viv. His gaze lingered on her hair and he ran a few fingers through the curly strands. "Like it better down. Kinda wild."

Her heart tripped, and the last bit of logic left in her brain poofed to nothing. She clenched the steering wheel and swallowed, grateful to find her mouth wasn't hanging open.

He winked and stepped back. "Take care, sugar."

The car door thumped shut, muting out everything but the quiet strains of Shinedown and Callie's muffled snore.

She put the car in drive and forced her eyes to aim straight ahead. She wouldn't look back. He might've nudged her long-dead sex drive out of a coma, but he was bad news. Everything about him screamed danger and headstrong alpha, and she'd sworn she wouldn't have that kind of life for herself. One look in the backseat showed where that landed a person.

Still, making a right turn onto Highway 75 for her townhouse in Uptown instead of circling the block for another peek was tempting as hell.

Buy ROUGH & TUMBLE by Rhenna Morgan, now available wherever Carina Press ebooks are sold.

www.CarinaPress.com

About the Author

Rhenna Morgan is a happily-ever-after addict—hot alpha men, smart women and scorching chemistry required. A triple-A personality with a thing for lists, Rhenna's a mom to two beautiful daughters who constantly keep her dancing, laughing and simply happy to be alive.

When she's not neck deep in writing, she's probably driving with the windows down and the music up loud, plotting her next hero and heroine's adventure. (Though trolling online for man-candy inspiration on Pinterest comes in a close second.)

She'd love to share her antics and bizarre sense of humor with you and get to know you a little better in the process. You can sign up for her newsletter and gain access to exclusive snippets, upcoming releases, fun giveaways and social media outlets at *www. rhennamorgan.com.*

If you enjoyed *Guardian's Bond*, she hopes you'll share the love with a review on your favorite online bookstore.